I0819875

ALARUMS OF REALITY

Novels published by Midnight Fire Media

Your Own Fate
Night on Earth
Dreams Belong to the Night
ShadowWalk

The Janus Clan series:

The Defenseless
The Slaves
Birds Flying in the Dark

Poems:

Amos Keppler: Complete Poems 1989 - 2003

(A few of the) novels to be published:

The Afterglow trilogy
Season of the Witch
Thunder Road: Ice and Fire
Falling
Black Dragon

For a «complete» list of current and current future Amos Keppler and Midnight Fire Media projects see the back of the book and the Midnight Fire/Midnight Fire Media web pages.

Alarums of Reality

By

Amos Keppler

MIDNIGHT FIRE MEDIA
2012

Midnight Fire Media

http://midnight-fire.net/mfm
For more about Alarums of Reality:
http://midnight-fire.net/aor

E-Mail:
ak@midnight-fire.net
manofhood@yahoo.com

Cover, text, design, premedia, art and photos Amos Keppler

ISBN 978-82-91693-13-2

First book:
GRAINS OF SAND

CHAPTER ONE

He can't quite make out the words, can't hear the sound of his own voice. His lips move, but there is no sound.

– You've always been here, the woman says.

She stands in a corridor filled with twilight. Her body is in shadows. Only her face is clearly visible. She wears a white, translucent mask. The mask moves, as if being a face, as if being alive.

– Take this ring, as a token of my love.

And he wakes up in his own twilight bedroom, wondering what's real and what's not.

Colin rose from bed as he did every morning. He stretched his body, his muscles, soft and laden after a night's sleep, after days of inactivity. Looking at his watch, checking the time, registering he had sufficient time, as always. The alarm clock had probably sounded some time ago, even if he hadn't heard it. It had indeed brought him out of his slumber. He had always hated rising early in the morning.

Five steps to the bathroom, only five steps. Marion continued to sleep soundly. She had thrown off most of the blanket covering her body. Her nightgown had slipped a bit, exposing her large breasts. The sight instantly made his prick rise hard and painful. He splashed cold water in his face, looking at it in passing in the mirror. He removed his own night-suit, stepping into the shower. Water pushed against his body, surrounding it. He noted absent-mindedly that his cock still kept at it, half hardened, which he found quite unusual considering the previous night. Marion had been quite eager. They had both been after a few days absence.

She had visited her mother, left him alone.

There was breakfast, hardly noticeable. A few minutes later he couldn't actually recall what he had eaten. He tried to, as he stopped before the front door, shook his head and moved on.

He walked to the bus stop, the short distance from home. Autumn had come to the area just a few days earlier. Yellow leaves covered the streets, the sidewalks, floating in the air. He stopped a bit by the crossroads, as he always did, looking for the bus. If the bus emerged from the top of the slope he would have to run to the stop. He saw no bus. His eyes caught something in a heap of leaves close to the drain. He went there to pick it up. To his surprise he found a ring, a golden ring, somewhat downtrodden, with a curious red glowing stone. Who could have dropped it here? Whoever the owner might be couldn't have been wearing it on his or her finger, or he or she wouldn't have lost it. Luckily there hadn't been raining tonight, or it would certainly have been flushed down the drain. It could have been anyway, by the wind, along the heap of leaves, if he hadn't discovered it.

The bus had already stopped by the stop. He saw it leave it. And he, looking about found himself on the same spot by the crossroads. He started waving frantically, even though he knew, in his heart he did so in vain. Slackers had no chance with this bus company.

He couldn't claim his work to be easy; he couldn't claim it to be hard. But still he arrived home in the afternoon absolutely dead tired. Marion, too, did always look haggard, exhausted. She studied physics at the local university.

– If only it could be physics, but it's math, math, math all day long. I've got four years of math to look forward to.

This was her favorite subject each time work and school surfaced in the conversation. He couldn't very well complain about it. He had his favorite subjects himself.

He slipped the ring into his pocket, wondering why he had thought about what he thought about just now. It had been like a flash of revelation, not a tired memory.

The bus moved slowly through the city traffic. There was ongoing construction work going on somewhere ahead. They always did some construction work or road construction work somewhere. Bulldozers entered the neighborhood with their slow, inevitable pace and started bulldozing away some topsoil, some green spot. They had started working on the green spot by their home, a lawn where kids had played soccer in the afternoons last week. Nobody knew why, nobody cared. Construction work played an integral part in people's lives.

He would be late. Colin accepted it with a resigned shrug. Another reduction in his salary, another nick in the chief's book. There had been some of them lately.

A man spoke to a woman a few rows ahead, seemingly a mind reader:

– The bus is always late… or early. I swear to you, it's been impossible to keep track of time recently. Others have noticed it, too.

– So why haven't I, or anyone I know noticed it, except you? She said sarcastically.

The man fell silent. Everything fell silent. No one really spoke on the bus. One had to raise one's voice to be heard above the buzz…

But no one spoke.

They finally exited the cluster of suburbs and reached a bit of open land. On their right was a church. It had seen better days. The white paint had started to scale off several places. Even most of the white chalk on the brick wall wasn't white anyone.

On their left was an old castle. Nothing special about it, really. Just an old castle. Nobody had lived there for twenty years, after the owner had died. The way Colin had heard it he had been killed by a rowing band of drunks a stormy Saturday night. The city council and one of those societies working for the preservation of old castles had shared the expenses and kept its exterior somewhat shiny. Not many had ventured inside. The rumors of the place being haunted were very persistent.

They drove through a forest. Not a very big one. Just ten seconds or so, a glimpse of trees and they found themselves on the highway on the other side.

– Did I sleep? The woman in front asked the man in front.

– Sleep? He said.

– Yes, I got tired. She kissed him. – The life of the commuter is never easy. The queue seems to go on forever, doesn't it?

– There hasn't been a queue in these parts since they opened the new link-road, he sniffed.

– Oh, you old sourpuss, she declared, slapping him cheerfully on the cheek.

They hadn't completely completed the new link-road yet. There was still the question of the second lane. The bulldozers had started the completion work a few days ago. Green turned brown, turned gray. It turned black, completely black.

There was a girl speaking very loud. She had a very distinct voice and was easily heard. Everybody was treated to her long monologues every morning. Her friend didn't say much, except replying with one syllable or so now and then.

- I woke up this morning, the girl said, - and Sylvia had her period as usual, and she was in a very foul mood. I try to speak to her, but you really can't, you know. It's just one of those days, right?

Colin didn't really listen to the words, only to the phenomenon that was her voice. Everybody in the bus did, he wagered. The entertainment was really limited on buses.

Green turned brown, turned gray, turned black. Blue sky turned dark. There were no clouds. Suddenly the sky was filled with clouds.

Colin blinked and rubbed his temples. He hadn't slept much last night, but this was ridiculous.

He felt good really. The exhausting sex had reinvigorated him to a point of euphoria. At least he felt a few inches above his lowest ebb, something that hardly ever happened anymore.

The two of them sat facing each other on each side of the dinner table. Marion looked at him with a soft stare, a warm glow in her eyes. The candles lit her face, blushing her, burning him. Beyond the dinner table they saw nothing, heard nothing, sensed nothing. This was their time, their place. Nobody could reach them or disturb them here. Within these four (or five) walls they decided what would go or not.

And anything would go here.

The bus' journey through the rural and urban «landscape» was slow, exuberantly so. Colin yawned, a long, painful yawn threatening to break his jaw. The ride was slow, to the point of time crawling to a halt. He looked up again, out of the window. Had the bus moved, moved at all, since the last time? Its wheels had most certainly turned, but had it actually moved from its previous position?

He doubted it.

The day turned out to be one of those days, a day exactly alike the previous one, or the one before that.

They drove through a small piece of open landscape, before once again being immersed in the sprawl, the conurbation of modern human existence.

– You're off your guard, the girl said to the boy.

– No, you are.

– You, too.

– You, too.

On their left was a church. They had just painted it. The lawn had been cut. The city council kept it in top shape. Nobody would go on record for not supporting Religion.

On their right was an old castle. A spooky ghost house, if one ever existed. Windows had fallen out and a part of the roof was missing. Some society working for the preservation of old castles had been talking for years about funding a restoration, but talk was cheap. Nobody had given a fuck, since the owner, Marlon Caine had passed away 20 years ago.

The bus returned to the sprawl, the conurbation of modern human existence. The city rose around it, devouring it, immersing it between the cloud high buildings. The people shuddered in shadow. In the middle of the day the sun didn't reach them.

He registered at work 3 minutes past nine, three minutes late. Everybody looked at him as if at a leper. Everybody was closely watching everybody else here.

Michael Carnaby, the boss watched everybody from his office down the hall.

Colin's «office», like that of all the other lowly employees consisted of small cubicles, not really divided by walls, but by dividers on wheels, movable and flexible. Modern office space in a nutshell.

A desk, a chair, a computer screen, mouse and keyboard.

He and Sharon Wells, the dark-skinned woman next to him, greeted each other, exchanging looks before entering the cubicles. The video cameras caught that, of course.

The video cameras caught everything.

Not that they weren't allowed to say hello to their co-workers, but they had been late today. And when that happened «niceties» were at best frowned upon. And Colin felt a bit of the usual guilty pleasure. Perhaps he hadn't done anything wrong, but he sure felt like it. The all-seeing eye gave everybody a continuously guilty conscience.

He heard the sound of the tapping of his fingers against the keyboard. He didn't really feel anything. The work was monotonous There was no end to it. He kept tapping. It didn't really require any higher brain functions. He had thought he could dream only at night, while sleeping, but had evidently been wrong. Perhaps he was dreaming right now. He certainly was so close to sleeping as he could come without actually doing it.

Modern research suggested that parts of the brain turned itself off, well before people actually fell asleep. He could believe that.

Lunch-break already, after a thousand years. Lunch-break was part of the regulations. The firm abided by them, regulation by regulation. The first group of workers filed to the lunchroom. The other group would file in thirty minutes. Somebody had to work, at any given time, twenty-four hours a day. The machines kept going. Drechsler & Son had set its eye on the new, global economy. Colin, like all the employees worked night shifts once every third week. The twenty-four hours were divided in three working shifts, revolving continuously.

The lunchroom was big, big enough to fit almost the entire shift. Statistics said that twenty percent of the workers left the building during the break, either to smoke or eat or for other reasons and that assessment was about right.

There was a queue in front of the cafeteria desk. If lucky even those last in line would get a few minutes by the tables, not finding it necessary to wolf down the food too fast. The best workers sat closest to the boss, closest to the cafeteria, being the first in line when the klaxon horn sounded.

Colin wasn't among them.

He and Marion had agreed to work and study every second year, until they both had received a higher education, he in computer arts, she in physics. This was their second year. It would at least take them twelve more years to complete their self-inflicting task.

And that was just if nothing went wrong. Something always went wrong, but he had planned for that, in his planning, his calculations. If anything didn't go seriously wrong, they would arrive in twelve years, with a whopper salary as a result. Computer service, as he did now, was required practice anyway.

The klaxon horn sounded. Back to work. The walk back was uneventful. He hardly remembered it. A lot of E-Mails waited for him, accumulating during the break. It was always tough to catch up after a break.

He had to read, to study during his sleep year, too, of course, keeping his knowledge sharp and clear in his mind. It would have been a nightmare catching up otherwise. Time waited for no man.

Tapping again. He had kept this up for three months now, with just a little bit of unease. Even if nothing was said officially, there was a lot of talk about mouse and keyboard sickness, how it could disable you after a few, short years, turning you into a cripple. Both the keyboard and the mouse he used was the latest in ergonomic equipment, but one could never be absolutely certain, could one? Each new generation the last century had, after all, had their own, unique problems with the doing of monotone, repetitious work. It wasn't *fair*. Machines were supposed to make life easier.

Slowly, slowly he noticed the increasing smell of sweat under his arms, his bladder being filled, to the point of bursting. He rose and walked to the toilet. Toilet-visits were allowed. As long as they didn't turn out to be too frequent and too prolonged. The video cameras recorded everything, of course, including what went on inside the toilet. No one living today could truly imagine how it had been back then, before video cameras had been put up everywhere in public places. Colin, Marion, and their entire generation had lived with them since the cradle. He smiled a bit, shaking his head. Naturally he was unable to actually recall the hospital birth where he had been filmed the first time, but in a distant, intellectual way, he understood the point. One generation's nightmare was the next one's daily life.

Emptying the bladder felt like heaven. He had almost waited too long. The management expected rushed expediency of the workers. Another guilty pleasure. He could imagine how he looked, on the image of the monitor, with the beam of fluid erupting from his organ. If he had been an adult twenty years ago he supposed he would have grinned a bit. Now it felt completely natural to share what had been considered private space with total strangers.

Well, some of it remained, he guessed. The toilets still had walls, and even a locked door. Some atavistic practices always remained. It was kind of funny, though, how anonymous strangers were allowed to see you, but not people physically close.

He wondered a bit about all this, if most other people wondered about it. They probably accepted it with a shrug, without really thinking about it much. He probably pondered it more than most.

Tonight was Friday night. Something he hardly dared think about too much during most of the week, but now, with it merely a few hours away, he allowed himself to dream.

Friday night was the end of the week. There was no work tomorrow. One could shake loose, get slam bam drunk and the occasional headache could be nursed at home, within the five walls. Monday had to be the worst day of the week. Everybody knew then that they would have to work for five days before the week's end.

But Friday was bad, too. A poor ass had worked the entire week and all the seconds felt like hours. Time dilated to eternity. He took another look at his watch.

04.32.30

He waited, and waited. He waited a long time, before looking again. He looked hard, thinking hard, but nothing seemed to work.

04.32.30

– What's the time? He asked Sharon.

– Four thirty-two thirty, she said, and he swore he could spot black lines under the eyes on her brown skin.

Every watch was synchronized every morning. Another bold move from the management implemented two months ago in an effort to improve efficiency.

– Four thirty-two thirty, he mumbled. – Remember. *Remember.*

– What did you say? Sharon asked in a tired voice.

– Nothing, he replied. – Nothing important.

E-mails kept pouring in. Most of it was Spam, of course, of little value to the receiver. But within all the crap there could be gold, pure gold, and everybody had to sift through it all, just in case. There had been a case last month that had been broadcasted all over the wire services, about a guy who had skipped a lot of Spam… and missed a million dollar opportunity. Colin kept tapping.

He looked at the watch one more time, one final time.

04.34.12

Colin kept tapping.

The tapping grew louder, as if he somehow was able to hear everyone in the room tapping. The sound of one person tapping wasn't very impressive, but when one heard an entire office do it, it turned out to be quite impressive indeed.

He turned deaf after a while, as if there was no sound at all. The construction work outside their home had also been bad the last two or three nights, but had then seemed to subside into the background, into nothing. He couldn't remember actually hearing the klaxon horn at precisely five o'clock, what he supposed had been five o'clock precisely. But for all he knew it could just as well have been **05.05.54**… or even closer to **05.30.00**.

One just couldn't tell.

He found himself on the bus, on his way home, reading «Colors in the Night», a very colorful magazine. The bus took forever to move in the afternoon rush hour. In a rare show of creativity the company operating this particular route had started selling newspapers not long ago. Very few read the papers, but «Colors in the Night» was quite popular. But today it hardly mattered which paper or magazine one looked at, or opened or read. They all had the same screaming headline:

CHLOE WEBSTER MURDERED

And in «Colors in the Night» Colin read:

> «Chloe Webster is dead. Our esteemed investigative reporter died while pursuing leads on a story to be written for our magazine».

There was a picture of her, of an anonymous looking woman in her twenties. She had *something*. Colin could easily see that. Even on a bland black and white photo he saw the fire in her eyes…

But essentially, this described just another dead individual, another lowlife murder, nothing extraordinary at all.

Colin almost missed his stop. The door closed behind him the moment he put his feet on the ground. The irritated driver had threatened with closing the door in his face, «if such shite ever happened again». The bulldozer still went at it, and would continue doing so for at least a couple for hours more… before finally calling it a day. Its sound would eventually fade to a tiny buzz. Everything did. He had lived close to a construction site once. The first few nights it had been quite impossible to get even a moment's sleep, but after a few nights he had slept like a baby. The bulldozer reminded Colin of the bus driver, even though he couldn't say exactly why. The house suddenly appeared, right there in front of him. Marion greeted him in the door and everything was great again. The outside world faded like the fucking nightmare it was.

She had made sandwiches. He smelled them, even from outside, and inside, in the hall, the scent of them was very distinctive in his nostrils. He smelled Marion, too, of course, like he did the entire day at work. But now it overwhelmed his senses, overloaded them, like a wall of fresh flowers a rainy day.

- How was your day?

He looked sharply at her. She always asked him that, and it did irritate him occasionally, but her smile always washed away any grumpy feeling he might have.

The kitchen, cold and small. The living room warm and open, light colored walls, soft carpet on the floor.

Dark, now, candles being the only lights in the room, two hours gone like magic.

The party started at eight sharp. Very few people arrived late, even fashionably late. The Friday parties at Dexter's had grown quite popular.

– This is our place, Marion greeted the guests. – Everything goes here.

She had dressed up in an outrageous outfit. The virtually transparent black cloth had ornaments of devils and crosses and pentacles and god knows what. Everybody new to the Dexter's stared. She enjoyed that. The others just shook their head. Her firm, heavy breasts pushed at the cloth, the dress that seemed more like a part of her body than anything distinct from it. That, and the way she moved made more people than Colin horny and dizzy.

All electrical lights had been turned off. Only candles lit the dark place. Colin could hardly see more than shadows around him. Faces, brighter than the dark-clothed bodies, seemed to float in and out of sight in the darkness, drifting as balloons in the breeze. He danced with Ethel Wharton, sort of. At least she pushed her body at his, and he remembered getting a large and painful hard-on, before pulling himself backwards, floating away from the fire-red face. He leaned against the wall, drying sweat from his forehead. And as he did so, he heard voices speak in the shadows, the soft darkness surrounding him, comments coming from nowhere, making no sense. He couldn't be certain there was anybody there at all. He heard the voices, but they could just as well be tape recorders.

– Mathematics is truly the linchpin of the Universe, she said, Marion said, with her arms around Carl.

There were several candles on the table, illuminating the immediate surroundings. Colin and Marion sat on the couch with their arms around each other. Then suddenly, he was out in the hall, where candles were rare and everything seemed like a long, black tunnel, and he could just about make out other human shapes in the darkness.

Colin and Marion sat in the sofa with their arms around each other. Ethel was talking. Her voice soft and full, her eyes twinkling in the firelight of the candles.

– Poe was right, she said. – All that we see or seem is but a dream within a dream.

The sound of the words reverberated inside him. A strange echo in the room (the room had no echo).

– But that poem was nothing like the existential interpretation it has been given, Carl protested. – It was about his one-way love to a woman. His short time with her seemed like a dream. A silly love poem, that's all.

– Are you sure? Ethel crouched in the seat beside him, grinning wildly.

– It's about reality, another one said. – He wanted it to be solid, something he could grasp, at least for one moment in time. The moments were slipping away from him, at least all the good moments. He wanted, in his despair to save one, at least one from the roar of the eternal storm, one grain of sand from all those slipping through our fingers.

Colin sensed gooseflesh on his arm, huge as grains of sand. He looked at Marion, but she was busy conversing with Carl on her other side. He turned back to Ethel. She was snuggling with a man he didn't know. A big, powerful built man, which face he couldn't see, hidden behind Ethel's fire-colored curls.

– Ah, it's such a quiet place you got here, a girl sighed. – At least at night. It's like the world outside doesn't exist.

– Unfortunately it's just during the nights, Marion said. – The construction work down the road is certainly loud enough.

– There seems to be ongoing construction work everywhere these days, Sharon from work said, shaking her head. – I mean, there is *always* some construction work going on. Buildings and roads, and everything need to be constantly refurbished and upgraded, but lately the process of entropy seems to have gone into overdrive.

– Old Marlon Caine's haunt has certainly fallen into disrepair.

– Well, the historical society has kept it somewhat in shape.

– With a missing roof? You must be kidding. Out of shape, you mean?

Colin didn't really participate or even listen in on the conversation. Conversation and general details had never interested him much. He stood out there in the hall, surrounded by mirrors and shadows, blinking.

– Sleepy? He saw the silhouette of the firehair by the entrance table, a shimmering figure in the night.

– It's been a hard week, he nodded.

She held up an object, something twinkling in her hand.

– You found my ring, she exclaimed happily.

– It's yours? He sounded like an adolescent kid and knew it.

– Of course it's mine, you silly boy, it's always been mine.

A clock stroke midnight somewhere. Colin looked at his watch. He lifted a hand, a huge smile transforming his face.

He sat in the sofa with Marion by his side. Glasses were being filled. Bubbling fluid decorated the table and the furniture. He rose with his glass raised, before a gathering of candles, illuminating his flushed face.

– Marion and I, he began, interrupted by a loud cheer, looking down at her equally flushed face. – Marion and I have now been married for a year…

– A year filled with love and understanding, comradeship and challenges, he said, reaching out a hand.

She took it, rising with her own glass in the other hand, kissing him hotly on the lips, his sore lips.

Ethel lifted her own glass, standing in the shadows at the other side of the table.

– Good cheers to Colin and Marion, she cried, signaling with her free hand to the assembled party.

– GOOD CHEERS TO COLIN AND MARION, everybody cried, – MAY THEY LIVE LONG AND PROSPER

And they all drank. And the bubbles stirred his stomach in new and exciting ways the wine earlier during the evening hadn't been able to.

There was dance, and there was a lot of Champagne. And in the shadow he slept, and dreamed about the old castle on Marple Road. It was big. So big that the stairs went on and on upwards and downwards, into the sky, down below the Earth. He relived the old television programs with Marlon Caine, heard the man's insane mad shriek of a laughter echo in the tower of the castle, in its deepest depths.

He awoke on the couch the next morning with a splitting headache and in good spirits. Only a slight sweat revealed the existence of his intense dreams. Marion slept snoring by his side. He rose quickly, looking around, looking into the bedroom. The bed showed signs of having been used, but there was no one there now. All the guests had left, fortunately.

The house had fallen silent. The construction work down the road sounded muted and insignificant. He awoke in bed, with Marion snoring by his side. It was a quiet morning. No sounds, unfamiliar or not, disturbed the peace. He rose quietly without waking her, without even making her stir. He had long practice. She would like fresh bread for breakfast. She loved fresh bread for breakfast. He looked at the watch and then took a look out of the window, at the setting sun. Hmm, late afternoon already. He grinned.

There were still ten, fifteen minutes until the bus arrived. He took his time dressing, savoring every sense of cloth touching the skin. Outside, as he closed the door behind him, he breathed in the sharp air, the scent of spring. The lawn was green, but it had been green all winter. The trees were naked. They hadn't started growing leaves yet.

There was a crossroads close to the house. From there he was able to easily see the bus appearing from around the corner. There was no bus to be seen.

He stopped there, spotting something twinkling on the tarmac. He recognized it immediately as Ethel's ring. She had somehow managed to lose it once again.

Take this, as a token of my love.

He picked it up. When bending he experienced only the slightest sense of vertigo, but still regretting not starting early on the breakfast. Food was important after such wild nights as yesterday night. Everything started spinning, but he managed to rise to full height quite easily, and the dizziness faded fast enough. The bus… He realized with a start that it had passed him somehow, without him being aware of it. At that very moment he saw it slow down to a halt down the road, by the stop sign. He started walking faster, quickly breaking into a run. The queue, dreadfully short on Saturday afternoon disappeared into the bus. He reached the front door, just as it was about to close. By sheer luck he had exact change and put it into the greedy slot machine in front of the driver. The driver looked at him with more than a hint of suspicion and wrath. Why Colin couldn't say, and he didn't really care.

The driver stepped on the gas pedal, moving the bus out of the lane long before Colin and most of the other passengers, too, had found a seat. A man stumbled and almost fell, before managing to pull himself into a seat, using the next minutes drying sweat from his forehead. Colin sat in the front of the bus, where there were just old ladies, glaring suspiciously at him.

People, still tired after another hard week at work stared blindly ahead. Some stared out of the window, seeing nothing. There was a blandness in their eyes making him turn shitty all over. He looked in the mirror at home to scout for the same signs in his own eyes. He did so often.

The relatively short trip to the shopping mall was as uneventful as ever. Nothing ever happened around here. Nothing in public. The driver kept staring at Colin as he disembarked the bus. One moment it looked like the man would rise from his seat, and give chase, but he remained. And Colin left, hurrying into the many comforts of the shopping mall.

Flowers, there were flowers everywhere. The entire mall stank of flowers and antiseptic junk. He saw Ethel by the big palm tree by the escalator. She waved and he waved back.

The walls... He frowned. The walls here changed color. Or… perhaps not color… but consistency.

Wind ruffled his hair. The walls… breathed on him.

He shook his head, in wonder, over all the bullshit thoughts rattling him lately.

The two of them embraced. Ethel kissed him on the cheek and he kissed her back. They went arm in arm up the escalator to the upper floor. The upper floor was dedicated to restaurants and cafés, the smell of coffee and spices almost overpowering him. She walked by his side, smiling brightly to his face. He caught himself at smiling back, wondering if this was the girl from his dreams.

He heard water flow from a tap somewhere. He couldn't tell from where. There was no restroom nearby. But he could hear the water, hear its flow, like a river in his mind. He kept shaking his head. Ethel didn't notice. There was a flow, a release, and the river became a waterfall. He pushed his hands at his ears, but it did him no good. The sound just kept flowing, and it hurt. And when it finally subsided it was still there, like an echo in his mind.

They sat down in a coffee bar. He tried not to glance too hard at all the strange people around him, the people suddenly filling the place, but he found it increasingly difficult. He wondered where they had all come from. He wondered a lot.

– So, how has your day been so far? Ethel asked brightly, staring openly at him with those deep, burning eyes of hers.

– Well, it started fairly *late,* so I haven't managed to do much yet, not even having breakfast.

– Neither have I, she said.

– Marion was still asleep when I left, so I thought I would surprise her with breakfast… on the bed.

– Nothing wrong with having breakfast twice one morning, Ethel said huskily.

And she smiled ever so sweetly to him, and he couldn't help returning the smile. He had always found her…refreshing.

She was a big woman, taller than most men he had met. The blond hair had a touch of red, of sunset, her skin a similar touch of brown, her lips more Slavic than not. She was a strange creature, and he liked her.

They ate. And it was as if all the other people in the room weren't there. He was aware of them, but they were more like window dressing, like unmoving mannequins. They didn't give away any sound, didn't move or disturb the conversation in any way.

– I must say one thing about you guys, she said excitedly. – You know how to throw a party.

– Thank you, he replied, not really hearing the sound of his own voice.

– From the declaration of «Do what thou wilt» to the deep philosophical discussions. You don't experience that in many parties these days.

– One doesn't, does one? He nodded briefly, before once more being caught in her deep eyes, before another thought struck him. – Who was it that explained Poe?

– I thought I did, she grinned. You won't seriously claim that Carl did, will you?

– No. no, after you, after you both. There was someone…

– I can't recall anybody else. Carl got insulted and left, and that was it.

She shrugged.

– It was a pretty wild night, after all.

She bent slightly forward, taking his hands in hers, her eyes shining like black stars.

– I love wild…

He pulled back a little. She did, too, smiling in regret.

– I forgot something, he said, shaking his head again. – I can't believe I forgot.

He stuck his hand in the pocket, pulling up its content. Her eyes widened.

– You lost your ring again.

She looked at him with a sobering smile. She took the ring, looking closer at it.

– It's very beautiful, but it's not mine.

She returned it to him with a regretful smile.

– But you…

He hesitated, suddenly wondering if it had truly been her that night at the party. Oh, she had been there, all right, but he realized with a start that he had never seen the face of the girl claiming ownership of the ring.

– You found the ring somewhere? She asked curiously. – You actually found it?
– Just outside the house. One of the guests must have lost it.
– I didn't see it on anyone. She shook her head. – And I can't imagine it actually belonging to anybody present last night. I mean we're a loose bunch, but not that loose. And not that rich…
She inspected it from afar, as he kept holding it up.
– What *is* that stone? She wondered incredulously.
She smiled to him again, and once more he drowned in that smile.
– I *do* wish it was mine, she sighed.
They kissed each other goodbye, and parted. She waved and he waved back, more than a bit relieved.
The man behind the desk spoke a lot, as usual. He was one of those people who had been given a machinegun mouth as a gift at birth, and he never failed to take advantage of that fact.
– I saw her, you know.
– Who did you see? Colin asked, not really interested.
– Chloe Webster, the salesman said, almost proudly. – The very night she was killed.
– I would gather a lot of people saw her…
– Not that night, no. No one else saw, according to the police officers questioning me. Except for the killer, that is.
Suddenly the guy looked anxious, as if he had revealed something or had said too much, or he, unbelievably enough was afraid Colin would suspect him.
– She was killed far away from there, he said hastily. – Several hours later.
Colin just looked at him. Motormouth coughed and died. No more gas.
Colin Dexter looked at the driver on the bus on his way back. He made a point of looking at him. It wasn't the same guy, he was fairly certain of that fact, but he saw that… flash in the eyes of the guy causing him to not be hundred percent sure. There, there it was again. He drew breath, suddenly feeling a strong urge to breathe, a need for air.
– Are they *ever* gonna complete that crossroads work, a guy two seats behind him said to his companion. – I feel like they have kept at it for years.
– Try centuries, the other guy replied, shaking his head.
A lot of people were evidently shaking their heads these days.
– You see, that's exactly what I am talking about, the first guy continued. – They have kept it going for so long, now, that I don't know what I will do if they finally stop. Perhaps I have grown so used to it that

I will never be able to sleep in peace and quiet again. I fear I will go crazy, and that they will lock me up somewhere.

– What *are* you talking about? His buddy said.

– Am I talking? I wasn't aware that I was talking.

And then, a few minutes later:

– It's these bus drives. They're driving me nuts. I swear the bus is changing routes several times a week. I *swear*.

For some reason Colin looked at his watch.

07.02

It said.

He figured he had wasted at least 90 minutes with Edith. If he hadn't he and Marion would already have been half through the breakfast, and they would have started on the long, eventful, joyful evening.

The sun had set. A red glare darkened the horizon. Everywhere else was cast into the big shadow. The front lights of the bus hardly seemed sufficient for the task of brightening the road ahead. The construction workers had taken the weekend off. The road looked like it hadn't been worked on at all. An argument had broken out in the back of the bus, quickly ending in a wild exchange of blows and curses. Then silence. With luck they had knocked each other unconscious and wouldn't awake for quite a while.

Colin left the bus. It stopped at the stop for once. Colin left the bus. He walked the short stretch to the driveway.

There were a lot of cars ahead… in his driveway?

A lot of police cars.

It even covered the turn ahead.

He spotted a lot of spectators outside the yellow ribbons, the ones that said:

CRIME SCENE DO NOT CROSS

He reached the gate to the driveway. The entire path to the house was lit by blinking red and blue lights.

– What is going on here? He cried out to the two guards.

– Police business, sir, one said politely, – move along please.

– I MUST get in there.

– I'm afraid that's not possible, sir… And then, after a short hesitation. – Who are you?

– My name is Colin Dexter. I live here. What has happened here?

The two exchanged glances, and then stepped aside.

– Please, come with us, sir.

Two other uniformed cops took their place, as they were escorting Colin to the house. He looked around as if he couldn't believe what he saw. Red and blue lights turned everywhere, turned round and round in an insane dance.

– Why are you here? He insisted. – What has happened? Is it something in the neighborhood? Are you in all the houses?

But he saw that they weren't. He saw curios neighbors everywhere outside the police line, the red and blue yellow ribbons, and a terrible sense of apprehension cursed through him.

– Just come inside with us, sir.

A man, obviously the man in charge waited inside the door. His face was drawn. Colin recognized the face immediately. Not the man, but the face, of one who had seen too much, too many times.

– I am Lieutenant Elliott Lasko. The man extended his hand. – I'm in charge of the investigation.

Colin took the hand reflexively, suddenly finding it very difficult to breathe.

– The investigation? He exhaled in pain.

Lasko changed expression, evidently making a decision.

– Hell, there is never any easy way to say this… It's your wife, sir. I'm afraid she has been murdered.

– Are you insane? Colin protested weakly. – Are you sure? You don't know my wife, do you? Can't it just be someone that looks like her?

– I'm afraid there is little doubt, sir. She has been identified, positively identified by several neighbors. Will you come with me, please?

– Positively identified? Colin wondered dumbfounded. He wondered about that phrase, wondered a lot.

He was led further into the house, further into the Inferno, through the kitchen, into the living room.

And there, on the carpet he saw what made all blood, all blood leave his body. There was nothing but frozen ice left.

The body of Marion Dexter, of a strange, horribly alien Marion Dexter lay there on the carpet, in a pool of blood. He looked at the knife sticking out of her chest, her lovely bosom, her lovely body frozen there on its spot. It wasn't Marion at all, but some look-alike pretender.

He looked around the living room. Everything was in place. Everything was neat and compartmentalized, as it usually was. Everything was in place… except for the body on the carpet.

– I was… out, he said slowly, – buying breakfast. Marion loves fresh bread for breakfast

He turned to the Detective.

– Who did this? He cried out. – Do you have him, have him in custody?

– We don't know yet, sir, Lasko said, gritting his teeth, – but we will.

Colin Dexter sat down, right there on the spot. Coincidently there was a chair right behind him. He crouched on it, doing his best to hide as much of his face as he possibly could with his small palms, his shaking hands. He wanted to scream, but couldn't. Colin Dexter had lost his voice.

CHAPTER TWO

He sat in the police car on the way to the main police station. A man waved to him from the old castle. There was light inside of it, and it showed every sign of being inhabited. He turned away for just a moment, looking at the church, and when he looked back at the castle a moment later there was no man there, no sign of light or it ever being inhabited. The car drove a similar route to town to the one the bus took every day. But it was not exactly the same. It never was.

He sat in a room at the police station, realizing with an incredulous, dull pain that it was the interrogation room. He stared at the one-way mirror, and imagined there was an entire army of police officers hiding behind it, staring at him. In the mirror he could see, constantly see the image of Marion's dead body. He closed his eyes, and it was gone, but the moment he opened them again, and stared at the mirror she was there.

Lieutenant Lasko and his partner Albert Monroe entered the room. They looked grim. Their smiles looked grim, turning grimmer by the minute.

They sat down opposite him, taking their time, studying him without studying him. It was almost like in the office. Everybody studied, scrutinized each other, always wanting to find as much gossip as humanly possible. Monroe turned on the tape recorder. He tapped the microphone a few times before speaking.

– Interview with Colin Dexter, the victim's husband, starting at… he looked at his watch, – starting at 9.35 Monday evening. Present is also Tom Ruiz, the husband's attorney…

Colin turned off the rest of it, turned it all off. He knew there were many questions followed by answers. It just didn't seem to concern him.

– You stated that you were at the shopping center, buying «fresh bread» in the time leading up to the murder, is that right?

Monroe's voice was light, very light. Colin looked closer at him. There was something in his eyes that hadn't been present before.

– Yeah, that's right. Marion loves… loved…

– She loved fresh bread for breakfast, Monroe interrupted him impatiently. – You've told us that a hundred times.

There was a short, unpleasant silence. Colin began to feel bad, really bad.

– You see, Mr. Dexter, Lasko tuned in, – there is a problem verifying parts of your story… important parts.

– Not to my knowledge. He heard his own, hoarse voice, cursing himself.

– We checked your story. We always do that. Most murders are committed by husbands, wives or lovers. It's just plain statistics. So we checked it, to check you off the list. We saw it as a routine procedure, and didn't expect to find any, any… discrepancies… but we did.
– Discrepancies? Colin said dully.
Monroe leaned a bit over the table.
– As it turned out, Lasko stated. – Major discrepancies.
Colin wanted to catch his breath. He wasn't allowed to.
– Several of the neighbors stated that you arrived home about an hour before you said you did. Monroe stared at him. They all stared at him. – And that you left shortly afterwards, with blood-soaked clothes. They thought you had cut yourself… until they decided to take a peek through the living room window, that is.
– That's bullshit, Colin protested. – Ethel will…
– We spoke to Miss Wharton, too. Colin had to turn, turn to Lasko once more. The effort in itself seemed to cost all his remaining strength. – She said, in an affidavit interview… we have it on tape if you wish to hear it… that you two didn't meet at the Mayfair Shopping Mall on Saturday. She was supposed to meet you there, but she got delayed.
– But that's impossible. She was there. And she would never…
– Lie? We considered that, too. But people at the shopping mall, among them a reliable deli owner confirm that you sat there in the coffee shop all alone.
– But then…
– He also stated that you left a full hour before you said you did.
Their eyes seemed to turn huge and threatening before him.
A huge, black abyss opened up below him. He fell into it so slowly, so slowly that he hardly noticed, and he wondered if that was how it had been, how it had been for quite some time now, with him not noticing.
He sat in his cell. A week later, perhaps two, he wasn't sure. There was a sound somewhere. The cell door opened. Tom Ruiz, his attorney and friend entered with a serious expression on his face. There was no greeting from him, and none from Colin.
– It doesn't look good for you, Colin, he said, shaking his head. A lot of people were doing that these days. – I just got the word: it is your fingerprints on the murder weapon. They found bloodstained clothes in a dumpster that belonged to you, even with your hairs in the fiber. More witnesses have come forward.
– I didn't do it, Colin whispered. – I DIDN'T FUCKING DO IT, OKAY
He collapsed there on the seat.

– Someone is setting me up, he shouted in boundless despair. – Someone is DOING this to me.

– I believe you, Tom said. – I'm just saying it looks bad, okay. I, your lawyer, serve nothing lying to you about your chances.

– My chances… So, they're going to p-prosecute?

– Yes, that is a given, at this stage. They have motive, opportunity and a load of evidence and witnesses. I would say they are going to prosecute, all right, and I can assure you it will go to trial.

– M-motive?

Colin Dexter touched his face, his face covered in sweat and shit, and he moaned, a sound coming from a condemned man.

– I'm lost in a black, vast nightmare, he complained bitterly. – I'm not sure whether or not it started the moment I stepped off the bus that night at home, or earlier, but at some point something… happened, and everything turned inside out. Everything. And it happened so fast, as if someone, somewhere just snapped his fingers and *did* this to me.

– Most murders are committed by husbands, wives or lovers, Ruiz mused. – My guess is that they opted for that option early on, and ran with it. We can use that, I think.

Colin nodded, not really interested. He studied the pattern on the wall. It was constantly changing. Darkness surrounded him like a blanket. The entire room was drenched in shadow.

He sat there alone, unable to tell if Tom had ever been there.

– I'm thinking through the last few hours before I returned to the house, he said to Tom. – I see myself go to the mall, meet Ethel, and go back, and see the police outside the house, see the body on the floor, and that's all I see.

– All you see is the fucking prison walls, Lasko screamed at him. – That's all you gonna see for the rest of YOUR NATURAL LIFE.

The detective was red-faced. Spittle flowed from his mouth. And behind his eyes… wasn't there a hint of… malice, of glee, of a satisfaction beyond anything there should have been. Lieutenant Lasko's distorted, evil face haunted Colin's nightmares as he twisted and sweated on the hard prison bed.

They came and took him away one morning. They returned him at night. He could just about make out the courtroom during the day. Everything seemed dark, malicious, worse than any nightmare he had ever had. There was this guy with the club up there. He looked completely ridiculous. Colin giggled with an insane look in his eyes. He could just about make out the features of the stranger in the mirror. They cuffed him, hands and feet, before taking him away. He saw Ethel up there on the stand. She looked haunted and helpless, the way he felt.

– No, she said. – NO, I don't think he did it. I am convinced he did not. I don't know why he claims to have met me that day, but there was no reason for him to kill Marion. They loved each other. Everybody knew that.

She shifted and changed on the stand, as the courtroom shifted and changed, and nobody but him seemed to notice. He looked around at the people, the spectators gathered before the execution, and the insane glee was present in everybody's eyes. He looked up at the stern man behind the bench. There were no words, even though the fellow moved his lips. He didn't hear the sound of the club hitting the wood. The room… was it even here?

He was led out in chains, to the waiting car. The spectators were here, too, in the backyard, being present when the witch was being led to the heap of dry wood, the awaiting fire.

And it was Ethel. Among them was Ethel. He saw that easily now. But this Ethel was a different Ethel. She pretty much looked the same. She was a bit more muscular, wilder in her display, the hair more a hue of red, but she was the same. Where she more than anything was different, was in the eyes. Her eyes had the same color, the same glow of fire as the stone in the ring he wore on his finger.

– Keep the ring, she said, – and never take it off your finger.

The car moved through darkened streets. This was the final transport, the one taking him to the actual penitentiary, not another holding cell. The van was filled with suspicious individuals who he would have never chosen to spend an evening or even a second with, if he could avoid it. More low, downtrodden life like himself. The chains hurt. They burned his wrists and ankles, and he couldn't get enough air.

There were lots of lights visible through the bars-covered windows, muted, without color, gray and dirty. They were on their way out of the city, to a dark, dark place, where no one ever returned from.

He looked at the ring, imagining it pulsing and glowing in the night. After a while he started clutching it, like a drowning man. He didn't look at the other prisoners, but he saw them nonetheless, saw their faces, their mirrors. Everybody stared straight ahead, without ever changing the dull expression in their eyes, their bodies.

His nose started twitching. It did so long before the others' noses, he was certain of it. There was a loud crack. The ring flashed. He saw the driver, impossibly through the wall haul up his arms in a useless attempt to protect himself. Then there was the insanely loud sound of metal against metal, and everything turned black, turned white.

He stood there on the open road, breathing hard, breathing fresh air, laced with poison.

And the man with the club, the man behind the bench cried out in a high-pitched voice:

– … AND WHERE YOU WILL SPEND THE REMAINS OF YOUR NATURAL LIFE

The shock rattled him like snakes, as he stood there, frozen, in the middle of the road, as smoke, as mist and debris were all around him.

He looked down on himself. The chains were in tatters, torn apart in the crash, still attached to his ankles and wrists, but no longer able to hamper his movements.

There was the sound of church bells. He turned. On one side was the church, on the other the castle.

The air cleared. He looked closer at his immediate surroundings. There were blood and guts, and mangled bodies everywhere, pieces of bodies raining down on the crimson ground. Bones stuck out, at impossible angles. Two guys were decapitated. Their headless bodies met a bit above the ground, in a weird, horrifying embrace. The heads were nowhere to be seen. He looked around, walked among the bodies, among the debris. They were all dead, prisoners and guards alike. He was the sole survivor. He surveyed himself some more. There was no pain, no wounds he could see or feel. The driver was still in his seat, in what was left of the car. The roof, the doors, the walls were gone. The tires were gone. Everything had vanished, except the seat and the wheel in the guy's hand, the piece of sharp glass sticking out of the half severed neck. In the other seat was a gun, but there was no sign of the guard. The weapon seemed to have been placed neat, very neat there on the seat. No blood, no remains, only the weapon, the somehow very sinister weapon.

There was a bus, split in two, its passengers hacked to pieces and spread all over the place. Blood was a river. Flesh a stinking garbage heap of rot. A young couple still sat in their seats, holding hands, their upper body virtually cleaved in two. An old lady had lost, misplaced her feet. Two gaping wounds were where her knees were supposed to be. Her mouth was open, the tongue sticking out, bloated and coarse. Her eyes were red, red, red, tomato ketchup on a steak. A man was gutted on a shard of metal. Colin spotted his eyeballs on the ground. He couldn't take his eyes off the empty sockets. They seemed to haunt him, to persecute him into a red, red field of shadow. He could hardly believe it, believe it all. It was just too much, way too much.

Round and round the major vortex span. Car tires, wreckage and twisted metal pieces lay spread everywhere. Everything visible from the air and in the light cast from the powerful spotlights, like an indistinct shimmering twilight where all sharp edges were hidden. A curtain in a bedroom where light and shadow constantly moved. Indistinct phantoms becoming something alive, something tangible.

There were no more church, no more castle. They, he and the bodies, all the bodies were on the highway somewhere, a place he didn't recognize.

His attention, as if in a dream finally returned to the prison guard by his feet.

Colin spotted the flashing metal, the ring of keys on the guy's hip. He closed in on the guy, very slowly, very cautious. The guy didn't breathe, not a single wheeze. He didn't blink. Not a tiny hair of the eyelashes moved. There was no wind. Not a single breath of wind. Colin grabbed the ring of keys and pulled it free. The man still didn't move. Not an inch. Colin tried the keys. The third and fifth fit, and he got rid of the remains of the manacles.

He stood there, for a few seconds, undecided.

The man with the club, the man behind the bench cried out in a high-pitched voice:

– … AND WHERE YOU WILL SPEND THE REMAINS OF YOUR NATURAL LIFE

Colin Dexter ran off, fading into the pitch-black darkness.

He ran, and there was nothing else. No surroundings, no details, just his heaving breath and swinging arms. When he looked down he was unable to spot his feet and legs. They disappeared somewhere down his thighs, and he feared he had lost them, misplaced them somewhere. He felt a sudden, desperate craving to stop, to run back and *look* for them. He kept running.

The powerful sense of unreality kept overwhelming him. He ran and then he could no longer spot his arms either. It was just his torso moving and mouth breathing, as if he was about to turn invisible, indistinct.

The city rose around him, like a giant, fire-breathing monster. Steam blew from beneath its surface. Cars raced back and forth around him, and it was a miracle they didn't run him down. He once again saw the driver from the prison transport sit in the seat with the door gone. The corpse… winked to him. He sat down in a dark alley, breathing hard, as if he never could get enough air. There were police cars and police officers. He was like a ghost to them, because they didn't see him. During many a second he felt compelled to give himself up, to go to them and explain it all to them, that there had been an accident, a horrible misunderstanding. He sat there in the dark alley, breathing, crying, slowly pulling himself together.

He looked at himself, studied himself. He was still clad in the prison uniform. Fingers, hands pulled the clothes off, until he stood there naked. People walking by in the bright street outside the dark alley didn't see him. He remained a ghost. Nothing connected him to them anymore, nothing at all.

There was the bodiless head in the street, leering at him. He searched through the nearby garbage cans, suffered the smell and stench, until he finally found some leftover clothes. They even were his size, and they weren't bad. There were no holes in them. They weren't even worn. A bit dirty perhaps and certainly wrinkled, but all in all okay. He felt an enormous relief over wearing clothes again.

It brought tears to his eyes. He dried his tears, as he drifted through the streets, like cordwood down a river, with no goal in mind, no end in sight. He cried and he dried his tears.

– That's my clothes.

Suddenly a woman stood in front of him, speaking to him. She was his height, medium built, like him, and he could half on half believe her clothes would fit him, skinny as he had grown lately.

She rushed to him and banged her rather big hands at his chest.

– You're wearing my clothes, *my* clothes.

He struck her, struck her hard. She fell at the wall, fell to the ground. He grabbed her hair, lifted her up after it, and struck her again, and again. She turned limp in his grip. He dragged her into the nearest alley, the next dark place. There was a brick there, glowing in the dark. He grabbed it and started banging her with it, sensing skull and bones give in to the harsh onslaught. He pulled the bloody wallet from her pocket. The money, a thick pile of bills was clean. There was nothing red there, only green, green, green. He walked on, on the lookout for ghosts.

A ruby stone was glowing in the dark. Drops flowed from it like blood.

And there was a roar somewhere, a thunder in the dark alleys of the night, and he froze in his thin skin.

I give you this ring, as a token of my love.

The master is playing his fiddle, like a butcher's knife.

He stood on the corner, in the shadow, sweaty and with huge, staring eyes. The woman walked under the streetlights, passing from one bright spot to another.

– You're more beautiful than ever, he told her.

She gasped, and fainted on the spot. He dreamed, dreamed about a wooden ship sailing the seven seas. Ethel Wharton lay on the sidewalk, half in light, half in shadow. He lifted her up and carried her inside the building, up the four floors to her apartment. It took him a while to find the keys, looking through her purse. From the neighboring apartment he heard funny noises. A bus passed by outside. It stopped on the stop, and opened its doors, but nobody walked out. He found the keys and unlocked the door. Breathing hard he carried the headless corpse inside and closed the door behind him. He dumped it in the freezer in the room to the east, and closed the lid decisively.

He put Ethel to bed and splashed her face with water. She opened her eyes, slowly, painfully. A demon was laughing somewhere, and its laughter hurt his ears. She smiled to him, embracing him, dragging him into the bed.

She held him, held him hard.

– I'm so sorry, she cried. – Sorry, sorry, sorry.

There was silence. They just sat there for a while, saying nothing.

She touched him, touched his head.

– You're all bloody and dirty, she gasped.

– The… prison transport… there was an accident. There were bodies everywhere. I see heads. I can't stop seeing the heads. I just had to… get away.

He turned away from her, as he dumped down on the bed's edge, crouched there, and covered his face with his hands, and the tears burned like acid, as he shook, as he couldn't stop shaking.

She moved out of the bed, grabbing the remote, and turned on the television. He heard her, heard her move behind him, with the knife in her hand.

The news.

It didn't seem real. Not any of it. There were just more headless corpses, stretched out on slabs in the basement of the police headquarters. She didn't seem real, there on the slab, pale and still.

Marion Dexter was dead.

She opened her eyes and looked at him.

The driver opened his eye, and looked at him. He had only one eye. The other was gone, left somewhere on the highway. The police had closed off an incredibly large area. There were yellow ribbons everywhere. There were bloated corpses everywhere.

– It's a MASSACRE! The network reporter Andrew Fallon screamed into the microphone. – Guards, drivers, civilian people in passing cars, even the prisoners have been *slaughtered* to the last man, woman and child. What happened here? What happened to turn this peaceful scene of people driving home from work or returning from their early week shopping into such *carnage?* You may ask, but no answer is forthcoming. Not from any higher powers and certainly not from the police, which seem to walk around in a state of paralyzed, perpetual stupor. As we speak bodies are being hauled into ambulances, but they are not brought to any hospital, but to the dark, cold basement slabs of the police headquarters…

He saw, relived the collision. There was the hard hit, the screaming of breaks, the smell of burning tires. Cars hit each other on an assembly line, came at each other from all sides, as if they had all been lined up to crash. The sounds and images of it all just overwhelmed him. He sat there at the edge of the bed, shaking.

Ethel turned off the television. Overwhelming silence dominated the room. She turned to him, pale and timid.

– You… can't return to prison, she said, very definite. – They'll… slaughter you.

She walked to him, dropped the remote from a shivering hand. There was no sound as it hit the floor. He couldn't say if it ever actually did.

– I love you. I have always loved you.

She unbuttoned her blouse. Fingers moved down her body, as white blouse turned to white skin.

– You are big, he said. – I like that. I've always loved that. Your big, juicy tits are like clay in my hands.

– Don't say tits, she said, absentminded. – Please don't say that.

She pulled her pants down her thighs, removed the last vestige of clothes. He grabbed her. She fell on him. Her hands, her eager hands worked on him, pulling off his clothes. She kissed his lips, his bloody lips. He was naked now. His bloodstained body pushed against hers. His blood mixed with hers.

There was a smell of trees, and of salt from the endless sea, smoke in the eternal forest.

She bit him in the shoulder. Her teeth held on to him and the howl echoed.

Through the eternal forest.

He stared at himself in the mirror, the blond hair, the changed man. The man in the mirror didn't even look like him anymore.

– Am I good or what? Ethel snuggled behind him.

– You're a genius, he marveled. – A hair and body dresser extraordinaire.

And the sense of dislocation didn't leave him.

They snuggled in bed, and he talked.

– It is as if I'm still in the house, he said. – Seeing the body on the floor. Nothing is right. The very walls seem to shift and bulge around me, and my vision is totally off. I can't seem to see what's right in front of me.

– Your neighbors lied like hell, she snarled. – They must belong to some sort of cult or something, and they offered poor Marion up to some demon or similar.

He looked at her, suddenly pointedly, as if remembering something he didn't want to remember.

– The woman I met in the cafeteria looked exactly like you, he said. – She speaks like you, she behaves like you, she was you. She is you. There are slight variations, subtle differences I can easily see now, but at the time, it was impossible.

– At the party… Ethel looked at him, and he saw no deception in her eyes, but then again, he hadn't seen any deception in the other Ethel either. – You thought I had given you the ring. I saw you speak to a woman in the hall, in the shadows… and I froze to a statue in my mind.

She grabbed his hand, holding up the hand, displaying the ring.

– It's beautiful… and eerie. It's like it's staring at me, drilling into my mind.

They still stared at it, as they stared at the city from her small balcony. Her building was high up, on the rise, in the Pit at the center of town. They could look at the city from here, but they didn't. They looked at the ring, the ring of fire, and it was as if reality shifted, waxed and dawned around it.

– I'll make breakfast. She kissed him on the cheek and disappeared into the apartment.

It was four in the morning. The eastern horizon had just started reddening.

This was the part of the city called the Pit. Nobody could see him here. Everything was just smoke, just mist, swallowing everybody whole.

He was still not sure she wouldn't turn him in, but just now, it didn't matter. It was so peaceful, here, on the balcony.

He would just sit here for a while, and just wait.

Ethel stared down at him while he slept and laughed contemptuously. And the demon reared its head.

He sat on a chair in the bathroom in the morning. There were no windows here. No way to look outside. No way to look in. She kissed him on the cheek.

– Remember, she admonished him. – Don't answer the phone or the bell or anything. You're not here, remember?

He didn't mind being admonished then, still feeling distant from reality, his mind still reeling and screaming in dark places.

After seeing her walk through the alley, to the street beyond he rushed to the cold room, and opened the lid.

The body was gone. He just sat down, there on the floor.

He rushed back to the living room, to the window towards the alley. There was no one coming, not Ethel, not others and no sound of sirens. He stood there for a long time, before going to the bed and dropping down on it.

Days passed, as he stayed indoors, watching television. She brought food, brought herself. They fucked on the old, dusty bed. He watched television, watched the horror parading on the screen, the bodies, the blood and carnage. His ears listened, as he watched television, the silent images, the skull grinning at him, for heavy boots running up the stairs. But they didn't come.

He wanted to ask her about the body, but courage and initiative failed him.

The two of them walked out one night, in the cold and misty night. Wisps of smoke formed in the air every time they exhaled. There was an old lady searching through the garbage cans, searching for food perhaps, scraps of food, and faded memories. She mumbled to herself, muttered words he didn't understand. They passed around the corner, and the old lady faded behind them, burning in his memory, just like the talking skull.

– This is the world, isn't? He said to Ethel. – The world as it truly is?

She returned his look with solemn eyes.

And the skull faded. And the old lady took the place of the skull in his mind

A bell struck twelve somewhere. They walked in the middle of a heavy trafficked street, a noise overwhelming their senses.

They still heard it.

He was nervous every time people looked at him, but he saw no recognition in their eyes. Police cars passed by. Police officers passed them on the sidewalk. Ethel held his hand, giving it a comforting squeeze. The two of them passed homeless sitting against a cold wall, people packed in rags and newspapers, in their desperate attempts at keeping the cold away.

Ethel was also disguised, wearing a black wig, and also other details, making her hard to spot. He realized it made sense. The police would check out her, at least once or twice, check out all his friends and associates.

– They do look for me, I know that, he said. – But it doesn't seem like they do, does it? I feel like a ghost passing the living on the streets, knowing I can never touch them, never know them.
– It's a big city, she said, squeezing his hand some more. – A man or a woman can disappear here, never to be seen again.
There had been a shootout on the corner of Aldwich and fifth. It was filled with police cars, with police. And bloody corpses and blood and bones and guts decorated the street. Among them were several officers. The policemen and women looked very pissed and stared hard and hateful at the pedestrians. Colin imagined they stared straight at him. He kept staring straight ahead, kept staring curiously at all the bodies, like everybody else passing by.
The carnage faded, as everything did. This carnage faded, like it always did. They walked to the older, less kept-in-shape part of the city. The buildings were older, and not with the somewhat shiny quality of the new office buildings in the central parts. They passed many a construction site that had just faded and died before being truly born. Half made ruins of what could have been, a result of yet another economic recession. They entered a street lost in time. Newspapers and dry, yellow leaves blew in the wind and he glimpsed his own insane face. The wind, the ghosts of the wind whispered to them.
– Creepy, he remarked.
– Yeah, isn't it great? She grinned.
They stopped in front of a dark, foreboding building.
A sign said with huge, macabre, dark red letters:

THEATER OF BLOOD

They entered through the open door, pulled by the dark, shimmering light inside. Colin turned and looked back, and the door was already far behind. Geysers of smoke rose left and right of them, as they made their way through the long corridor and into the main reception hall. It was dark there, as well. They saw no electrical lights, only the lamps on the wall, the flickering fires. Tonight had drawn quite a crowd, most of them dressed in black, in black costumes, with heavily applied make-up. Colin felt a kind of relief. He wasn't hiding, wasn't in disguise in here. He was blending in.
There were sirens outside, rising and fading. They were overwhelming just as the cars passed the front entrance. Otherwise they were not.
– A concealed place, forgotten by time, she whispered. – Isn't it great?
He nodded. The fear and shock still very much present in him, but in here it was muted, indeed half forgotten.

The entire room gave the impression of being in shadow. There were mirrors, cleverly placed, not only on the walls, but on the floor as well, expanding the room, the sense of the room. Colin saw two people stand close to each other and he couldn't tell whether or not they were truly two or each other's mirror image.

– Isn't it clever? She said.

– Breathtaking, he nodded.

– This is no ordinary theater, she assured him.

The bell announced that the performance was about to begin. They walked to their front row seats. The inner hall and the stage were even more eerie. Demon statues on the walls. Carvings on the seats.

– I saw a man I thought I recognized out there, he said. – But it can't have been him.

– Then it surely isn't, she assured him.

He relived the image in his mind, unable to fathom why a wave of terror washed over him.

A big, older man with blond hair. There was not a shred of gray on that head.

They sat down. The seats were deep and comfortable. They sat a bit above the stage, in a room resembling an ancient Greek theater. The audience could, when a man entered the stage and put a finger to his lips, making them fall silent, hear the quietest rustling and most minutiae sound from down there, echoes enhanced, not fading.

There was shadow down there, even though the room itself was fairly well lit. The man with the long black hair slipped in and out of those pockets of shadow, endlessly disappearing and appearing. One step to the side, and he wasn't there, was there.

– THE STREETS ARE DEVOURING US, SWALLOWING US WHOLE

He SHOUTED.

LOUD.

Making people shake and jump in their comfortable chairs.

Colin, impossibly as it was, was, in a flash convinced he walked the streets, and that they bulged and stretched and reached for him, eager to swallow him whole.

– Good evening, good people, the man on the stage cried. – Welcome to this dark soirée. «Good evening», says the night. «I am Anubis, the mystery of death. And I am Mysteriam, the secret of life».

– That is Jason Gallagher, Ethel whispered mysteriously. – He is quite infamous.

Colin nodded. Even he, not really traversing in the circles familiar with Jason Gallagher had heard about him.

– We're living a *theatre absurd,* are we not? Jason chuckled.

– I saw a picture of him without make-up once, Colin whispered back. – He looks quite normal without make-up.

A woman a few rows below hushed him up. An expectant murmur rose from the gathered crowd. Low music traveled from the stage and from ear to ear, a whisper in the silent, silent night.

– Hello, hallow audience. The man's voice rose to an impossible level, stamping the audience' flesh like nails. – Welcome to our show. We walk in darkness and wade in blood. Welcome to our feast. We are the love upon which everything is made. Welcome to the milk and blood of existence.

A man rushed from the shadows, eager and hallow, halting before Jason like an adolescent admirer (and perhaps he was). Jason pulled a knife from his cloak and sliced through the dark air. He cut off the man's head in one, powerful stroke. The head, flying through the air hit the floor with a thump. The body slumped to the ground like an empty sack, with no sound at all.

And then all kind of normalcy was thrown out the window. For good, this time.

– There once was a castle, the storyteller told. – It isn't anymore.

The room turned dark. The many shadows were the only light they could see. They saw, easily the man down there cloaked and hooded in night.

– But I will take you back, now, take you forward to a time, a place there was a castle. You are visitors and I am your Guide.

– There is a flash, an image of a building in broad daylight the sun's rays can't reach. You see your Guide. He stops before the entrance, calling you inside with a wave of his hand, a withered hand appearing from the cloak.

A crow, a crying crow lands on his shoulder, taunting you, and he enters the shadow, and you follow him, follow the crow into the darkness.

The crow speaks like a man, very distinct, very articulate, of all things. It tells you about the castle's beautiful interior, about the carvings on the wall, about the carpets on the floor, about the shadows in the corners. You enter the castle and you see, experience the hall. There is a wall there, with a lot of paintings. It might be paintings, paintings looking like photos, photos resembling paintings, compelling images of an insane reality. There is a staircase, broad and tall, going up. Let us go, the Guide says. Let us walk up, up, into the sky. And you follow the crow as it walks like a man up the stairs.

There is an exhibition on the second floor, artifacts from a forgotten world. There is a feather, a raven feather hovering in a glass booth, flickering like a candle. You see it, feel it as it rattles your skin, your withered skin. There is a knife, a blade black and oily, bathed in blood. There is a sign with the word WELCOME, written in blood. The floor is red. The walls and ceiling are black. History is written in blood, ladies and gentlemen. There is fire and there is shadow, and that's all there is, the endless there is.

You ascend the stairs. There is no third floor, even though there is a third floor. You visit it briefly, like a memory you desperately try to access, but cannot quite wrap your mind around.

There is Order, there is Chaos in the Universe, even though it is never the way we expect. In fact it is so far removed from our expectations that both words are meaningless, like words, like everything really is.

You look down, and there is dust on the stairs upon your feet are treading, increasingly so as you ascend further on the endless staircase. So few walk here, so very few. You imagine you can see footprints in the dust, but you cannot really quite convince yourself they are there.

When you turn and look back, on the stairs you have just trod, there is nothing but dust.

You have reached the attic. You do not know how long you have walked, only that a very long time has passed since you possibly entered the gate far below. The attic is huge. You have walked here forever. In fact you have stumbled around here for so long that you can no longer tell if there ever were stairs anywhere.

The attic is a crossroads. From high places you can spot the end of the world. There is no end, no beginning. Everything and nothing can be glimpsed from this place. The attic is no place.

There is a ship, sailing the seven seas. The wind is fierce. The waves are tall. The ship hardly touches the sea at all. Its sails are tight as drums. There is thunder and lightning as it sails through silent mist, forever clouds in endlessly changing patterns.

He spotted them, indistinct figures on the deck, impossible to recognize.

There was a flash of shadow, a blink of an eye.

Colin walked, stumbled darkened streets. Loud sirens sounded and resounded around him. He fled the bright-lit streets and sought dark, quiet alleys. The Pit was filled with people tonight, creatures stumbling around in rags, confused and belittled, without any hope that tomorrow would come. He sat down there, on a box between two of the burning oil barrels the homeless gathered around.

He kept stumbling through darkened streets without any notion of where he happened to be.

– I know Jason, Ethel said excitedly to him in his ear. – Know him from old.

That was a strange expression… wasn't it? He stared at her, beyond curious.

– I kid you not, she assured him. – I'm fairly certain they will let us visit him behind the stage.

She pulled him with her, led him from the excited buzz of the stage-room and to the silence behind the carpet. There were no people there. He would have thought there would be hectic activity on this place, but he saw no one, heard no sign of anything happening.

He stopped. The door to the wardrobe had been opened. He stared in there, filled with incredulity and horror. Ethel drew a knife from her coat, and stabbed Jason Gallagher repeatedly with an impassive expression on her face, a cold glee in her eyes. He fell to the floor, blood flowing from his many leaks. Colin screamed in pain. He turned abruptly and ran away from the place, the demonic face of Ethel Wharton burned onto his vision.

He ran through darkened streets.

Colin Dexter ran through darkened streets, between bulging walls, surrounded by red and blue flashes. He ran so hard that his lungs burst.

The shaking figure leaned against the brick wall, coughing while breathing, breathing while coughing, desperately attempting to breathe.

His feet were firmly planted in desert sand, but the walls were still there. He smelled the scent of bricks and of desert, its hot, arid air. His hand… it was light, without the heavy load he had carried on it. He looked down at the dusty street. The eye stared at him, glowed at him, penetrated his very being.

Ethel walked towards to him. She smiled to him, the sweetest of smiles.

She walked to the ring, bent down and picked it up. Her smile sent chills to his very bones.

Ethel picked up the ring. She put it on her finger. The stone glowed, and her eyes glowed as well. Her skin changed to a darker hue. Cold trickled down his spine.

– I take this ring, she said. – As a token of our love.

She turned a bit, as if sniffing in the air, as if taking in the surroundings, not really looking at him, not really talking to him.

– These streets don't feel real to me. They would to you, of course, but not to me.

He tried to sneak away, but Ethel turned back to him, proving beyond doubt that she was truly there.

– I made you, she whispered, her voice filled with love. – Made you from nothing. I won't let you go. I will never let you go.

Just as she was about to put the ring on her finger something incredible happened. Another woman seemed to step right out of the air and charge her. One of her hands clutched those of Ethel's hands clutching the ring. The hand opened, and the ring fell to the ground. The ethereal creature caught it as it as it fell, and she pushed Ethel away. The two women measured each other, hatred burning in both pair of eyes. The newcomer threw the ring to Colin. It flew through the air towards him. He reached out a hand to grab it.

– Take this ring, she cried, – as a token of our love. And never let go.

She and Ethel clinched, and reality itself seemed to blink, and everything turned into mists and shadows.

CHAPTER THREE

They had seen a David Somby flick at the movies last night. What had happened after that wasn't altogether clear in his mind.

He woke up in Ethel's bed, her warm body snuggling tight to his. She reached for him, half asleep, releasing content, joy-filled throaty sounds.

They sat by the table, having breakfast, sitting tight, doing a lot of heated snuggling. He disengaged himself with a laugh, standing up, looking frantically at his watch, looking apologetically down on her where she sat with her arms reached out and embracing the air he had occupied.

– I must go home, okay. One night away might be acceptable, but much more than that and she will start growing suspicious. It was bad enough that our anniversary party was cancelled.

– Please, don't go, she whimpered, her pale skin turning even another shade of pale.

He backed off.

The door opened behind him. The door closed behind him.

He left the apartment, left the bright, nice neighborhood, with a frown on his face. Wasn't there something, something he was supposed to remember?

But it slipped away, like water on ice. If he had ever remembered, he forgot the moment he stepped out in the bright sunshine.

He looked at his watch. It was still fairly early. He had time to go shopping. An idea, or a beginning of one began forming in his head. He shook his head in denial.

The bus stop was right down the street. The bus had already stopped by the stop. He hurried, to the point of running, and made it just as the doors slammed shut. The driver stared accusingly at him. The doors slammed shut right behind him, like a disappointed jaw being cheated of its meal. He didn't quite make it to the seat before the bus began moving, and he lost his footing and landed on it with his butt, not too hard. The driver whistled cheerfully in the far front. Colin wanted to walk back forward. He was sorely tempted.

Saturday afternoon on the bus, a fairly different crowd compared to the weekdays, but not that different.

A woman spoke in her phone. Colin had major difficulties even spotting the small thing, there in her hand, pressed against the ear. He imagined he could see the damaging microwaves surrounding her head and making a mush of it all. The woman rubbed her temple, clearly nursing an approaching headache.

He heard her voice. It was clear and present like a waterfall in his mind, a loud, clear voice without even an indication of distortion.

– I'm sitting inside in a room. I can't see outside. Outside may be anywhere. It might be the streets familiar to me, those I just left… or it might be something completely different.

There was a reply, and her response was clearly one of irritation, of annoyance.

– Yes, I know that. No, I wasn't imagining it. The room didn't seem real around me. The walls bulged and I got the distinct impression that they weren't there at all.

The voice in the other end of the line spoke some more, and the annoyance in the strained face turned to rage and fear.

– What are you *talking* about? Who are you? Do I know you? How did you get this number?

The woman's voice grew loud and shrill.

Colin looked at his indistinct reflection in the window. It was a dark day, dark enough for his reflection to be fairly clear. His dark hair was long and curly. Marion wanted him to cut it, but Ethel liked it. Marion didn't seem to like anything about it lately. He wondered what had happened, when it had started to go… wrong.

The dark and foggy day stared back at him, as the bus moved slowly through the city traffic.

– More construction work! A young boy cried it out in misery. – When will it end?

– Never kid, an older man replied with clear malice in his voice. – Ongoing construction work is a major part of modern life. Everybody knows that.

Every-body.

He took a bow, and the other passengers chopped off his nasty, little head.

They sat there, with a dull expression in their faces, not moving, not moving at all.

The road vanished into a misty hole appearing to the west. Some of the cars stopped, but others kept driving, and they, too, followed the road into nothingness.

It was sunny and mostly blue skies by the time they finally arrived at the mall. The urban landscape was, as always, coated in dull gray. People filed past Colin, until he was the only one left on the bus, and almost didn't make it out before the bus drove on. The door had teeth this time. He was positive.

Colin crossed the large parking lot. Families arrived here from all over the southern part of the city to catch up on everything they hadn't been able to do earlier in the week.

– Today, a father told his children. – Today is Saturday, and we can enjoy life.

The pained look on people's faces, as they were pushing themselves through the crowds didn't exactly confirm his words. He, himself, looked anything but pleased.

The buzz of the crowd was clearly audible outside, as well, but inside, when it echoed between the walls, it turned into an indistinguishable cacophony of noise.

Colin had visited this mall a thousand times, but today it seemed somewhat… different. He couldn't tell why that was, only that it was. It was a kind of vague impression he couldn't pin down. He recognized the man in the newsagent booth, halfway nodding to him and receiving a nod in return. Newsagent salesmen recognized everybody. They had the memory of an Elephant.

There was the girl behind the counter of the leisure store. She was quite the looker, and clearly memorable in more ways than one. He waved to her. She didn't wave back. He kept walking. This was the same mall he visited, and had visited virtually every Saturday for a long time. He recognized people and places constantly, as he made his way through the prevalent Saturday afternoon chaos.

He began noticing the familiar scent of flowers, of flowers everywhere, overpowering that of the antiseptics used all over the place. The combination created a jumble of smells making him nauseas and dizzy. He bought the newly baked bread at the baker vendor at the corner, and headed for the cafeteria. It was full, but he managed, by a miracle to secure a place right in front of the counter. The man behind it stared at him, in a way quite similar to that of the bus driver. Colin heard the sound of the waterfall in his ears, and couldn't fathom why it sounded so familiar to him.

– Someone is taking a leak somewhere, a girl insisted to her boyfriend at the neighboring table. – It's like a waterfall, that's what it is.

Colin listened in, focusing on her very special voice. Everybody in the cafeteria looked at her as she spoke, even though it was hard to fathom why. She was a looker, but it was more than that.

– You're such a laugh riot, Chloe, her boyfriend holding her hands shook his head.

– Thank you, Malcolm, she grinned. – You say the nicest things…

And the boy didn't like that. He didn't like that at all.

Colin found he was hungry, too hungry to wait for the breakfast with Marion at home, and he bought a few sandwiches to the coffee.

– The food tastes like paper, a man a few tables away said in despair. – It always does at this place. I don't understand why I keep returning to this shithole. I just don't.

His wife comforted him the best she could, but she didn't really look that happy herself.

Colin wolfed down the sandwiches. He didn't really taste them, just devoured them at a staggering speed. They were gone before he had truly been able to appreciate them. He shook his head in dismay.

– Something is wrong, Chloe's boyfriend complained. – Something is very wrong.

And it was so out of character that it gave Colin goose bumps.

There was an airport nearby. He heard the sound of the planes taking off and landing fade in and fade out of his ears. The prevalent whispering in the room found its way to his table, somehow. All that noise and buzz, and he was still able to hear the whisper.

The black, black coffee surface seemed to expand as he stared at it, as he was drowning in its abyss. The coffee stayed warm, and never seemed to turn really cold. He kept sipping it, as the minutes passed by.

He bought another cup of coffee. The man behind the counter, the owner kept talking as if he was paid to do so (and he wasn't).

– Exciting days, with the new airport, and all, you know, he stated. – Brings a lot of new business here.

– Is it? Colin shrugged.

– Exciting days, the man repeated. – Exciting days.

Colin left early, a sense of urgency almost overwhelming him, leaving the excited man behind. The guy looked at his back with a puzzled expression in the face. Colin drank up all his coffee as he walked, drank it in a few turns, threw the paper cup in the nearest wastebasket, and hurried outside. The traffic outside was staggering, with both people and cars moving back and forth like confused insects. He managed to push through it all somewhat sane and was lucky enough to catch an unscheduled bus.

– Is everything all right? He asked the driver.

The driver looked at him as if he had lost his marbles.

– Is everything all right? He repeated.

The driver did not start the bus until Colin had reached the backseat and sat down safely.

The bus reached the highway, the foggy, foggy notion highway.

– Is this the same route? The girl asked her boyfriend.
– What do you mean? He wondered.
– The same route the bus took earlier today? She insisted.
– I can't tell, he shrugged. – Who can, in this gray shit they call air?
The mist seemed to penetrate the bus. All the windows were closed, and the internal heat was turned on, but it was still cold and wet inside.
Colin stared out the window, attempting to discern any details in the eternal gray out there. It was hopeless.
There were stops and the bus picked up new passengers. That much was certain, since new people actually entered the bus. That was an empirical fact.
But they saw nothing outside, not even the stop sign.
– This isn't fog! An older lady cried. – I know what fog is like, and this isn't it. A fog is… foggy, but you can discern some details, at least a few steps away. This is a white wall, falling on us all.
– That was a rhyme, a man in a suit barked a laughter.
Colin shook his head and turned away from it all.
They all heard the sound of other vehicles passing, but they saw nothing.
– This is insane, a woman said. – We can't see shit. The driver can't see shit. We're gonna crash. It's common sense.
Nobody objected to her statement. They kept staring out the window.
– I want to leave, she wailed. – We should stop. *Listen* to me! We should *stop!*
She remained seated, distraught drying her foggy tears.
For some reason Colin looked at his watch.

6.02

It cried.
They heard the sound of the ongoing construction work, heard the roar of the thousand engines. It rose like a scream in their mind. The woman attempted to dry her foggy tears and cover her ears with her palms simultaneously, with spectacularly bad results.
And then there was another screech of tires and banshees, and people's terrified stares into nowhere.
He walked with them all among the dead and the dying. They were no longer inside the bus, and he had no idea where the bus had gone, but it just wasn't there anymore. They waded through body parts, through pools of blood, a gray soup of mist that seemed to go on forever. There were cops and paramedics present, but they didn't seem that interested in him. Both those in white and in blood grabbed him, as they grabbed others, and he had no idea why that scared him so much.

Some of the others were led off and made to sit down in the trench, but not he. He seemed fine and didn't need coddling. People spoke, but he didn't hear a thing. Not their voice or the noise from the engines or that of the beyond extensive wreckage being removed.

What happened? A woman cried. What in God's name happened?

Colin didn't hear her, but he saw her move her lips.

The policeman heard her, but he shook his head, just as baffled as the rest of the people present. Confusion and chaos ruled the scene, leaving nothing to choice. Colin recognized his surroundings now. On his left was the church. On his right the castle, the newly refurbished castle, with spires reaching into the sky. They seemed to fade into the blue and the gray, and where the blue came from he couldn't say. He walked there, walked to the castle door. It was open, open to all the people filing through it. There was a Japanese couple with cameras. Colin saw a nasty looking man resembling everybody's idea of an Italian mobster. And there were others.

He spotted Chloe Webster somewhere in front, just as she turned her head and returned his interest.

– But you're dead? He blustered.

She looked at him with humor in her eyes, evidently not getting his drift.

– I read it, too, a man said sarcastically. – National Enquirer says she is, so it must be true.

– Everybody does, Chloe grinned.

Hearty laughter dissolved some of the tense mood. National Enquirer was the rag of rags, as far as «newspapers» were concerned. Their stories were half completely made up by the staff, half the wildest rumors in print. Nobody, not even the touchiest movie star would bother with litigation against them.

The castle's reception hall opened up to them, like someone opened a book. Colin shook a bit, as the cold trickle descended his spine. Before his half closed eyes he saw a row of newspapers at a newsstand, including National Enquirer, saw a tall, bold headline:

CHLOE WEBSTER IS DEAD

The Guide stopped at the center of the large hall, very professionally, very friendly. They formed a half circle in front of her.

– Welcome, dear friends and fellows interested in preserving this castle, welcome to the Caine Castle Exhibition.

Polite applause. Colin glanced around him. There were a few people among the entourage that fit the guide's expectations, people with fat wallets that might be interested in supporting this enormous conservation project.

But there were also clearly at least one other category present, represented by himself and Chloe Webster and a few others. They fit in because they didn't, pure and simple.

They… observed.

The guide began her lecture in a dry, controlled voice.

– Marlon Caine rose to fame thirty years ago, while producing Night Terrors, one of David Somby's most infamous works…

She droned on, as she guided them on the tour through the enormous space that was the building.

– As we walk from room to room you will experience one of the greatest collections of art ever assembled under one roof. Caine was an avid, even fanatical collector. Some say he collected people as well. I'm certain you've heard the rumors about his dungeon, supposedly a hidden room in the cellar where he hid, displayed his supposedly numerous victims.

Gasps of joy-filled horror rose from the assembly, drowning in the giant aerie they walked through, as they passed countless walls of paintings.

Colin stopped in a room where there were only three. Something about them resonated in him.

On his right he saw a picture of a tidal wave engulfing a city. In front of him a woman caught behind a window in the rain. And to his left a face, half in, half out of shadow, one constantly shifting and changing to the point that he couldn't be sure of who or what he saw.

He turned, and the rest of the group wasn't there anymore. In the other part of the room, where he imagined there had been a wall, there was a set of broad stairs leading up, far, far up. He imagined he couldn't see its ending.

Hours later he still walked upstairs. There were many floors, countless levels, but he passed all of them. He saw people on those floors, but they seemed ghostly, ephemeral, not truly there at all, revenants belonging somewhere else. One man, a man with a very familiar face looked at him, looked right at him, and Colin was convinced it was in fact him the man was looking at.

He stopped in a hall with a giant painting, one covering an entire wall. One of a ship in a harbor. There was wind in the sails and the mooring rope was tight. The waves struck the ship and the harbor relentlessly. He smelled the salt of the sea. The wind ruffled his hair. The hand he reached out with turned wet.

– What is it?

He turned and Chloe Webster appeared behind him.

– The paint is still wet, he stated.

– I saw it, she whispered.

He looked closer at her, at her distant and clearly distraught demeanor.

– I saw the ship sail the seven seas.

– The seven airways, he said.

Unable to decide why he said that.

Her eyes widened. She looked closer at him, scrutinizing him as if her eyes were about to burn straight through him.

– My name is Chloe Webster, she said nervously, giving him her hand. – I write for «Color of the Night».

She smiled obliging, the nervous twitches around her mouth not disappearing.

– I know, he said gallantly. – I've read your articles.

– It's sooo nice of you to call them *articles,* she grinned. – Most…

– Most people tend to call them something quite different. He nodded. – I know.

– I won't say my bad reputation is totally… undeserved, she said hastily, the nervous twitching returning. – I have taken shortcuts, not done my work properly…

He looked astounded at her, at her brutal honesty.

– … but recently I've come across a story that changed all that, changed *everything.*

She began pacing back and forth on the floor, the misty floor.

– I came here, pursuing a lead, she said. – Because several people came here, and I've been investigating them in a number of ways recently. There are a few that haven't come here to observe art and shine in the light of their perceived generosity. They have far darker motives than that.

Chloe said.

They stood there for a while, in silence.

– So how does all this strike you? She wondered, both anxiously and with a strangely calm smile. – How do I strike you? Am I sufficiently paranoid?

– I am speechless, he admitted, in a hopeless attempt at joking.

She stepped forward, into his arms, very anxious.

– I don't believe it was a coincidence that we met here. She spoke fast and passionately. – I think we both have stumbled on to something, something both amazing and terrifying.

She stepped back, embarrassed, clearly out of her wits.

– I believe you, he heard himself say. – I believe every word you say.

But had she truly said much? A few unclear statements, a few veiled truths, and nothing besides. He shook his head.

There was a splash behind him. He turned to look at the painting, but it was still just a painting.

He turned back towards her, and froze. She was there no longer. He ran from room to room, looking for her, silently calling her name. He stood there, frozen. There had been no sound of steps, no sign that she had walked off. It was like she had simply faded away there and then, while his attention had been… had been diverted.

Colin Dexter walked from room to room in a daze, yet another daze. He eventually returned downstairs, unable to tell how long time he had been gone from the visitor group. Looking at his watch did him no good.

6.02

– I've stopped using a watch, a man by his side shrugged. – The sun still rises in the morning and sets in the evening. That's enough for me, at least these days.

He looked okay, but several other people scrutinized Colin with wicked eyes. A chill trickled down his spine.

A fire was lit in the large living room. He stopped there for a while, warming himself in front of the fireplace.

It was like his feet still moved, still descended the stairs on his way down. He walked down the stairs, and there was no end in sight.

A man entered the room. Colin saw him half in, half out of his vision, as he stood in front of the fireplace with his back turned. He could no longer hear the visitors or the loud, screeching voice of the guide. The other man stopped in front of the fireplace, at Colin's side, reaching out his hands towards the fire, heating his open palms. Colin stared at him.

– A good fire is essential, the man said. – If done right it may heat an entire house or building, even settling in its walls, and even remain long after the original fire is put out.

He was fairly old, with silver hair. But his face seemed quite youthful, and his body looked quick and agile.

The old man turned, and Colin could no longer move.

– My name is Marlon Caine. It's such a delight to meet you, Colin, to meet you at last.

He reached out a hand and Colin took it, numb and anxious and terrified and shocked beyond belief.

– But you're dead, Colin stammered.

The other man laughed, contemptuously, triumphantly.

– I'm not dead. You are.

Colin remembered the photo from the old newspaper. There was no doubt. This was Marlon Caine's face. And somehow, beyond words, beyond appearances Colin also knew that this was Marlon Caine.

– Let me guess, Caine grinned, a perfectly normal grin. – You're curious, anxious for answers, are you not?

Colin wanted to speak, but he couldn't. It was as if his everything within and without was frozen.

– I will give you some answers. Caine nodded. – I always enjoyed it, in the old films, when the villain of the story explained his motives, revealed his grand plans, giving the hero time to act.

A brittle hand stirred the fire, and it grew and obliterated the shadows in the room.

– Time is fixed, you know, destiny is decided from the first electron to the last. That was, at least how it was, how it used to be.

He grinned.

– Or perhaps not…

What are you talking about? Colin wanted to ask him, to cry out to him.

– There are so many misconceptions, such an endless row of silly approaches to it all. Most people are totally clueless, and most of all those professing to possess pieces of the puzzle, the puzzle of time… and space. Reality is fluid, bendable, like a spoon. By moving a few well-placed mirrors everything becomes unraveled. Things were right once. They're not anymore. They are now…

The room was suddenly filled with shadows.

– Call it Hyper-Reality if you want, but it's an unnecessary, intermediary step. It is Reality. There is a ship, sailing the seven airwaves, and we're all its passengers. You can't leave it on a whim. No one can. And you are therefore a victim of nature's causality, of any gust of wind, any wave hitting its side, throwing it off course, throwing you off course. There is no right course, no wrong course. Everything is random, and everything may transform from one moment to the next to something new and unrecognizable. I was dead. You were alive. Now, I'm alive, and you're dead, and I swim like a fish in the sea.

Colin ran. He couldn't exactly recall leaving the castle, running from it gasping for breath, but he recalled the run, the endless run through the infinite night.

Colin Dexter sat on the bus, on his way home, clutching the fresh loaf in his hands. He whistled a tune, a melody he couldn't quite recall. There were other people on the bus, a score of them, on their way home from the Saturday shopping.

– What a wicked tune. A girl snarled at him, stared at him. – What a wicked, wicked tune.

An old couple sat a few seats behind him. He saw them, saw them as well as he heard their tired voices.

– Saturday is a day off, right? The husband said. – But since no one really have time to shop much the rest of the week, they have to shop on Saturdays, and since everybody shops on Saturday it's quite the ordeal. And we all go to bed early, just as exhausted as all the other days. And Sunday we rest, too tired to do anything else. And we never get enough sleep, and we wake up just as exhausted as when we fell asleep.

– That's quite an optimistic view of the world you've got there, fella, a man cried sarcastically. – Some of us are trying to actually enjoy ourselves a bit, you know.

– If you want to wear blindfolds that's up to you, the other countered.

– Better blindfolded than delusional…

The other other cried sarcastically.

The banter stopped, after a brief, heated exchange of insults. Colin didn't hear the rest of the words, and he didn't care doing so.

The bus made the final turn into the long, broad road plowing into the quiet neighborhood. A bulldozer worked its butt off somewhere. Stone and soil were caught in its gap. The sound of stone hitting stone hammered at Colin's ears. The bus stopped, and everything turned eerily silent. He left the bus, not hearing the sound of the doors closing behind him. There was no light in the kitchen, or any other room in the house that he could see, as he walked up the driveway. The door was open, opened wide. He walked inside, walked inside and stopped.

His wife stood in the kitchen, with a knife in her hand. He stopped a bit, rubbing his eyes. A dream? Had it all been a dream? He saw her incredibly clear in the bad light from the sunset outside.

He couldn't believe what he was seeing. His eyes burned as if he had been rubbing them for days.

– Listen, Marion, he said. – Be calm, okay? Something weird, something really weird is going on here, and…

– Don't come any c-closer. Not one single s-step.

She stood there, rigid and crazy, holding the kitchen knife in both hands.

– What are you doing, Marion? Why do you act this way? Do you actually believe I will hurt you?

– You want to kill me, she gasped. – I know you do.

– That's ridiculous, Marion, he almost laughed, his jittery nerves working overtime. – And you know it. Calm down, okay?

She stood her ground, the point of the blade still pointing at him, making him feel nauseas and strangely scared. He didn't know what was going on, but he was scared. His throat was dry, and his gut tied itself in knots this very minute.

– Calm down, he repeated. – Please, let's talk about this.

– I saw it, she gasped. – I saw you…

– It must have been a nightmare, don't you think? You haven't really been sleeping well lately, now, have you? Please, put down the knife, and let's discuss this as adults.

– I saw it, she said whimpering, heaving for breath.

The hands holding, clutching the knife slowly fell down. She started shaking. She leaned against the wall, tears running down her cheeks, eyes dull and lifeless. He carefully stepped forward, touching first one of her shoulders then the next.

– Calm down, he whispered, about to take her in his arms. – There is an explanation for all this, a rational explanation. We just have to find it, that's all.

She leaned against him, crying against a shoulder, shaking like a leaf.

– I had a nightmare, she sobbed. – It was h-horrible. You k-killed me, and left me in a pool of blood on the floor. You smiled horribly, and left me there, on the floor, dead and cold.

He kissed her on the brow, holding her head between his shaking hands. Cold sweat erupted from his skin, all over his body. It was as if he had been locked away inside a storage freezer room without clothes on his body. He sensed her calming down, slowly, painfully, as his warmth spread to her cold, cold body. Silence reigned in the small kitchen, closing them off from the world outside. She slowly relaxed in his arms, even though her body kept shaking in violent sobs.

– It will be all right, he whispered in her ear. – Everything will be all right.

– Do you think so? She sobbed, hardly able to form coherent words. – Do you really think so?

– I know it will, he said. – Trust me.

Eventually she was almost totally relaxed, to the point that she could hardly stand, and he had to hold her up, hold her steady in his grip.

He carefully took her weak hand, her knife hand, and grabbed the knife's handle, pulling it from her hand.

– NO! Suddenly her eyes reopened, wide and insane once again. – YOU WANT TO KILL ME, KILL ME, KILL ME

Her suddenly strong fingers clutched the knife and pulled it back, away from him.

– DIE! She shouted enraged, and stabbed him. – DIE!

He looked astonished at the blade sticking out from his chest.

She stabbed him again, and again, and again, pushing him back. The sound when the blade punctured his skin sounded shockingly loud, a sick, sucking sound. Somehow he was able to hear the roaring sound of the bulldozer down the road. It rattled him, overwhelmed his other senses, as everything turned black, as he could only smell the red fluid flowing, gushing from his body, from his heart, from his throat. He stumbled back, until his back hit the wall.

– DIE! She shouted.

– DIE! She repeated and kept repeating, mumbling as he slid down the wall, leaving a broad trail of blood.

He sat there on the floor, leaned against the wall. Warmth leaked from his wounds. Life left him. He stared. He stared incredulous. At her. At his wife, at the insane stranger clutching the knife. And also at something else.

The door to the living room was ajar. He could just about glimpse a body in there, as the darkness in there illuminated it, and an even bigger shock rattled him. He wanted to cry out, but couldn't for lack of breath.

The body of Marion Dexter, of another Marion Dexter lay there on the carpet, in a pool of blood, exactly as he remembered it. He looked at the woman with the knife in her hand frozen there on her spot.

– You can see it? She asked him dumbfounded. – You can see it, too?

He wanted to move, to nod, but he just stopped breathing. He died there on the spot, and his eyes turned dead and cold.

The uncanny rage left Marion Dexter and she sank to the floor like an empty sack, hiding her face in her bloody hands. The knife fell to the floor. It started spinning a bit, before it stopped and remained still. Everything was still.

She sat there, like that, unmoving, sat there for hours and days, until red and blue lights filled her vision, and the uniformed people came and took her away.

Part 2:
The Lady of the Lake - The Chloe Webster story

The water is still. There is hardly any movement on it, any at all. The mountain reflected on its surface is virtually a complete, unchanged copy of the one above.

This is the story about Chloe Webster.

No, more than that.

This, more than anything is *the* story about Chloe Webster.

Chloe is dead…

She was an investigative reporter for the magazine «Colors in the Night» and she was killed while pursuing the story.

Sorry, make that *a* story. Sorry.

She was murdered. Whether or not the murder is related to the actual story she pursued isn't clear. It still isn't clear, even after all this time. The case is open, the case is closed. The police haven't found out, even after eight weeks of extensive investigation why Chloe was killed or who did it or precisely how it happened. One can say, with a bit of added candor that they haven't really found out much of anything here. Some would claim that this isn't unusual, but that is clearly wrong. The police always find out something. They just hardly ever get the full story.

In this particular instance, in that regard they have indeed surpassed themselves.

Chloe Webster is dead and no one seems to know why…

CHAPTER FOUR

A car races along a deserted highway. The driver stares straight ahead, as if there is nothing to the sides, only ahead.

– … Nobody who is talking about it anyway.

Andy lowers his small, handy tape-recorder, just a second before raising it again.

– Now, that is certainly not unusual. The world is full of mysteries, tragedies and unexplained incidents. One can even say that the great Enigma, human life in general is largely unexplained. Even the most fanatical science convinced scientist would admit that, following some torture. Anyway, in this case there is very little to go on for anyone.

The hand is lowered again and the tape-recorder is left on his right knee.

The highway was dusty, but one could still see far ahead.

– Chloe Webster is dead, his desk editor had told Andy a cold morning two weeks ago, as if he didn't already know. – I want you to write a piece on it.

– Why? Andy had asked flat out.

– Because everyone else is doing it.

A very straightforward answer. Andy had nodded and before long he had been on his way.

Marion Dexter looked dead, her face sunken, her eyes swollen. She sat completely still on the chair in the interrogation room. He couldn't decide if she was even breathing.

Marion Dexter was dead.

– He wanted to kill me. He tried to kill me. He wanted to kill me.

She repeated it like a mantra over and over again. Her voice sounded ghostly, like it didn't actually come from the room, like she wasn't really there.

– He wanted to kill you? One of the detectives interviewing her attempted to get a straight answer. – He tried to kill you? Which one is it?

She started to cry, huge heartbreaking sobs, cutting to the bone.

Her lawyer put a hand on her arm.

There was a break. A female officer accompanied her out of the room, probably to the bathroom.

– I killed him, she said, with just a hint of life in her voice, in her unmoving eyes. It was like she had never cried, and certainly not just a few minutes earlier. – We had quarreled the night before and it turned into an ugly fight. He threatened to kill me. Anyone can confirm that. I stabbed him, and I kept stabbing him, until he was dead, until I noticed he was dead, and I just sat down, waiting for someone to come, and you came.

Fallon stood behind the one-way glass with his friend and contact within the police department, Elliott Lasko. Fallon had started on the Chloe Webster case where he always started on his stories: in the newspaper's archives.

All the articles already written had been spread out on the desk in front of him.

Andy Fallon read them once, and then read them again.

– This isn't saying much, is it? No details, no… curiosity. Even the National Inquirer does it better.

Peter Askiew, the desk editor shrugged. He wasn't really interested.

– I mean, I can see why you want me to write a piece on it. There is a lot of uncovered ground here, and as the truth-seeking, idealistic newshound you are, you surely want me to expose the Truth.

Before it could become ugly there was a knock on the door.

Nobody entered the room. Fallon and Askiew glanced at each other.

– ENTER, Fallon cried.

The door didn't move. Nobody entered. Fallon rose and walked to the door. He opened it with quite an impatient swing of his hand. There was nobody there. He looked at Eleanor Wingott at the closest desk, at least ten steps from the door. She shook her head in bewilderment.

– There was nobody there, she said, shaking her head.

He wanted to ask her if she had heard the knocking, the banging on the door, but didn't. He wanted Askiew, who most certainly had heard it, to confirm that he had indeed heard it.

But he didn't.

– There was nobody there, she said, shaking her head.

His cell phone beeped. Several others reached for their own, but he was certain it was his. And uncannily enough, it was.

There was one short message:

`I'm outside.`

The others stared at him, but he ignored them. He grabbed his jacket and went on his way.

The wind rushed against him the moment he opened the door. Pages of a newspaper almost struck his head and levitated a considerable distance down the street. He saw no one at first. The entire street was empty. The wind and the rain made people stay indoors. Finally, after waiting for maybe ten, twenty seconds and already growing impatient he saw movement in the dark alley across the street. He saw Elliott Lasko's pudgy face appear from the dark gray of the city. There was a wave and

Fallon crossed the street. There were no cars, but he still felt a tingling in his nerves. Lasko pulled back into the alley, making sure nobody could see him from the newsroom above. Fallon wondered what was wrong with him. He acted like he was an informer, a snitch doing work for the police, not a policeman tipping off a journalist. Or even worse: A convicted felon on the run.

– I've got something for you, Elliott Lasko had told Andrew Fallon.

– What is it? Fallon had asked, an image of infinite patience.

– You'll see, Lasko whispered hoarsely.

– What is it? Fallon asked, as they made their way to Lasko's car.

– You'll see, the policeman repeated hoarsely.

And Fallon saw. He saw Marion Dexter sit in the interrogation room with her lawyer by her side, hearing her ghostly voice. Fallon and Lasko were the only two inside the observation room. Fallon had been in many such a room during his considerable time as an investigative reporter and he couldn't remember a single time when there hadn't been an extra set of detectives there.

– I saw myself on the floor in the living room, bathing in a pool of blood. When he grabbed the knife I just… it was like a switch turned in my mind.

The interrogating detectives exchanged glances. Then Fallon got it, whatever he had come here for. Lasko's reaction, his increased fidgeting confirmed it. Fallon sensed the familiar thrill down the spine, one he had developed after chasing all kinds of stories for years… and this one was a doozie. There was a worry in those glances, in those eyes, beyond anything that could be described as ordinary.

Marion was brought down to the basement. Lasko and Fallon followed her, her lawyer and the two detectives down, down to the morgue, the vault, where all the bodies were stacked. A steel door was opened. A body on a table was pulled out of the wall.

– Mrs. Dexter, one of the detectives said formally. – We would like you to make an identification, please. We would be extremely grateful if you would help us out on this.

The other pulled the coverage off the stiff, and the room suddenly turned that very much colder. Marion pulled a hand to her mouth. Fallon just stood there. He couldn't claim to have a single thought in his mind at that moment. Not a single one. Everything had turned to stone. A hardly perceptible nod from the woman, and the cover was refitted over the stiff on the slab. The likeness, in spite of the frozen expression of the corpse was unmistakable and beyond uncanny.

Marion Dexter was dead.

– The knife that was stuck in the dead woman's chest…The husband's bloody fingerprints is on it, unmistakable. We're fucked. There is no way we can prosecute the woman in there, whoever she is. For that matter, there is no way we can prove she is *not* Marion Dexter. We can prove there is another Marion Dexter… or we could have, if we wanted to.

Lasko had for years been very useful to Andy, in revealing the inner workings of the city's police homicide division. Fallon had never seen him in a condition even close to this one.

It was a week later. Nothing had changed from the everything a week earlier.

– We asked her, of course. We keep asking her, if she has a twin sister. She says «no». We don't believe her, of course, so we check birth records. We talk with people at the hospital she was born. There is no mystery there. Then we start digging deeper. We get the coroner to do an autopsy, *convincing* him of its importance, a beyond reasonable thorough autopsy. As it turns out the diseased woman has exactly the same teeth-fillings, the same scars as the live one and a slew of other shit being exactly the same. They even have the same broken bone. We checked. Marion Dexter had a serious fracture in her leg when she was eleven. The coroner will never repeat it in public or record it anywhere, but what he pretty much says, beyond the fear and technical mojo is that the two of them aren't merely identical twins, but that they are definitely, beyond doubt… the same woman.

Lasko looked like he was about to croak and fall over that very moment.

She stood outside the police station, talking with the lawyer. Fallon approached them from further down the street. The lawyer got a very poised look in his eyes when discovering the journalist.

– It's all right, Fallon heard Marion say. – I'm all right.

– Hello, Fallon greeted them.

The lawyer just stared grimly at him, without a word.

– Hello, Marion replied, her voice dead and even.

– Listen, Fallon said, without really knowing what he said. – You don't know me, but I would very much like to buy you a cup of coffee. At least we have a pretty dramatic turn of events in common, right?

– Sure… why not? She shrugged.

She turned to the lawyer with a soft look in her eyes.

– Thank you, again, Tom, she said. – I can never thank you enough, but I'll try some day, if you need me.

Tom mumbled something and left.

They had that cup of coffee, had it in a dark coffee bar a few blocks down the street. Or he had it. She didn't even touch her cup.

– I should go back to the house and pack, she said quietly.
She finally spoke.
– Why? He turned to her with a puzzled look.
– There is no way I can remain here after your story is printed. The house will be besieged by journalists and weirdoes from all over the galaxy. I have to change my looks and move to a place nobody knows me.
– Listen, he grabbed her arm carefully.
She stiffened, but then she relaxed. He kept his eyes at hers, speaking slowly and deliberately.
– There is no way I can write about this. He shook his head. – If I could it would have been out the day after the murder, hot off the press. My editor won't touch it. No serious newspaper editor would. Even «Colors in the Night» wouldn't print it. This is typical National Enquirer stuff. You're safe.
– Safe, she echoed with her hollow voice.
He didn't know what to say, so he didn't, for once say anything.
– It's all right, really, she said in that horrible, hollow voice. – I don't want to go back to the house anyway. You can never be sure what's w-waiting t-there, can you? And anyway, I don't want to ever see it for my eyes again.
But she did anyway, and it was like it swallowed her whole the moment she crossed the threshold. Fallon waited in the car, but that didn't make her feel any better.
She deliberately walked through the kitchen, took the detour through the living room, to the bedroom. There was nothing in the kitchen, no spots, nothing except for the strong, antiseptic smell. The stain on the living room carpet remained, and the stench of rust as well, no matter how much antiseptics that had been poured into the human imprint on the floor.
The bedroom was silent and had a neutral smell, quite fresh, since the windows had been open all week. The mirror looked just like a mirror. She had some problems fitting her breasts inside her blouse. She always had. It felt very uncomfortable. She kept dressing, and after she had done that, she packed the small suitcase in a rush and hurried out of there.
She returned to the car, hurried inside. But even though Fallon quickly started the engine and drove off, she remained inside the house. She walked through the living room one more time, frowning, and in a dark, dark corner she imagined she saw her husband's diabolical face. It was leering at her, and at a point it seemed to grow and reach out to her with the long, long tongue. And in the passenger window of the car, she feared she saw that leer again, and she shrunk in her seat.

The last thing she saw before they drove off and turned the corner was the ongoing construction work on what had once been a lawn. She looked away.

Tom Ruiz stared at the house. He held a hammer in one hand. The big sign in another

– Something is very fucked up somewhere.

He shook his head and didn't think twice about it. A lot of people did that these days.

He stuck the pointed end of the pole in which the sign was attached in the ground and started hitting the top of it with his hammer. Shaking the sign a bit after a while he nodded somewhat content. It stood solidly planted in the ground. He took another look at the dark house lit by the sun's evening rays, and walked off.

Yellow leaves blew in the garden filling the empty driveway.

On the huge sign there were painted two words in big, big letters:

FOR SALE

There was more coffee, and always on packed places, but being surrounded by the lot of people could never chase off the feeling of dread and cold shaking her.

– I keep seeing myself on the floor and on the slab, she whispered. – And there is the look of absolute shock on my husband's face the moment he realized that I had stabbed him.

She spoke quite loud. The other guests heard her, and shivered in their seats as well. Even those farther away that couldn't possibly have heard her visibly shivered in their seats. It seemed to be contagious, like a plague.

The next day she finally returned to the university and followed her first lecture in weeks. She sat there, attempting to listen to the words, but the man down there could just as well speak gibberish as far she could tell. She didn't fathom any of it.

She hurried outside, into the pale sunshine, filled with shadows, and stopped in the middle of the yard, out of breath.

Her cell phone rang. She took it from her pocket and stared suspiciously at it, stared at the message:

UNKNOWN CALLER

– H-hello?

– He was no threat to you. He just wanted to talk.

– Ethel?

– Do you *sleep* well at night? The raspy, ominous voice cried calmly.

– Ethel, wait!

The line went dead.

She looked at the phone for a long time before putting it away. People passed her, kept passing her, walking around her in huge circles, to avoid touching her, avoiding her like they would a leper. Their stares, their secret stares burned her. She walked, walked all the way to the Pit. At one given moment she could no longer properly recall, she had decided to enter a bus. The bus had sighed then, and glared at her with its cold and reptile metal eyes. She reached the Pit at dusk. Marion Dexter stood at the event horizon of the Pit and stared downwards, into the wet and misty air between ramshackle buildings.

Ethel's apartment was on the right, a few floors above the ground, close to the bowl's edge. Marion knew where it was. She had visited the place a few times in the distant past. The stairs in the darkened hallway creaked under her feet, as she made her way up. She heard, *easily* people breathe beyond closed doors, leering at her with blind eyes. A prevalent voice kept shouting silently at her: Get out get out get out get out

The door to the apartment stood ajar, the light from the room flooding the dark hallways. Marion Dexter stood at the center of the apartment, the nice, ordered apartment, with no recollection of how she had gotten there. Ethel was nowhere in sight. Marion called her name several times more. There was no reply.

There was a creak from the bedroom, very loud and very, very creaky.

– Is that you, Ethel?

There was no reply. Marion didn't move.

The phone rang, very, very loud. Marion realized startled that it wasn't her cell phone, but the one on the night table inside the bedroom. She carefully crossed the room's threshold, moving her eyes back and forth, in a never ceasing flicker.

She ran to the bed and grabbed the phone, lifting it off the hook.

– H-hello?

– Do you sleep well at night? The raspy, ominous voice spoke calmly.

A man's voice. One she didn't know.

– I don't live here. I'm not…

– I don't think you do, Marion. In fact I *know* you don't.

She strived to speak, but couldn't. Her mouth opened and closed, but there was no sound coming from it.

Her hand put the phone back on the receiver, but she felt no connection to it, to her hand. She turned and kept turning, looking around the room with an insane look in her eyes, staring at every dark corner she could spot. She kept turning until vertigo hit her, and she lost her balance and fell on her back on the bed, and she saw the dark corners dance on the ceiling, and she moaned in the deepest terror. Her body pulled into an extreme fetal position, and she couldn't stop shaking, and she was unable to move, until she hours later finally fell asleep, and she didn't move at all, except twisting and turning in bed, dreaming restlessly and endlessly.

It was dark, still dark when she woke up. The door to the apartment was still ajar. It waved to her, winked to her, with its cheerful grin. She sat up in bed, studying herself in the mirror, the large mirror opposing the bed. Her face smiled at her, a lingering, pleased grin. It was Ethel's face.

The car raced across the highway in a pile of dust.

Marion approached Fallon just after he had started the engine and he was about to leave the driveway outside his small, suburban house. She was sweaty, as if she had run for miles. He opened the door for her, the passenger door. She sat down, breathing hard.

– Is your offer… me as your assistant… is it still on?

He nodded, fairly out of breath himself.

The car raced across the deserted highway in a pile of dust.

Andy left the tape recorder on his left knee. Marion smiled as she grabbed it and put it away inside the glove compartment.

– It is such a beautiful day, isn't? She smiled seductively to him, winked to him.

They had left the city behind, driven through a hole in the air somewhere, and the world had changed around them, the higher elevation quickly noticeable. The dusty road and remote landscape changed to that of a lake and a few streets, a picturesque image of peace incarnated.

– So, this is it? She nodded.

– Yes, he confirmed, – this is the place Chloe Webster supposedly spent the last seven days of her life.

There was a village, a few houses and a rather sizeable estate building reminding Marion of a castle.

– So, where do we stay? She queried. – You didn't bring camping gear, did you?

He stopped in front of the building's main entrance.

– In there, he said dryly. – It's a hotel. I'm told quite a lot of people come here from the city to unwind, especially at weekends.

– To get away, at least for a little while, from their unbearable lives, she said, very, very sober, her big eyes locked on his.

– That, and the excellent fishing opportunities in these parts, he replied, forcing a grin.

Their room was spacey, cozy and bright. She… liked it. It comforted her somehow, without her being able to tell exactly why.

He opened his suitcase, and the file he pulled from it, spreading pictures and articles meticulously across the floor. One picture caught Marion's eye. It was one of the lake and the house beneath the mountain. She stared out of the window, at that very image. On one hand there was the lake, and then there was the mountain, and between them was the house, the house where Chloe lived, where she still lived.

– She rented the house, the entire house?

– That she did. There are the craziest rumors as to why. Some say she practiced witchcraft, that she worshipped Satan, there, in the empty house. And there are crazier stories still.

– Is that possible? She gave him that lingering, seductive smile.

He blushed like a schoolboy.

The flames in the fireplace began to stretch and reach pleasantly into the room. She froze under their ruthless scrutiny. And her smile, in turn froze him.

– Time for dinner? He queried lightly.

– I'm ravenous, she nodded.

The hall was practically empty and silent. This was off-season. The hotel and the entire area would close in a month, when the snow came. They walked to the dining room, where there actually were a few people. A waiter approached them.

– Good afternoon, he said pleasantly. – How can I be of service to you?

– A table for two, please, Andy replied cheerfully.

– Certainly, sir. One by the window, perhaps, with a magnificent view of the lake?

They followed him there, and it was indeed a great spot, was a magnificent, breathtaking sight, like a painting view. The lake was perfectly still, mirroring the house, land and mountain on the other side.

– Is it raining? Marion frowned.

He didn't reply, but looked at her inquiringly, looked at the light and shadow of the sun dancing in her face, with a shiver passing down his spine. There had been a quality of absolute sincerity in her words.

– I can swear I heard the sound of rain. She giggled embarrassed, apologizing with her stance and lowered eyes.

There were people filling up five of the other tables. On one table in particular there was a very vocal and noisy group, evidently celebrating something, celebrating *a lot*. Fortunately the very thoughtful waiter had placed them at the other side of the room.

Andy added in his thoughts.

Their laughter made Marion wince. People didn't need to be in her vulnerable state to wince in the onslaught of spiteful laughter, but she had gone through so much lately. He put a hand on her cheek, touching it briefly. She looked at him, meeting his eyes for a moment, a grateful expression touching her face.

They sat down, both highlighted by the room's lamps and the dying brilliance of the late afternoon's sun. The appetizer arrived, just after they ordered it. The main course arrived, not too late. They sat there in silence for a while, doing mostly small talk. She ate swiftly, almost as if she was ravenous, as if she hadn't eaten for many hours and even days. Most of the women he had known ate like birds, but she didn't, at least not now. She wolfed down the food, tore the meat to pieces in her mouth before chewing it. They sat there in silence, savoring the meal, enjoying the quiet evening.

She looked at him. He noticed startled. She had the most wondrous eyes, and he wondered why he hadn't noticed that earlier.

– Who was that woman? She asked him, aggression noticeable in her voice and entire posture. – It was me, wasn't it, down to the last hair, the last molecule?

– It wasn't you, he stated hoarsely.

– Come on, don't play games with me! You're chummy with that policeman. I saw it. I'll bet he gave you the entire muddy picture.

– It was you, Andrew Fallon stated, somewhat calmly. – The extended coroner examination couldn't find one, discernible difference. On the contrary, he was able to cross off on a long list of absolute likeness, impossible likenesses.

She rubbed her shoulders. It was cold in the room, as if the chill from the morgue had followed them here.

– There is an archive in the newspaper, like in most newspapers, a non-existing we never really talk about or just mention in passing during our most extreme binge drinking.

His voice was both flat and strangely excited. He just kept talking in an even, uninterrupted flow.

– You wouldn't believe the crazy stories gathered there.

The flames in the fireplace seemed to pale, to dwindle into insignificance. One of the waiters lit the two candles on their table and the room, the air around them seemed to heat up again, to become real. Her right hand shook. He saw it, even after she had hidden it under the table.

There was low-keyed music in the room, soothing still raw nerves. Desert was served. She wolfed that down, too, as if it was her last supper. There was something in her eyes unnerving him. There always had been, right from the first time he had seen her sitting in the chair in the interrogation room. He discovered that his hands were shaking, too. She noticed, and nodded to herself. He felt both shame and relief and couldn't distinguish the one from the other.

– This place is so different, she said, – so different from the city. It looks unreal, like a painting.

He nodded, half conscious of doing so, half not.

The hotel was an old, renovated castle. It became even more obvious than during the day, when they strolled through its halls and hallways after night had fallen. It was quiet wherever they went. There was activity, quite a lot of it actually, but it was as if the carpets and even the stonewalls absorbed any loud sound.

There was a painting on the wall, looking eerily real. They stopped and studied it.

– That's Marlon Caine, a voice said from behind them, – the infamous film producer.

They turned around, fairly anxious. There was just a man standing there, a man and a woman, dressed like they were themselves, in formal wear for the evening.

– And you are? Marion queried, slightly pointedly.

– Oh, forgive me, the man grinned. – My name is Victor Matushe. My lovely companion is Desire Lowell.

– Nice to meet you, Andy replied automatically.

Marion didn't say anything.

– There are ghosts here, Desire said abruptly, softly, looking, staring at Marion. – They dance in the walls, and on the carpets like specters of a forgotten past.

– Very poetic, my dear, Matushe coughed.

– You're from National Enquirer! Andy raised his voice accusingly.

– Guilty as charged, Matushe grinned. – And you are the envoy from the Post, I trust, arriving late, but good at the scene?

– The scene of the crime? Andy blurted out, unable to help himself.

Matushe laughed heartily. He had a very distinct laughter, very ironic and very powerful, and invasive.

– So, why are you here? He asked lightly. – Why have you come to this place, where Chloe Webster spent her… final days?

– My editor pointed out that every other paper in the world had featured a story about her, and he didn't want to be left out in the cold.

– And honest reply. I just *love* those!

– But you could have written a story, a perfectly… «acceptable» story from your city desk. Miss Lowell took a step forward, startling him some more. – Why didn't you? Why come here? Why *bother?*

Fallon felt that he couldn't speak, that his tongue was locked somewhere in his mouth.

– Because Andy is among the last of a dying breed, my dear, Matushe laughed, – the curious journalist. He's not content merely to sit on his ass and write about an event or to rehash other's writing. He has to go out there and *experience* it.

Fallon looked closer at the man. Suddenly there was no irony or malice in his voice. If he hadn't known better he would have said Matushe was… excited.

– That is strange, a strange compliment coming from you, Andy said hoarsely.

– Considering where I work, you mean?

Andy shifted uncomfortably his feet.

– Don't worry, (Matushe laughed), – I won't hold your prejudice against you…

Desire Lowell stepped forward, a strange gleam evident in her eyes, in her soft, inviting and sinister smile.

– We were on our way to the bar. Do you care to join us?

Andy and Marion looked at each other, nodding slowly, simultaneously, and without really knowing why they followed the couple from National Enquirer down the darkened hallway.

The bar was well lit, or the light was strategically placed, lighting certain areas, leaving the shadows. An unexpected thrill shot through Andrew Fallon, one equal to those he dimly recalled from his younger days.

Victor leaned forward, sipping his strong drink, taking a large sip, not really noticing himself doing so.

– There is a *mystery* here, he stated intensely, – one ancient and powerful, and one people don't bother to seek or even acknowledge anymore, because they, in their fear and fearful complacency, are content sitting in their chairs doing nothing, and letting life pass by.

A piano played somewhere, and somehow overwhelmed the sound of chatter, and the clink of glasses and buzz in the room. It wasn't a standard background tune either, but heavy, fairly heavy chords, tinged with sadness.

And mystery.

He turned to Marion and Desire did, too. And Desire spoke, very deliberate, with excitement in her voice.

– Usually, when a person encounters one's Doppelganger it is a sign of one's imminent death, but you are alive, Marion, and your Doppelganger is dead.

It dawned on Marion that she hadn't introduced herself, that she hadn't been introduced to the two. She wanted to leave, half up from her chair the next, unfathomable moment, before she let herself fall back on it, tingles of both excitement and terror riding her spine.

– You followed us here? Fallon said flatly.

– Both yes and no, Matushe grinned. – We're here to investigate in detail, the life and death of Chloe Webster. Our esteemed readers' interest in her keeps soaring. They can't get enough, and here's the thing: They are unusually well informed, far more so than the so-called readers of established newspapers. If we write bull or simply invent stuff, they'll see through it in an instant. So we come here, to this place, where no journalist so far has tread, to dig a little deeper, look a little closer at the truth.

– Imagine our surprise when we found the two of you here, Desire said, with her penetrating stare, – representatives, such as you are, for the esteemed Post, digging in the same sewers we dig in. It's almost poetry in motion, the way I see it.

– Desire here, is a Seer, Matushe told them, suddenly very somber. – She sees ghosts and shadows, and things hidden in the dark corners of the world. But very few believe her, and she is generally ridiculed and chastised for her talent, and so she is a bit rough around the edges.

And the piano sounded even closer, as if it was right beside them, striking its own tangents with invisible fingers. A man sitting there played. Marion saw his grin, saw his half exposed skull, devoid of flesh grin to her.

And just like that, he was gone.

She pulled herself together, pulled hard. A smile touched her face as she faced the couple.

– So why tell us all this? She said, suddenly with luring, eerie eyes. – I mean. What do you hope to gain by it? We are, after all, your competition… as it is?

– You are very perceptive, Marion, Desire nodded. – Somehow, I knew you would be. Why is that, you think?

– Generally speaking, you would be right. Matushe nodded, too, practically in tandem with his companion. – But this is big enough for all of us, and there might even be more to it. There might be no coincidence that we were… thrust together on this far shore, and we should honor that, I think. Yes, I definitely believe we should.

Marion and Andy nodded to each other and shrugged, their smiles joining that of the other two.

A waiter brought a bottle. Matushe grabbed it and broke its seal. There was a popping sound, shockingly loud in the noisy room. He filled the four glasses with liquor and additions, with the most burning of spices.

– I worked as a bartender at one time in my life, he grinned. – I've crossed most boundaries when work is concerned.

Marion grabbed her glass and lifted it, held it up.

– To silver-tongued devils, she cheered darkly.

Matushe actually reddened a bit, just a bit.

Laughter, loud and brittle. Marion drank. They all did. The strong content of the drink burned in their throats, filled their stomachs and slowly, consequently, inevitably their entire bodies. It made its way to their brains, a balm on sore minds.

Andy danced with Marion on the slippery floor. Marion whispered in his ear:

– I need this. I need to get as far away as possible and this is far, far away.

There is loud, loud music. The piano picks up speed, and the dancers break into a wild, wild jiggle. The two of them return breathless to the table.

I need this, the face of wrath hissed at him. I need the death, and suffering and sacrifice.

He shook imperceptibly, and she still noticed.

– What is it? Marion asked, clearly worried. – What is wrong?

– Nothing, he mumbled. – Nothing important.

The table… he almost passed it. For one moment there, he thought it was on a completely different spot compared to how he remembered it. The foreign woman, so familiar, sat in Victor's lap, with her arms around his neck, a paragon of desire. Andy blinked, and time passed as the blink passed, passed incredibly slowly. In one moment was eternity.

Desire posed for Andy, clearly, undeniably, her breasts hanging out, the edge of her dress pulled far up on her thighs. The four of them cheered again. Glasses met and parted. Thirsty lips met and parted with the chilled glass' edge (and fire flowed down their throat). Marion sighed as she sat by Andy's side and leaned closer, completely different from how he had learned to know her.

Andy sat there shaking his head, amazed, tasting his every word as if it was his last.

– The hypocrisy of the current media is incredible, he stated amazed and disgusted. – We present ourselves as truth-seekers, as paragons of virtue and honesty, but we're nothing but.

– Hear, hear. Matushe raised his glass.

They all did, yet again, and there was more cheering, more laughter, loud and strong.

– We're the fourth, *supporting* estate, Fallon spat in contempt. – We're eager supporters of the other powers, not a corrective, the way we falsely present ourselves.

– The world is an illusion, Desire sobbed. – Reach for it, for anything, and it dissolves into mist before your eyes. Touch it and it turns to dust in your hands.

She smiled to him, and her eyes were dry as desert sand.

The sobbing, shivering Desire, the laughing, sensuous Desire… they both looked real to him. He shook in the loud, hot, quiet and chilly room. The candle on the table… in a slow blink of an eye it turned into a campfire, and they sat outdoors, in the darkness, in the distant wilderness.

They left the restaurant, left one section of the castle, and headed back to the guestroom section. One incredible bridge connected the two. Its walls and ceiling were mostly glass and they had an amazing view of the lake bathed in moonlight.

Desire stumbled a bit, holding on to Andy not to fall. She looks at the three of them with clear ambiguity in her eyes and expression, one bit joy and one bit terror.

– In one of my visions I cross this bridge, she told them, the texture of her voice very distinct. – There is daylight, but a strange form of daylight, one I've never before experienced. There is no sun, but yet there are shadows. I'm alone, and I am haunted. Perhaps I'm even fleeing from something, something sinister chasing me. I can't tell. I have painted my face, and I don't do that, and I don't look like me at all. As I walk my eyes are moving constantly back and forth. I turn my head and look behind me, look forward, and there is nothing to see, but still I look and seek, seek for something dancing in the air in front of my very eyes. And then suddenly I stop, and when I look around this time, there is no glass anywhere on the bridge. There is nothing but stone, and the stench of fire in my nostrils, the sight of flames burning my eyes. I look to my left, and then I see it, whatever it is, but I don't see anything. I see my eyes turn wide in fear, and I dissolve into nothing, and only the bridge is left.

Somehow, as Desire's voice is fading, they, the lot of them end up in Victor and Desire's room. It's a nice room, about equal to that shared by Fallon and Dexter. Fallon is drunk, so drunk that he can hardly stand on his feet, and he dumps down on his ass on the bed. Desire sits in his lap, loosening his tie, and it feels incredible. Suddenly, Fallon can actually breathe, feeling like air is actually reaching his lungs, his boiling blood. Marion is kissing Victor. She's kissing him, kissing Andy, his sore, burning lips. The room is darkening, as one by one of the lamps in the room are turned off.

The four are in bed together. Desire giggles and removes her dress, and now he's positive he can see her breasts, her pointing nipples. And then they touch, skin to skin, body to body.

He is writhing on his back on the bed. The other couple embracing there, in the darkness seems far, far away, on a sandy, sandy beach. Marion moves on him, back and forth, as she covers his body with her own, as she smiles enigmatically down at him.

– You're a brave man, you know, bedding a confirmed murderess.

She's embracing his cock with her hard and muscular thighs, crushing it sweetly in her grip. He pushes against her, as the itch grows, as the pleasure expands, leaving his body, spreading to the entire bed, until the four of them are not one, are not two, but a many-headed beast tumbling and moving in the night.

– I enjoy seeing the fear in your eyes, she whispered.

And he pushes against her, pushes himself into her, falling into the black hole beneath. And there is nothing there, nothing but the dark fire surrounding him on all sides, and that's all he can ever sense.

CHAPTER FIVE

The First Day

– I saw her, the old woman squeaked. – I saw her on the hill, the naked hill. I saw her dance there, and do her unholy deeds.

There was heavy, ongoing construction work not far from the hotel. Some enterprise or two were building yet another holiday resort. The four of them walked past it, and the noise was so terribly loud that they couldn't hear each other speak.

Chloe Webster moved into the Victorian house across the lake. She didn't bring much, only a small suitcase with the most necessary change of clothing and such. She parked her car in front of the main entrance, and just left it right there, as she hurried inside, into the dusty old house.

There was a squeaky sound, as the large double doors were pushed open. Marion Dexter coughed as she crossed the threshold into the half blue, half crimson ebon air. The sunlight was still deep red, even though the sun had been up for quite some time that day.

The wheels of the tape-recorder turn and turn, as the various voices emanate from it.

– She seemed… off base from the start, the pleasant hotel manager said. – She paid for a week for her room, but moved into the house the next day.

Marion Dexter speaks into the microphone:

– The hotel manager fell from grace. He became a bum, unable to keep up with the rat race of modern society, and was forced to roam garbage cans for a scrap of food and old glory.

The four of them stretched in bed, waking up in a fever of half-remembered dreams.

– It's such a beautiful day, Desire cried. – Isn't it a beautiful day?

She smiled and kissed them all on the lips, lazily sliding out of the bed towards the bathroom, wriggling her butt, her skin covered by hardened semen.

The large bedroom in the lake manor looked exactly as Chloe Webster had left it, even with her suitcase opened on the bed. Everything was still there, except Chloe's tape-recorder.

– The police had it, Desire nodded.

– Had it? Marion wondered, turning towards the other woman.

– Yes, and they lost it. At least that's what they keep saying. And not even a substantial coaxing on our part could persuade them otherwise. I think they are telling the truth, and that they are embarrassed.

She stopped, considering it, frowning.

– Yes, I definitely believe that's the case. Embarrassment was what I «got» from them. They can't really hide anything from me.

– So, you're truly a… a psychic?

– Don't say it like it's a dirty word, my dear. Desire laughed, sobering as she spoke. – Yes, since I was a little girl. I saw and sensed things and ghosts and specters, both dead and not everywhere, and no one would ever believe me.

– I'm sorry.

– Don't be. You do believe me. At least you do, now, because you know there are things unseen out there, because you have experienced it.

There was acid in Desire Lowell's voice, a hardening expression in her face only slowly softening.

She stepped closer to the other woman.

– Last night was amazing, wasn't it?

– Yes, Marion whispered.

She recalled it in vivid detail, also the moment she attempted to rise from the bed, and the sheet had stuck to her butt, to her sticky, sticky butt.

– I have never experienced anything like it before, Desire said hoarsely. – You may not believe me, but it's true. Not with Victor, nor with anybody else.

She stepped even closer to Marion, grabbing her arms.

– You sensed it, too. I know you did. We all did, the four of us, the sense of recognition, of familiarity between us, like…

– … like we've always known each other, Marion finished the other's sentence.

Chloe walked around in the large bedroom, taking it in, getting a sense of it, touching the shelf above the fireplace, getting dust on her fingers, staring into the mirror.

Marion blinked, imagining the marks of Chloe's fingers in the dust still being there. She blinked again, and the marks were gone.

– Day One, Chloe spoke into her Dictaphone. – 12 PM. I have arrived.

– Chloe is still here. Marion spoke into her Dictaphone. – There is something here of her that won't go away. Her body may be long gone, but she is still very much here. Her spirit is soaring through these rooms, these dusty halls and hallways.

A shiver passed through her, passed through Chloe, passed through Marion.

– I like this, Marion reported excitedly. – I really love it. I wasn’t sure I would, but I am, and I’ve got a talent for it, for finding information, for interpreting it. I can see myself with the others, and I *belong* with them.
– It is impossible for us to know what Chloe actually did in the house, Andy said, frustration clearly present in his voice. – There is no known record of it, not anymore, and no one ever visited her here. No one we know of.
There was a village, a rural village not far from the lake, with a few stores, and a few blocks with homes.
– She was a witch, the old woman cried in pain. – She cast spells on us, and cursed us to our last soul. I heard her, heard her mumble her incantations, heard her swear, and I saw her dance on the hill, around her fire.
An orderly came and took her away. She looked distressed beyond belief. Oddly enough there was an entire retirement home in the village, serving several neighboring villages. Chloe had been here. For what reason no one could say.
Marion recalled an eerie moment the last night, when she had witnessed Andy return from the bathroom. His cock was still partly rigid, and dangled between his legs. She had been half into the dream state, she knew that, but she had still been awake, at last that very moment, and she had seen his eyes glow in red and fire.
The two of them interviewed the administrator of the retirement home. The man looked both full of himself and very, very uncomfortable.
It was hard to read him. For all intents and purposes it was like there was a wall there, between him and the two across the desk, keeping them from accessing him fully.
– So, what did Chloe ask you about? Andy asked the man behind the desk.
– It’s hard to tell. The man sat there with his ten fingers pressed against each other, a frown appearing on his brow. – She didn’t really ask me much.
– But she asked you something, didn’t she? The follow up question, journalism 101 came easy to Marion, and she felt Andy’s warm glow of approval.
– Nothing that made much sense. The man behind the desk sadly, very sadly shook his head.
– So why did she come here, anyway? Andy wondered. – What story was she chasing?
– She asked a lot about the history of this building, the man in the suit replied ecstatically circumspect.

Andy and Marion sighed.
– I have to say, sir, she responded sweetly, – that is such an astounding revelation…
And thus it went, with no real information, no true facts, like swimming through quicksand, frustrating beyond belief.
Marion looked out at the garden. There was a shadow there, one in an open spot where no shadow should be.
She rushed to it afterwards, with Fallon in tow. There was nothing there, nothing she could fathom. She stood there, on the open spot, a bundle of raging emotions.
– Boy, was that man slick!
– An expert, Fallon nodded admittedly, absentmindedly. – I'm still not sure if he's just an idiot, or if he's actually hiding something.
– We will find out, of course.
She walked to him, grabbing his hands.
– We will find out everything there is to know. It's our distant goal, our *fate*.
– Absolutely, he joked, not sure how to respond to her intensity, to her beyond intense glare.
She held back, taken aback, suddenly noticing, growing aware of herself, in a way she never before had been.
– Wheels, she whispered.
– What? He shook. – What did you say?
– Wheels, she said in a ghostly voice. – Wheels within wheels within wheels on a never-ending path.
And then she felt it, the cold shadow, felt it embrace her, expand her, fill her up, until nothing else was left.
And her eyes turned black.
The fire warmed her. She stood with her back to the fireplace, but it still warmed her front. The four gathered in one of the bedrooms in the evening, comparing notes. It was strange… eerie how easy it felt between them, sharing. There was suspicion, but it didn't stop them from showing and telling.
– I think we have basically mapped Chloe's moves the first day, Desire concluded.
– She arrived at the mansion at twelve fifteen PM, Victor began. – She spent less than ten minutes there, before leaving, leaving without locking the door behind her. The motel manager saw her, probably through his binoculars. A fact a few of the guests probably could have confirmed for us, if they were still here.

– But let's leave that point open, Desire nodded, – for the sake of argument. Let's keep pretending we know nothing, nothing we haven't confirmed thoroughly to our satisfaction.

They recorded this, too, recorded all their own sessions, brainstorms.

We are great together.

The thought struck Andy from nowhere, warm like an early autumn stream.

– She drove right to the retirement home, he said. – The drive there from the manor is only five minutes. She arrived at 12.30 precisely, as the visitor's log confirms.

– Two hours have passed, Marion continues, – when she logs herself out, having spent virtually every minute at the administrator's office. Two hours asking questions, repeating questions, redirecting questions. Her writing in the log is now erratic, unbalanced. Something has happened. She has found something. There has been some sort of discovery, realization. Perhaps not what she came there to find, but something nonetheless.

The wheels turned, and words were spoken, recorded voices echoing in the room, the empty room.

– She returned to the hotel for dinner, Victor noted, – clearly out of it, a fact noted by all the staff present that day. She was abusive, paranoid and downright scared. After less than twenty-four hours in this place she was shaking like a leaf.

They returned to the mansion, to the house by the mountain, by the eastern shore of the lake. Night was falling. They returned, and Chloe Webster returned with them. They saw her, felt her presence in their midst.

Chloe rushed from the dining area of the hotel, spilling sauce on the waiter's arm as she rose abruptly from the table.

I see her. Marion spoke in darkness. I see her naked face.

The house is slowly heating up, from floor to floor, room to room. There is gas heating in addition to the various fireplaces. They imagine they can sense how it's spreading from room to room, moving through the air, as well as the metal pipes.

This is an old house. Even though it has been recently renovated, the electricity is still scarce. There are still gas lamps on the walls, and they feel a kind of dislocation, as if they aren't there at all.

– She received a visitor sometimes after dark. Desire's voice echoed through the empty space. – We don't know who that is. Nobody saw anybody arriving, or actually walk in the front door, but passing pedestrians heard two voices from the house, and saw two shadows move on closed curtains.

– Brrr, Victor grins.

They stand outside, looking in, staring at the shadows dancing on the curtains, surrounded by the sound of approaching and departing steps.

It is thunder, soft and loud in their ears, vicious laughter cutting to the bone.

– We walk in her footsteps, Desire said frostily. – We walk in a dead woman's tracks.

– Exactly, Marion exclaimed, – and that will lead us exactly to what we came here to find, to the exact point we want to go.

Her voice echoed in the void, and Andy shivered, as he lay on his back on the bed, nude and sweating, lonely and scared, surrounded by a wall of darkness, where nothing and everything patiently waited and hid, and bid its time.

The Second Day

Chloe woke up early, after a bad night's sleep, sore around her eyes. She had evidently been crying. Mrs. Henderson, walking by, saw her as she peeped through the window, carefully, for a second or two brushing the curtains, the heavy curtains aside, before pulling back into the quiet darkness of the house. Mrs. Henderson was a gossip maker, one of the foremost in the area, essentially infamous for those particular skills.

– That girl had pro-blems. She exhaled. – You hardly needed to look at her, to spot the nervous twitches of her lips and fingers. It's a telltale sign, if I ever saw any.

Victor and Desire exchanged glances, fairly humorous, with a touch of gallows humor. There was no problem getting Mrs. Henderson to talk. She excelled in it. But the main problem remained the same: to actually get her to say something.

– Of what, Mrs. Henderson? Desire wondered with both humor and exasperation in her eyes.

– Of marital problems, of course. The fat woman blew a cloud of smoke across the table, making them cough, cough hard. – Surveys say that nine out of ten problems young women experience stem from that fact, you know.

Desire rubbed her temples, rubbed them hard.

Mrs. Henderson turns into a rotting, stinking corpse before her eyes and nose, one still smoking, smoking, smoking.

The warm sunshine outside is insufficient to warm her. She shivers uncontrollably, and Victor has to take her into his arms to warm her, and he is, his heat stronger than any sun, any warm day.

– She was married, wasn't she?

He nodded.

– Not a well-known fact, but yes, she was.

Chloe stepped outside, locking the door behind her, walking to her car. A boy in his middle teens, Oscar Larner, passed by, on his way home from school.

– It's a warm day, she told him, – but I can't get warm, no matter what I do. I shiver in the midst of a heavy sweat. The cold drops are acid, burning my skin.

He hurried away.

– All people living in that house turn weird after a while, he tells Desire and Victor. – But she was weird, and she hadn't stayed there more than a day, a day and a night.

The four gather information, also from other days and nights of Chloe's final days, but still strangely linear, as if they are truly reliving everything.

– I followed her, the boy stated, suddenly, unexpectedly, – followed her into the mountains.

They stared at him. This was something new, something he had never told anyone before, at least not anything reaching the public.

He took them there. It was a hard trek, through uneven terrain and remote wilderness. They were soaked in sweat when he finally stopped at a clearing in a small forest somewhere directly east of the house.

They knew that. The sun was in the same, the exact same spot in the sky.

A pentacle covered the ground. There were five little dolls there, each standing on one of the five bases of the pentagram.

– She drew it by hand, Matushe noted, – and I'm willing to bet it's completely symmetrical, at least down to very detailed measures.

Desire looked up, startled, and for a brief moment the sun had become the moon, and its intense rays supplanted by the cold silver rays of the moon. And the moment lasted forever, and Desire couldn't breathe.

Chloe stood there, chanting, lighting five small fires, and they grew, and the ghostly flames seemed to engulf her, and she breathed their fumes, and her eyes turned huge and spooky and deep.

– You're lying, Desire told the boy, gasping, sweating hard the cold droplets, – whatever happened here happened at night.

Oscar froze, his eyes lit by hatred as he stared at her.

– You were not supposed to know that, he shrieked. – You were not supposed to *know* that!

He raised a pointing finger at her, looking like a vulture scared of the predator.

– Thou shall not suffer a witch to LIVE, he shouted insanely.

And he set off, ran away, and just like a puff of smoke, he was gone.

They didn't see him, didn't hear him anywhere. There was no sound of him breaking through the dry underbrush of the surrounding vegetation, no sight of him as they rushed to the cliff's edge, and surveyed the valley below where he clearly had been headed.

The two of them stood inside the pentacle, sensing the tingling of their skin.

– So, she was a witch, Victor noted, somewhat pleased.

He bent down, sifting through the ashes of one of the fires. There was something there. He frowned. There was something, a dark flame, glowing like the sun. He found a ring in the ashes, and without thought he picked it up. It wasn't hot, wasn't warm at all, in any way, but rather cold to the touch. He held it up, studying it. It had a stone, a stone resembling ruby, but… different.

There is a breath or a wind, something he can't quite make out. He stands in a hallway in an old castle, somehow recognizing the stone walls and oozing torches, the bluish light coming from nowhere.

He can't quite make out the words, can't hear the sound of his own voice.

– You've always been here, the woman says.

She stands in a corridor filled with twilight. Her body is in shadows. Only her face is clearly visible. She's wearing a white, translucent mask. The mask moves as if being a face, as if being alive.

– Take this ring, as a token of my love.

And he's reawakening there, inside the pentacle, wondering what's real and what's not.

Desire screams at him. At first he can't identify the words, but then they scream at him:

– Don't put it on your finger!

Desire shouts, frantic, almost in panic.

He looks at her, frowning.

– I wasn't going to. What's gotten into you?

She stands there, breathing, a deep frown digging into her forehead.

– I don't know.

She looks bewildered at him, shaking her head in confusion.

He hands her the ring. She backs off, refusing to touch it.

– You keep it.

It slipped into his pocket. It felt very heavy there, very much like a much bigger rock. He sifts through the rest of the piles of ashes within the pentacle, but there's nothing more to find.

– I guess she attempted to destroy it, he said, nodding to himself, looking at the woman in his presence.

– It can't be destroyed, she stated dully, chillingly. – It's not of this world.

– So it's alien then? He probed her, attempted to provoke a clear answer from her. – Small green men made it from a neutron star or something?

She shook her head hard.

– It's not of this reality.

He reproduced it from his pocket, studying it harder. Rubbing it, most of the ashes came off. He set off, moving in a determined pace to the nearest rock. She followed, still slightly out of breath. He put the ring on the flat rock. Grabbing another, smaller rock, he lifted it up, and brought it down, brought it down hard on the ring. There was a loud, piercing sound. They looked at the ring, stared at it. Both the ring and the ruby were undamaged. They were unable to spot a single dent or even a scratch anywhere on it.

Fear shook them, rattled them like the strongest of earthquakes.

– It's h-heavy, isn't it? She stuttered, like an insecure teenage girl on her first date.

He nodded, unable to speak, to voice his thoughts.

– Than let's throw it in the lake. It will sink to the bottom, and r-rot there.

She grabbed his hands, and dug her nails into his flesh, drawing blood. He stared astonished at her. She gasped in shock, and let go of him, backing away, almost to the edge of the cliff before stopping.

They hurried back down, walking as fast as they possibly could without actually running, panic lurking like crawling ants beneath their skin.

He rowed, rowed hard. The oars shook loose on more than one occasion. He rowed to the center of the lake, and there he stopped. The boat was instantly caught by a strong underwater current and pushed back towards the shore. He grabbed the oars again and kept rowing, keeping it there, in a fashion, at the center of the lake.

She looked at him. He nodded.

– Get rid of the shit.

She looked down, into the depths of the lake. Then she saw it, saw the ghostly image of the body, the pale face of Chloe Webster, without expression, life or eyes.

He looked down, too, and fear froze, totally froze his features.
– You see it? She said dumbfounded. – You see it, too?
He leaned back, for a moment more astonished than frightened.
– That was my first ghost, he confirmed, quite stricken, not really able to keep up the pretence of himself joking.
Because there wasn't anything like a body down there, below the surface. They knew that, before confirming it by sticking an oar into the water, perforating, but not really touching, disrupting it in any way, the indistinct flickering image of Chloe Webster slowly, slowly fading before their eyes.
There was laughter in the wind, unmistakable, cold, cruel and vicious. Desire threw the ring into the water. It hit the surface, and sank instantly. There was nothing special or spectacular about it. The metal and ruby-like stone simply sank below the surface, like any rock, any heavy object. They imagined they could actually see it, falling, into the depth, into the darkness.
Lethargy and dizziness swept Victor once again, before he pulled himself together and began rowing back to shore. It was like there was no resistance in the water at all. The boat seemed to fly above the frothing surface.
Chloe stood at the shore, staring at some point at the center of the lake. She rowed out there, somewhere, but what she was actually doing once she got there, no one watching could say.
Victor and Desire sat close to the fireplace, unable to get warm, hardly even feeling the sizzling heat.
– They observed her. Marion consulted her notes. – She was the talk of the town from the moment she arrived, and she didn't become less so, as the days and nights progressed. Everybody being close to the lake saw her that day, from all corners of the valley. They saw her sit there for hours, doing absolutely nothing.
– Yet she seemed strangely agitated upon returning to the house, Fallon said. – As if she has actually seen something, something truly disturbing.
Chloe left the house at the stroke of midnight, stepping into a landscape illuminated by the full moon, its lights looking like slivers, stabbing her and making her bleed. Arnold Jenkins, the butcher met her on the narrow path leading away from the main road. He's able to describe it all in vivid detail, everything that didn't happen, two full months later.
– Her face, he gasps. – Her face was covered in blood.
She went to the mountain cliff, the clearing in the forest, and she drew the pentacle, and she placed the dolls she had brought with her at the five

bases of the form. The moon and the fire warred for dominance in her face.

– She carried a… pouch, Jenkins continued. – She had her dolls in it…

He paused, as she stared insanely at them.

– I followed her, he stated, – followed her, as she light on her feet walked on a trail she had never before walked, and she did so as easily as anyone would have done in broad daylight. I witnessed as the witch did her magic, her unholy deed and conjured her demons and other dark servants of the netherworld.

His voice mixed… mixed with the choir surrounding them, those of all the voices they had heard in recent days, and of the many machines from the ongoing construction work outside. It was like the metallic sound reverberated through the walls, the stone and hit them like knives. Even the flames in the fireplace looked metallic, lifeless, cutting where knives couldn't reach.

They slept and their sleep was troubled, troubled beyond belief. There was no rest.

– I heard her sing, a woman said troubled. – But it wasn't really singing, but more of a chant, one right out of a satanic ritual. I got scared. I got really scared.

– How can people live like this, Marion cried, bitterly complained to Fallon, – live in constant flux, with nothing to hold onto?

Desire heard them, saw them stand in the other room in front of the fireplace, saw them shift and burn.

It was Night. The full moon was up, dancing on a high-wired sky. A dark night, filled with shadows.

There was water all around her. There were no bubbles, only dark, cold, still water. It didn't move her at all, but kept her in place, frozen, dead, undying.

Desire Lowell saw Chloe Webster rise from her watery grave, rise bundled in a grin and rotting flesh, and

The Third Day

Desire awoke in a lake of sweat, sitting up, gasping, gasping, unable to stop gasping, unable to close her wide open mouth where air was supposed to come through.

She looked around. There was no one else in the bed. She was alone. There were sounds from the bathroom. She heard Victor hum while brushing his teeth. Hands moved by themselves, brushing off hair sticking like glue to her sweaty, sweaty skin. Suddenly, shockingly abrupt she threw up, puking her guts out, there on the bed, and she couldn't stop, not until there was nothing but thick, acid slime left in her stomach.

The bathroom mirror appeared before her. She stood in front of it, shaking, shaking hard, looking at her pale complexion. Eyes were huge and insane, and she feared she would just fade away, and the mirror would be everything that was left.

Victor wasn't there. He was always there to comfort her, when she needed him, but now he was nowhere to be seen. She rushed back to the larger room, but he wasn't there either. He was Nowhere. She choked, and once again she had trouble breathing.

She walked across the bridge, and it turned dark there, dark as night, and flapping wings surrounded the single lamp in the ceiling, and loud shrieks hurt her ears.

The stench of vomit filled the room. The bright light hurt her eyes, and made tears flow down her cheeks.

She walked towards the other three at the breakfast table, the special table, with the scenic view of the lake, a young, confident woman with no worries in her life.

Smiling to the other two, she bent down and kissed Victor on the lips. She grabbed the menu the moment she sat down. Silver rays of the moon crossed her face, also touching the other three around the table.

– She was scared. She was scared all the time.

Fallon sat in his room, speaking into his Dictaphone, his small, portable tape recorder, occasionally taking notes.

– Who was Chloe Webster? That depends on whom you ask, and where you are asking it. It's striking how virtually everybody here sees her as a kind of witch, a sorceress, a woman living in shadows. Her colleagues and acquaintances in town have quite another impression of her. Colors of the Night was, is a magazine clearly «dabbling» in the supernatural, but it's not that obvious.

Fallon sits by his improvised desk, and it turns darker. He turns on the night table lamp, but it doesn't really help much, to bring light to the room.

– Not much happened, really, on her third day at Lake Mountain. She kept asking around, speaking to people, asking her… her offbeat questions. She asked about the Lady of the Lake, an old legend in these parts, one that won't go away, no matter how civilized people become. According to the lore, and also, astonishing enough, to current sightings the lady rises from the lake at the full moon, visiting the surrounding villages and townships. She's a stranger, one no one recognizes, but she isn't unfamiliar.

– She was a Seeker, Desire told the other three softly at the breakfast table. – She sought the Unknown and the Strange and the Colors of the Night. Her day job was just yet another means to that end.

– But why? Marion wondered, clearly struggling with something, to vocalize her thoughts.

Desire stared at her, in pain and befuddlement.

Marion put more film in the camera. A fairly awkward act at first, it was quickly becoming a natural process, becoming second nature. She took another picture of the arc, the bridge crossing the gap between the two parts of the castle. She looked at Victor. He returned her look, his humorous appearance in place.

– Bridges on and off old castles aren't uncommon, she noted. – But they are usually there to cover a river or water surrounding the castle, one of several protection-spells against potential invaders.

They both looked down, beneath the arc, at the lawn, the green, flat, mundane lawn.

– I've seen a lot of such stuff, of seeming contradictions. He shrugged. – And after a few years in this line of work, you will have, too.

Andy and Marion walked up the mountain, to the pentacle. It wasn't really hard to find. There was a trail up there, indistinct, but still clear as day, and more than one chill passed down their spine. In the brightest of days they were surrounded by Night.

They had dressed for the occasion, acquiring training gear in one of the tourist shops near the hotel area, and brought food and enough to drink, but it was still a hard trek.

– We're both city people, aren't we? Andy snickered. – Unused to the hardship of nature.

She looked softly at him.

It took forever to reach the special, grassy spot on the cliff. Fallon glanced at his watch. It was not yet noon.

The eerie sight of the five piles of ashes, and the five dolls met them head on, as they rounded the large rock.

– Is it fair to say… He looked at her. – … that, except for Desire and Victor's… brief visit no one has disturbed this particular scene of the crime?

– It's fair. She nodded.

Chloe walked to the old house at the end of the road. It had turned dark, and only a single lamp illuminated the last stretch of the street, and there seemed to be no light coming from the other lit lamps at all. Everything was so distant, so far away from where she walked.

She rang the bell, and an old woman opened the door, one clearly addled, but with strangely clear, awake eyes.
They sat down by the fire in the living room. The wheels of the recorder spun as they had their conversation, their dance of questions and answers.
– Mrs. Haverhsen… I have heard you have actually seen the Lady. Is that true?
– It certainly is, the old crone nodded. – I have even spoken with her. She comes to my house, and asks me questions I can't answer. She's a very curious one that one.
Matushe sits there with them, in a third chair. He asks Mrs. Haverhsen questions, slipping them to her in able moments, when her eyes clear.
It isn't often, as the evening stretches on. She mostly sits there, totally oblivious to the world or at least to this room and everything and everyone in it, including himself.
– I want to meet her, Mrs. Haverhsen.
Chloe asked.
– Is that possible?
– You're such a curious girl, Chloe. The old crone shook her head, the flames from the fireplace dancing in her eyes. – You always were.
Matushe stares into the old woman's eyes, and what he sees reflected in her eyes is the same room, but with Chloe sitting in his chair.
– What did you tell her? Victor urged her, leaning eagerly forward. – What?
Mrs. Haverhsen turned towards him, and it startled him.
– You're such a curious, boy, Victor. You always were.
He rose, abruptly, and walked out with fast, measured steps.
The drive back to the hotel seemed to last forever. He looked into the rear mirror often, very often, but there was nothing there. The road ahead of him seemed to, at least in glimpses and feverish flashes to disappear altogether. At some point he lost control of the car, and it slid from side to side several times before grinding to a halt, stopping with a piercing sound of the tires finally making renewed contact with the dry, dry road. He sat there for minutes in the dark, while the smoke surrounding the car slowly faded.
The engine had died. He realized he had been sitting there in silence for minutes. After some hesitation, after looking one more time into the black, the pitch-black darkness outside the car he made the first attempt at restarting the engine.
No cigar. There was a stutter, before the machine died unborn.
There were no road lights on this place, no lights anywhere. The no man's land seemed to go on forever out there.

He made another attempt, and another, and another. The engine stayed dead, dead as a doornail.

He made another attempt. The engine started with a mighty roar. The lights turned themselves on. In a flash, in a blink of an eye, he saw

The world changed. It turned itself inside out, or so he imagined. Dark turned bright, turned gray, turned mist. Branches on the nearby trees transformed into claws, and the trees themselves looked more like fangs than any trees he had ever seen. The landscape looked strange, totally alien, barren, without any known point of reference. None he could identify.

It lasted just a moment, but in that moment was Eternity.

He crossed the bridge into the hotel's entertainment area. The river below seethed and boiled, washing its shores hard. He felt it, felt the currents hit the barren land, each new drop burning like acid or lye on his skin.

The barroom seemed so peaceful, almost serene. The others, his three partners in crime, waited for him in the corner, the corner dark and lush. He sat down, the scent of palms stuck in his nostrils.

– It was just another crazy old hoot. He shrugged. – This area is full of them, and they're all full of it.

Desire pulled close to him, leaning heavily against him, her full lips tasting his.

People talked around them. He heard a lot of shards, incomplete phrases, bits and pieces of conversation making no sense.

– The fire makes me feel the fire, the man by the fireplace stated, a huge furrow appearing on his brow.

Shades of fire danced in Marion Dexter's face.

– I'm subtle, a woman insisted. – I can make people listen to me for hours without anyone having any idea of what I'm talking about.

– Gurd! A man jumped to his feet, nodding.

Chloe sat by the fire, listening in on people's conversation.

– Interviewing all these people is getting to be tedious, the man with the greasy hair sighed. – Everybody says pretty much the same, but no one is really saying much.

– There was no pentacle in the mountains, Fallon insisted. – Or if there was, we couldn't locate it.

– You couldn't… locate it? Matushe said, staring pointedly at the other man.

– I want to kill them, a woman mumbled, a mumbling coming from everywhere simultaneously, from many lips moving, from one voice speaking. – I want to kill them all.

Matushe danced with Desire. The music was low-key, hardly heard, hardly more than felt in the background noise of the room.

The five dolls danced their stiff dance at their designated base of the pentacle, as the warm sunlight slowly turned blue and cold.

The warm light from the numerous dark lamps burned in his face. Slowly, slowly the light turned blue, turned to ice, and he no longer danced with Desire, but a stiff, lifeless mannequin without blood, flesh and soul, and with dead, unmoving eyes.

He pulled free, abruptly. The mannequin stood there, for a second or two, for an eternity balancing on her rigid feet, before loosing her balance, falling and hitting the floor, and breaking in a thousand pieces.

Desire stood in front of him.

– What's wrong, Victor, she cried, slightly panicked, – what's wrong with you?

He blinked. He blinked again. And it was still Desire, warm blooded and wild standing in front of him.

– Excuse me, he mumbled.

He pulled back, pulled away from her, rushing out of the room, the dead, dead eyes burning a hole in his neck.

The restroom called to him, and he rushed there, to its large mirror, the sight of his own full-figured image, his large, insane windows against the world. The door to a cubicle called to him, and he opened it, suddenly very, very close, close enough to grab the handle and pull open the door. He rushed inside and closed, locked the door behind him, and sat down, sat down fully clothed, without pulling his pants down, on the wet seat.

He sat there, and when he finally looked at his watch over an hour had passed. Shadows danced around the watch, around his head, and he couldn't think, couldn't hear his own thoughts over the loud, loud beating of his own heart, the gasps of his wide-open mouth. He sat there, reaching out with a shaking hand, almost reaching the handle before the hand fell down, bathing in the shit and fluid on the floor. He could no longer move, no longer do anything but listen to the horrible noises outside, the sounds of a mouth chewing, chewing, chewing, forever hungry, forever chewing.

Victor Matushe sat for hours on the toilet seat, shaking violently, not daring to move, totally unable to rise and open the door, and see with his eyes what moved and breathed and grinned outside.

CHAPTER SIX

The Fourth Day

The old woman sat in her attic and painted. She painted the bridge over troubled waters. Her hand was steady and her brush quick.

Desire awoke with a start with the others. They awoke in the king-size bed in the house that Chloe had rented.

– Is everything all right, honey?

Victor held around her, kissing her ear. She looked disoriented at him, at her surroundings, her eyes wandering around the room, the luxurious room where Chloe had slept.

– The light hurts my eyes, she whimpered.

Marion stood up from the bed and walked to the mirror, stopping in front of it, staring straight ahead, staring at nothing.

– I can't see myself, she stated, her voice low and dead.

A car was driving by outside. They heard the music from the over-dimensioned speakers quite clear. The music lingered in their bones, haunting them. It was as if it stayed in the room, as if it was actually played in the room, now. It evoked the thoughts of ghosts, specters and ancient times.

Marion looked down to her right. There was a piece of paper on the floor, its corner sticking out from the curtains. She bent down and picked it up. It was a note, scribbled in haste. She brought it back to the bed, and they all took a long, hard look at it. It was hardly readable, a few letters on one line, a few more the next, a few less below that.

Fallon brought a sheet from the map on the night table, his Chloe Webster file.

– It's jumbled, erratic, he compared the two samples, – but it is Chloe's writing.

– I hear voices, Marion read, timid and scared, with glazed over eyes. – I hear them all the time, even in my sleep when everything else is silent.

And they could swear there was this eerie other voice reading it with her.

Many voices called to them, in the dark, dark corners of the house.

Chloe sat there, writing, doing her best, in vain, to overcome the vicious shaking of her hands.

A car raced through a tunnel bathed in an eerie, dark blue light. Marion stretched her arms above her head, in her place in the passenger seat, stretching her body as far as she could in the limited space, smiling to the driver.

Chloe sat by a table in a cafeteria in a small, cozy street, nursing her cup of coffee. She sat in a corner, glancing nervously at the entrance.

Fallon frowns, as if grasping at something, a thought just beyond his reach.

– Let's walk today, he declares. – Let's have a walk.

They walk down the cozy, narrow street. They pass the cafeteria and imagine they see Chloe in the window.

They pass a window, and in the window there is a lamp, and that's all.

The room beyond the lamp is dark, mysterious… empty. A chill passes beyond Andy Fallon's frown.

The day is still young, a baby crawling on the floor before the proud parents. Chloe stretched her long body on the bed, smiling slightly to herself.

The village people looked at her as she walked down the small and cozy street.

– They stare at us, Desire grinned.

They did, from all vantage points, out of the corners of their eyes. Even where there weren't any people they felt the stares on them. The attention was tangible, in the very air around them. Desire's grin faded and was supplanted by anxiety and muted distress, a haunted expression in eyes and features.

There was a cafeteria at the end of the street. They shivered as they spotted the lamp in the window, the lamp standing out. It cast a cold and soft light, and illuminated the street in the shadowy day.

– There is an entirely different world in that window, Desire whispered, – and we're not there. I can see it, easily see it. I don't even have to try.

Marion looked at the window, and for a moment there, it was as if she was unable to see the four of them in the reflection. There was an entire street there, but they weren't in it. The four of them looked around with wild eyes, at the people that were there, the people staring at them with cold, fish-like eyes.

They walked inside the cafeteria. The darkened atmosphere and smells of a bar seemed to embrace them for a moment, before the room once more returned to being a cafeteria. Marion blinked, and kept blinking, until tears filled her eyes.

– Is the smoke bothering you? Andy asked her.

She shook her head.

There were a few people sitting by simple tables in the fairly bright room. Some digested an unidentified meal, but most nursed a cup of coffee. The man behind the counter wore a giant apron, and squinted his eyes suspiciously at the four newcomers. They ordered both coffee and food, and sat down at a midpoint table, deliberately taking the center stage of the room.

– I look at the wall, she said. – And sometimes I get the crazy feeling that it isn't there. And I see a gallery of faces floating in mist.

Andy blinked and in that blink he saw an expanding dark cloud, bright as a billion streetlights, and he became the cloud and the cloud became him, and the thousand few voices condensed into just two, no more than two, two joining that of his own, and in that choir, that multitude of voices the world was born.

He heard a sound from somewhere in the room, but he couldn't identify the direction from where it originated. It seemed to come from everywhere at once. It hurt his ears, and he flinched.

– Are you okay? Marion studied him with a concerned look on her face, seemingly totally different from the anxious creature at his side only a few seconds earlier.

– I'm okay, he replied calmly.

Elephant feet trickling down his spine.

They sat at the bar, drinking, watching the bartender polishing glasses. Marion coughed every second breath. She kept waving a hand before her, attempting in vain to keep the thick cigarette smoke lingering in the room from reaching her.

– So, what are you guys doing here? An old fellow that had more than a bit too much to drink wondered. – Except for the odd Japanese bunch and other weird foreigners we don't get that many tourists during these out of season times.

– We're journalists. Desire, who had also had too much to drink, grinned. – We're investigating the death of Chloe Webster.

The room turned dead silent, dark and ominous.

– Chloe is dead, the no longer so drunk old man stated.

– Precisely, Desire droned on happily. – And no one seems to know why.

– She was here, the bartender finally nodded, after a break that had lasted seemingly forever. – She sat on the stool before me, like you are doing now.

Suddenly they experienced it as if all the people in the room gathered around them, as the four of them sat there, surrounded by endless chatter. Marion sat on her stool, rocking to the music, the moody music.

– She came in one day, and remained for hours, the bartender mused. – Why was never clear, and she never volunteered information of any kind.

– She sat by the window, a girl said, – and a blond man sat down by her table.

– No, he wasn't blond, the bartender insisted. – He definitely had dark hair, and she never sat by any of the tables. It was a dark haired man, and he joined her, by the bar, where you are sitting now. I know. I'm a trained observer. I've worked behind this desk for thirty years and know my craft.

Marion drew the various scenarios. Andy stared fascinated at her, and her work, as it became alive on the paper. He saw Chloe Webster on the stool, with the bartender and another man with a dark complexion and hair. And then he saw her sit by the window, with the fair-haired man.

They walked in the park afterwards, the sound of the Grasshoppers in the bushes kept surrounding them, dancing invisibly in the slowly darkening air.

– It's all so *confusing,* Marion complained. – There is no lack of information here, but the various pieces are contradicting each other *endlessly*. Everything we've found may be true. Everything or nothing.

Chloe walks in the park, back and forth, laughing with the man with hair by her side. His face is indistinct, shifting, never truly the same. The color of his hair seems to shift as the light shifts.

– I'm all things and none, he says, – and you are, too.

Marion froze in the warm autumn evening.

The two females sat on a bench. The two males were nowhere to be seen. Marion could remember sitting down, but not much beyond that. It was all a blur of fevered emotions. Desire fingered with her hair, laughing into her ear. Marion shook when she felt the wet tip of the other woman's tongue, when she heard her thrilling laughter.

Marion drew a picture, but on that picture was a bridge, the bridge. That was evident as the image took form, as the castle was suggested by its edges. Marion heard Desire speak.

– I see the bridge, too. It's like a painting. And there is a girl there. She stands at the middle of the bridge, staring at nothing.

Desire crouched slightly, shivering.

– The girl in the painting… that is Chloe Webster… isn't it?

Marion said.

Desire grabbed her breast, cupped it in her skilled hand, her enticing fingers. Marion bit her lip, trying to move, to get away, before relenting, giving in. Fumes of hot air blew in and out of her open mouth. Desire turned her head, and kissed her on the lips, her playful tongue slipping in and out of that very open mouth.

Chloe sat on the bench. She was with a woman. Marion knew her, but couldn't quite place her, not in her fevered state. Desire fumbled between her legs, laughing throatily when Marion released a load moan. Marion saw the world through Chloe's eyes, and recognized Ethel Wharton.

Not far from there, Andy and Victor writhed on the ground, in each other's arms, sullying their clothes. In a flash images burned themselves into Marion's mind, of Andy pushing down his pants, of removing Victor's pants and pushing his giant cock into Victor's arse, immediately breaking something there. She smelled the scent of shit and blood as if she was there and gasped aloud.

Desire eagerly unbuttoned Marion's blouse, exposing her skin to the humid night air. But everything yet felt so hot, so very hot. Desire smiled, so sensuously and enticingly and impossible to resist. Marion returned the smile. The two of them sat there on the bench, writhing out of the final fabrics of their clothes, caressing each other in hungry gasps. Marion pushed herself at the other woman, biting into Desire's soft shoulder tissue, drawing blood, and the color of rust and dawn filled her mouth.

The next morning wasn't really the next morning. It was still last night as the sun rose on the sky.

– I know you from somewhere, don't I? Chloe asked Ethel.

– No, you don't, Ethel replied enigmatically.

Desire walked through the park. Yellow leaves blew around her feet. She walked through the castle hallways, looking at the paintings. One of the paintings depicted an old woman painting the bridge over troubled waters. Suddenly she was no longer in the castle. At least it no longer looked like the castle, but a place filled with stale air. The floor was covered in mud, and the walls looked like they hadn't been cleaned for years. She whimpered. There was a sound behind her. She turned her head and heard the cruel, triumphant laughter, and she ran. She ran so hard that her chest hurt, and her legs turned to jelly, and she feared they would give in beneath her, and that she would fall into the mud, the mud moving and grinning to her as if alive, a grin revealing huge, sharp fangs, and a huge gap.

She moaned in Marion's arms. And there was pain and joy. And that felt right, that felt real. She looked at the other woman covered in cold sweat, looked at her with insane eyes. Marion returned a blinding smile. Desire moaned in fear and joy, and she could no longer tell which was which.

Chloe rowed to the center of the sea. Every time the oars dipped into the water she sensed it, as if the surface was her beyond sensitive skin. The house was on her right, the castle on her left. They seemed to push at her, flatten and squeeze her, pull at her and pull her apart. It was all written in her face, her expressive face.

Ethel, a very different Ethel from the woman Marion knew, sat at the opposite side of the boat.

– I'm going to show you what things are like, now, she said. – I'm going to reveal the Universe to you.

Marion shivered in the cold moonlight.

– You are Chloe, Ethel grinned, and Marion gasped by the onslaught hitting her. – You are now. And by the snap of my fingers… you're not.

Marion awoke on the bench, the wide bench. It was night. She was nude, but she didn't feel cold. Desire was still sleeping, a wide smile painted on her expressive face. Marion reached for her clothes, but they weren't there. She smiled, too. She knew that, as if she was able to actually see her face from a given point beyond herself. Marion saw herself walk on a trail between the trees, and trees were the only thing she could see. Ethel levitated before her, evidently as much at home in the air as on the ground. Marion felt fear, but she couldn't act on it, couldn't express herself. Her attention and wonder were locked on the ethereal specter hovering above her like… like a Goddess.

– I'm going to show you wonders, and you, like the pathetic creature you are, will crumble under their weight like paper.

A hard, solid hand touched Marion's head. Ethel didn't move, but a hand, a third hand appeared from nowhere, and the world changed, transformed around Marion Dexter.

The scream, the howl from the grave woke Desire from her slumber. She sat up startled. The scream echoed through the park. She dressed quickly, covering the most necessary parts of herself and rushed in the direction from where she had heard the scream.

She found Marion crouched by a tree, staring at nothing with eyes big as footballs. Kneeling down she carefully touched the distraught woman. Marion noticed her. Her eyes, her head began moving, back and forth, and it didn't stop, and it chilled Desire to the bone.

– The world turned inside out, she wailed.

– What *happened?* Desire cried, sensing her distress beyond distress.

She touched her lover, and images, emotions, sensations, alien and horrible touched her, and she backed off in horror. Marion smiled to her, a horrible beyond horrible smile.

– Inside out, Marion moaned. – Inside out, inside out, inside out…

And she never stopped.

The Sixth Day

– I go, Chloe said. – I go where no one will find me.

Andy looked through her journal. He strained his eyes. He was almost able to actually see her, see her as a flesh and blood creature ahead of him, as he turned page by page with his numb fingertips.

Marion sat in the chair, nude, resting her head in her palm, staring blankly at him, at nothing. She was dirty. Practically her entire body was covered in dirt, and partly in mud. The mud part was strange, was strange, too. There had been no rain, and there was no mud he knew of around the Lake.

– She reaches out for us, she recited, – through time and space, to catch up with us all.

She rose, rushing to him, grabbing his collar.

– Have you seen the room? She whimpered. – There are dollies there, dull-eyed, and transparent like glass, dirty like ink.

– Take a shower, he snapped. – Clean yourself!

«Tianuc Merde is walking down the road», he read.

– Tianuc Merde is walking down the road, she sang from the bathroom.

He heard the sound of the shower, and it sounded like the heaviest of waterfalls.

– I need a taxi to the city immediately, Chloe shouted to the bell clerk.

– She sounded really out of it, the bell clerk told the four of them.

– Is something the matter with your car, Ma'am? He wondered.

– It's a big, BIG MOUTH is what it is, she whined in terror.

– The cab was late, very late, and she got more and more agitated, not really herself at all.

– Herself? Desire smirked, leaning across the desk.

– Yes, he quickly countered. – We had gotten to know her real well during the week, but now she was like a completely different person, like a stranger to us.

– He's lying, Victor stated firmly in the hallways right afterwards. – Or at least lying about something. He knows something he isn't telling.

– Or he's just vain. Marion shrugged. – The way I see it at least a million people, considering all the people bragging about it, must have spoken to Chloe Webster the week before she died.

– The rumors *are* true! Victor exclaimed astounded, lightening up like a Christmas tree. – There *is* a magnificent mystery here. Something spectacular did indeed happen to poor Chloe. If we can just penetrate the shroud of… of secrecy surrounding her death and final days we will most certainly expose events that will make us all rich and famous beyond words.

– Beyond words! Desire's oriental eyes twinkled.

Marion photographed the bridge from yet another angle. The stench of darkroom chemicals filled the house, and turned the air dense and hardly breathable. She dropped the pictures on the living room floor afterwards, covering most of the available space.

– Are you done soon? Desire complained loudly, incessantly (and endlessly), resting in Victor's strong arms.

Marion frowned. Her head hurt. She shivered when looking at the sick gleam in the other woman's eyes. Desire stared at the images on the floor. She never took her eyes off them. Marion studied them, too, from all angles. There was something there, something giving her the creeps.

There was no one at the bridge, no people at all.

– I took my photos during the entire day… she began.

– And there's no one there, Desire said frostily.

Victor cuddled her softly. She sent him a grateful look.

The sea of pictures on the floor began to swim before her eyes. She crossed the bridge, stopped halfway, and stared down at the bridge's frothing currents. The wind was blowing, and she could hardly keep her footing. She found herself in the pictures, found herself on the bridge, staring at a given point, at something she could never quite see in paralyzing fright.

She saw herself from a given point outside herself. The camera, or whatever recording device there was, zoomed in on her face. She stared partly at the camera, partly to the side, a haunted look in her face, and she never got to see what it was, what was there.

Andy walked off on his own a bit later in the day, as was his want.

The police station was down the road, by the main harbor. He turned a bit, looking at the Lake. It was big the Lake. One could only glimpse the opposite shore from here. It was fairly narrow, but quite long. Steam rose from it, and created a misty haze in the hot day. The fairly short walk was sufficient to make Andy sweat. The chill inside the building welcomed him like a blanket.

Everybody in there stared at him, or so it felt like. The heads of everyone in the room staring at him bulged and twisted, and he felt a profound sickness in his gut, bile burning like acid in his throat.

– What can I help you with, sir? The smiling desk sergeant asked him.

– I'm here to speak with the investigating officer in the Chloe Webster case, Andy stated somewhat calmly.

The smile turned broader, and Andy's incredulity and sense of unreality even stronger.

– There was no investigating officer in the Chloe Webster case here at our station, sir, the desk sergeant smiled, – but you may speak to our public relation officer if you want?

– It was unreal, Andy related to the others later, – like walking into a scene of keystone cops or something.

A female officer led him down a long hall. He looked at her swinging hips and muscular thighs. Sounds from the walls distracted him, and there were *noises*. He believed they originated somewhere below, in the lower floor or in the actual floor, but he couldn't be certain.

– Have you worked here long? He asked the cute female officer.

– Practically my entire life, sir, she replied brightly.

She frowned, clearly studying him.

– We are a very peaceful town, and there is very little crime here, really.

He stared at her, attempting to keep himself from staring, in an effort to decide whether or not she was being ironic or if there was a touch of menace or implied threat in her voice, in vain.

A stocky man reached out a hand, and Andy took it, absentmindedly, attempting to concentrate. He sat down in the very comfortable chair, feeling anything but comfortable.

The man cleared his throat. Andy kept studying him with a bad feeling in his gut.

– Thank you for seeing me on such short notice, Andy began.

– We don't get many journalists here, the man coughed.

It was at this point Andy got seriously spooked.

The light sifting through the windows got darker. The draft on his legs more pronounced.

– I'm here about Chloe Webster, Andy began.

– She was here, the Chief nodded.

Andy frowned, but kept up the attempt to gain some semblance of normality, some sort of upper hand.

– Yes, so I understand, sir, he began, began again. – But there still seems to be a lot of confusion in this case, and my colleagues and I have come to this beautiful village in a yet another attempt to find out what exactly happened to her.

– I will help you to the best of my ability, of course...

The Chief said.

Andy caught himself, pulled himself together by the hair.

Words from his nebulous career of journalism, advice given him by older, experienced newshounds echoed through his mind, and he grabbed that, grabbed those words and held on to them… to the best of his ability. Gallows humor erupted from his insides, and once again he caught himself just in time.

«Rely on what you know. When things go screwy and everything seems totally out of whack, return to the basics, and proceed from there».

– I would like to begin at the beginning, he said, – and go through everything in detail. I want to make sure we don't leave anything out.

Did the Chief give him the eye, or was it only his overactive imagination? Andy couldn't tell, and found there was very little to hold onto here, in this whirlwind of confusion.

– We were asked to contribute to the investigation, the stocky man related dryly, as if speaking about the weather or some similar *dry* topic. – Asked to trace Chloe Webster's movements the last week of her life. We found that it wasn't hard, not hard at all, really. We are a very open community here, with few or no secrets, as I'm sure you can attest to.

Fallon stared at him, giving him his own eye. Was this guy for real?

– I have to commend you, Fallon, the Chief droned on. – You and your people have basically walked in our footsteps here. You have interviewed every single individual even remotely connected to the case. Miss Webster arrived here on Friday the twenty-third and left us almost exactly to the hour one week later. We have documented her stay in immaculate detail, I'm proud to say.

Fallon nodded sympathetically without really thinking about it. He foresaw one hell of a boring (and wasted) afternoon, but saw no way out of it. They needed this information. There was something… something he couldn't quite grasp, something rotten in Denmark somewhere. His bloodhound instincts kept screaming at him, even on mute.

– She arrived at the hotel late in the evening. After settling down, she walked straight to the top of the mountain, and there, as we understand it, she performed a satanic ritual.

– She was a pagan, Fallon corrected him absentmindedly, – not a Satanist.

– She performed the satanic ritual for about three hours, the Chief continued unabated. – The clerk noticed her when she returned to the hotel, dirty and haggard.

Fallon took notes, even though the Chief spoke into his microphone. He always took notes. For some reason it had always felt as natural for him as breathing.

– The next day she announced, out of the blue that she intended to move into the house across the lake.

Andy crossed off on his list as the chief kept talking, as he never stopped, as he droned on endlessly.
The hotel manager observing while Chloe was leaving the house… Check.
Old woman in retirement home claiming she observed Chloe dance naked on the hill… *Check.*
Chloe meeting with the retirement home manager… Check.
The manager being evasive… Check.
Chloe being clearly distraught while leaving the retirement home… Check.
She returned to the hotel for dinner, still very distressed… Check.
She spilled sauce on the waiter's arm… Check.
Passing pedestrians hear two voices from Chloe's bedroom… Check.
They see two shadows on the curtains… Check.
Mrs. Henderson observes her the next morning… Check.
Oscar Lerner lying… Check.
People watch Chloe row to the center of the lake… Check.
Arnold Jenkins meets her at night, on her way to the mountains… Check.
He claims her face was covered in blood… Check.
He describes her pouch… Check.
He follows her and sees her work her magic… Check.
A woman, Miss Cartwright, hears singing… Check.
Chloe asks the villagers about the Lady of the Lake… Check.
Chloe visits Mrs. Haverhsen…
– Mrs. Webster visited the cafeteria in the village, the Chief said.
Fallon stared at him, unable to help himself.
– Didn't Chloe visit an old woman, Mrs. Haverhsen?
– There is no one by that name in this town. The Chief looked at him as if he was mud.
Fallon stared incredulous at him, set on staring him down. The Chief seemed to stare back, but his look is blank, expressionless, like that of a dead body.
Chloe tells the clerk at the motel to call a cab… Check.
She claims her car «is a big, big mouth»… Check.
– She was here, the Chief stated.
– She was here? Fallon wondered.
– I talked to her myself, the Chief confirmed. – She wanted to know about the Lady of the Lake. I told her that it was just an old story, and that it had never been substantiated in any way, at least not any way that would satisfy a formal investigation. Miss Webster asked where the

restroom was. I told her where, and she left. I found out half an hour later that she had stolen a police car, leaving all her stuff behind.

Andy frowned, realizing that he still didn't get it… whatever it was.

– So what happened? Fallon wondered.

– Happened? The Chief voiced.

– Yes, Fallon nodded. – Can you give me the specifics of her death? You did find her, right, found out, at least in part, what had happened to her?

The Chief leaned back in his chair, leaning forward, towering above Andy.

– I'm afraid you have been misinformed, sir, the nice man sighed. – It's amazing how information can go awry in this day and age. You see, she wasn't killed here, but in the city, in the Marlon Caine residence, at Marlboro Hill. You will have to ask the Metropolitan Police for further information, I'm afraid.

It was amazing how many times he could incorporate the word «information» in just a few sentences like that, and in such a short time.

Andy stared at him, stunned beyond belief.

He wasn't really there, as he left the building a few minutes later. His surroundings didn't seem real, didn't seem real at all. He hurried back to the house, the house by the lake. The others caught his distress immediately. He began his report in an even, dead voice.

They sat there, all of them, shaking their heads.

– How could people not ask that question? He cried out afterwards. – How could we not do it, until now?

– We even picked up her journals at the Metropolitan police station, Marion sighed.

He looked at her with fond eyes. She was such a treasure.

– We saw what we expected to see, Victor pointed out. – I see a lot of that.

– Appearances rule the world, Desire stated firmly.

Andy and Marion glanced at each other and nodded.

– I began shaking in there, he said. – I still do. Something was so very, very *wrong*.

The Chief had looked at him with his dead fish eyes, and he had felt like a dead fish himself.

Marion rubbed his arm, comforted him.

– And he was lying, too, even though he clearly didn't lie about the bombshell he dropped. But he was at least holding back something, not telling the whole truth.

– Who is? Marion wondered.

He showed them his notes.

The hotel manager observing while Chloe was leaving the house… Check.

Old woman on retirement home claiming she observed Chloe dance naked on the hill… *Check.*

Chloe meeting with the retirement home manager… Check.

The manager being evasive… Check.

Chloe being clearly distraught while leaving the retirement home… Check.

She returned to the hotel for dinner, still very distressed… Check.

She spilled sauce on the waiter's arm… Check.

Passing pedestrians hear two voices from Chloe's bedroom… Check.

They see two shadows on the curtains… Check.

Mrs. Henderson observes her the next morning… Check.

Oscar Lerner lying… Check.

People watch Chloe row to the center of the lake… Check.

Arnold Jenkins meets her at night, on her way to the mountains… Check.

He claims her face was covered in blood… Check.

He describes her pouch… Check.

He follows her and sees her work her magic… Check.

A woman, Miss Cartwright, hears singing… Check.

Chloe asks the villagers about the Lady of the Lake… Check.

Chloe visits Mrs. Haverhsen… *There is no Mrs. Haverhsen.*

Chloe tells the clerk at the motel to call a cab… Check.

She claims her car «is a big, big mouth»… Check.

– That's a bald faced lie! Victor said, clearly agitated.

He raced out of the room. They followed him, followed him to his car, quite puzzled. He sat down behind the wheel, and they jumped in just before he started the car and drove off.

The drive seemed to take forever, or maybe it was done in a blink of an eye, they couldn't tell.

He stopped at a clearing at the end of the road. There were quite a few houses on that stretch, but none where he stopped.

– It was here, he insisted as the four of them left the car. – The old hoot lived her. You were here with me, all three of you. Then… you weren't. I drove back to the hotel alone, and everything just faded away into nothing.

A flash visited Fallon's inner eye, a vision of a fireplace and an old woman with fire in her eyes. In a flash it was gone. He shuddered and forgot about it.

They were back in the house by the lake, back there packing. Andy and Marion were alone in the bedroom. They stood close and spoke in low voices.

– We don't really know Victor, do we, or Desire for that matter?

He said hesitatingly.

They looked out the window, at Victor and Desire loading their luggage into the back of the car.

Marion grabbed his hand.

– I think you're right. She nodded. – They were just here when we arrived, very conveniently here.

She kissed him on the lips, a little tenderly, a little desperate.

– The fuckers don't even have a car.

The two of them left. Marion turned in the door, and saw Chloe sit on the bed, smiling to her. It was such a weird smile, and it gave Marion the willies.

They closed and locked the entrance door behind them. The air outside was crisp and clear. They faced their two companions by the car.

– What did we *do* yesterday?

Marion frowned, as if striving to remember.

– We walked in the park, Victor smirked, – or don't you remember?

– No, that wasn't yesterday, Marion protested. – That was the day before. I…

Four pair of eyes met, or didn't meet. A shiver passed through Marion, and a moan escaped her as she hurried inside the car.

– Let's get away from here, Andy said. – Let's get as far away as we possibly can.

He practically jumped into the car, in front of the wheel, or at least he tried to. His head hit the edge of the ceiling, and so hard that he was practically dizzy when he fell into the seat behind the wheel.

Fingers produced keys from his pocket. His hand was shaking as he put the key into the ignition hole, and switched it on.

There was a coughing sound as the engine fluttered and died. He tried again.

– Don't do it, Marion said weakly, – not so quickly.

The engine roared as it came to life. Smiles lit their faces. In front of them appeared a massive black space. The smiles faded. They stared right ahead. Andy stared. He could see through the darkness, barely, to the other side. It was as if it was an integrated part of the very air, of existence itself.

Andy drove straight forward, determination darkening his face, drove right through the shimmering cloud, appearing on the other side, and there was nothing there, except the totally familiar and ordinary place they had come to know.

Marion looked back as they drove away from the old house by the lake. She saw Chloe Webster stand in the window, beckoning her. Marion turned her head back, and stared demonstratively forward, glimpsing her pale face in the right outside mirror. The mirror was twisted at an impossible angle, for a brief moment, until it was once more «right», in the correct position.

Andy drove off in a not too fast, not too slow pace. They drove along the lake, past the hotel, the medieval-like brick building resembling a castle. He didn't stop there, didn't even slow down. The others merely shrugged.

– It's funny. Desire laughed short, ghastly. – I have money and most of my belongings in there, but I don't want to stop and pick them up, not for anything in the world.

Nobody commented on her outburst. They just looked glumly straight ahead.

They left the lake, and the two buildings behind, and didn't look back, not once. It faded in their memory, as if it had never been real, never been there in the first place.

They were back on the highway. The long stretch of gray seemed to go on forever ahead of them. Marion leaned against Andy, careful not to disturb his driving. She yawned, and she was sniffing a bit, something catching in her throat.

The sun settled behind them. Victor looked at his watch. There were several motels along the road. The four of them looked at each other, looked at each other again.

– Just keep driving, he insisted. – We'll keep going, no matter what. We'll take turns, you hear me.

His voice rose and cracked.

They kept driving throughout the night.

CHAPTER SEVEN

On The Seventh Day

Images shifted and flowed like lightning, or a landscape bathed in lightning. Each new flash brought another jigsaw to the puzzle. They flowed like mercury dancing at the heart of a volcano.

Marion woke up on the bench in the park. It was morning. Her eyes opened to behold Desire's smiling face and exposed body. They were both nude. The morning dew covered their skin. The parts of the women's bodies touching felt pleasantly warm. The parts exposed to the environment had turned cold. A chill fired through Marion, one not influenced the slightest by the warm, rising sun.

Desire yawned and stretched her body. The happy smile remained as she kissed the other woman on the lips.

– Good morning, she grinned.

– Good morning, Marion mumbled, a little off.

The warm sun boiled her blood, stirred a memory she was unable to recall.

– A good thing it's summer, is it not? Or we would have surely frozen to death.

She frowned, the grin widening.

– Or perhaps not.

They dressed. Their clothes were wet and difficult to put on, but they managed, with a little help from the other.

It's funny, Marion giggled darkly – I keep hearing the sound of whining tires.

She frowned, unable to locate her shoes. Desire couldn't find hers either. They searched a bit for them in their immediate surroundings, but they were nowhere to be found.

They walked barefoot on the trail between the trees. Yellow leaves danced by their feet.

– It looks so different, now, in daylight, Desire said.

She heard the sound of the lake, of its water hitting the shore. It felt so peaceful, so right.

Marion saw the hotel between the trees, quite the comforting sight. A strange tingle shot through her. Andy and Victor sat on a bench in front of the hotel. The women waved and the men waved back. Clouds gathered above the castle. Marion saw them, saw them pull together and embrace like living creatures.

– Are you all right? Desire asked her lightly.
– I'm fine, thank you. Marion squeezed her hand.

The road split the two women and the two men. Marion quickened her pace to avoid a noisy car.

She rushed into Andy's arms. He looked strangely uncomfortable, but returned her sultry kiss.

– What is it? She wondered.
– I fell on my ass last night, he said. – It hurts like hell.
– He fell on his ass. Victor chuckled.

They all laughed. It was funny.

But there was a strained look in Desire's eyes when she looked at Victor, when she walked to him, and kissed his lips.

She hardly remembered anything about their breakfast at the hotel. It had been totally uneventful, as far as she knew.

The hotel rose around her. She wanted to stop it from doing that, in vain, in hopeless, hopeless vain.

A man sat by the neighboring table. He seemed to be in a good mood, a very good mood, practically dancing on the chair.

A woman sat by the bar in her training gear, looking very fit and very healthy. She drank orange juice, looking like she had been running, and running hard, her short hair clinging to her sweaty skin.

Desire recalled her gut reaction at the time. It felt wrong, totally wrong and fake. The trickle down her spine scared her.

She remembered fragments of the four of them having lunch on the lawn of the house. Chloe stood there looking at them, staring at them, staring at *her*. She remembered that, vividly.

– Guys, she said, she whimpered. – Guys…

Her hand moved by itself and grabbed hold of Victor. She pointed what she imagined was a bony finger. All three of them turned towards where she pointed. She knew, knew they saw nothing, except the air, the transparent air.

– It's her, she whispered. – It's Chloe. She's staring at me.

And then she realized that the others didn't hear her, didn't see her, as if she wasn't really there at all. Victor didn't even notice her hand.

– You are lost to this world, Chloe told her, holding a shoe in her hand.

Everything seemed frozen, even though it moved. Her three companions looked distant to her, far away, unreachable.

– You are lost to this world, Chloe told her, the shoe gone from her hand.

Everything moved, but Desire didn't. She didn't feel the air she breathed, the ground she stood on.

Panic gripped her, but she couldn't move, no matter how much she strained. She stared straight at the sun, but she wasn't blinded. There were no wind, no smell, and no scent, only sensations. They overwhelmed her, made her almost shut down in desperation.

Suddenly, there was movement, as she saw through her neck as easily as she saw through her eyes. She saw herself enter the garden through the kitchen door carrying a tray with glasses and that was the point where her three friends had directed their attention for what seemed like ages ago. A flash inverted her world, and she became that woman of flesh and blood. She remembered now. She had gone to the kitchen to fetch lemonade, and then… then…

She put the tray on the table. The others looked at her, acknowledging her existence, and she experienced a sickening sensation of relief, coupled with the lingering fear.

– I was here, she said.

– You were… here? Marion covered her eyes with her hand.

– I went to the kitchen, but suddenly I found myself back here, with you. You didn't see me. There was nothing I could do to make you aware of me.

– So, you went out of your body? Marion wondered. – What is it called, spirit walking?

Desire nodded, half occupied.

– I saw Chloe, she finally said. – She spoke to me.

The others looked at her, stared at her.

– What did she say? The interest in Victor's eyes warmed her.

– She said I was lost to this world.

It turned quiet as she sat down, as she took a huge sip of the lemonade, as Victor kissed her and comforted her, as was his want.

– Has anything like this ever happened to you before? Andy wondered.

– No. She shook her head.

– Your powers are growing. Victor nodded to himself. – This case, what we're experiencing in connection with it, is clearly pushing your limits, opening you up.

He looked so excited, as if he had been just been given a new toy, or as if the toy had been somewhat upgraded. She wanted to be angry with him, but his winning smile won her over, as always. So, she sat down in his lap and kissed him passionately.

– Like a flower, he added. – A sweet, sweet flower.

She saw the flower in full bloom, its full power, saw it wither and die because of lack of sustenance. Her lips kept seeking his. She pushed herself against him, not passionately, but desperately. He didn't notice.

The view and sense of the garden faded in her mind. They walked from the house to the village. Desire walked closest to the quay, to the black, black water. It seemed to reach for her. She imagined the many ghostly arms and hands do their dance in the shadowy air. There were blue skies and blinding sunlight, but it didn't reach her.

They walked through the village, up and down, up and down. Desire led them, pulled them with her.

– What are we looking for? Marion wondered, clearly irritated.

– I don't… know, Desire replied despairingly, desperately.

People looked at them, to the point of being impolite. There was an eerie quality to their eyes that made Desire very nervous.

– They stare at us, Andy said.

– They always do, Marion shrugged.

The small, pointed eyes never let go.

They stare at me, Chloe wrote in her diary. I'm not saying this because I'm imagining things or because I'm being paranoid, but because it's *true*.

The four of them sat on a bench in the park, the small lung of green behind the city hall. Desire watched the people passing by.

– The clerk is drawing my suspicion again, Marion read. – I mean, every clerk I've ever encountered is curious. It goes with the job, but this guy is clearly over the top. He follows my every move, as if I am a leper, or something.

The words did something to Desire. They dug deep in her, and didn't let go, and she couldn't understand why.

It wasn't Marion. She read the words with the passion of a rock. If she had been an actor acting her lines, she would have been drowned in rotten tomatoes.

– A leper doesn't belong, Andy said suddenly. – A leper is an outsider, no matter where he or she goes.

He sounded surprised, as if he had just come by this conclusion.

– Was that how others saw her or how she saw herself? Victor wondered.

– It's usually a little bit of both, Desire said lightly.

She looked at Victor, studied him, pondering what she saw, but she didn't recognize him.

They walked down an auspicious, small street. It was the only one with any real number of stores in the village. They sat on a bench at the street's northern end. Marion sketched with fast, confident moves. The street came alive on the paper before her.

– I draw the world, Marion hummed happily. – I dream of things and make them real.

Desire sensed the street, felt it and its people move. She found herself out there, among them, in a chaotic whirl of visuals and sensations. It slowed down, almost to a crawl. She moved, while the others didn't or hardly did. The world had virtually stopped moving.

– The world is yours, a woman told her.

The woman had auburn hair and strange, ruby eyes. Desire didn't know her, but noticed the ring with the ruby stone on her finger.

Desire sat on the bench, staring at Marion's drawing. A man stumbled from an alley. Desire looked up, and there he was. He looked sick, very sick. The man stumbled, desperately attempting to straighten, to walk straight, but failing miserably. He coughed once, coughed twice, and fell on the ground right before the four on the bench whirling up a cloud of dust. Desire coughed, and looked at the man on the ground through a film of tears. He was unnaturally pale, covered in sweat, stinking of it, the skin around his eyes red and swollen.

The four stood around him, unable to move. Desire wanted to, but couldn't. She stood there, frozen like a statue.

– I make films, the man gasped. – At least I thought I did.

She knew him, or at least she thought she did.

His clothes were in tatters. They looked more like rags than clothes. They suspected he hadn't slept indoors for quite a while, if ever.

He coughed. His cough turned worse, far worse. His entire body shook, and the next time he coughed, he coughed blood. It flowed from his mouth like a waterfall. Not bright pink cleaned blood from his lungs, as one would expect, but a dark and festering red puss. The river of blood flowed towards Desire's left foot. She stepped back, racked with sudden panic.

– I... know him, Andy said hesitatingly. – Why can't I remember him?

People gathered around the coughing dead man with a curious look in their eyes. It felt completely morbid to Desire, but she couldn't stop looking either. It felt like a compulsion, one emanating deep below, irresistible.

The man shook one final time, and died. He lay still, covered in dust and blood and other things none of the onlookers dared to vocalize, not even in their paralyzed minds.

Desire stepped back, and stepped back, and stepped back. She kept doing so, until the crowd no longer filled her vision. She turned with a pained expression in her face.

Marion called to her, but she didn't hear anything. Marion's lips moved, but there was no sound.

Desire stopped before the window. The street was bright, mirrored easily in the dark window. Denise saw herself in the mirror, but she was… misplaced. She didn't stand on the place she did… out here. All the rest stood where they were supposed to stand, but she didn't. And she didn't look like herself at all. She looked… haunted. Beyond haunted. The expression in her eyes that of nameless fear.

Make up smeared her face. It covered her skin, and made her almost unrecognizable, but Desire knew who she was looking at.

She looked at a pottery plant in the window. It faded away and vanished before her eyes. Her entire expression turned incredulous and changed into terror.

Marion called to her, called her name, and this time Desire heard her. She returned to the three. The crowd had dispersed, even though a few of them still lingered in the street and immediate vicinity. The police and medics had come to take the dead man away.

– This isn't today, she told them, suddenly determined, nausea gripping her like death.

They looked incredulous at her.

– What do you mean?

Victor looked patronizing at her.

– This isn't today, she said. – It's the day before yesterday when we…

– What are you *yapping* about?

The hostility in his voice shocked her.

Something happened. It turned quiet again, really quiet. She saw her three companions and herself in a spin. The four of them seemed to shrink, to grow, and she couldn't tell, couldn't decide what. The village loomed above them, below them.

The coughing dead man stared at her. His left eye had fallen half out of its socket, and the left side of his mouth was lowered into something resembling a leer.

– Oh, God, she whimpered.

She stepped back. The man coughed, standing there, right behind her three friends, but they didn't see him, didn't even suspect he was there.

– What happened? A wail rose from her throat. – Something happened to us, but I can't for the love of me say what.

Her eyes turned inside out, turned white. The shock in the others' expression hurt her. It hurt her terribly. She fainted. Everything turned black, turned shadow. Consciousness left her, even as sensation embraced her. She fell, slowly, fast, and hit the ground on her back, landing in the pool of dust and blood. The others rushed to her, but they felt distant and far away. She didn't believe they could save her.

On the seventh night

The four returned at late dusk, avoiding each other's eyes. Their feet had long since turned sore, after miles of walking.

– We should send someone after the car, Desire said apprehensively.

– Tomorrow, Victor said hastily.

They glanced to their left, seeing the house, and to their right awaited them the hotel, everything they had sought to leave. The main street of the village was lit with something resembling Chinese lights. It wasn't electricity. It looked like giant fireflies swarming and buzzing. They hurried into the hotel.

Andy approached the desk. The others remained by the entrance.

– Hello, again, he greeted the man behind the desk.

– Hello, Mister Fallon, the clerk replied politely.

– We've had an accident with the car, I'm afraid, and will have to stay at your excellent establishment for at least one more night. Our old rooms are still available, I trust?

– They are indeed, the clerk confirmed. – This late in the season we are quite flexible that way.

Fallon stared at the man, looking for anything resembling smugness or triumph, but there wasn't any, not any that Fallon could discern.

They didn't carry any luggage this time, of course, but the clerk still insisted that the bellboy followed them to their rooms.

He led them through dark and long hallways. The lights dimmed further. Everything turned completely black for a moment, before the dim lights blissfully reappeared and blinded them. Marion sought close to Andy. He put his arm around her, and squeezed her gently.

Their rooms hadn't changed. In fact they looked exactly the same. The beds hadn't been made. The four of them checked out both rooms with a nervous flicker in their eyes.

– Looks like they knew we would return, Victor cried, almost shouted.

– We can't say that for sure, Andy assured him. – As the clerk pointed out: it is off-season. They are probably only sloppy or late with the cleaning up.

– That's ridiculous, Marion snapped at him. – Why don't we go and take a look at the other rooms and see for ourselves how «sloppy» they are.

He stared astounded at her, at her pale visage. She ran into his arms, and she shook and cried there, while he desperately attempted to comfort her, to brighten her spirit.

Victor nodded to him. He took Desire's shaking hands, and the two of them left the room. Andy nodded back. He closed the door and returned to Marion's sagging figure, her wide-open, suffering eyes.

– It turned completely black, she said, whimpering.

– Yes, I know. He shook his head. – And in this place, in these circumstances…

– NO! She shouted, changing in a blink of an eye from whimpering to aggressive. – You don't UNDERSTAND! It didn't turn completely black. It turned completely nothing. Everything vanished. When I tried to sense the walls… or anything, I… couldn't. The floor we stepped on just wasn't there anymore. Everything disappeared, as if someone… or *something* had turned a switch.

She sat down on the bed, sobbing, completely beside herself. He wanted to go to her, but he couldn't. His feet seemed to be glued to the floor, and pure, crystalline ice cut open his heart.

– My feet hurt, she complained, and he hated the childish taint in her voice.

He didn't comment on her words.

Desire and Victor knocked on the door a few minutes later. Neither Andy nor Marion had moved by then. Now, they did, painfully, with great difficulty. The horror of the room gave way to the glittering lights of the dining hall. There weren't many people present, mostly people enjoying the leisure of old age.

– It's quiet, Marion whispered.

They glanced at each other, at the pale faces, the sunken eyes, and terror took hold in their hardly beating hearts. The bleak fear that had grabbed them earlier in the day held them in its fist.

A man sat by a table drinking. He drank fast and intense, like he was drowning in a desert of water. Andy studied him, or tried to. There wasn't much to see, really, except yet another drunk getting drunk.

– I wonder, Desire said, looking down in her glass. – Can a person, any person find quantifiable proof of his or hers existence or will reality, once reached for slip away like quicksilver the moment you attempt to touch it?

– Heat is real. Victor shrugged. – Cold is real. But you can't touch it.

The man at the other table got ever more intoxicated. He stared into his glass with a dull expression in his eyes.

– It doesn't work, he said aloud. – Nothing does!

Marion leaned forward, almost over the table.

– We should never have returned here, she hissed, – but quite simply kept walking.

– That's ridiculous, Victor cried. – We would have needed to walk for days, just to get to the nearest gas station. We're in the middle of nowhere, or haven't you noticed?
– We are nowhere, Desire whispered.
– WAITER! The man at the other table shouted.
Desire jumped in the chair.
No waiter came, or at least didn't come instantly, and the man at the other table rose on unsteady feet and stumbled towards the bar. They heard a loud rumble as the poor guy evidently fell over some chairs. Marion hid her smile, and the non-audible giggle behind a hand. Her eyes had turned large and shiny.
Andy glanced at her, worry visible in his eyes.
Someone played a piano somewhere, haunting, eerie music. It rumbled through the hall and hallways, and they heard it as a kind of enhanced, not fading echo, enchanted like a forest… or a dance. The chords, the very sound of it sent shivers through them all.
– Where is the PIANO? The man on the floor wailed. – I never saw a fucking PIANO here!
The four giggled. Marion chuckled cruelly, her eyes bigger than ever. Andy's shiver increased a notch or two more.
– I need to go to the restroom, she said lightly, casually, very correct and polite. – Will you all excuse me for a minute?
– Certainly, Victor said, sipping his drink. – We will just sit here and relax while you are exerting yourself.
– Do you want me to follow you? Fallon asked concerned.
– That won't be necessary, my dear, she said. – I can take care of myself, in this and other *exiting* endeavors.
Her reply felt like a rejection and hurt him a bit, but he concealed it, and just nodded encouragingly to her, though she had already left.
The piano music changed. Somehow it metamorphosed into lengthy organ tones. There was no transition or sense of transition. One moment a piano was playing, the next the organ.
– How could we have forgotten? Desire wondered.
– Forgotten what.
Victor sipped some more from his newly filled glass.
– Forgotten the coughing dead man.
– But we didn't forget him, my sweet. I can honestly say I remember everything.
– You do now. Desire grabbed his hand. – But you didn't before.
The two men looked at each other, totally bewildered. They shook their heads and had a toast.

Desire sat there, anxious and alone, desperately attempting to put her worry into words, but no words came.

Marion returned, her walk confident, her eyes calm, a large pool of calm.

– Have you seen our friend, my dear? Victor wondered.

She looked inquiringly at him.

– The drunk? Victor explained. – We can't seem to locate him anywhere, and I suspect we wouldn't have, even if we had actually tried to do so.

– So, he has vanished, then? She nodded. – Good! I didn't care much for his loud act.

She smiled, and bent down and kissed Andy on the lips. He felt her hard nipples stab his skin further below. There was an odor coming from her he couldn't quite identify, so familiar that he was amazed that he didn't recognize its imprint.

A man, another man screamed. He wasn't far away. They saw him when they turned around, saw him sit in his chair, saw him fall off it, and hit the floor.

– NO! He howled. – NOOOOOOOOOO

He kept repeating it, not letting up, not getting up, but remaining on the floor as if his ability to walk or even stand had been taken from him, been plucked brutally from his brain, and he no longer had the actual ability to use his legs, or even remembered that he had any.

A woman sat by the bar, drinking. A row of glasses had been lined up in front of her, and she took on them all, and there seemed to be no end to her endurance. Her long and dirty hair hung from her bowed head, and occasionally it swept the floor, and picked up even more dirt.

The floor had clearly not been cleaned for days.

– Let's leave. Marion shook her head in disgust. – The clientele here isn't exactly desirable company, and certainly not up to our standards.

She smiled, a smile freezing tongues and larynxes, keeping voices from being heard.

– Everything moves so deliciously slow, she grinned dreamily.

The others, sick to their stomach, were only happy that someone finally took the initiative, and they could hardly wait to get up and walk off, out of there. The woman in the bar, with a downright eerie smile started throwing the glasses at the mirror. It broke, and broke again, until it was in a thousand pieces, but yet had to fall off the wall. Desire looked into the mirror as they passed it, and she frowned at first, but then she shook, hard and viciously in Victor's arms.

Victor walked behind the bar, grabbed a couple of bottles and four glasses, and they were off. They didn't see the bartender or anyone resembling a bartender anywhere.

The hallways were as quiet as always. They half expected the bellboy to join them and insist on following them to their rooms again, but they didn't see him, didn't see him anywhere.

They glimpsed the clerk, on his post, grinning at them with his faceless smile.

The four of them returned to their rooms, to Victor and Desire's room, for some reason. Victor opened the bottles, both the bottles without delay, and poured four stiff drinks to them all. They drank. They emptied the glasses in one single swallow.

Victor coughed as he fell down on the bed, his face covered in sweat and greasy hair. Desire sat down beside him, and kissed him and rubbed his back in a useless attempt at comforting him.

– My God, he cried, – what a shitty hotel. Do you think it gets any recommendations in the tourist books beyond the polite, useless «stars»? I will certainly not give them any.

His comment seemed totally out of context. No one replied.

There was music somewhere, coming from somewhere, the dark, ominous organ music. It made Desire shiver, shiver to her bones.

– Something isn't right here, she whimpered.

– What are you talking about? Marion chastised her. – What are you yapping about? Everybody is perfectly fine. *Cheers!*

They had a toast, actually had a toast, and they drank. Desire stared at Marion, studying carefully the face constantly shifting in shadow and light. She covered her mouth with her hand, and ran to the bathroom. The others could hear her throw up in there.

– Somebody can't take their liquor, I guess. Marion shrugged.

She turned towards Andy.

– I think I'll go to our room for a while, honey, she said, – picking up some things. Don't worry, I'll be back. And then we can have some fun, the four of us.

She kissed him on the cheek, and left, first leaving the door and then both doors between the rooms open. He saw her in there, walking back and forth, heard her as she was humming to himself.

Desire returned from the bathroom. Victor handed her a filled glass. She shook her head and sat it down on the table.

The building shook.

– What the hell…

Andy was on his feet immediately, looking around him, but there was nothing to look at.

Desire looked at the table, stared at it as if hypnotized, at its constant movement, almost forgetting that she wasn't alone in the room.

– There is a rhythm to it, she said sleepily. – I can both sense and see it.

– I just see it move, Victor blew some air.

She looked at him as if it was the first time, seeing him for what and who he was. She grabbed the glass and drank, drank a lot, the liquor burning in her mouth, throat and stomach. Not long afterwards she began seeing the room in a gray, pleasant haze.

Andy looked out the door, and into the other room. For a time now he had seen Marion walk back and forth in there, but now she didn't. He frowned.

Desire began unbuttoning her blouse in front of Victor, dancing, swaying before him. He grabbed her and pulled her down on his lap. She sighed happily and let herself be grabbed and pulled, pushing herself at the man without a face, rocking in his lap.

– I'll be right back, Andy said with a remote look in his face.

He didn't really know whether or not he got a response, and didn't really care. The hallway had turned dark, the room ahead of him a little less so. He spotted Marion by the wall. She just stood there, frozen, staring at nothing. He rushed to her.

– Is everything all right? He asked softly.

There was no reply.

– Is everything *all right?* He shouted and shook her.

There was a reaction this time. She turned and looked dully at him.

– Behind the wall is nothing but the void, she whimpered.

He stared nonplussed at her. She didn't look like herself, like Marion at all.

He opened the door, and looked into the other room.

– It's just a room, he told her.

– Behind the wall is nothing but the void, she whimpered.

She began backing off. He attempted to grab her, but she pulled her hand away, pulling away from him.

And just like that, she had turned. Her feet began moving by themselves, and her body never seemed to quite catch up. She ran off. And she never stopped.

She stood still, two steps away from him. He stepped closer, close to her. She didn't move.

– Tell me what to do, Andy said. – Please let me help you.

– Anything? She whimpered.

– Anything, he nodded.

Relief flooded her features. She rushed to him and embraced him, hungrily kissing his lips.

– I was so afraid. She choked. – So very, very afraid.

She kissed him, holding his head between her hands.

– Touch me, she hissed.

He did, rubbing her breasts, touching her nipples, and she sighed happily in his arms. Suddenly she was grinning, a hungry grin her huge, opaque eyes made very spooky.

– Is something stepping on your grave? She inquired, very, very strange.

He nodded, not able to vocalize his words, his concern.

– On mine, too, she nodded.

She led him to the bed, eager like a girl. Eager hands undressed him. He felt her nails scratch him, and he felt himself harden below. She grabbed him below, and he hardened even more. He choked. She chuckled throatily as she pushed him down on the bed. He lay there on his back, staring up at her, at her far above, as she undressed, as she writhed out of her clothes. The snake hissed at him. Fear grabbed him, and he wanted to sit up, to rise from the bed, desperately attempting to vocalize his concern, but she put her finger on his lips, and stopped him from speaking, stopped him from moving.

– Hush, she said softly. – Hush, my love. Don't strain yourself with speech, or by moving. I will speak and move for us both. You lie still, little boy, and move no more.

There was something in her words, her wording that chilled him to his heart. And they charmed him, froze him in place. He couldn't move, couldn't even bend a finger. And he saw nothing but her lips, her lips moving, spewing soothing words.

She chanted and hummed, and both the chant and the hum rose to a choir, rising from a multiple of throats.

Ropes. He imagined she held ropes in her hands, imagined that she tied them around his wrist and ankles, tying him to the bed, strapping him to it like butchered meat, and fear filled his dying thoughts.

Victor emptied himself in her. Desire sat in his lap and received his warm flow. Her head rested on his shoulder as she smothered him in wet kisses. He fell back on the bed, snoring in his alcohol-induced sleep before his head hit the linen. It missed miserably the pillow.

Desire dismounted him and rose unsteadily to her feet. A hand sought the bottle. She poured full the glass, but instead of drinking from it she put the bottle to her lips and drank from that. There wasn't much left. She put the empty bottle back on the table and picked up the glass.

For some reason she looked down in the glass, at its swirling mists.

In the glass she saw some kind of darkness grow like a plant from the central part of the bottom and upwards, and slowly spread through the entire fluid. She dropped the glass and it hit the floor and broke in a thousand pieces.

She found herself in a corridor, a hallway dark and moist. There was nowhere to go, both ways up and down gone in a swirling, dark mist she couldn't see through. She reached out with her hand, and it faded and turned into that very mist. A song called her. She pulled back the hand, and it once more turned into flesh and blood. The song pulled her. She entered the other bedroom, entered through a door ajar. Fear rattled her like a snake, but that couldn't move her, not like the hissing hum rising from Marion Dexter's throat.

Marion sat on Andy, with one knee on each side of his limp body. Andy's eyes were open, but they were hazy, unresponsive. Desire saw the ropes tying him to the bed, immobilizing him.

– You want to see? Marion asked her. – I know you want to…

And the twisted, demonic features made Desire whimper and shrink in her tracks.

– You knew about Andy and Victor, didn't you? You know what they have been doing?

Desire attempted to speak, but she couldn't move her lips

She saw the doll and bone and needle by Marion's side.

– Come to me, sweet girl. Come to me and be sweet.

Desire's feet moved. She stood by the bed, at Marion's side.

– That's a good girl. Now bless our dollies. Drown them in holy water.

Desire noticed that there were two of them. She kissed their heads, and drowned them in spittle.

– Not that, Marion hissed. – Be a woman, not a girl, sweetie.

Desire relented to Marion's superior and terrible will, and put the dolls between her thighs. She pushed the dolls' heads into her wet, flowing hole and pushed them up and pulled them down, and opened her mouth in a silent moan as the dolls' heads roamed in there.

– That's so much better…

Marion broke the large bone in two, and handed one to Desire.

Marion grabbed one of the dolls, and with a large, sinister grin pinched it with her bone needle, her broken bone. Andy shook on the bed. His body shook, but his face remained frozen and unresponsive.

She chanted, and the words soothed Desire, made her turn drowsy and dull.

Dead is dead

Cloth is fire
Tooth is sharp
Dead is alive
In all the myriad
Corners and closets
Of my mind

Desire handed her a knife, one large and sharp, one she didn't know she had held in her hands, until that very moment, curtseying deeply and respectfully as she did so. Marion accepted the knife, held it up, looked at it as it twinkled and shone in the shadow… and then she pushed it deep into Andy's chest. He shook a few more times and lay still. She cut open his chest quickly and effortlessly, in a clearly expert kind of way. Desire watched it all in a detached manner, not really seeing anything, moving the doll up and down, up and down in her wet, wet hole. Marion pushed a hand into the opening she had made. Desire saw his heart beat in there. She saw Marion grab it and pull it out, and she saw the white sheet turn red.

She began backing off. Marion took one bite of the heart, and chewing on the tasty snack, she turned slightly, offering it to Desire, too. Desire ran from the room, the image of Marion and Andy, dead, dead Andy stuck in her mind.

Marion Dexter sat there and devoured his beating heart, bathing in the red waterfall, filling a shoe and drinking from it like she would a cup, as the walls shook and the room shivered and shifted around her, and she howled in delight.

Desire recognized the shoe. It was one of the two pairs she and Marion had lost in the park. She stumbled into the other room, rushing to the bed, rushing to Victor, but he wasn't there. Sweat burned in her eyes as she bewildered scoured the room. Then… A motion caught her attention, and she spotted Victor. He hung in a wire from the ceiling. His face was bloated and his tongue stuck out like a flower. Desire doubled over and threw up. She kept throwing up, until all content was gone from her aching stomach. Desire walked. She didn't know where. Some time ago she had fought herself on her feet and run from the horrors of the two rooms. She walked and stumbled on. Strains of the floor and ceiling, and walls reached for her like vines, coiling around her feet and waiving arms.

She found herself in the restroom downstairs, the one situated close to the bar. There was no air, only mist, one she couldn't breathe. She told herself she had died a long time ago, and had simply been unable to realize that fact. Shaking hands bathed and washed her face. She stared at her pale mug in the mirror, her large, mirror-like empty eyes. There was nothing there, nothing reflected in those vast pools.

On the floor lay what was left of the shouting man from the bar. She couldn't remember turning. At the least she believed it to be him. His head had been totally severed from his body, and had been thrown into a corner. Its face leered at her. On his chest had been placed a pair of shoes. Desire recognized that pair, too.

She could recall entering the restroom, the men's restroom. She had no memory of having left it.

But here she was, walking through the hotel's empty vestibule, looking neither left nor right, and not even straight ahead. She just walked, totally oblivious to her surroundings.

The coughing dead man sat with his back to a wall. He was still coughing, and the fist he pushed at his mouth was covered in blood.

– I make films, he cried. – I am one of the most innovative artists of our time.

She hurried past him, and when she fearfully turned her head and looked behind her, he was gone. He was no more.

The sound… the sound of his bad cough echoed in her ears.

– Victor! She cried, her cry turning into wail. – VICTOR!

He was nowhere, no matter how long she searched.

And she sought hard and along. She stood still, imagined she returned to the room upstairs, but he wasn't there. The door to the other room remained open. Marion still sat on Andy, devouring his flesh. Desire Lowell opened the other doors. All the rooms were empty, gaping holes of nothing. Denise looked at her hand, and she saw only wisps of mist. She walked and there was no end to her walk. Her hair turned gray and her face old and ashen.

She passed the paintings on the wall. They seemed very lively, animated to her, not really paintings at all, but windows, portals to other worlds. She walked on the bridge, not having any recollection of having entered it. Wings flapped around the lamp, only wings and nothing else, around the lamp up there, in the open air, in the ceiling she couldn't see. The shaking, empty-eyed woman heard the river boil and rage below. She stopped in the middle of the bridge, staring at the castle walls ahead, at her own sweaty and sweet girlish, ashen face. Her head turned slightly, but she didn't know what she was looking at, her long, dark hair coiling around her beyond shivering body. She just stood there, frozen, while everything turned to Nothing around her.

A car raced across a dusty, worn highway. There was a loud crack, as one of its tires blew. The cars screeched and howled as it slid across the road, all the way, almost to the edge, until it screeched to a halt, and stood there spinning round and round, until a vortex formed, and the car could hardly be seen anymore, except as an indistinct image a misty and dark morning.

The sky cracked open above the lake, followed by the sound of droplets hitting the water and land everywhere, and the rain began pouring, began whipping the dark water, and already muddy ground.

The droplets formed pools, the pools forming rivers flooding the roads.

A woman stumbled through the rain, the beyond heavy rain, and the deep mud covering the shaking ground. People stared at her and she couldn't understand why.

– What is happening? She asked with a hoarse voice. – What is happening?

They looked at her with totally incomprehensive stares, pulling away from her, but not fleeing. They followed her with fearful but beyond curious eyes.

She stumbled through a strangely familiar street. The sight, her current experience evoked memories, but jumbled, as if they had happened to somebody else.

A newspaper headline glared at her from afar. She rushed towards it, blinking the acid rain momentarily from her eyes.

CHLOE WEBSTER IS DEAD

The black hair flooded the woman's face and eyes, but she saw well enough, as she attempted to squint her eyes, to see through the fog of confusion riddling her life.

Chloe Webster stared at herself in the window.

Part 3:
TALES OF MYSTERY AND IMAGINATION
DAVID FALLON SOMBY

CHAPTER EIGHT

David Somby is dead.

This is only half the story. The rest is shrouded in half-spoken riddles, mystery and imagination.

David Somby is dead. David was a famous movie director, one of the truly great and innovative artists of our time.

Somby was a bum, traversing garbage cans for a shred of food, a glimpse of hope. Those who knew him say they can't really say whether or not David Somby was ever alive.

He was always looking for something, people crossing his paths said, but they never knew what.

The police cars moved through the city, through streets of fire and bedlam. It was one of those nights. Homicide Lieutenant Elliott Lasko plowed a hand through his busty, graying hair.

– It's one of those nights, his partner Albert Monroe told the air in front of him.

– Tell me about it. Lasko shook his head in dismay.

– I mean… Monroe, a white blond powerful built man in his early thirties continued, as if Lasko hadn't spoken. – Some nights you can just tell will be bad, right from the start. Even before it gets dark you can hear the howls rise from the alleys and the toilets of the city. And then it gets dark, and everything is worse than you ever imagined it would be.

Monroe looked particularly shitty tonight. He always looked shitty, but tonight he looked worse than ever.

There was a brief congestion on the road, one that not even having the power of driving a police car could dissolve quickly. A gang of youths used the hood to hammer a drum solo. The noise was deafening. Lasko pulled his gun and fired without aiming through the open window. Boys and girls ran like rabbits.

– That showed them. He laughed loud and shrieking. – That showed them. He he.

Five bodies. The two detectives shook their head. Five stiffs waited for them somewhere ahead.

Lasko smelled fire somewhere. He even saw the flickering light the flames cast on the walls they passed.

But he didn't see the source of it. It seemed to be somewhat beyond him, beyond the range of his senses. People moved through the streets with a glee in their eyes. He imaged they carried clubs in their hands.

But he didn't see any.

Mayhem and bedlam waited for them.
A huge neon sign saying

CLARION HOTEL

appeared in their line of vision. A row of police cars already decorated the building's main entrance

Monroe couldn't drive their car all the way to the scene. The congestion of police cars was just too tight. Fallon had found that this was increasingly often the case. One would think that someone would learn something eventually, and avoid such occurrences, but no such luck. Monroe stopped the car in the middle of the street, and they left it there. Waving their shields they easily passed through the various checkpoints. Well out in the street outside the hotel a patrolman was busy dispatching the characteristic yellow ribbon saying:

CRIME SCENE DO NOT CROSS

Another uniformed officer approached the two Lieutenants with a strange expression in her face. Lasko shuddered, realizing in an instant that this one would be bad.

– I heard there were five bodies, he said gently to her, as she stopped in front of him.

– Yes, there were, Lieutenant, the black officer replied hesitatingly.

– Yes? He prompted her.

– They… left, sir.

– They WHAT?

She straightened, as if being confronted by a teacher or a military superior.

– There are several witnesses, sir, among them a number of police officers arriving at the scene. The five bodies stood up and left, one of them reportedly with a huge knife sticking out of his chest.

She didn't look good. There was a thick film of greasy sweat covering her face. Her eyes wandered constantly back and forth. All in all he suspected she was one of the witnesses mentioned.

– Ok - ay, he said aloud, surveying the stage, preparing to take charge of the situation.

There was a commotion over by the entrance, making him hesitate. A guy with a cap on his head and a bullhorn in his hand attempted to breach the crime scene sealing.

– LET ME THROUGH, he shouted through the bullhorn. – I repeat: I want to speak to the man or woman in charge, THIS INSTANT!

Lasko signaled for the guards to relent. The guy with a cap and a bullhorn rushed towards Lasko with a threatening speed and killing look, making it tempting for the good Lieutenant to draw his gun.

– Who are you? He demanded, boiling with impatience. – What's the meaning of this *intrusion?*

– I'm police Lieutenant Elliot Lasko, sir, Lasko said patiently. Those who knew him would say that he at that moment was infinitely patient... – I'm a homicide detective. This is my partner, Albert Monroe. We got a report about five murders at this hotel.

The man's reaction was not in any way close to what Lasko had expected. He froze, that was «in character», but then he flat out started laughing. He laughed loud enough to overwhelm any sound in a wide proximity.

The guy got to be a singer, Lasko thought unprompted. Only trained singers have that kind of volume.

The guy (with the cap and the bullhorn) turned towards the other people within the sealing, those who had stared angrily at the policemen for some time now. Lasko noticed quite amazed that one of the gentlemen in question had a huge knife sticking out of his chest.

– ITS OKAY PEOPLE. THIS IS ALL A BIG BEAR, A WHOPPER OF A MISUNDERSTANDING. WE WILL TAKE A BREAK, AND RESUME THE ACTION IN HALF AN HOUR.

Another man, angrily waving a pile of papers in front of him approached Lasko and friends.

– We have permission to do this, man. I have the personal authorization from the hotel manager right here in my hand. We also have all the necessary permits from the mayor's office and the central police headquarters.

– And you two are? Lasko managed to push out.

Those who knew him would say that he was close to a crucial breaking point at this time.

– I'm sorry, Detective. The man with the cap and bullhorn dried his tears as he simultaneously managed to somewhat calm down the man waving the pile of papers. – I do recognize you, now, by the way. How *horrible* of me to not do so sooner. I am Edgar Allan. I am a movie director. This is my assistant, Peter Sardè.

He took a break, to help Lasko catch his breath. It was not the success he hoped for.

– We're making a movie about David Somby… the famous movie director… a name that should be very familiar to you, Lieutenant…

There was a question mark at the end of the sentence. Lasko frowned angrily at the energetic man in front of him.

– The name is known to me. But he died years ago. Why the sudden interest?

– Oh, it's not *sudden,* believe me, Edgar Allan, the movie director stated proudly. – Somby has been a pet project of mine for years, which now, finally comes to fruition.

– He made crime and horror movies with a further, existential twist, Sardè said proudly. – He was an artist, one of the true geniuses in our time.

– And even better, Allan added, – his death and life were just as dramatic as the stories he told.

Lasko looked at him, calling for his entire, complete attention.

– And this is a movie set?

– Precisely, Allan replied, very good humored, now. – We didn't reveal anything to the hotel guests. We even hid the cameras. We wanted their reactions to be spontaneous and true. Somby himself used that very same technique quite successfully. Even though I doubt he was ever *this* successful…

There was a beep from Lasko's pocket. A look of irritation crossed his face as he collected his cell phone. It stopped ringing almost before he had freed it from its confines.

– Damn thing never works properly, he swore.

He looked at Monroe, who shrugged with an apologetic smile.

– I forgot mine at home, he said.

– Use mine, Detective, Allan offered graciously.

Lasko shook his head, and managed, unbelievably enough to both smile and look irritated simultaneously.

Another phone called somewhere. Everybody stuck their hand in their pockets, producing the small, electronic wonder. Most of them looked disappointed at the display and put it back where they had found it.

There were more calls, and several people talking in phones simultaneously.

– Now what? Lasko exclaimed.

One of the officers spoke in a phone.

– Yes, sir, it was just a movie set. No, sir, Lieutenant Lasko's phone is out of order, sir. Yes, sir, everything is in order, sir. They have all the necessary paperwork worked out… Yes, they're making a movie about Somby, the famous movie director…

There was a brief silence.

– You want to speak to the Lieutenant? You wish to speak to him about…

The officer turned to Lasko, a study in confusion.

And the sense of unreality, only briefly leaving him this evening, once again overtook the detective.

– You better look into this, sir, he said hesitatingly, offering the cell phone.

Lasko took it.

– Yes, this is Lasko. Another brief silence, then: – Yes, speaking. What is this about? Yes, it's just a coincidence I was on the premises. I was just passing by, really. This is my night off, the first one in weeks, actually. Yes, I know Somby is dead. I was the detective in charge of the investigation, remember?

The Lieutenant's face was one of the most expressive Allan had ever seen. And there was a frown there, suddenly, visibly growing as he was speaking. And suddenly Allan felt it himself, as he felt the first birth pains of a palatable, familiar growing excitement.

The senior Detective disconnected the cell phone almost as an afterthought. He was clearly distressed to his guts where he stood.

– I must go…

– That's okay, Lieutenant, we will wrap things up here, one of the officers said.

Allan smiled. Another movie slogan that had migrated to official language.

Lasko remained on the spot, undetermined, not really intending to reveal anything, but it just slipped out of him, like mercury on a plate of gold.

– David Somby is dead…

– Yes? Allan prompted him, completely unable to conceal his excitement.

– You don't understand. He was found dead this morning, with a huge knife in his chest.

There was laughter, slowly turning into stunned silence as Allan made a very deliberate move with his hand, a hand already infamous in the world of cinema.

– One… one of the coroner's assistants was a movie buff. He recognized him, and he finally convinced someone to start the procedure of genetic testing. The results are yet not in, but everybody is… everybody is convinced they will turn out… conclusive.

A rush of incredulity, excitement and fear touched the crowd, moviemakers, policemen and spectators alike.

Allan had always had an image in his mind, a half forgotten dream one forgets a few minutes after one wakes up in the morning, of himself sitting in a comfortable chair in a big, luxurious house. Now, abruptly it was clear and distinct in his mind.

Lasko turned in a daze and started walking away, the look in his face clearly showing a man who wasn't there.

– Lieutenant, Allan cried, catching up to the policeman in a few, fevered steps. – Wait up.

– Yes?

Allan spoke fast and eagerly.

– It's my bet that you may need me, in this matter, Detective, need my unique expertise. After all, there are very few people who know more about David Fallon Somby than myself. I would do anything to convince you, sir. Just give me a hint of what I must do, and I'll…

– Okay, Lasko said distantly. – You may come.

That was all.

One moment Allan was too shocked to react, but the next his famous survival instinct took over, and he grabbed the tiger by its tail. He turned towards his crew and actors.

– Okay, people. The production is delayed. We will meet again in a week to discuss further implications of the latest events. The script will have to be rewritten, of course.

– *Again*. A man, standing in the shadows with a bowed head and a doomed expression on his face moaned. The executive producer.

Allan spoke constantly in the car on the way to the central morgue. Lasko turned him off, letting him speak without letting any of his ravings intrude on Lasko's own chaotic thought-processes. The drive back to the station seemed, if anything, even crazier than the drive to the hotel, to the temporary movie studio. Lasko saw everything, every move, every excessive expression in the people he observed.

A man jumped up on a garbage can, balancing there, while moving his big mouth and shouting his rhetoric at the people below. Lasko didn't hear the sound of his voice. He just saw the lips move, move, move.

– The world is insane, isn't it?

Allan's voice suddenly penetrated the fog of indifference, and Lasko turned, facing the director's widening grin.

Then he just turned back, and kept slumping in his seat.

The police station appeared in their vision, glum and dark. When they stopped there a few minutes later it looked exactly like that. Lasko stared dumbfounded at his two companions.

– We were at the bridge, he faltered. – We…

He rubbed his temples. Dark, flashy shadows danced behind his close lids. He wanted to scream, and looked insanely at an unknown point somewhere ahead.

Allan rushed into the station, rushed in again. They saw him. He saw him, too. The mirages slowly settled into one, somewhat coherent moving image. The three of them walked up the stairs to the station, entering its murky halls and hallways.

Everybody looked funny at them the moment they entered the precinct. Lasko began sweating, and he didn't understand why. They took the elevator down to the basement, the vault, the morgue, the place with a thousand names.

Connor and Hesky met them the moment they stepped out of the elevator.

Word gets around, Lasko thought.

The five of them walked to the Freezer.

– We were the investigating detectives. Isabel Connor enlightened him, quite unnecessary. – He was found in an old dump on the East Side. The room had a bed and a chair and nothing more. The bed was soaked in blood. This murder raised more than a few flags right from the start, in spite of its location. We took a lot of pictures, and forensics was all over the place. Everything was done by the book.

She seemed to be doing her best to assure him of her dedication to the case, to appease him.

The East Side was infamous for its bloodbaths. Murders were as common as grass there. It was the pit of the Pit. While the Pit was bad as a whole, this particular part of it was the bad of the bad.

She nodded to the attendant welcoming them. He opened the steel door and pulled out the slab. Lasko noticed that his hand was actually shaking a bit when he pulled off the sheet.

They all stared at the man on the slab.

David Fallon Somby was dead. There was no doubt about it. Lasko nodded, as if he was a relative. He recognized the dead man without looking at him.

– It is him, he confirmed, totally unnecessary. – He is older, of course, further marked by life, but it is he.

It was twenty years ago today. He remembered it as if it should have been yesterday.

He noticed they hadn't even begun the autopsy. Someone had been using their wits, for once. It made him feel a little better, amazingly enough.

– Wow, Allan whistled.

The movie director hovered in awe above the body, spittle practically flowing from his mouth.

– WOW! He repeated.

Lasko studied the body from all angles. He thought he might be moving while doing so, moving his feet, but he wasn't sure. The ghastly stab wound in Somby's chest was a dead giveaway, a kind of comfort. The rest of him didn't seem real, somehow. Monroe looked at him, looked at him a lot. Lasko pretended not to notice.

The five of them left the room, not truly leaving it. It stayed with them, lingering, festering in their guts. Monroe glanced back, did it to such a degree that he had problems turning his head back forward. He rubbed his neck, attempting to work out the kinks in it.

Connor and Hesky brought them to a room without windows, a place where the sun didn't shine. Lasko noticed instantly the two distinct sets of tables. A quick glance confirmed it: These were sketches showing the two deaths of David Fallon Somby. Allan walked back and forth among them like an eager kid, Lasko somber like death.

The recent photographs showed a ramshackle apartment. It showed Somby on his back on the bed with a large, very familiar knife sticking out of his chest. A pentacle carved on the floor with strange symbols inside and poles with an unfathomable purpose surrounded the bed.

– Yes, this is indeed a scene from Dark Shadows in Bright Lights, the one we were recreating tonight, Allan cried. – See the knife, the distinct pattern on the shaft? We were just able to get a copy, but I am willing to wager with you that this is the actual knife used in the original shooting.

– So, this is a setting, in your opinion?

– I would say that is a dead giveaway, Allan confirmed. – Was he brought here or found here, I wonder.

– Which is it? Lasko asked him, clearly irritated.

– I don't know, Allan grinned. – I'm not the detective. I don't know.

Lasko nodded to himself. Allan was undoubtedly correct. This was a deliberate setup, for a purpose, not a random slaughter.

– What I wonder about… Allan paced through the room. – Is the Cult of Beelzebub revived? Is it the old gang, or some unknown members of the old gang, or copycats celebrating the twentieth anniversary?

Lasko stopped nodding with an effort of will. He walked to the other table, to old photos, old, sinister memories.

A bunch of hoodlums had been on their way to the home of Marlon Caine, Somby's producer and collaborative genius, but they were diverted and decided to off Somby instead. Bringing the very special knife they broke into Somby's house a few minutes before midnight, and precisely at midnight they sacrificed him to the hungry god Beelzebub, leaving obscure messages written in blood all over the house.

They had nailed him to the wall, and buried the knife in his heart, and had been dancing and singing while he had bled to death. A neighbor had heard them, and gone to join the party, but luckily enough for him he had noticed Somby on the wall, and fled, and called the police. The Cult of Beelzebub, or those present anyway, had still been celebrating when Lasko, a young detective had arrived with his crew.

– Fallon is a girl's name, isn't it? Monroe spoke up, feeling he had to express himself somehow, tearing Lasko from his murky thoughts.

– No, originally it was a male name. Allan chuckled. – You can write this one up as one more example of what television does to people…

– They're all dead, Lasko said.

– Who? Monroe inquired perplexed.

– The Cult of Beelzebub. Either executed or died of natural causes or just dead. At least those caught at the scene.

– Marsten, too? Allan said incredulous. – How?

Marsten had pleaded temporary insanity and it had worked out for him. He had spent five years in an asylum, and then been released.

– He threw himself off a roof last month. Lasko enlightened him, not without a certain level of satisfaction. – A very high roof.

– I didn't know that, Allan cried. – Why didn't I know that?

There were old videotapes on the table. Everything had been put before them, had been arranged for them to study. Lasko almost felt like a king, parading before his missing subjects. It was all downright weird, eerie even.

He grabbed the tape marked MARSTEN ONE, and put it in the old VCR. Evanard Marsten's angelic face filled the screen.

– … initial interview with Marsten, Evanard, Lasko heard himself say from twenty years ago. – Also present is Marsten's attorney Evelyn Ash. The time is seven fifteen PM.

Marsten looked at him with a huge smile painted on his face.

– Why did you do it Ev? Peter Coleman, Lasko's old partner, asked in a very intimidating voice.

The smile faded. Marsten glanced anxiously around him, staring at a lot of people that weren't there.

– I don't *know,* okay? Nobody told me anything. I don't even know why I was there, or how I got there.

– Oh, don't give me that BULLSHIT! Coleman blew his horn.

– It's TRUE! Swear to God and hope to DIE.

Marsten jumped up. Coleman and Lasko grabbed him and put him back in his chair.
Ash whispered something in his ear.
He sat there for a while, unmovable. The two detectives watched him. Then, suddenly, he burst into tears.
– It was such a beautiful picture (pit-ure, he said beside himself). They wanted me to take the pictures. That's all. *Honest!*
He cracked the smile again.
– It was such a beautiful painting, he said dreamingly, – such wonderful composition… I take it just as the sacrificial lamb dies, exactly the moment the light leaves his eyes. It's a masterpiece, a masterpiece, I tell ya…
Lasko remembered Coleman at that moment. The big man wanted to be angry, to be enraged, but words and courage failed him. Lasko fingered the photograph, the old photograph. It seemed as good as new to him, fresh… and stained in blood. But this was a newly developed copy from a digital image made from the old negative.
– There are no witnesses this time, Lasko said. – Not any we know of, at least. It's… different.
– It's a stage like the last time, Allan said. – But there was no open celebration. The neighbors, the people in the Pit may be used to quite a bit, but they would have remembered that.
– No writing on the wall, Lasko nodded.
Monroe just stood there, mute like an oyster.
Marsten's cracked features gave way to Carter John's totally insane and completely rational mug.
– Beelzebub is the Universe, he preached. – She's the provider of us all. We spring from her loins and she sees to all our needs and desires.
– She? The young and old Lasko said.
– Precisely. History and its heretics have for some insane reason pegged her as a male. That is merely one of countless indignities visited upon her, but her vengeance is coming, and it will be vast and terrible.
John's lawyers had also, against his explicit wishes made the insanity plea, but it hadn't stuck, perhaps because of the utter calm and ice-cold rationality he exhibited.
Lasko still felt his eyes on him, even after all these years. He had been present at the execution, the eyes had been present, too, even when they had been closed in death.
– You solved the case, Allan said. – And it made you a living legend.
– There was no case to solve. Lasko shook his head. – We merely picked them up, and we never found out anything, about possible accomplishes

or anything. Everything turned into a mirage, a specter of horror and unsolved mysteries.

– Something fitting quite well with Somby's life. Allan shook his head, too, in bewilderment and excitement. – The part of his story detailing his last breath was just as enigmatic as the rest of it.

Monroe kept cracking his neck, and weird sounds reached the other two's ears while his joints seemingly kept realigning themselves.

The five of them kept working, working through the evening and the early hours of the next day, after midnight, when the night turned even darker, when it turned pitch black, and they hardly were able to glimpse a hand in front of them. They studied old reports until it all turned blurry and they couldn't see the trees for the forest.

– It is important, Allan insisted. – We need to study the script in order to understand it.

Monroe gave him his evil eye. Allan didn't seem to notice.

– I read, I study, Connor said, – but I just don't see it.

– Understanding may elude us, Allan nodded, – but that makes it more important than ever to study the script, to find its finer points, to gain at least a modicum of realization, of what it's attempting to convey to us.

– You think this is a script? She suddenly cried dumbfounded, indicating the case files thrown across the tables and on the floor before them, as if something had just dawned on her.

– As stated, yes, he frowned. – It's a recreation of Somby's life and art, and as such a riddle to be solved or not, but certainly one to be studied with meticulous zeal. This…

When he indicated the room and its content he did so with far greater panache than that of Lieutenant Connor.

– … is just a part of the puzzle, though, mostly about his death, not his life.

He paced a bit before walking towards the door. He turned, as he was about to leave the room.

– Are you coming?

The others, the three policemen looked sheepishly at Lasko. He nodded.

Outside seemed strange now, different from how they remembered it. It was still noisy. A wail rose from the city, as it always did, hitting them like a sharp blade. It was the same arid air. But outside still seemed strange, seemed different.

– I wish it would rain soon, Monroe said to no one in particular.

And no one voiced a reply.

They stood at the top of the stairs for a moment, before walking to the car.

They drove yet again, through the streets, in two cars. But not to the heart of the city like last time, but to the Hills, the low hills to the east. They arrived at a place surrounded by tall fences, the Planet Studios, one of the bigger independent studios in town. It was heavily guarded. Allan, even though the guards clearly knew him had to show his identity card two times on their way to one of the larger buildings on the property.

The two cars stopped before the main entrance. It was dark and quiet there, with no people outside. Allan used his keycard. The light on the lock shifted from red to green, and there was a beep, and they were inside, heading into dark hallways and increasingly brighter halls of a modern building of steel and glass.

– Yeah, I know. Inspiring, isn't it?

And they couldn't tell whether or not Allan was being ironic.

There were posters on the wall of the production company's previous successes, among them Dark Shadows in Bright Lights, Somby's greatest triumph, both commercially and as a cult «phenomena».

– The critics… those assholes didn't like him from the start, Allan commented, – but when it seemed to matter even less than it usually does to determine people's taste and preferences, their persecution of him turned to hatred, turned downright ugly. And for every new scathed attack on him his reputation grew some more. A colleague of mine, usually when he is quite drunk says Somby was beyond earthly matters. With that he means matters confined to the movie industry, of course.

Lasko studied the image in the few moments it took for them to pass it. The man on the poster wasn't Somby, but the actor that had played the main part in Dark Shadows in Bright Lights, Howard Measly, but he looked just as disturbed, just as Gone. Lasko blinked. For a moment it had seemed to him that the man's eyes had… had *moved.*

Monroe looked strangely at him with fidgeting eyes, but Lasko pretended not to notice.

The hallways were silent, to such a degree that everything seemed on mute, like in a silent movie. Lasko stamped on the carpet, and it sounded like thunder in the quiet place they moved through. Everybody glanced at him.

They entered something that clearly was a library of some kind, not containing books but reels and scripts.

– Here we will find everything worth knowing about David Fallon Somby, Allan bragged. – In his *art* we will see what isn't written explicitly elsewhere.

The hallway expanded into a theater. The doors were locked in open position, inviting them in. Lasko tried to shake off the feeling of discomfort, in vain. A man met them inside.

– Hi, Ratman, Allan greeted him.

– Hello, Mr. Allan, the man replied. – Welcome.

He didn't look like a rat, really, didn't look like a rat at all. Lasko wondered about that. He wondered about that a lot.

– We want the works, Rat, Allan said, – the highlights of highlights.

– I understand, Mr. Allan, Ratman replied. – It will all be ready shortly.

They sat down in the theater, five people in the midst of five hundred seats or so. This was at the very least as well equipped as any public theater Lasko had ever visited. He shrugged and began focusing on the screen. The flickering images began its mad dance in Lasko's vision. Fifteen cigarettes and an even fouler taste in his mouth later, he still hadn't really seen much. It surely didn't feel that way.

A man walked down a street with an insane look in his eyes, his bulging eyes. The camera filmed him from his left side, but his face and his eyes (his bulging eyes) were also, for some reason also visible on the brick wall behind him. The face laughed silently, and the laughter's echo whispered enticing words from the hallway outside. The door was wide open, even though Lasko was positive Ratman had closed it. Lasko heard scratching sounds. They came from behind, and occasionally from the front left corner (and from the hallway). He frowned and looked at the others. They didn't seem to be hearing anything, anything…

Lasko sat there shaking his head, sweat pouring down his forehead.

Nothing of interest happened, really. They sat there, watching the dull masterpieces of David Fallon Somby. Connor released a loud scream of delight. The growing ulcer somewhere in Lasko's stomach gave protest in a loud and foul manner.

– Amazing, isn't it? Allan sat there with wide open eyes, never removing his attention from the screen.

Connor nodded eagerly. Lasko and Monroe mumbled something. Lasko had no idea what Hesky was doing just then.

The music in the room, in the film turned loud and whining. It sounded like a banshee and Lasko shivered in his chair. He heard it again just after dawn, from somewhere. He knew it was dawn, even though there were no windows anywhere. It came from below, not from the speakers at all. When he looked at the others they kept gobbling their popcorn, and seemed totally unaffected.

Ratman brought them to one of the empty apartments used by the production company's executives. It was lavishly equipped, luxury wherever they turned. To Lasko it looked old and worn.

The movies, for some reason kept playing themselves out in Lasko's mind. He made repeated attempts at purging it all from his consciousness, in vain.

There were more than enough bedrooms for everyone. Even when each of them had taken one for themselves there were still several left. Lasko removed his coat. He had wanted to remove it for hours, but never managed to actually pulling himself together and *do* it. Uncomfortable and weary he fell down on the bed and pulled the blanket over himself. He knew he should remove the rest of his clothes as well, unless he wanted to wake up feeling worse than he already did, but he couldn't make himself bother with it, with that either.

Connor looked shyly at them, before retreating to her room. Lasko couldn't be certain, but he imagined that Hesky and Monroe exchanged grins. Lasko closed the door to his room, and suddenly he was alone, and he felt extremely lonely. The noise of the long day vanished in a moment, and he was alone.

He found himself on his back on the large bed, listening for sounds in the adjacent room, but there were none. The walls looked very dark, and he heard not a single sound anywhere. He knocked on the night table and he did hear something then, but it was distorted, eerie, not like knuckles on wood at all. The lights in the room seemed to be concentrated at the center of the floor. Even though the lamps were seemingly evenly distributed throughout the room all the light seemed to be pulled to the center. And the walls… the walls seemed to draw all the darkness. When he looked at the wall, actually looked at it, he saw nothing, nothing escaping the black hole hiding there, lurking there, waiting patiently for him to be sucked in.

He closed his eyes, deliberately, with an effort. Sounds reached him from somewhere. He still hadn't fully undressed, and lay there writhing under the thick cover, attempting to feel sleepy, to let the strife of the day tire him even further, to the point of him actually feeling sleepy.

Weary eyes opened wide, with a loud crack. He wondered if he had slept. Sweat poured from his skin, his flabby skin. He held up his hand, he *knew* he did, but he didn't see it. There was nothing there, no light whatsoever, nothing he could focus his wide open eyes on. But when he turned his attention to the wall it revealed a pattern to him, unrecognizable, alien, a swirling movement drawing him in, sucking him into its hungry maw.

His hands shaking he jumped from the bed, and instantly, without even considering it he pulled the bed the vast distance to the tiny light at the center of wherever he was (wherever he was it wasn't a room). And there, looking back he was, after squinting his eyes a little (a lot) able to glimpse the walls, real walls, and he sighed in sick relief. He crawled back into the bed shaking like a leaf, like a dry leaf, shaking to bits in the storm.

Lasko and Monroe sat in the mess hall at the police station the next morning (afternoon). The light through the windows had a fairly bright quality. In a sense it looked like morning, like dawn. Lasko poured sugar in his coffee. Monroe didn't notice.

– The taste of bad coffee in the morning makes me want to puke.

Monroe stared down at the black pool as if it hid great secrets.

Lasko didn't notice.

– I need coffee in the morning, you know. It helps me get through the day, helps me not to stumble around like a fucking sleepwalker.

Lasko nodded and mumbled something unintelligible. Monroe ranted on.

– I see the sleepwalkers every day. They are creepy. It doesn't look like they have a single thought in their head.

He rubbed his face with both hands, doing so for quite a while before giving it up.

– My face has turned… unmovable. The skin feels so stiff, stiff to the point that I can hardly smile anymore.

– The weather seems promising today, Lasko said, shaking his head for no apparent reason.

Monroe frowned, lifting his head, staring at Lasko.

– Most people are as wooden as actors in a bad movie, with no real emotion.

Time passed. How much wasn't clear, but it felt like a lot.

– I think you've got a point there, Lasko finally said.

Silence fell between them. Two pair of eyes met, not really meeting. They both sat there, squinting their eyes, not really seeing each other, attempting to glimpse something, anything through the thick mist the world had become.

CHAPTER NINE

Bart Bohrman played Howard Measly, the actor who had played Peter Morgan, the main part in Dark Shadows in Bright Lights.

Allan had taken up filming again, sort of, claiming that «he was too inspired to not do it», and that «it would help the investigation».

– SPACE and TIME, Morgan tells his wife on his deathbed. – It is real, as far as it goes, but only as a limited way of looking at reality.

He dies, in a totally unspectacular way, drawing one last breath, his eyes staring blank at the ceiling.

His wife utters a tiny squeak, hiding most of her face in her shaking hands.

– CUT, Allan cried, racing forwards. – That was great people. That was so fucking great.

The funeral is a strange scene. People, the known and unknown alike, stare at each other with uncertainty in their eyes. Peter rests in an open casket, totally without moving, and they half expect him to. Alicia Pendergast played Victoria Arness, the actor who had played Judith Morgan, the second main part in Dark Shadows in Bright Lights. Judith looks glum, looks enigmatically at the gathering, as the rain is pouring down at the small cemetery and threatening to drown the now closed casket.

– He will rise again, she told the uncomfortable relatives and friends and attendees. – He's dead again, and will rise again, as both Satan and God are my witnesses.

Howard Measly played by Bart Bohrman is alone in his wardrobe. Victoria Arness played by Alicia Pendergast hesitates a bit before knocking on his door. He cries ENTER, and she does, with fidgeting, nervous moves, quickly closing the door behind her, rushing into his arms. They stand there, after a while, only reluctantly, very reluctantly breaking contact.

– He is quite mad, you know, Measly says, – totally bananas.

– Perhaps, Arness grins, scratching her arm absentmindedly, – but he is also brilliant beyond words.

– He makes us do things I don't understand, Measly cries, catching himself, lowering his voice, looking around him with paranoia in his ever moving eyes. – He acts like he is… possessed… or something, like he is Ahab, leading his ship and crew to disaster, and like Ahab, he doesn't care.

Arness wants to say something, wants to contradict him, but she is unable to give voice to it, to both her disagreement and visible concern. Measly nods slowly and her eyes grows wide and fearful, and they just stand there, while the room grows darker around them.

They leave the room, returning to the set, becoming once more Peter and Judith Morgan, recreating themselves for the stage, and the shudder becomes even more pronounced.

– I will die and you will live on, Morgan tells his wife, – but I will never leave you, and after not so long ago in time, we'll meet again.

– I know, Judith says calm and centered, – I know it is possible, is feasible, and I will do everything in my power and beyond to achieve it.

The two stands there and the world is fading away around them.

– CUT, David Fallon Somby cries. – That's good people, but we need a little more… a little more panache and awkwardness.

David Fallon Somby was played by Leonard Friedman. Lasko noted yet again that he had a certain resemblance to the man Lasko had only seen on pictures and as a body on a slab.

– Which one? Measly speaks up, almost in a whisper.

– What was that, Howard? Somby wonders, a cat to the mouse.

– Which one is it, awkwardness or panache?

– I said awkwardness and panache, Howard, Somby grins like a wolf. – That shouldn't be too hard to understand, now, should it?

And they reshoot the scene, time and time again, and the entire stage turns darker and dank.

– CUT! Allan cried.

The lights are turned back on, and the mood lightens a bit.

– THAT'S GOOD, PEOPLE, Allan cried. – WE'RE GETTING THERE. JUST ONE MORE TAKE.

A sigh passed through the people gathered in the studio.

– He said that ten takes ago, Monroe whispered to Lasko. – Methinks he takes his emulation of Somby a bit… too far?

They were all gathered here, to participate, directly or indirectly in Planet Studios' new production HAUNTED LIGHTS, based on David Fallon Somby's life and art.

Marlon Caine, the producer, played by Roger Fremont goes to Somby afterwards.

– This can't go on anymore, David, he tells the agitated director. – You're taking it too far. People call us and say they will blow up the studio if this keeps up. We have even received direct death threats.

– There is no such thing as «going too far», Somby replies acidly. – And what if I am? This is my film, *my* masterpiece, and no one will be allowed to ruin it, do you *hear* me?
– I hear you, David, Caine replies.
There had been several witnesses to this altercation. Lasko had spoken to several of them. What they all had in common was the fidgeting, the nervous glances and the contradictory emotion, as if they still couldn't decide how they felt about David Fallon Somby.
– Watching this gives me the creeps, Monroe kept whispering. – One set, one reality seems to be superimposed upon another. It's an eerie, disconcerting feeling.
Monroe seemed to have developed a rational, analytical mind lately and that was quite disconcerting in itself.
Lasko imagined he heard his colleague's whisper long after they had parted company, and a shudder, one he couldn't suppress ravaged his body and soul.
He passed a board, one of many posted on the set, containing the cold facts concerning Somby's life and death.
YEAR ZERO: Born 19 January in Tobruk, «The Rain City», to Elizabeth Arnold Somby and David Somby.
YEAR TWO: After the disappearance of his father and sudden death of his mother Somby is adopted by his aunt and uncle, the wealthy couple of John and Joan Arnold, a lawyer family in Jaynagar, «The City of Dreams».
YEAR SIX: He moves abroad with his adoptive parents, and lives there for five years.
YEAR ELEVEN: Returns to Jaynagar.
YEAR EIGHTEEN: Goes to University, but leaves after a few months. It's rumored that he lost hundred thousand dollars playing Poker. The persistent rumor states that his father had to pay the debt. He joins the family firm, but leaves after a few weeks, and is subsequently kicked out of the Arnold home. Little is known about the next few months. It's rumored (again) that he changed his name, and moved east, even though he resurfaced in Jaynagar before the year is over. He begins making short movies at a local amateur club, while working as a waiter, and playing poker during the nights.
YEAR TWENTY: Adoptive mother Joan Arnold dies, leaving her personal fortune to Somby against the expressed wishes of John Arnold. Somby's film, HILARIOUS LIFE, called «an absurd study of student life» by the critics, made with money from his inheritance, is accepted at a short film festival.

YEAR TWENTY FOUR: He is given a three movie offer by Planet Studios. Two days after that milestone event he has yet another - and final fallout with John Arnold. He starts working with his first feature full-length movie, MIST ON THE MOOR. John Arnold dies two months later, leaving his adoptive son nothing.

YEAR TWENTY SIX: MIST ON THE MOOR, after several delays, rewrites of the script, and sacking of actors is finally completed. It opens to less than enthusiastic reviews, and is generally hailed «as the worst debut of the decade» by the critics. Contrary to everybody's expectation it is a modest hit, and actually makes money. But far more important is the cult following it is eventually attracting, and subsequently their ditching of the reviewers, and, as a result those very reviewers' prevalent, life-lasting animosity towards Somby and everything he does.

YEAR TWENTY SEVEN: It's here that it gets sketchy and even dicey. During the preproduction of his new film he vanishes for six months, to reappear out of the blue one day, married to Angela Dorman. Speculations about his disappearance and subsequent reappearance rage on for years.

YEAR THIRTY: After an even more turbulent and prolonged production his film Dark Shadows in Bright Lights is finally released. It's a major economic success. No matter the hassle the film and Somby get from the reviewers people rush to the theaters in droves. The enmity between Somby and the reviewers grow to an uncanny degree when he smugly calls them «the parasites of the industry».

YEAR THIRTY ONE: He completes his novel «The Undiscovered Country», «hailed» by the reviewers as «a morbid piece of garbage». It's about a man who becomes a component in his own, incomplete painting. Some Somby biographers later more than suggest that he foresaw or even planned his own death.

YEAR THIRTY TWO: He moves into his dream house, Wonderland with his pregnant wife, seemingly quite enjoying the spectacle his life has become, and enjoying even more doing his frequent attack on reviewers.

YEAR THIRTY FOUR: Wonderland burns to the ground, killing his wife and two children. Somby escapes badly burned. He retreats from public life altogether, reportedly living as a hermit. Wild rumors fly about him participating in witchcraft and magical rituals, in an attempt to bring his loved ones back from the dead. It is here that it gets sketchy again, very sketchy. He vanishes for a while, totally disappearing from the face of the Earth to reappear a month later, a frail and sick man.

YEAR THIRTY FIVE: He starts writing reviews for Horror Magazine, an irony certainly not lost on his detractors. One review in particular eventually draws everybody's attention. On the surface he comments on what is widely seen as «a Somby clone», a certain Wilfred Manners making a film called DANCING TWISTERS, but the review is later seen as Somby's rebuttal of his own works, as his way of rejecting his own past.

YEAR THIRTY EIGHT: He finally completes his third and final movie, a total break with his previous works. It's called ORDINARY FOLKS, and deals with the daily problems of a suburban nuclear family. After tripling the original budget, after numerous scandals and delays and what the actors later called «a sick attention to detail» the film is a total flop, causing Planet Studios to go bankrupt. Somby is hospitalized not long afterwards, raving about flowers whispering to him and dark figures with knives lurking outside his house at night, cutting up his flowers. Later that year he marries Adelaide Robinson, a young, aspiring actress.

YEAR FORTY: He signs a deal with the new Planet Studios, and returns to work. The title of the new movie, announced at a press conference not long after that is CHILLY NIGHTS, clearly a return to basics, to his roots. He seems upbeat, ironic and more his old self. One night he is found stumbling through the streets of Tobruk, dressed in another man's clothes (a certain Albert Royce actually files a complaint, but he is never tracked down and his identity is never really confirmed in any way). He is brought to the hospital, but is discharged the next day and returns to Jaynagar. The police are called to the Somby residence the next evening, to what is clearly a domestic dispute. The screaming contest between Somby and spouse continues long after the arrival of the police officers. She leaves before the officers. They manage to calm down the distressed man and after spending hours in the Somby home they leave as well. Later that night the Cult of Beelzebub breaks into his house and sacrifices him to their hungry goddess, leaving him as a part of their incomplete wall painting. David Fallon Somby dies under very mysterious circumstances.

– What do you mean, «mysterious circumstances»? Lasko asked Allan later. – He was quite simply killed, though in quite the unusual way. Nothing mysterious about it.

– That wasn't quite the case even before the latest development, Allan grinned. – And it's certainly not true anymore.

They sat in the at-the-set cafeteria in the besieged fortress the set had become. Security was generally tight during most modern filmmaking projects, but since the news had gotten out about the body at the central police headquarters it had turned insane.

Allan followed Lasko's line of vision as it wandered along the tall walls surrounding the compound, read his mind and grinned some more.

– A non-numbered script was sold to a well-known magazine last year, he said. – The movie was one of the most eagerly anticipated for years, but it flopped due to the fact that everybody knew the story long before it reached the theaters. Since then most copies of a given script are numbered, and security is tighter than the bank.

Lasko let Allan yap on.

A fly buzzed outside the window. Lasko didn't look at it, but he saw it anyway, how it worked ceaselessly with its front legs, gathering necessities only it knew the value of.

The actors left the cafeteria. They did so well before Allan, the way he desired it. They filed through the door like lemmings towards the river. The image appeared in Lasko's mind, totally irrationally and he let out a bark of laughter.

– You need to start seeking out the old gang, Somby's compatriots, Allan said abruptly, casually, very casually. – You'll have to do so without me, I'm afraid. They won't see me, won't let me come near them. They've made that abundantly clear, even done so to the point of getting restraining orders from various courts, both domestically and abroad.

That's certainly a relief, Lasko thought, striving to keep his face impassive.

Monroe appeared in the door down the hall, saving him from further imposition from the intense man at the other side of the table. Lasko rose, nodded to Allan, and walked off, striving to keep an even pace.

They drove up the hills. Monroe was behind the wheel. Lasko frowned, as if there was something he couldn't quite recall or grasp. He imagined he saw the car from the outside, from the above, in front and behind, an experience he found quite disconcerting.

That word again. He couldn't keep himself from shuddering. It didn't matter how hot it was in the car. The heat seemed, in a beyond eerie manner to make the shuddering take a turn for the worse.

Somewhere down to their left, he glimpsed the Caine Manor and the old, shiny church, and another unpleasant feeling flickered down his spine.

– We will visit Caine Manor last, I trust? Monroe stated, certainty tangible in his voice.

Lasko nodded, not surprised anymore that his dislikes and stuff were well known in the police department.

– You met Caine quite a few times twenty years ago, I guess, Monroe nodded, more to himself than to the man in the passenger seat.

Lasko glared at him. Monroe seemed to be very talkative, *unusually* talkative tonight. If he said two words during a given evening it was deemed sensational at the precinct.

Howard Measley and Victoria Arness, husband and wife lived in a fairly unspectacular home, in a fairly quiet neighborhood, at least compared to other places in the Hills. A simple sign at the gate revealed their names.

It had been very noisy outside, in the streets in the sphere around the car. Suddenly, the moment they drove through the gate everything turned quiet and still, as if someone had snapped a finger or two.

Lasko kept hearing the cries from the journalists gathered outside. And among those sounds he heard even far more disturbing sounds, a jaw he imagined in his head, one chewing, chewing and never stopping.

The car stopped before the main entrance. Lasko opened his door. Monroe opened his. They both stepped outside. Monroe took two steps forward and rang the bell. They heard the sound of some commotion inside, quickly fading, and the sound of steps in the hall.

A woman opened the door. Lasko recognized Victoria Arness faintly in the wrinkled face, over an abyss of twenty years.

– Yes, is there anything I can help you with?

She gave no evident indication that she recognized him, but she did anyway, he could tell, actor or no actor.

– We are here because of…

– I know why you are here, she said abruptly, suddenly evidently tired of the game.

She retreated back into the hall, down the hallway, leaving the door open. Lasko and Monroe exchanged glances and walked inside.

Howard Measley sat in a chair in the living room, the unusually bright living room and stared out of the window, intentionally or unintentionally in the direction of Caine Manor. Measley's chair had wheels. He turned it around and faced the detectives, speaking in a dramatic outburst.

– So the ghost refuses to stay dead, does he?

– I'm afraid so, sir, Monroe replied when Lasko refused to do it.

– He is dead, actually, Lasko added with dry humor.

– Dead Again.

Measley continued his performance.

– I always enjoyed that movie, you know. He frowned. – I don't really know why. Perhaps because the woman actually was the man, and the man actually was the woman…

– Would you like some tea? Arness interjected hastily.

– Thank you, ma'am, Lasko replied. – That would be lovely.

She rushed to the kitchen in her eagerness to serve her unexpected guests. Lasko and Monroe sat down on the couch opposite Measley.

– So, the ageing actor exclaimed, – how is the police dealing with this *highly* unusual situation?

– That one is easy, sir, Lasko replied lightly, very lightly, – by doing basic, good police work. We seek and interview witnesses, friends and possible enemies of the diseased, research various motives, crossing off on the lists of suspects. In short we seek to find the murderer.

– And as we all know good ol' Dave had a rather long list of enemies, Measley chuckled. – Tell me, detectives, have you exhumed the old grave yet

– Not yet, Lasko said, – but we expect to get the necessary permits in just a few hours. We will do it!

– You took your time, getting there… didn't you?

– As I said, Lasko stressed, – during extraordinary circumstance, and this case certainly qualify, we tend to fall back on basic police work. We've taken our time and not rushing things. We want to get everything right, in the event of a trial.

The room turned quiet, unnaturally quiet. The buzz from the fly in the window frame rose above all other sounds from the far outside in the men's ears. Lasko looked at Monroe, and the young detective pulled himself together, as he pretended to consult his notes.

– You, yourself counted among those enemies, sir, a very vocal such as well, the way I've heard it.

Measley shrugged it off.

– That wasn't and certainly isn't a secret. The man was totally intolerable, on his good days. There were a lot of us dancing on the tables when those loonies did our job for us, that's for sure.

– So, where were you, on the evening of March 12, sir?

– I was here. Another shrug, another wave of the hand. – We were both here the entire evening, and unable to provide a single witness to that effect, I'm afraid.

Arness brought the tea, during what had become a very uneasy silence. Arness joined them around the table. The four of them all sipped a bit, putting the cup back down, as the fluid was yet too hot, like they had known it would be.

– So, who do you think did it? Lasko asked Measley, laying off the pretence of politeness.

– It could be any given person on the list, the long list, but if I was you I would have looked among his less outspoken antagonists. In my experience most people boasting about doing something drastic, like murder makes it less likely that they will actually go ahead and do it. I, myself certainly belong in that category.

– I guess that someone realized he was still alive, somehow, Arness said with a pale smile, – and decided that such a state was completely unbearable.

– Oh, be quiet, Judith, Measley snapped at her.

The two of them sat there, holding hands, casting fond glances at each other, very much like young lovers.

Lasko kept himself from frowning. Only decades of experience kept him from doing that.

– So, there is a… queue? He asked lightly, deflecting his astonishment as best he could.

– Of course there is. Arness said with a pale smile. – You know that as much as anyone, Lieutenant. Many even felt cheated when he was whacked twenty years ago, because others took him out before they did. I would imagine that if people found out he was still alive there would be quite a race to get there *first*.

Monroe drank the tea, taking a huge sip. Lasko drank, too, quickly putting the cup back on the tray. He had never cared much for tea.

The conversation went on for some time, a considerable amount of time. Lasko and Monroe pushed the couple quite a bit, went at them with all their experience and muster, to no avail. It was like hitting a wall, one they had no hope of circumventing without having anything more substantial to go on.

Lasko rose eventually, and Monroe joined him.

– That would be all, for now, he said politely. – We will be in touch if we need more information from you.

– Thanks for stopping by, Measley grinned. – Please feel free to return anytime.

There was something in that grin. It made Lasko's unruly stomach voice a silent protest. He felt the sting of pain there, as he often did, but stronger, more potent.

The air outside felt uncommonly fresh and clean. Lasko took a deep breath.

– HEY, Lieutenant, one of the pack of newshounds gathered outside the gate cried, – what's the score here?

– No score, Lasko shouted back, – only quite the ordinary information gathering.

They dumped into their seats and shut the doors, ignoring the hungry mob of newshounds. Monroe started the engine and drove off, parting the sea of sharks momentarily keeping them from leaving the place.

– I want to run them down, he mumbled. – Sometimes the need is so strong that I can taste it. I really can. It isn't just an expression.

Monroe worried Lasko sometimes, he really did.

They drove on, through the twists and turns up the Hills. Almost at the top, at the very top there was an estate surrounded by high fences and a lot of both two-legged and four-legged attack-dogs. The two-legged carried big guns, but aside from that they didn't appear that different from their companions in the harness.

Or those with microphones, cameras and loud mouths camping outside the perimeter.

Lasko and Monroe and the sentries did the usual dance. The officers showed their credentials. The dogs phoned their employer or a representative, and then they opened the gate.

There was a long way to the front «door», to the palace-like building, at least the equivalent of several blocks. No one showed up to greet them, as they disembarked the car, and walked up the short stairway to the large doors, these doors, when wide open inviting guests to lavish parties, even though there had been fewer of them lately. Lasko knew they were being watched, studied. He knew that feeling from a long time back.

Monroe knocked on the door, the left door in the set of two, as it happened.

It was opened from inside. An old man, impeccably dressed appeared before the two detectives.

– Please, come in, the old man said pleasantly, before they managed to speak. – Ms. Robinson is expecting you.

The butler did it, Lasko thought, totally unprompted.

The detectives followed the well-dressed man into the building, into its bright halls and equally bright hallways. Adelaide Robinson welcomed them in thc library. She looked practically the same as she had done twenty years ago, just a few facelift-operations later. The room was located at the center of the building. There were no windows, not even the smallest spot of daylight there, but an eerie glow seemingly originating from nowhere, nowhere Lasko was able to pinpoint, anyway.

– Welcome. Adelaide reached out a rather a large hand. – Thank you for coming.

– Thanks for welcoming us, Lasko said lightly, taking her hand, her eerily strong hand.

She was well known for her eccentricities, her reclusive ways, and hadn't been seen in public for years.

In fact she hadn't been seen in public since her husband's horrible death (first death?).

– I remember you, she said somberly. – I must thank you for what you did.
– I didn't really do anything, he coughed.
– You did *something,* she insisted. – That was more than most. And now… you're doing it again.
He was astonished to notice lines of tears in her face, and didn't know what surprised him the most: the fact that she had been crying or that the tears were still there, that she hadn't cleaned her skin, concealed the obvious signs of her distress and sorrow.
She sat down in the sofa, crossing her legs. The two detectives sat down in the chairs across the table. The butler served tea.
– He was a brilliant man, Adelaide Robinson said, – simply brilliant. He saw so much more than most people, saw corners and edges of existence the rest of us weren't even aware of.
She sniffed.
– He taught me so much.
The distraught woman pulled herself together with a visible effort. She looked at the two ill-at-ease detectives.
– No, she said, – I didn't know he was still alive. I sincerely believed he died twenty years ago. I saw his body, or what I believed to be his body. If that was intended to be a hoax of some kind it was a doozy. If I had known, if I had discovered that he pulled something like that, had done that to me, I might have butchered him myself.
The distraught woman looked quite mad then.
The two detective exchanged glances. The walls in the already confined space closed in on them.
– I was here when he was butchered, she sniffed. – I haven't left the house in a month. A number of people, of his enemies and friends and loved ones could have killed him. The poor baby was always so damn *honest*. He could never keep his mouth shut, and I loved him for it…
When they were done Lasko and Monroe knew positively that they had asked her questions, even pointed questions, at least giving an impression of an interrogation, but they couldn't actually recall asking them, not a single one.
She followed them out. They didn't see the butler anywhere. She left them with one final thought.
– He was always looking for something, you know. No one I knew of knew exactly what, but one look at those wandering eyes told an entire story, you know. I fear he finally *found* it.
The thought stayed with them, as they kept driving through the Hills and beneath, visiting friends and foes and acquaintances of the late, *late* David

Fallon Somby. On the fourth day, or perhaps the fifth they sat at a corner table at a restaurant consuming their burger and fries. A fly or two was buzzing around somewhere, making a low but irritating sound. Lasko shook his head in a futile attempt at getting it out of his head. He couldn't see the fly (or flies), but knew they were there somewhere.

– It's amazing. Monroe shook his head. – No one seems to have the same impression of him.

Him. For some reason they were reluctant to mention his name, to take it in vain.

– I mean, there are clearly two camps basically split along the middle, one admiring him far beyond any healthy manner and the other, pretty much hating his guts, but there are endless variations within each side.

Lasko nodded. That was unusual.

– It's damn unusual, Monroe concluded.

They looked through the crime-scene photos again, yet again. Other dinner-guests looked at them while walking by. A few of them, suddenly in a hurry ran straight for the restroom.

But most merely shrugged and moved on, or didn't react at all.

Late on the seventh day they made the final stop on their journey, in front of the proud and shiny Caine Manor. In an area of wealthy neighborhoods this was clearly the jewel of the crown. The manor had recently been refurbished and so had the church across the road. They stepped out of the car, to the silence and emptiness lingering in the air.

– There are no journalists here, Monroe whispered. – Not a single newshound in sight.

It was said that Caine had his ways when it came to keep both paparazzis and all kind of chasing journalists both off his property and away from his person. Those few that had been granted an interview with the lord of the manor were considered legends in the business.

– It's downright creepy, Monroe added.

When they stepped from the sidewalk and onto the fairly short road leading to the house they felt a tingle, nothing pronounced, but still unmistakable, as if they crossed a boundary of some kind. Lasko looked up. The building towered above them, to a point where it seemed to pierce the sky. There was no button to push, but an actual bell hanging above the door. Monroe rang it, after first casting a hesitating glance at his superior. It sounded unnaturally loud in their ears.

The butler opened the door.

– Come in, sirs, he said. – We have been expecting you.

– You have, huh? Lasko wondered, stepping inside. – How come?

– Please, sir, the last week you have been visiting everybody in the Hills with even a remote connection to David Somby. It stands to reason that you saved us for last.

– It makes sense, Lasko nodded.

He studied the butler. Something was off there, at the edge of the man's eyes. Lasko could always tell, tell such things. It was a knack he had gained early in his career.

– Master Caine is awaiting you in the living room. If you will come with me…

It was quite the long walk, to the large, cozy room, long, dark hallways, before they finally reached their destination in the large and drafty old house.

The old man warmed himself by the fireplace, standing close enough for the flames to touch his legs and hands, but they never did.

He turned towards them the moment they crossed the threshold to the room.

– The detectives Lasko and Monroe for you, sir, the butler coughed discreetly.

– Ah, gentlemen, Marlon Caine cried, – there you are. I have been *expecting* you…

The red dark flames seemed to reach for him as he stepped away from the fireplace.

– May I offer you anything? A drink? Tea? Coffee?

– Nothing for me, thanks, Monroe mumbled.

Lasko didn't reply.

– Shall we retire to the library, then, to a more… appropriate setting?

The library, it was always the library. Lasko shook his head.

– We've been served tea all week, he said, staring pointedly at Caine.

– I can imagine, Caine replied pleasantly, very pleasantly.

They walked up the stairs. The butler had vanished without a trace. Lasko looked around for him and couldn't spot him anywhere. He had seen him when he had turned his head and looked back just a few seconds earlier, but now he just wasn't there. The two detectives followed the surprisingly agile old man up the endless stairs. On the fourth or fifth floor Caine finally took off to the right and opened the double doors to the vast library inside.

– Welcome, their host cried, – to the Library of Time. All secrets of the Universe are gathered here.

It seemed to go on forever inwards.

– That's one of the best mirror-tricks I've ever seen.

Monroe whistled impressed.

– Yes, isn't it? Caine grinned.

He walked to the fireplace and the flames seemed to welcome him and embrace him. The flames danced around the bulky body. At least that was what the two detectives imagined or told themselves they imagined. He turned towards them, his grin still in place.

– So, what can I do for you, gentlemen?

– David Fallon Somby is dead, sir, Lasko said formally. – He was murdered, stabbed with a knife by an unknown assailant. We are the main investigating detectives on the case, and we visit all his old… acquaintances.

– So, it is true then? Caine asked, and Lasko was stunned to actually notice a frown on his brow. – It's no setup or hoax?

– We're confident that there isn't, sir. Lasko allowed himself his own, small grin. – The man currently lying dead in the police headquarters *is* David Fallon Somby. So far we haven't been granted permission to dig up the body of the man that was murdered twenty years ago, but we will, and we will establish his identity.

Caine was an actor. He had played in quite a few films both before and after he had become a producer in his own right. But Lasko knew people. He had learned to see beyond appearances and acting, and right now he was stunned to see fear and more beneath Caine's calm exterior.

The man was *shaken* to his core.

– You were confident that the man that died was Somby, I take it? Monroe, unusually perceptive asked the suddenly very old man.

– I certainly was, Caine replied, distracted, distraught. – I knew him well, both in good and bad ways.

Suddenly he sounded and seemed almost human, not at all like the almighty demigod he looked like in the interviews and media appearances, and Lasko's curiosity was peeked.

– So, in your humble opinion, was his death twenty years ago a snow job?

– A… snow job? Caine uttered perplexed.

– Did he fake his death? Lasko inquired.

– No! Caine shook his head decisively. – Surely not.

Was there a question mark at the end there? Lasko couldn't tell.

– Surely he must have? The policeman suggested. – There must have been a snow job of some kind or he wouldn't have been alive to be killed last week?

Caine *looked* at him, and Lasko suddenly felt very cold. The old man's eyes seemed to contract and expand at the same time.

– That is quite the logical point of view, detective, Caine granted. – At least when speaking of conventional logic.

A roar rose in Lasko's ears. There was no sound. The roar was so loud that he couldn't hear.

– Unfortunately for you… detective, conventional logic is *shit*. It has no bearing what so ever in the real world.

Lasko couldn't say for certain later when the conversation had… turned. If he would dare to venture a guess, he would say it had been when the man had *looked* at him, but he wasn't sure, was no longer in any way sure of anything. Everything had turned, and he stood there sweating in he heat from the, oh, so fiery fireplace.

Caine walked to the far shelf and pulled out a book, an old book with a worn, decrepit cover.

– I will tell you boys a story, he said, turning the pages, making dust whirl in the air.

Monroe coughed. Lasko didn't have the strength to.

– There once were two boys walking into the woods, Marlon Caine read.

His hypnotic voice drew them in. They drowned in the sea of his eyes and gasped helplessly for air.

– They were warned to not enter the dark and dangerous forest, but disregarding the countless warnings and foreboding signs they headed into its vast depth without bringing any weapons to protect themselves from the countless horrors lurking between the trees, the trees studying them with dark, envious eyes…

The surroundings changed around them, from the safe (but eerie) library to the dark, dark forest. It seemed so real, so damned real. Caine vanished as they looked at him, and in his place stood a large, dark-haired wolf with a steaming gap and illuminated eyes sending shocks of terror through them.

– To better EAT YOU, BOYS, it growled and lunged forward, and the gap opened wide, and they were devoured, and digested as teeth ripped them apart and their remaining pieces flowed down the throat bathing in the digestive fluid, one with acid-like properties dissolving everything into a soup ready to be sucked into the bloodstream, until there was nothing left but a few stray thoughts and dull, dull, dull pain.

Lasko sat up in bed, gasping and sweating like a sick man. The lamp burned in the corner, hot as the sun, searing his skin.

He splashed his face in the sink below the bathroom mirror. When he looked, looked at himself there was hardly anything there, not even a grinning skull. He stood there, frozen, attempting to think, desperately trying to draw more than a blank on yesterday's events. They had left

Marlon Caine's residence, Caine Manor after a lengthy conversation. He and Monroe had parted company, and he had returned to his apartment, returned here… and nothing had happened, nothing out of the ordinary. On the contrary, it had been a thoroughly uneventful evening, spent in front of the television.

Caine's grin haunted him. He had waved to them, from the library on the second floor, like a royal did from the balcony when his subjects passed by. Lasko looked at his watch. It showed just a few, indistinct numbers and didn't tell him shit. He looked out through the window, confusion painted in his face. It was still night. He squinted his eyes, straining them in an effort to glimpse the street lights he usually easily saw.

But it was pitch black out there.

He stood there until dawn, and he finally was able to see the poles at the other side of the street.

The sound of the electric razor seemed dull and far away. He looked at his swollen eyes and the large bags under them. The surreal drive through the empty streets demoralized him further. He stared through the window, at the vast emptiness out there. The police cars were lined up on the parking lot outside the headquarters. He glimpsed the ghosts moving back and forth like puppets. Dawn came with a bright, blinding light. He sat in the cafeteria for an eternity before it was filled up with people. Monroe spoke with Connor. They were laughing about something, sharing a moment and having a hell of a time doing it.

A man walked down the street with an insane look in his eyes, his bulging eyes. Lasko saw him from the side as he was turning a corner, just before arriving at the police station. The man looked at him and everything just went away.

He remembered taking the bus to someplace or another, but couldn't tell where. The sound of the engine buzzed in his ears. He recalled the sensation of sitting in the seat.

When he looked outside there was nothing there.

It was a bright, sunny day, when they stepped out into the yard of Caine Manor. The house's master followed them out. The butler (the butler did it) was nowhere in sight. Caine shook their hands (their huge, clammy hands).

– Was that all, gentlemen?

– That should be all, sir, Lasko nodded. – We may come back to you eventually.

– Sure, Caine shrugged. – Feel free to return at any time.

They walked to their car. The entire street was empty, like on a Sunday afternoon.

– It's a beautiful day, isn't it? Monroe said.

Lasko heard birds sing. He didn't hear what his partner said, didn't hear him speak at all, except as a distant rumble somewhere beyond the horizon.

They drove off.

The week ended as it had begun, on the movie set. Nothing had changed, really. Allan looked even more like Somby than he had a week ago. It was profoundly eerie, and the shiver down Lasko's spine didn't end, but was an ongoing, unending thing.

A man stared at Lasko, stared at Lasko, not at Monroe standing right beside him. The staring man had the most remarkable and terrifying eyes. Lasko almost felt something akin to pain, and crouched slightly, before straightening, sweating and breathing like after a run.

Judith Morgan cried out at the vigil, standing by her partner's open casket:

– DEATH IS BUT A TRIFLE. THE TRUE DEATH IS NOT THE GRAVE, BUT THE DECAY OF THE SPIRIT BURNING WITHIN THE SHELL OF MAN.

And the cameras hummed and buzzed around them all, recording everything there was to record. Lasko dried the sweat off his brow. He had removed his coat, but it did him no good. The sweat kept pouring and kept burning his eyes, weakening his ailing vision further.

He tried reading the script. Allan had given one copy to him and made him sign for it.

– This is one of the few copies in existence. The director had grinned to him. – Now you're privy to secrets people will kill for…

Lasko sat down to read. People moved around him and he didn't see them, except as indistinct shadows moving back and forth in a rush of wind.

INT. BEDROOM - DAY

Judith Morgan is dancing on the floor around her bed. The bed stands at the center of the room. She hums a melody. No one hears it but her. She dances with a dazed look in her eyes.

Except it isn't Judith Morgan, but Victoria Arness playing Judith Morgan, and even that isn't correct. It is, in truth Alicia Pendergast playing Victoria Arness that played Judith Morgan in Dark Shadows in Bright Lights.

She stands in front of the policeman, slightly bent forward, sending him sweet kisses through the air.

JUDITH/VICTORIA/ALICIA

Am I guilty, detective? Did I kill my husband? Did I kill my fellow actor, or instead some complete stranger, a poor smuck I met on the street?

Lasko looked up. It was as if the curvy female form faded in his hazy vision. He rubbed his eyes, but his vision remained hazy. Colors and lights kept shifting around him.

Victoria Arness grinned at him with her practically naked skull.

He gasped and jumped on his feet. The script fell from his hand and hit the floor with a loud thud. He rushed to the restroom, and to the nearest mirror, turned on the tap, filled his cupped hands and splashed his face as he bent down, and got most of his first try-out on his clothes. He repeated the performance and this time it splashed his face right on. His body straightened practically by itself and he stood there, staring at his swollen skin.

A sound behind him made him turn. Someone flushed the toilet. The sound made him *cringe*. He stared dumbfounded as the door opened. He didn't recognize him, didn't recognize the man from the movie set staring at him with a steady, menacing look.

– My name is Albert Royce, the man grinned. – Nice to meetcha.

There was something in that grin that worried Lasko, worried him terribly.

Then Royce's skull showed through the skin, too. Lasko squealed. The name was *known* to him, but no matter how hard he tried he couldn't wrap his mind around it, and unveil its secrets.

Minutes, hours had passed. He stood there alone. Vapors and mist surrounded him, and the air reeked of a foul stench. He didn't want to breathe, but had to, and the stench entered his body and mind, and poisoned him, poisoned him terribly. It might be imagination, but he glimpsed people walking in and out of the restroom, in and out of the stalls while he stood there, frozen like a statue, like a dead man, unable to move, but able to think, while the remnants of life slowly left him, and he began rotting there, as if he had been rotting in the grave for years, not realizing he had died.

CHAPTER TEN

It was a dark, dreary and wet day when they dug up the remains in the old grave. The permits had finally been granted just a few hours earlier. The rain poured down. The smell of dirt and other, even less comforting smells tore at the nostrils of everybody gathered here, both those inside and outside the yellow ribbon.

A crowd had gathered here today. Electronic flashes exploded and fizzled in the rain. The sound of voices faded and died the moment it crossed the many pairs of lips. The flashes were so numerous that it created a constant illusion of lightning, but still, still, it couldn't overwhelm the persistent darkness hovering above the cemetery. Monroe listened to music through his earphones. He seemed to be lost to this world. The people exposing what remained of the coffin kept glancing around them, relentlessly moving their wary eyes.

Lasko stood there, wet and uncomfortable under his umbrella, staring into the pitch black hole in the ground. It seemed to draw all the light from its surroundings, not like a black hole, but exactly like a black hole. He felt hot and cold alternately, and couldn't tell which was which, and shivered hard in the boiling, freezing rain.

He stood absolutely still, looking blindly at his surroundings.

The spectacle ended, eventually, hours, days later. The forensics team pulled the remains of flesh and blood and bones from the ground, from the Abyss and brought it to their shiny laboratories, and brought the prevailing gray darkness with them. They picked the dry and wet bones, studied them under their microscopes and in their reactive fluids and humming machines.

Lasko sagged in his chair in his office, finally reading the report. The words turned indistinct before his eyes and he skipped to the end, to the inevitable conclusion.

The remains in the grave belonged to David Fallon Somby, and so did…

The body of the recently murdered man was also David Fallon Somby.

Their genetic prints were identical.

– «The conclusion is clear». Lasko read. – «There is no margin for error».

Monroe had turned off the music, but forgotten to remove the earplugs.

Connor and Hesky didn't say anything, didn't move or doing anything identifying them to Lasko as human beings.

– This changes nothing, you know, he told them. – We still have a murder to solve. That hasn't changed.

They nodded. Of course they did, being dedicated, duty-bound police officers.

He studied the photographs, both old and new again, yet again, until they began dissolving before his eyes, turning into something even more eerie and sinister. His tired eyes blinked and the photographs were once more only photographs.

A few days later all four of them went to the hospital where Somby had been born. They drove all the way to Tobruk. He knew he could have, should have sent Connor and Hesky, but he wanted to check it out in person, see it with his own eyes, sense it all beyond all senses.

The hospital was a dump. It had been a source of joy and pride once, according to Dr. Brucker, Jeff Brucker, but had fallen on hard times.

They had seen a lot of bugs, of cockroaches and spiders and worse in the hallways and saw even more of them here. They saw one cross the man's palm. He didn't seem to notice.

– No, no, the old, geriatric Dr. Brucker assured them. – There was no twin. I was present at the birth, and it was just one little tyke coming out of that bloody cunt.

He sounded even more insane than he looked and he looked quite insane.

– The hospital was a source of pride and joy before that birth, he repeated, – but afterwards it fell on hard times, and things were never the same since, since that *horrible* day.

The good doctor followed them, stalked them when they left, all the way to the exit, and even outside, to the car.

– His mother was a witch, Brucker grinned wickedly at them, – and his father a demon, a hell-spawn coming to our world to prepare the takeover.

They heard him, even as they closed the doors and drove off.

THE END OF THE WORDL IS COMING. THE DEMONS WILL COME THROUGH US. THEY WILL GROW IN OUR MINDS AND OUR HEARTS, IF WE DON'T REPENT AND GIVE PRAISE TO THE LORD

– He sounded more like a priest than a doctor, Connor said, clearly shaken. – Brrr.

Lasko had trouble holding on to the wheel, to keep the car straight. The old building had seemed more like a morgue than a hospital.

There was a four-hour drive between the cities, at top legal speed. The road was wide, with no turns and hardly any deviation from a straight ahead norm. The sunny day imposed itself pleasantly on them as long as it lasted, but dark clouds lingered in the horizon the closer they came to Jaynagar. They weren't hungry, even if they hadn't eaten since early morning, but stopped at a drive-in anyway, in a desire to postpone the inevitable.

The cafeteria was filled with afternoon dinner guests. They found one table for four by the corner window.

– Are they staring at us? Connor wondered. – They are staring at us… aren't they?

It sure felt that way. Lasko had never been the most sensitive guy in the world, but now he had a very powerful sense of being watched. He saw people's eyes from the corners of his own. The other dinner guests… glared at them.

He looked outside. The landscape seemed to be changing, changing in an ever-shifting pattern. He looked at the hill across the road. One blink and it was no longer a hill, but a shopping mall. The change seemed so casual, so… natural that it gave him chills all over. He didn't rub his eyes, just stared, until his eyes turned dry and dusty, and he felt like he had been sitting there for ages.

They ate, ate a few crumbs on their plates, not hungry. The lack of hunger was… profound, such a devastating sense of… nothing, and Lasko had never experienced its like.

Hesky finished his lack of meal quickly and began reading the case files. He did that often, being described by his scoffing colleagues as the archetypal eager beaver.

He frowned. The other three studied him, waiting with infinite patience.

– I read and read, but I don't see it, he said.

– What is it you don't see? Lasko asked him.

– Anything… substantial, Hesky said. – The list of suspects is... large. I've never seen anything like it, and we haven't really made any progress since we started, have we? There is nothing there, nothing… pointing to itself, no meaning or substance at all. The guy was disliked by many, a very controversial figure, but there is no motive, not really, especially given the case's unusual circumstances.

– Perhaps those circumstances are merely a smokescreen, Connor suggested, – a way of concealing what really happened, or is really happening?

Lasko looked almost grateful at her. She was bright, energetic and logical, even when fatigued, as she was now.

– But in that case we have to wonder what *is* happening, Hesky cried. – We have done *basic, good police work* for weeks now, and come up empty.

Lasko knew that was a jibe directed at him, but he refused to act on it.

He stared at the warehouse across the road. One of the windows, one of the many eyes… winked at him.
They finished their meager meal, taking their time. Lasko looked astounded around him. The place seemed almost empty, and he realized that it had happened slowly, imperceptible. People had just drifted off, through the entrance door or elsewhere. They did, too, in a slow march, a long queue making its way out of the room.
Hesky, with a very green face rushed off to the toilet. Lasko, suddenly very alarmed wanted to hold him back, but couldn't find the voice or the will to do it. They heard him, saw him in there, kneeling over a toilet bowl, puking his guts out. He returned to them, pale and sweaty, with swollen eyes, giving them a dead man's grin worse than Lasko had ever seen.
The place had changed, slowly being filled up with shadows and mist. Lasko's phone was ringing. This time Lasko knew it was his phone. He pulled it from his pocket and answered the call.
– *Listen,* the demonic voice said, – *and listen carefully.*
Lasko didn't say anything. He just stood there, frozen in time.
And the horrible voice rhymed and hissed:
Patty has her home in the sand
The golden sand falling from her shoulders
And she smiles at you with her playful tongue
The silence was filled with noise, with loud, snarling voices. The face he spotted in the mirror of the window looked pale and dead, and he couldn't fight off the profound sense of dread.
– What? Lasko said nonplussed.
– The little boy is lost. The laughter was like a knife's edge. – And he will NEVER home his way find.
Suddenly it was as if the voice didn't come to him from the phone at all, but from someone standing right there beside him. He turned abruptly, but there was nothing there, nothing but empty air grinning at him.
He looked outside, just before they opened the door, and what he saw through the window wasn't the parking lot at all, but another vast room in a house, and gripped in panic he grabbed the doorknob and pushed it down and pulled the door open, and when he saw that outside was outside after all, he breathed a sick sigh of relief, and the cold fear churning his insides let up a little bit.
The city grew in their view. Connor's fingers around the wheel looked like bare bones. She smiled to him, and he turned hot, oh, so hot under the collar. The police station late at night looked like an old church, abandoned and neglected. Connor stopped the car at the parking lot, close

to the eastern wing. The full moon cast long shadows as the four of them left the car. The city grew in their view.

Lasko rubbed his temple, as they entered the building, his fingers turning wet of cold sweat.

He sat in his office, alone, looking at the photograph of the apartment where David Fallon Somby, the modern version had been killed, had been slaughtered. He heard Ben Winstone, one of the in-house photographers speak.

– Great composition, isn't it?

Lasko looked at him. Winstone had been the photographer on duty that day.

– I don't mean the photo, of course, Winstone caught himself. – I mean the *room.*

Lasko recalled Evanard Marsten's insane raving. He heard it, too, whispering in both his ears simultaneously.

– It was such a beautiful painting, such wonderful composition. I take it just as the sacrificial lamb dies, exactly the moment the light leaves his eyes. It's a masterpiece, a masterpiece, I tell ya…

The sacrificial lamb.

– So you're saying a professional photographer did it? Lasko asked Winstone.

– There is a distinct possibility of that, yes, Winstone stated proudly, before once again catching himself, and finishing meekly: – At least there is a great likelihood of one taking the actual photos.

– We have been looking for… a connection between the two murders, Lasko told the other three. – Perhaps this is it. Perhaps an *artist* did both.

Winstone shrunk to nothing before him.

Lasko sat alone, staring at the photograph. The pentacle carved on the floor in the ramshackle apartment seemed to glow and pulse.

He walked home alone, living nearby, just a few blocks away from the station. A sound, a shriek to his left caught his attention. He had his hands on his gun in an instant. The gnawing sound reached him, one he couldn't properly identify. He stopped. A man appeared from the dark alley, turning visible under the streetlights.

– Good evening. My name is Albert Royce.

– Haven't we met before? Lasko wondered faintly.

– No, Royce replied decisively, – this is thc first time. There will be other meetings later.

He gnawed his teeth. Lasko realized that startled. The man gnawed his teeth, and it was as if he wasn't alone in doing that. The sound, the now so very familiar sound surrounded Lasko, and it was as if thousands of teeth joined those of Albert Royce.

– Have you heard the story about the man who returned home after a prolonged journey abroad and found his wife dead on the floor? He was later arrested because neighbors swore to the police he had returned home five hours before he said he did. And he was convicted of the murder, even though accounts proved he had been aboard the ship Queen Elizabeth when the murder actually happened.

– I believe that to be only an urban legend, Lasko responded weakly.

– It most certainly is not, Royce stated very convincingly. – I know for a fact that it did happen… and so do you.

– What…

– ADMIT IT! Royce shouted. – YOU KNOW IT'S TRUE, GODDAMN IT, SO GET YOUR ACT TOGETHER MAN AND START ACTING LIKE A MAN

The moon hid behind a cloud. There was such pressure in Lasko's ears that he feared his head would burst. He choked and felt like he could start crying any minute.

– That's better, Royce said softly. – That's so much better, isn't it?

– Yes, Lasko nodded, bowing his head, staring at the ground.

– *Good* boy!

The moon appeared again, peeking from behind the cloud, at the two figures in the wide street. Lasko stared dumbfounded and speechless at the skeleton grinning at him. He finally recalled, through his dimwitted mind who Albert Royce was.

– You are stupid, you know, the skeleton said casually. – I am dead, you see. What a fool are you, having a conversation with a *dead* man?

The jaws kept gnawing, gnawing, gnawing.

Lasko blinked one, single time, and he was alone. He stood there, a lone, shaking figure among all the whispering, snarling shadows. The shadows grinned at him. He heard the gnawing jaws, but faint, far away, but the moment he focused on them they were there again, surrounding him like vice. Rattlesnakes hissed at him. He choked and rushed home, to the safety of his so very familiar apartment.

The walls seemed to move, as he walked along them, to move like waves on a beach, making everything blurry and eerie. He heard voices from inside his apartment when he stopped in front of the door and fumbled with his keys. In a frenzy of anxiety and sweat he kicked open the door and rushed inside with the gun in his hands. He ran through the rooms with his gun pointing straight forward, ready to fire at anything that moved.

Nothing did. He didn't see a single soul, not even when he entered his bedroom, the room where people were talking. There was no one there.

The radio, his old, antique radio was on. Two people had a conversation with people in the audience or with fake laughter. He kept breathing hard, only slowly, very slowly relaxing.

– Have you heard the story about the man who returned home after a prolonged journey abroad and found his wife dead on the floor? He was later arrested because neighbors swore to the police he had returned home five hours before he said he did. And he was convicted of the murder, even though accounts proved he had been aboard the ship Queen Elizabeth when the murder actually happened.

– That's just an urban legend, man. No one can be that stupid.

– Except with the exception of our excellent judiciary system.

Fake laughter. Lasko sat down on the bed, still clutching his gun, clutching it so hard that his hands started to hurt.

– Why are they laughing? Lasko complained aloud. – It *isn't* funny!

– Wilma Erin Jones, the rather large actress fell from the top floor of her condo last night. The metropolitan police are treating it as a suspicious death. The coroner had a field day with her luscious body.

– Man, that's sick!

– Not as sick as our excellent police force.

Laughter, laughter, laughter. Lasko, without thinking twice about it fired at the radio, one, two three shots. The old antique was blown to pieces. The loud noise shook the building, the echo only slowly fading in his ears.

He sat there, waiting on the bed for minutes before frowning and looking up, looking at the open door to the hallway. People should have come running by now, but nobody had come, nobody came. The building was totally silent. He sat there for a long time before rising and stumbling into the hallway, the empty hallway. The frown deepened on his forehead. He knocked on the door to his closest neighbor, good old Mrs. Hansen. There was no response.

– Hello? He cried. – Is anybody there?

There was no reply.

He kicked at the door. Nothing happened, except for the instant pain in his foot. He kicked again, kicked in the door. His right foot hit the wood hard and the door was kicked off its hinges, and landed in a dustbin at the floor inside. He searched good and hard inside. Everything was in place, the furniture, the lamps and the fridge and oven in the kitchen.

Except for the people.

He didn't see a soul.

The dark space under the bed stared at him with its cruel, cruel eyes. He got the shivers all over and couldn't stop them. When he rushed out of the bedroom and out of the apartment and back into the hallway he almost stumbled and fell several times.

The next door down the hallway was tougher to break. He had to make several attempts before succeeding.

– Hello! He cried, after having reached the living room. – Hello?

There was no answer.

The dark space under the couch stared at him. He yelped once, twice, in helpless despair, before backing out of there, turning his head constantly to see if there was anyone standing behind him, without ever taking his eyes off the dark space under the couch.

He went totally berserk, and started screaming and shouting after that, and hardly remembered a thing before he stood at the opposite end of the hallway and stared blindly at all the broken doors.

Breathing was so loud in his ears that he feared his lungs would burst.

And another even worse notion burrowed its way into his feverish brain: that the sound he heard wasn't of him breathing, but something else, something much, much bigger, surrounding him, squeezing him like a vice.

He returned to his own apartment, the only one with an unbroken door. It was ajar, and he couldn't recall whether or not he had closed it. He stepped inside, rushed inside and slammed the door behind him, locked it with breathing so rapid that it hurt. Anxiety and perspiration drowned him when he turned back, but he saw nothing there but his own nondescript living room.

The kitchen sighed when he entered it. He frowned, as he walked to the kitchen sink. Droplets of water hit the metal below in a steady beat. The sound didn't thunder in his ears, even though he imagined it did. He grabbed a huge glass and filled it up, and drank all of it in what was indeed a noteworthy display of thirst. One glass didn't quite do it for him, and he downed a second without thinking twice about it.

The thirst… remained, as if he hadn't really been drinking anything. He downed a third and fourth glass before putting it down. The water felt like sand and he wanted to puke. He stumbled through the living room to the bedroom, to the bed, removing his clothes as he walked, almost falling when his underwear was caught in his foot. A muscle stretched snapped somewhere. There wasn't much pain, but further discomfort threatening to break through the surface of his mind.

He went to bed, pulling the blanket over himself, hungering for warmth in the warm and moist room. The bed squeaked, even when he wasn't moving, and he tried desperately not to do that. Something scratched on the floor. He couldn't tell if the sounds were close or far away, coming from the middle of the floor or from right under his bed. The lamp burned in his face. He wanted to turn it off, but… couldn't.

Minutes ticked away. He heard them tick, heard his watch tick. The numbers on it looked completely indecipherable and incomprehensible. He made several attempts at reading them. It seemed to him like there was no *time* anymore. If there was a problem it had to be that. His watch was certainly functioning well enough… just not in a way that he could comprehend.

He feared forever had passed since he first put his weary head on the pillow, and that morning was still far away. Something scratched on the wall right behind him and he turned abruptly, totally beside himself with fright. There was nothing there. He turned back, out of breath, after hearing heavy breathing behind his back. A fly buzzed in the ceiling. He looked up. It grinned wickedly at him with its powerful jaw gnawing at the meat in its mouth. Someone chuckled darkly under the bed. He wanted to look, wanted to do so more than anything, but didn't dare. He woke up in the middle of the night sometime, in pitch black darkness. Panic gripped him and persisted long after he had, after several attempts turned on the light.

– Did I turn the lights off? He said to the air. – Please tell me I turned off the lights.

Slumber claimed him at some point, but never sleep, never that deep, satisfying dream state that brought rest. He walked in sand, through the darkness, and it sucked him down, a vortex, a meat grinder with grinning jaws, and he whimpered, unable to utter a single sound to give voice to the dull, dull pain.

He awoke with a start, with light flowing into his bedroom. Relief flooded his being. He began laughing, as the bright morning gave him not only relief but also giddiness and pleasure.

The light transformed the room, transformed his existence.

The laughter followed him into the bathroom, into the rinsing water. He dried himself on his way to the kitchen, suddenly filled with a new kind of energy and purpose. The food and water still tasted like shit, but he didn't mind, didn't care.

He sat by the kitchen table, yet again sifting through the crime scene images of the two David Somby stiffs. A door slammed somewhere in the building, making him frown, for some reason. David Somby had been murdered twice, twenty years apart. The latest looked older, was obviously older, but the lack of deviation in resemblance still felt uncanny to Lasko.

Especially given the fact that the resemblance was skin deep.

The older Somby had all the signs of the younger, dental works, broken bones and stuff. The younger, he who had died first lacked some of the scars of the older man. Lasko had always believed in forensics, and genetic testing had been just a prolongation of that, but now he wasn't so sure… if not for the fact that everything else fit, too.

There were no deviations, period!

The body on the slab winked to him. He shook and wanted to rise, to pull back abruptly from the insanity that had come to plague his life, but he couldn't move.

He just sat there, shaking like a leaf, and couldn't stop.

Looking at the salad on the sandwiches made him want to puke.

Brushing his teeth felt weird, eerie. The toothpaste and water tasted like sand, with grains falling from his mouth like water. He stared at his mirror image, unable to see anything but the unmoving face he spotted there in the invisible mist. The bathroom loomed in exquisite detail behind him, but he didn't seem to be able to grab hold of it in his mind. Everything seemed elusive, unreal.

He grabbed his coat on his way out, like he always did, without conscious thought. Left hand opened the door. Right hand fumbled with the keys in his pocket. It was routine, nothing special, comforting, familiar, the back of his hand.

The hallway was dark. He noticed it just as the door slammed shut behind him. It wasn't supposed to be dark. He glanced at the two large windows at each end of the hallway. There was no bright light shining through them, no light at all. He fumbled with his keys, fearing in a moment of panic they were gone, before finding them as he returned to the door. The key slid into the lock and the door opened.

The apartment was pitch black, too. It was supposed to be morning, for God's sake, with bright light flowing everywhere, but there was none. He stared into the black hole and whimpered and slammed the door shut.

It was as if someone had turned off the light, the light in the sky, by turning a switch, like on a… film set. Yeah, big, bright lamps used to simulate daylight had been turned off. He choked.

He walked, taking one and one step forward, unable to tell how long he had walked. There had been the familiar, now so very unfamiliar hallway at first, but now, at some point it had changed into something strange and unrecognizable.

He imagined he was crossing a bridge, a feeble construct shaking in the storm. It felt so real, from the bow on the ground to the sound of the running water below.
Then it was just the house again, a vast building where he saw no end in sight. He had walked for hours, and nothing had changed from an hour ago, or two or three or ten.
His watch showed no time, no time at all.
Something finally changed. He arrived at a large, open space, a room, with a large staircase at its center. The stairs went up and down, and he could see no end in sight either way. He looked to the right and saw a painting of a giant wave flooding a city. It looked wet and smelled of salt. He looked straight ahead and saw a woman behind a window, drowning in rain. And to his left he saw a man's face, half hidden in shadow. He looked back, at where he had come from and saw only a wall, solid to his touch.
He left that place, too, and headed downstairs. Or at least he imagined he did. After a few minutes walk he was so breathless that he feared he was climbing a steep hill.
Mist rose like heat through an opening ahead. There was no door, just a wide narrow portal he passed through, stepping into a nice and cozy living room. At first it appeared empty, only the table and chairs. Then he turned his head just a little, and he spotted the silver-haired man.
Marlon Caine sat in front of the fireplace, staring into the dancing shadow fires.
– Ah, there you are, he said, without turning. – You took your time.
Lasko wanted to say something, but even though he opened his mouth and attempted to speak, he heard no sound, not even a cough to clear his throat. Caine rose and turned, but not exactly turning, but twisting, like a snake. Lasko felt a cold, hard fear twist his insides when he looked at the nice old man.
Marlon Caine's grin invaded Lasko's vision and settled, remained there, no matter how much he blinked or rubbed his eyes.
– What do you mean? What the fuck is going on here?
– Why do you ask? Caine wondered quite fascinated. – Do you have something particular in mind?
– First I was there, Lasko said confused and depressed. – Then I am here.
– Ah, that explains everything, doesn't it…
The butler entered the room. He carried a tray with two cups. Caine took one.
– Tea?

– No thanks! Lasko replied.

Caine sipped his tea and taking great pleasure in doing so.

– You really should. Nothing is like a good cup of tea. Let it be known that it's delicious and that you're doing a great mistake in not enjoying its pleasures.

Lasko blinked, unable to shake off the confusion haunting his eyes and mind.

The butler left the room again. Lasko once again stood face to face with Marlon Caine.

– It's a virus, you know, Caine said. – It's burrowing its way into your brain and devouring it in an orgy of a feeding frenzy.

The old man's smile turned demonic and his laughter drowned Lasko in a pit deep and wet.

– I'm afraid you're done for, old chap. Nothing can save you now.

Lasko stood there, with bowed head, and couldn't, for the life of him draw anything sensible from the current conversation. It was just so beyond him, and he felt lost, lost beyond words.

– Lies and truth are both overestimated, old chap. Caine lit a giant cigar, and once he started puffing on it the smoke filled the room and turned to thick, thick mist. – None are of any consequence. Both are deception. A person's power of deception is the only worthy value today.

Lasko had trouble seeing the other's face, his eyes flooded with tears.

– The tea was poisoned, of course…

– But I haven't had any tea? Lasko yelped.

The old man in the mist laughed out aloud.

– But that just isn't true, my dear man. You've had tea quite a few times during your life, and upon your own admission quite a few times the last week alone.

Caine grew to a giant in Lasko's eyes, and his facial skin faded to the point of being transparent and the skull being clearly visible. Lasko gasped painfully. He backed off, and ran away the fastest he was able, ran until his breath was ragged and he was hardly able to do anything but gasping. The house, its very walls was whispering to him, laughing at him, and the massive contempt assaulting him made him shake even harder.

There were two doors ahead of him. One led outside and the other further inside the shadow and mist of the Caine Manor. He threw himself through the open door to the outside world, and drew fresh and life-giving air into his pained lungs.

He emerged into the wealthy neighborhood, with the manor, the church and an entire street of luxurious homes. There were lots of cars there, but none he recognized as his own, and he shook his head in bewilderment and distress, unable to comprehend how that could be. People stared at him. He felt them staring. The next street looked pretty much like the one he had left, except for there being no church and no manor. Everything looked the same and everything dissolved into mist before his eyes. He finally found a bus stop, and sat down there, hiding his face in his hands, sitting there for minutes, shaking to pieces.

The bus finally arrived. He entered it, paid the fare and sat down. It took time before he could sit down, having stumbled most of the way to his seat, but the driver didn't rush from the stop, like most drivers Lasko could recall, and Lasko shook his head in incredulity. This was just too much, too much to take in.

The bus drove on, in a sedate, pleasant pace. People in a wealthy neighborhood could enjoy life more, at a slower pace, he supposed.

They had cars, and their cars didn't vanish without a trace. He sniffed a bit and dried tears from a wet cheek.

He stepped off the bus in some quiet street he didn't recognize. It was at the center of the city, close to the police headquarters, that was all he knew. The city looked completely alien to him. He could just as well have landed on Mars.

The parking lot loomed before him, quiet and insanely vast. His given spot wasn't that far off, that far away from the exit, but it felt like a marathon run.

His car wasn't there. It just wasn't. He shook his head in confusion, glancing around at the neighboring spots, with no success. Boundless bewilderment revealed itself in the flickering eyes.

His cell ringed, with a tone, a melody he didn't recognize. He drew it from his pocket and tentatively pushed the green button.

– Yes?

– You will find your car at the parking lot of the police headquarters. He recognized Caine's caustic voice.

He looked around a few more times.

– It isn't here, he heard himself say.

– Of course it is, *old chap,* Caine insisted. – I had it towed away from my yard. We couldn't let it stand there, of course.

– Why… not? Lasko croaked.

– Because you will never leave the castle, Caine chuckled. – We couldn't let it stand there and rot, you know.

– WHAT ARE YOU TALKING ABOUT

Lasko whispered.

– Don't you worry, the deeply condescending voice kept hassling him. – It is parked there, right now.

– But it *isn't,* Lasko whimpered.

– Of course it is, and it will stay there until you are declared dead, and they will sell it for a nice price to one of your younger, brighter colleagues.

The click sounded like thunder in his ears. The cell phone slipped from his hand and hit the ground far below. What would normally be a sharp crack sounded muted and dull in his ears. He had a notion after that, of wandering through the halls of the police headquarters, but didn't feel confident in its authenticity, no, not at all. On the contrary, everything he saw, everyone he encountered looked fake, like carbon card copies of the real thing, and they were no different from them all like they usually appeared to him, as the real fake people that made him throw up in contempt. He did, or at least he believed he did. His left hand dried vomit from his jaw. He felt his hand turn wet. He did did did

There was a mirror and a man, a total stranger staring at him with insane eyes. A brief flash, lasting an eternity, and it was gone, not more than the puff of smoke he feared it would be, and he wanted to scream, but couldn't utter a single sound, and he screamed his lungs out, a scream exempt of happiness, devoid of release.

He found himself in the Pit, without any idea or notion of how he had ended up there. A man ran, ran so hard that no matter how hard he gasped he couldn't breathe.

The Pit was filled with people tonight, stumbling back and forth without hope, without any expectation of a better tomorrow.

A man stood there, frozen in his tracks, staring straight ahead, his eyes never shifting or focusing on all the passing people. He repeated the same sentence again and again and again with the same dull voice and expression, without hope of ever receiving a reply.

– I'm looking for the Man with the Plan. Have you seen him? Have you seen the Man with the Plan?

Lasko walked on, never looking back. He saw, or believed he saw the pained expression of Albert Monroe somewhere, but if he did it faded away the moment it appeared. His partner was just one of many ghosts staring at him from the corner of his eyes. It was all so intangible, so horrible. He grabbed the nearest traffic light pole, and held on to it for minutes, just to make sure it was solid, and it was, solid like mist a chilly morning, before the sun rose and blew it away. The choke rising from his throat seemed real, though, like a kick in the groin. He stumbled on.

– Things can go wrong so fast, you know. A total stranger stood there and grinned at him. – With a blink of an eye everything may have changed and you're fucked.

Lasko fled from him, from all the silent stares.

There was a square at the heart of the Pit, Altman Square, called Pit Lake for some unfathomable reason. It appeared to him as a large gap, swallowing him whole. He felt its teeth, heard them gnaw against each other, and he wanted to scream his heart out, and he did, but no sound came, because it was stuck in his throat, like everything else.

He saw a woman cross the square, the lake and felt like he was supposed to recognize her, but she was a total unknown, a person he had never before encountered.

A large, two-legged monster with an alligator head entered the waters of rock and dust. It grabbed the nearest people passing by, and it began devouring them, cutting them to pieces with large, shiny teeth.

Lasko screamed, screamed himself hoarse. He sat down on the closest bench. It had been newly painted and stank of paint. The monster burped, and swam to its hideout at the edge of the lake, where it smiled content and laid itself to rest.

A man sitting on a newly painted bench cried out to all those busybodies passing by:

– I'm looking for the Man with the Plan. Have you seen him? Have you seen the Man with the Plan?

Fields, fields of rotting grass stretched on forever. There was no end to it, no matter how far he ran, and he ran far. A drunken moon swayed and burped as it crossed the sky on its way to nowhere.

Lasko just sat there, on the rotted bench, and he kept sitting there, long after they had come and taken him away. He stared straight ahead and never moved his eyes again, not even when they moved a flashlight in front of his face. Some of the doctors wanted to pronounce him braindead, but that clearly wasn't right either. Some wanted to pronounce him dead outright, but since he was obviously breathing, to some extent, in a way that was measurable by precise instruments, though not obvious to human observers they didn't. They stored him in a dark room and forgot about him.

He sat there, staring at nothing, smelling, tasting, hearing, sensing nothing. Grains of sand fell in an even flow from his open mouth.

The city rose above its citizens. Its night descended on the revelers wandering its streets and alleys tonight. A group of four fire-breathers performed in the presence of a large crowd in a narrow alley in the shadow of the Square. The crowd swayed in drunken pleasure, and hummed to the beat of the muted, broken drum. A man with two teeth in his mouth broke into laughter, and its jagged edge made them all bleed.

The bar was filled with smoke and sweat. A woman entered it through a door hidden in mist. The sportsbook room inside turned indistinct, almost absent in his mind. She took one of the drinks in the line of glasses put before her by the bartender. She took two. Then she… stopped. She just remained there on the stool for a while, allowing it all to sink in, feeling the weight and space of the heavy roll of bills in her pocket, the even heavier weight of the money note in her wallet, the knife in her pocket. There was a sense of desperation in her worn features, in the beautiful doll-face making every male stare crazy as a loon at her.

– I am the WoMan with the Plan, she grinned to the bartender, and the bartender croaked and fell hard on the floor behind the bar.

In the sportsbook room players waved their worn bills, and screamed at the fate clouding their minds.

Many tales are told about the WoMan with the Plan, in many different places and lands. It changes with times, with viewpoint and circumstances, as the centuries race on.

Some people claim to recognize him (or her), in a glimpse, at the edge of the eye. Others say, cloaked in terror that they have never before encountered anything even similar to such a being. The fates, the stories told by the fires say both claims are true.

It is said that the bartender waited with infinite patience until the place was empty, and then began drinking. It is said he is drinking still.

The woman that is a man, the man that is a woman (or women) wandered a thousand fires. It is said It is wandering still.

The hotel manager (whoever he was) fell fast from grace. He couldn't cut it, the story goes, and lost his footing, never to find it anew. It might just be an urban legend, but they say he became a bum wandering the city, searching the garbage cans for a scrap of food and old glory. He had taken a wrong turn once, they said, and never recovered from that series of unfortunate events. Long and shiny teeth welcomed him and everybody else like him in the darkness, in the gnawing teeth of the city and never let go.

Part 4:
The Lady of the Lake - The Chloe Webster story

«What are questions, except more questions? What are answers, except an endless row of mirrors showing nothing but your own face staring back at you? What are riddles, except cries in the night, fading away to confusion at the coming of dawn»?

Tales of the thousand fires
Chapter 3, verse 16

CHAPTER ELEVEN

Eternity passed and passed again. What had been no longer mattered. They had once been gods. Now, they had become something far more.

They were three creating the world, creating reality long ago, three creatures floating in the ancient void, in a slowly cooling energy sphere.

And in that cooling sphere energy turned to matter and matter to flesh. What had once been became once again.

They remembered. Slowly they began to get a sense of themselves again, to feel, see, smell, taste and sense, and not only be. They had become mind again, mind scattered across the vast Space the sphere had become. And suddenly, as they turned aware, as they noticed each other, as they regained their individuality, their sense of Self... perhaps what they had been mattered more than ever.

2

Across the square there was an old warehouse, abandoned to time and dust.

The young woman moved into the derelict old apartment building one chilly night. She didn't bring much stuff, hardly more than the bag she carried on her shoulder, the small suitcase in her hand, and the fairly new camera she wore in a chain around her neck.

Chloe Webster moved into the apartment in the Pit at November seventeenth. Her new neighbors stared at her, through the walls, as she moved through dark, moist hallways. Their eyes lingered on her sore skin and burned her bones.

She walked through the practically abandoned bus station late in the evening, having just stepped off the last bus for the day. Stairs from platform eight led, like from all the rest down to a long, broad and chilly hallway. She walked past seven, and six, where there were no longer any stairs, but just a wall of concrete where the stairs once had been, and five and below, and entered into the fairly warm entrance hall with quite a few shops and restaurants and stuff. The burger joint was still open. She wasn't hungry and walked right outside, into the moist and cold air.

The station, a part of a large wasteland between what most people considered the real city and the Pit loomed behind her. Steam rose above the dark mass ahead of her, surrounding it like a mushroom. There were just a few more steps and then the Pit swallowed her whole.

She ascended all the stairs in the dark hall and hallways, breathing hard, but never stopping, not for a second. Her apartment loomed at the end of the fifth floor. She looked at the key in her hand as if it was pure gold, a single shiny trinket in a garbage heap. It fit the lock, and when she turned it, it unlocked the door. She opened the old, heavy wood with an effort, feeling a sense of relief. An intruder would need a truck to break down this door.

She looked out through the dirty window, at Altman Square, at Pit Lake, at its countless lights and shadows, and shades of neither. People crossed it back and forth in what was both a predestined and random pattern. She walked through her fairly big apartment, her new home. It wasn't so bad. She had seen worse, much worse. The walls had scratches. The carpet in the living room had holes. The tap was dripping. Things like that stared her in the face. But it didn't annoy her or bothered her, really.

The suitcase and the bag called to her, waited for her to open them, to undo them. She waited a little while longer, before taking on the task, the bittersweet task.

Her possessions were brought out in the open, one by one. They didn't amount to much and hardly seemed to make any impression in the fairly large room. From the bottom of her bag she pulled four small rag dolls and put them in a chair.

– Greetings, Marion, Desire, Victor and Andy, she said softly, in an eerie voice. – It's good to meet again, here, in this place of our dream.

They didn't voice any reply, but sat there, staring at her, with their deep, dark eyes.

She drew, with obvious skill a pentacle on the table, and placed the five candles at the five points of the star.

– I have been fasting the entire day, she whispered. – And prepared myself strenuously. It's time! It's finally and inevitably time!

There was no hunger anymore, no pangs of pain in her stomach, just the light sense of floating and of fatigue. She lit the candles, using one matchstick to light each. The five ebony surfaces cast their shadow across the table. She picked a book from her small selection and opened it on a specific page. It was clearly a diary of sorts, filled with handwriting and drawings of strange symbols.

– I was so lucky in finding this, she marveled. – It was as if it sort of *fell* into my possession. I knew when I first spotted it that it was *special*. There is a *mystery* here, one ancient and powerful, waiting for me, or someone like me, to uncover and grab.

There were a few more items on the table. She removed some of them and positioned the others better.

– I go, she chanted. – I walk the Path. I go where no one has gone before me.

She walked to the kitchen and tapped herself a glass of water, and returned to the living room, the large, expanding space in her immediate surroundings. There were five seeds in her hand. She put them all in her mouth and swallowed them with a fall of water, burning like acid in her throat and stomach. A sound of a dark bell shook her and the air and the space itself. It shouldn't be. It was too early, but here it was already. She hadn't yet begun, but it had begun still. Excitement and anticipation shook her.

– I begin the Long Walk, she cried. – I reveal myself to the world and it reveals itself to me.

To me!

She undressed slowly, crouching slightly as the first pangs of pain revealed themselves. The clothes faded away as she picked them off one by one. She began drawing symbols on her skin. One of a half moon on her belly, one of an ankh on her left breast, an incomprehensible sign that was a mix of a snake and a lion and a latrid spike across her thigh. She imagined the latrid spike in her mind, its sweeping cuts and deep wounds, its constantly changing features.

And on her thigh the spike and lion and snake began to change, to flow and rise, until it floated in the air before her lips, and she took the bite of the air and devoured it whole.

She gasped as she climbed the table, as she sat down on her naked ass at the center of the pentacle, as she crossed her legs and embraced herself with her snake-like arms.

– I die and I live, and in the great scheme of things it's all the same.

The same!

The echo sighed in her ears, and her ears started bleeding.

– In six and one days I recreate the world, the sound of a sleepy, powerful voice filled the expanding space. – I reach back into the Void, creating everything from nothing. I have no name. I name myself!

I name myself!

– We walk this path the five of us, she cried. – We Fall down this road of nothing, decorating it with our blood and guts and sinew and bone.

She grabbed the knife and began cutting herself, in a wild frenzy, making blood and skin hit the table and floor in a totally unpredictable pattern. It didn't make any sense to her and she kept cutting herself, kept working herself up.

The room fell silent. The loud screams and wails faded. She heard one final sound as the knife fell from her hand and hit the table, hit the floor.

The markings on her skin and the paint on the floor dissolved and solved in her eyes, in her deaf ears, as a dissonant sound rose from the depths of the Void and filled the creature that had dared to venture these scattered lands.

The creature gasped. The face no longer a face crumbled. The body fell on the side, fell hard, making walls crack and break. All the candles were put out. The room turned dark and hot and moist. The body rested unmoving, there on the slab. Wax and blood kept flowing into the void, becoming the Void, being… born.

Being born!

On the first day

She looked out through the dirty window, at Altman Square, at Pit Lake, in the sharp morning light.

The suave, young woman moved into the worn down hotel in the early morning. The man behind the desk didn't look up until she had taken many steps inside the hall, but kept looking at his papers until she had almost stopped in front of him. Very professional, very competent, Chloe Webster thought.

– Good morning, ma'am, he greeted her. – May I help you?

– I would like a room, please, she said sweetly.

– Certainly, ma'am, he replied, with a slight, audible irony in his voice. – We have rooms. What kind do you have in mind?

Chloe blinked. Was that a rhyme?

– One high up, please, with a view of the lake.

He looked at her, now, wondering if there was a hint of sarcasm in her voice.

– I regret to inform you that the elevator is out of order, ma'am.

– That's perfectly okay, she said sweetly. – I'll use the stairs.

He relented, sort of and began filling out the papers.

– It's still early, she stated. – Is breakfast still available? Will that be okay? I mean, I have arrived today, but I would surely appreciate it.

– Yes, ma'am, he replied, reddening above the collar. – That will be quite okay. Breakfast will be available for at least another hour. Just bring your keycard.

She walked the stairs, the many stairs. The hotel was really two buildings, with the bridge over to its other, equally worn down part. The young woman felt suspended in the air, when she looked out through the glass walls, at the world far below. She stood in her room and looked out through the dirty window, at Altman Square, at Pit Lake, in the sharp morning light. People were scurrying back and forth down there, in an undetermined pattern. She raised her head slightly and looked across the lake at the darkened building there. There were lights in a few windows, but aside from that it looked dark and abandoned.

Breakfast was a pleasant surprise. The room and tables were clean, and the food was actually quite okay. Chloe enjoyed the simple setting, drinking a lot of juice and milk to the sandwiches. An old lady with a thousand wrinkles in her face looked at her with disdain. Chloe pretended not to notice. She was quite practiced in ignoring people casting her that kind of attention.

Chloe had coffee. She had tea, and she actually felt pretty good when the meal was done. With the pleasant memory of good, tasty sandwiches, good tea and good coffee she retreated to the small garden by the bridge afterwards. She danced a bit, hummed a bit, before her shyness got the best of her and she retreated to her room. The bathroom was nice, too. The water was hot, and she remained in the shower for quite some time, before she felt she had to leave. She grabbed one of the towels and began rubbing herself strenuously.

She stopped before the mirror, the cracked mirror and looked at herself, at the dark hair, the ivory skin, and flushed face and greenish eyes, hard muscles and generous forms and... Her lips moved, as if speaking, as if she was breathing hard. No one looked at her, she knew that, but still felt as if someone did. She dressed leisurely, deliberately taking her time, as if challenging the unseen eyes, savoring the unusually powerful cold trickle down her spine.

– I have arrived. She recorded her thoughts with her cell phone. – I can feel the *mood* wherever I go, but most of all in the house across the lake. It reminds me of one of those old, Victorian houses.

She paused.

– I will go there, of course, but taking my time, bidding my time, approach it slowly, at a natural pace.

Outside the hotel there was this dusty construction site. No work had been done on it for ages, obviously. Trees had been growing tall since the last worker had left. It was a mere ruin, really, with a few suggestions of what could have become a building. Passing by or stopping both was a strange experience.

Chloe crossed the lake, glimpsing herself in the water below. She walked right into the old, derelict building, up the stairs, to the large space at the top. A push, a little effort, a hard push, and the large double doors squeaked open. Daylight flooded her eyes through the large open window. The entrance, strangely enough was at the bedroom. Chloe walked around in the large, vast space, taking it in, getting a sense of it, touching the shelf above the fireplace, getting dust on her fingers, staring into the mirror. There was a large twin bed to the right. She walked further into the apartment, to the living room, stopping before the large table by the window.

A shiver passed through her. She stood there, frozen for a while, without any discernible thought in her head, not any she cared to remember, anyway. Then, abruptly she hurried out of there, back into the warm, warm sunshine.

Her watering eyes noticed a worn bench in the southeastern corner of the Square. She walked to it, but didn't sit down. It had been painted recently, amazingly so, but its appearance was still marred by the fact that someone had sat on it before the painting had dried, creating an imprint that looked almost alive in her eyes. She consulted her watch and walked off. Those looking at her could see that she was clearly in a hurry.

She walked a few more blocks, to a retirement home at the edge of the Pit. It gave her pretty much the same impression as the rest of the area: Someone had forgotten about it long ago, and left it to rot. If they had ever had a gardener on the payroll, he had clearly retired, too. The lawn wasn't mowed. The plants grew wild.

A wild garden, Chloe beamed encouraged.

The gate squeaked when she open it and squeaked differently when she closed it. An old woman, another old woman sat in a chair staring down the overgrown driveway, staring at Chloe, hissing at her, spitting at her, as she approached and passed her, and entered the building.

A young girl with large bags under her eyes and a cigarette hanging from her lips and a sour, very sour disposition sat behind the desk in the reception. Chloe decided to go straight to the point.

– My name is Chloe Webster, she presented herself. – I work for the investigative magazine «Colors in the Night».

– Are you expected? The girl shrugged, clearly poised to become very inhospitable.

– I have an appointment with the administrator, Jason Wynyard in… thirty seconds, Chloe enlightened her, deliberately looking at her watch.

The girl consulted her book or pretended to do so.

– Mr. Wynyard will see you now, she shrugged.

A little bit of ashes fell from her cigarette and into her already suspiciously looking very stinking coffee.

Chloe knocked on the door at the end of the long, dank hallway. She imagined she heard a muffled «come» and opened the door.

She noticed something about him, sensing it almost instantly, from when she saw him rise from his chair, saw him smile and welcome her by reaching out his hand. When she blinked he didn't look like Jason Wynyard at all, but someone else, someone completely different. It was hard to keep her hand from shaking when she turned on the recorder and placed her cell phone on the table, and even harder to understand why.

– Mr. Wynyard, she began curtly, courteously. – I'm investigating the Keller-building at Pit Lake and the entire Pit, really, investigating the numerous *sightings* there.

– I figured you would, Ms. Webster, but why come to me? I'm not one to believe in sightings, really. Your magazine is *way* too speculative for me. Science is my trade, or used to be, before… before things got out of hand.

– I know there are more things between heaven and Earth than are being dreamt of in any philosophy, Mr. Wynyard. She leaned forward, leaned back in her seat. – I have seen it, not only one time, but many, and I always do extensive research before I begin on a project, and know which stones to turn. I have a knack for it, you see.

– And you dabble, where you should dig, spending your entire life searching for what is always just out of reach, forced to work with a… questionable rag like Colors of the Night, everything they print, every evidence you find blatantly and deservedly ignored by the ignorant public. Poor Chloe!

His words… made the pain inside grow, and she stifled a gasp with the greatest of efforts. Images floated behind her eyes, meaningless, indistinct, and out of sync.

She wanted to shrug, to show him how little his therapist tactics meant to her, fearing he would look right through her.

– You knew Justin Keller, didn't you, knew David Fallon Somby and have kept your close relationship with Marlon Caine to this day?

– I did, and I do, but so what, Chloe? Wynyard grinned. – May I call you Chloe?

– Please, Jason. Chloe smiled wickedly. – Between the three of you, you were so steeped in the occult that you would drown in it.

– Poor David certainly did, Wynyard grinned even wider. – But we wouldn't. We've mastered it. But you are, you know… drowning, I mean.

– Excuse me.

Suddenly she felt panic, wide and bad, and she couldn't for the life of her see why.

– You don't know what you are, do you? His smile vanished completely, from one breath to the next. – You don't remember who you are, and you are lost beyond repair, in your confusion and denial. That's so satisfying, such a reason for celebration. You have come here, and thus placing yourself at my mercy.

She wanted to move, to scream, but found she couldn't do either. It was even impossible for her to follow him with her eyes as he rose and moved around, behind her back.

He placed his ice-cold hooks in her neck, and now she was able to scream, at least inside.

She sat there, interviewing him, and nothing spectacular was happening. He answered her questions, patiently, if somewhat unsatisfying, never moving from his chair, hardly ever moving at all. She frowned, unsure at what was wrong, if anything was wrong. Sweat kept pouring from her brow, blinding her, keeping her from seeing clearly, and fear settled in her gut.

Why won't you tell me what I need to know? She whimpered and begged him.

– C'mon, she retorted to one of his replies, – you can do better than that.

– I'm afraid I can't, Ms. Webster, he said with (false) regret, dismissing her with a wave of his hand. – You just have to take your badly phrased questions and ill-suited inquiry elsewhere.

That should have angered her, and certainly should have made her ask a pointed follow-up question, but she found herself unable in both regards, and she wondered what was wrong with her.

She left, and when she looked at her watch, she was shocked to see that two hours had passed. Stepping out, into the bright sunshine was like stepping into a freezer. She shook violently. The frown didn't fade, but deepened as she returned to the Pit, as she sat on the painted bench and listened to the recording, unable to tell what it was there, between the words and fairly pleasant conversation (she had experienced worse) that frightened her so.

He cut her open, and she howled in misery and eternal pain.

She decided, on a whim to have dinner at the hotel. A woman with dead eyes and pale, beyond unhealthy skin stood unmoving on the corner ahead.

– CAN YOU SENSE IT? She shouted. – CAN YOU FEEL THE WORLD'S SUFFERING RISE FROM A CROWD OF PUTRID CORPSES?

The walking corpse cried out in about thirty seconds' intervals, to everybody passing by.

Chloe didn't feel it was directed specifically at her, but at anyone, and wasn't sure if that fact made her feel better or worse.

The dining hall was only half full this early. Chloe slammed her keycard on the table in front of the half-asleep waiter. The woman looked at her with dull eyes, more dull eyes.

– I know this isn't a five-star hotel, Chloe said icily, – but it is still a hotel, right?

The waiter started moving somewhat. Chloe walked to her table.

He cut her into pieces, and she was beyond screaming at this stage and just looked at him with huge, begging eyes.

– You're just another broken toy, now, a free-for-all means to an end.

The spoon shook in Chloe's hand, and she spilled hot soup on her finger. She swore out aloud, making everybody sitting even remotely close cringe in their seats.

Time disappeared for her. Minutes could go away without her having any idea what had happened in-between.

Take this ring, as a token of my love.

– I must be going mad, she whined loud and clear.

She ate her steak, but didn't really eat, except by picking crumbs from her table. Suddenly she sat there with wet cheeks and discovered that tears fell on the plate in front of her and mixed with the sauce.

– Is everything all right, ma'am? The waiter asked her.

Chloe jumped to her feet, spilling sauce on the other woman's arm. She rushed from the dining area without looking back, and didn't stop until she reached the vestibule, almost unable to draw breath.

The sound of the labored breath wheezed in her ears. Whispers rose from all the corners and dark areas in her surroundings. She halted in her tracks and suddenly looked straight at the old movie poster depicting Marlon Caine. Rage and fear warred within her, none making sense.

She wandered the streets in circles for hours after that, never really leaving the Pit, as if she couldn't, as if it pulled her in, never letting go. The pained look in her face never went away, revealing itself to her as reflections in windows and shiny surfaces, a horrible, distorted expression on the fender of a car.

The area around the bus station was fairly peaceful in the evening. After the afternoon rush hour it turned quiet, even ominous. She sat there, on a bench, unable to stop shaking.

She forced herself to open her laptop, to begin receiving the data transmission. It would take some time to download. She had to go at least this far to do it. The Internet didn't work anywhere inside the Pit, a fact that various providers and scientists had made desperate acts attempting to counteract for years.

A bird almost landed on her, before putting the full breaks on, and with a loud screech once more taking to the skies. Chloe looked in disbelief at the bloody wings falling to the ground around her.

She sat there, for a long time, slowly calming down, settling into a state of something akin to apathy, a deadly calm she didn't understand and didn't care to probe.

There was a commotion somewhere. She frowned again, attempting to focus, to return to the world.

A man ran back and forth, from one part of the yard to the other.

– Marian? The man cried. – Marian? WHERE ARE YOU, MARIAN?

She noticed him after he had shouted a few times, after he had run a few times back and forth.

People scurried back and forth across the high walking bridge between the bus station and the railway station. She studied them through the glass walls.

The buses and the trains left the stations far more infrequently. She saw less and less people, as darkness fell and night drew close. A bus left, and silence fell and perception rose. Tall buildings swayed in the wind, the restless, silent wind. Her ears heard it. Her skin didn't feel it. But it was there. She sensed the whispers, but didn't hear them.

The download was complete. She closed the laptop, but didn't move from her spot.

She sat there, enjoying the late, very late Indian Summer night.

The man from earlier that day approached her, finally. She had expected him for quite some time.

– Have you seen her, seen Marian?

Then he seemed to catch himself, in his infinite sadness and despair, and a glimmer of reason returned to his eyes.

– Have you seen a beautiful woman with black hair pass by here?

– I'm sorry, Chloe shook her head. – I haven't seen anyone.

Reason left his eyes anew and he ran off, shouting the same meaningless phrase.

– Marian? Marian? WHERE ARE YOU, MARIAN?

Sounds rose from below, cutting into Chloe. She bit her lip, bit it hard. The pain made numbing fear go away, and give way to anger. Chloe rose and her feet steered her back to the Pit. It once again swallowed her whole and spat her back out. A cold draft hit her, chilled her. Blood filled her mouth. She had bit herself somewhere, unable to tell where.

She walked back alone, through the pitch black alleys and narrow streets of the Pit. Creatures hissed at her as she passed them, as she spat blood at them. They looked human. To her eyes they looked normal, but to her

Sight they appeared as the vilest of forms. If they had ever been human beings they had rescinded their birthright long ago.

The hotel still looked fairly bright, compared to the rest of the Lake. She returned, briefly to her room to pick up her stuff. It didn't take long. A few pulls and pushes, and she was done. She descended the stairs and felt everything, felt herself change, felt wild hope and abandon cross and criss and whip her mercilessly. The clerk had practically fallen asleep, as usual. She dumped the keycard at the counter with a loud crack. The clerk's eyes opened wide and shocked.

– I'm checking out, she said. – I'm moving to greener pastures.

She grinned when he looked in disbelief at her.

Desperation and despair gnawed at her, at her insides like razorblades, but didn't quite reach the surface. In her lowest moments she wanted it to.

He didn't get the joke. How could he?

The grocery store nearby was fairly well supplied. They did have food, and they also had other, more exotic ingredients she could use to mix her potions and cast her spells.

– So, what are you doing in this neighborhood? The rather heavy woman behind the counter asked, not really interested. – It isn't really your turf, is it?

– It is exactly my turf, Mrs. Henderson, Chloe replied. – I have been pulled to places of mystery and imagination and the hidden treasures of the world since I was a little girl.

– So, you are that sort, are you, the woman snorted. – And have you ever found anything making it all worth it?

The old woman tried to keep herself from staring.

How did you know my name?

I know everybody's name, Louisa.

I've found love, friendships and countless joys, Chloe replied lightly, Louisa's startled and annoyed reaction giving her momentary satisfaction. – And that's just the start of it.

She caught a glance of herself again, of her troubled expression in the window, on her way out. It didn't go away, no matter how hard she tried to make it.

A man appeared before her, startling her, until she realized, again that he wasn't truly here.

– Poor Chloe, born so gifted and forced to squander it on trifles, working for a rag like Colors in the Night, begging for favors, picking crumbs at the table of life.

Go away, Malakay, she shouted at him, suddenly even more dizzy and queasy.

He faded away, like the specter he was.

People stared at her, like they always did. She knew they stared.

They always did, god damn them.

She walked across the Square, to the old Keller building. It welcomed her, like a second skin, and she sighed in gratitude. The walk up the stairs seemed endless. She pushed open the doors to the bedroom. The echo of her sigh returned to her.

White (gray, dusty) sheets covered everything, the bed, the chairs, the tables and a broken television set. She removed all the sheets, and clouds of dust filled the apartment. The very air seemed to move around the tall woman, drawing shapes in the dust.

She dusted the entire apartment afterwards. It was therapeutic in a way, at least a distraction from all the shadows surrounding her.

There still was electricity here, even though it flickered constantly, as if it didn't really came properly through whatever obstruction that kept it from asserting itself. There were no working light bulbs, though, except for the one on the nightstand, for some obscure reason. She had lit a number of candles in every room.

The sound of the vacuum cleaner faded, its many coughs re-delegated into her memory.

She opened her laptop and turned it on. After a while a number of images started flickering across the screen. Chloe wanted to look away, but locked her attention at the screen. Some were horrible documents of mutilated corpses, but she had seen a lot of that and was sort of used to it, sensitized to its reality. What most people would call obscure signs and symbols worried her more. Contrary to most people they weren't meaningless to her. She knew their meaning, at least to a point.

On a wall was drawn in blood ancient Egyptian symbols. She stopped the slideshow.

– «Here lies Beelzebub, Lady of the High and Low Places. One day she will rise again».

This was partly the evidence from the investigation into the murder of David Fallon Somby. Some would claim the case was solved to everybody's satisfaction. Others would scream foul and bloody murder.

And Somby's grisly death was only a part of it. The Cult of Beelzebub was another factor. There were a dozen others, thousands of smaller and bigger pieces of the puzzle, to those daring to put it together. Chloe rocked back and forth on the bed, on the cold fabric covering the bed, unused for so long, dead to the world, but now she sensed its heat, felt it grow, as her butt and thighs turned numb and cold.

She opened the final file. Violet Connors appeared on the screen.

– That should be everything, she said to the camera in front of her. – You owe me one, and keep me out of it, will ya, whatever happens. I can't be implicated. My career is already in shambles because of you.
– Thank you, Chloe mumbled. – I can't tell you how much I appreciate your help.
– Are you sure you wanna *do* this anymore? What has it brought you but hassle and grief?
– And your invaluable input, Chloe mumbled.
She started pacing back and forth on the floor, so fast that the curtains moved when she passed them. Once in a while she would stop and stare at the curtains, to see if they still moved. They didn't. She walked from one end of the room to the other, replying, occasionally to the one-sided conversation of her old friend and acquaintance, as if this wasn't a recording and Violet wasn't miles away.
– There are rumors that the Cult of Beelzebub is revived, Connors said. – No solid evidence, but enough for lone, investigative reporters looking for them to be *worried.*
– You're calling me an investigative reporter? Chloe struck out with her hands. – That's so nice and so generous of you…
But then, right afterwards:
– What are you doing, anyway? This isn't your job. You're not a cop and you're working for a rag called Colors of the Night, one that would just as well print pure fallacy. There is no need for you to risk anything, to chase shadows the way you do, especially not in a cesspool like the Pit. You should pull out as fast as you can.
– I have to stay, Chloe cried. – I have to, need to keep searching.
The curtains flickered. She froze. The curtains moved, as if a great wind swept through the room. But there was nothing like that. There was a cold, cold draft, but not the sort that moved her hair or her clothes.
But one that hammered her spine like an Antarctic wind.
– Well, take care of yourself, Violet sighed. – And please, don't be a stranger.
– I am a stranger, Chloe stated.
She turned off the laptop and closed it. The last sound in the room faded to nothing, and she heard the hum, what she had always heard, and would always hear.
It pulled her in, like a vortex, and she answered its call.
She rested on the bed for a while, fully clothed, uncomfortable and anxious. The sounds and dancing shadows so prevalent in the room both attracted and repulsed her. She grew hungry, as she was bound to, as she

hadn't eaten all day. Fasting, either deliberately or by default, always made her feel giddy and volatile.

Fasting, emptying yourself opens you up, brings out in the open everything hidden within, Malakay, her old teacher in Magick had taught her.

She could practically hear his dry, spiteful voice, sense him, as if he was here, with her, as if he always was. It made her shudder in loathing. She wanted to stay here, wanted to leave. The window pulled her, and she slid out of the bed and walked to the square opening ahead, looking outside.

Almost all the streetlights were out. No one or only idiots changed light bulbs in the Pit. People sought this place, from all over the world because they enjoyed the darkness. She certainly did. It drew her in like a sponge. Her stomach growled. She rushed to the door, and opened it, and the pitch black Void opened up to her, and froze her in place. It threatened to swallow her whole, a giant mouth wanting to chew her and spit her out.

She slammed the door shut and ran back to bed and crouched there, shaking badly, her body pulled into fetal position.

Time lost all meaning. The growling in her belly turned to dull pain, turned to a dull nothing. She could feel herself open up, as she more or less deliberately cut herself, opened up like the sweetest and foulest of flowers. Her body writhed on the bed. Her spirit flowed through the Void, creating worlds and the deepest and most powerful strands of night and fire.

She descended the stairs and walked through the streets, the streets of dancing flames and shadows.

There were people outside, always, a lot of them strolling around, grinning to other wanderers in the night, and Chloe found herself grinning, too, even though she knew more than them, more than most of them about what was out there, lurking in the corners and alleys of the world.

It felt so pleasant, the sensation of the night breeze on your sparse clothing and naked skin.

She had a burger at the nearest kitchen, a worn, forlorn place at Winslow and sixth. It tasted like the most delicious culinary meal.

It filled her as she walked, the difficult to digest food wrangling itself through her system, making her even more queasy and delirious.

People had lit a fire in an old gasoline barrel. They gathered around it in a circle, warming themselves, even though the night air was swelling with heat. There was a lot of that here.

This particular group wasn't dressed in rags, but in fairly new clothes. Their poverty and desolation weren't exactly in their visible, outward appearance, but in their eyes and the shadows in their faces.

Space Lout was a downtrodden bar and tavern on the south side, right across the street from the bus and railway stations. So close, so far, far away. Chloe grabbed some kind of dark beer from the bar and headed into the deepest recesses of the spacious room. She sat down in the corner, covered by the shadows of broken bulbs. The music and the buzz warred for her attention, and she rejected them both. A part of her rocked to the music, another listened to those in the gathering she could actually hear fairly easy… and yet another listened to the far deeper rumble rising from beneath.

She sat there, with half closed eyes, and took in everything in her surroundings, both seen and unseen. The room felt both small and infinite. The world stared at her from beyond the walls of three-dimensional space and thrills and chills coursed through her in waves.

There was a sportsbook room in the other section of the building, reached through a long, dimly lit hallway. Betting was fierce and they heard shouts of triumph and despair during the few moments the music let up. Chloe walked through the dimly lit hallway seemingly for an eternity. She sat there, studying the players and the dancers, of both rooms. The rooms mingled in her mind and turned indistinct. They were one and the same, and the people were the same, and everything blurred.

She rushed outside and stood there unmoving for minutes, unable to tell why she was shaking like a leaf.

People passed by her, and she hardly noticed them. They blurred around the edges at first, and then a woman's face changed, until she had completely new features and hardly could be said to be the same person anymore. Chloe stood there, stood still. A man stood at the corner. She could have sworn he was studying her, but no matter how much she strived she was unable to be certain of that fact.

She walked back inside, deliberately, making sure she didn't clench her teeth, but she still feared that anyone studying her, any of the thousand eyes watching her would easily see through her façade of confidence, see her indecision, her shaking insides.

Time haunted her. She feared she didn't get it right, no matter how many times she looked at her watch. There was a large clock on the wall, an old-fashioned mechanical watch. She heard it tick, heard it beat, like a heart. The man from the corner outside entered the room. He didn't look at Chloe. To her it seemed like he went to great lengths to avoid looking at her. She shook her head, amused and bewildered by her own paranoia. It didn't seem like her at all.

People sat by the bar, having their obligatory conversation with the bartenders, getting drunker by the minute. A loud, very loud hunk dominated the «conversation».

– Did you know that the Pit was an entire lake once? It's said that pumps are working ceaselessly far below to keep the water from flooding the area.

The laughter was loud and noisy.

– That's one of the most obvious Urban Legends I've ever heard, man.

– It's true, the hunk cried, exercising his considerable frame to intimidate his opponents. – True!

The laughter wasn't so loud anymore, but there was still laughter.

– Oh, what do I care? The muscular man mumbled into his glass, before taking yet another large gulp of beer.

Something snapped inside Chloe, so unexpected and shocking, like a wave flooding a beach from nowhere, leaving her weak and drained. She rose from her position opposite the tall and handsome man, and threw her glass in the mirror, beer and all. Everything splintered in a thousand pieces.

Chloe stood at the middle of the floor, in the suddenly deadly silent room. Everybody stared at her with dull and swollen eyes.

– That's the problem with you lot, she shouted, she screeched. – You don't fucking CARE! None of you do! What a piece of yahoos you are!

She backed off until reaching the door. Then she turned and ran off, into the lonely and silent night.

Chloe returned to the house by the Square, by the Lake. She recalled only in dim glimpses what had happened. There had been drinking, a bit of dancing, of caustic laughter and that was all.

Piecemeal images and sensations kept haunting her as she ascended the stairs, the bitter taste of the light beer, of the piss water, the warm glow inside, as the rage swelled in her, briefly, the loud music, and other, unidentifiable factors. She pushed open and closed the big doors, like she had done so many times.

The wind was blowing outside. It shook the house. Its banshee whine hurt her ears.

Everything looked quiet outside, almost serene. Nothing seemed to be moving. Pit Lake looked like a painting. She shuddered in her memory, unable to tell why.

She wanted to put on her headphones and listen to some music, she wanted, yearned for the silence, the quiet, eerie darkness surrounding her.

The apartment was so big, almost like a house. To walk from one end to another was like crossing a field. She walked out on the balcony. There was no discernible, qualitative difference between the inside and the outside, no noticeable line to cross. She still sensed it, inside, where it counted, a ruffle of feathers, a light touch in the belly, a scratching on her soles.

Wings flapped before her in the darkness. She sensed the air push at her, gently and rough. A flash flared at her, not white, black, pitch black. It hit her like a wave. A mouth, the large, terrifying gap opened and the hot, moist air bathed her in its lap.

She retreated inside, to the bedroom, to the bed. The doors to the balcony slammed shut, hard. She went to bed with her clothes on, shivering hard, unable to stop, never quite getting warm.

Time stretched as she crouched there, in fetal position, and she couldn't make it speed up or slow down. Everything just stopped. She did, too, as she crouched there frozen and dead. Ghosts of grinning skulls danced before her closed eyes, and she couldn't make them go away.

Finally her eyes closed, and finally a long time after that she fell into a pitiful and troubled sleep.

CHAPTER TWELVE

On the second day

In a fever dream of distorted images and confusion she sailed a vast sea. They sailed for days and nights without number without spotting anything even resembling land. She attempted repeatedly to focus on her fellow travelers, but every time they just slipped away from her, into the mist surrounding both them and the ship.

When she finally woke up it was bright daylight. Her throat was parched and she was sweaty and uncomfortable. The finger with the ring hurt, and she winced in pain when she touched it. She remained in bed, haunted with indecision. The bed felt unpleasant, like bathing in stench and days-old body fluids, but she still dreaded the world outside its pleasant boundaries.

It took an effort to get up and out. She stood there in her damp clothes and looked down at the Square through a chink between the curtains. Mrs. Henderson returned from the grocery store, carrying two large and full plastic bags, smoking one of her stinking cigars. Chloe removed her clothes on her way to the shower. That, too, took an effort. She attempted to remove the ring, but it was stuck on her swollen finger and wouldn't let itself be removed. A choking sound pushed itself from her throat. She pulled hard, pulled until it hurt, in vain.

Water hit her. It hammered her, making her gasp for air. One minute it hit her, the next she was outside, in the bedroom again, drying her sensitive skin. The shower energized her, inevitably, but she still felt dizzy, out of whack. She dressed, choosing, after giving it some thought her brighter, flashier clothes. The image in the mirror smiled to her. She combed her hair, doing so thoroughly, using her large brush. It felt pleasant and decisively calmed her, her raging insides.

The hallway stayed dark, no matter how bright it was outside, but she was able to see slightly better and didn't need to hold onto the rail. The Square was busy. People heading for work rushed to the bus and railway station. Most of them worked far away from the Pit. Children and youth heading for school took their time, their good time. Disgust and a generally sour exposition dominated their features.

– It's a warm, warm day, isn't it? She says out of the blue to a boy passing by.

He looks at her with suspicion and contempt.

– It’s hot outside, she insisted, – but I can’t get warm, no matter what I do. I shiver in the midst of a heavy sweat. The cold drops are acid, burning my skin.

– Crazy broad, he mumbled.

He hurried away, fear evident in his eyes.

Everybody had their eyes on her when she entered the store. She knew that, even though very few actually looked directly at her. It was tangible, like a glow on her skin.

She picked her groceries in an ever-growing calm frenzy. Her stomach began growling in its vast emptiness. She couldn’t recall the last time she had eaten. The fat guy behind the counter glared at her. She ignored him and it made him glare even more. He took her money with his sweaty hand and she winced, and knew he wanted to strike her. She knew such things.

A guy tried to sneak in the queue, a woman stepped forward and stopped him from advancing further, and a rather tense mood developed. Chloe ignored it and returned outside, carrying her two full bags of groceries. She sensed how the water hit the shore of the lake, sensed its vast depths, right there, by her feet.

She had fruit first, had a banana, as she stood by the window and stared down at the Square, at its vast depths. The banana was devoured in a feeding frenzy and she proceeded to the apple, sensing the sugar rush almost immediately afterwards. She closed and opened her eyes. The texture of the world seemed… to grow, becoming something more, compared to what it had been.

Her stomach hurt. A mechanism unused for days turned to life again. She began pacing. It hardly felt like walking at all, but more like flowing, as if there was no floor there, no floor at all. A skull appeared there, beneath her. She forced herself to stop and look at it, glare at it with flashing eyes. It pulled back and faded away, and triumph and exaltation flowed through her in waves.

She wanted to go outside, but crawled back into the bed, lay there in fetal position. Every time she rose from the bed, she wanted to crawl back in. She jumped, as high as she was able, but she didn’t reach the ceiling, didn’t even come close to its watery, transparent surface.

Hours passed. She started making dinner early, deliberately, foreseeing her premature hunger. It came to her, as it always did like pangs of pain, beyond anything resembling reason.

The smell of food and spices filled the apartment, tickling her nostrils ever so pleasantly, but no matter how powerful the scent it couldn’t overcome the overpowering stench of rot.

She sat by the kitchen table and had her dinner. Flashes of taste, smell and sensations came to her. She spoke into the microphone of her cell phone.

– The building is *old,* she recorded, – far older than it is. It speaks to me like few other places have.

There was a long break, without her turning off the recording.

– Or… is it *me?* Have I coming here released something within me, something long dormant? Is the world opening up to me, like I am opening up to it?

She had her dinner, her steak, her vegetables and her desert, her soup, her water of spices and aromas. It was all so strange. She didn't usually have soup or any desert, but she was so hungry, so very hungry. Dizziness overwhelmed her. She would have fallen if she hadn't been safe there on her chair.

– Bits and pieces of the whole are everywhere, and I experience it here and there, but I am not content with it, with mere scraps and crumbs. I seek the place where I can find *everything…*

The words and the voices, the *choir* echoed through the room. She looked around her, looking for others, but she was alone.

– No, that doesn't sound presumptuous to me. I've always dreamed of that place, that state of mind. I can't ever remember not dreaming about it.

And just like that the visions, the feverish images and sensations began, about five people at the deck of a ship sailing the eternal seas. She blinked, attempting desperately to reject, to hold on to the sight unfolding before her. They faded, as she sat there, listening to the sound of her own breathing.

And she felt both bad and relieved.

Her right foot hurt a bit. She attempted to recall when she might have hurt it, in vain. There was a slight limp when she carried the glass and plate and stuff to the kitchen. She regained her more secure footing during the first few steps.

But the sense of being *dislocated* didn't leave her. It rattled at the periphery of her consciousness and made her glance around her, being almost constantly on edge.

She rushed back on the bed and turned on her laptop. The pictures from the two murder scenes of David Fallon Somby once again, yet again flashed before her eyes. She opened an illustrator program, and began drawing the pentacle in a 3D environment. The image formed in her head before she saw it on the screen. Her hand and fingers moved fast and confident. The pentacle formed by the final piece of the circle, and it seemed to glow slightly as she squinted her eyes. She added the other symbols, drew everything like the main photographs, from those various perspectives from the second murder, but then, upon completion she changed it, made it look at the room from a point above, from above the ceiling even, until the entire floor had been included, and…

It resembled, clearly the wall in Somby's house, the «painting». She had now two images, and they sort of complemented each other. Her heart raced as she imported the photographs, as her hand moved swiftly and anxiously. There were several hundred of them, and when all had been put together she saw it clearly, what had been only a dim scenery in her mind.

What was missing in one place was present in the other. Put together the composite image created what could be said to be a completely different scene.

It created an eerie effect of being a different room altogether, compared to both the two scenes making up the reinvented place. Police officers, both in uniform and not, tended to end up on some of the photographs, no matter how much the photographers complained about them blocking the shot. They tended to stand at the edge of the initial images, but when those parts became components of the whole the impression changed dramatically.

There were six of them, six people standing in the empty room. They were not exactly the police officers and detectives, but… different. Impossibly enough Chloe recognized Carter John, and the five other cult members, all of whom had been executed twenty years ago. At the very least there was a more than a passing resemblance. She anxiously checked the single images of the various people present, but none of them had any notable resemblance to John and the other five. They had placed themselves at each of the five points of the pentacle, and they glowed in a dark light. John stood at the base of the star, by the bed where they had placed Somby, by the place on the wall where David Fallon Somby had been strung up.

Chloe saved the composite image, closed the program, reopened it and recalled the image and it hadn't changed. Carter John stared right at her with his lustrous eyes. He stood by the tied up Somby with a knife in his hand.

Somby lay on his back on the bed. He was strung up on the wall. Chloe's impression of it changed with the viewpoint.

Evanard Marsten took the pictures. He was a study in ecstasy and elation. Tears flooded his cheeks and he smiled, smiled a lot. He looked completely insane.

Chloe stopped in front of the mirror by the entrance door. She looked at her perspiring face, and noticed, absentmindedly the visible pearls of sweat. Her hand touched the door knob, and opened the door, to the darkened hallway. She looked back at the bed briefly. The laptop was still there. She remembered turning it off and closing it.

The images flowing behind her eyes were impossible to turn off. They kept churning and churning like a meat grinder in her head, constantly mixing and changing the output.

The stairs leading upwards were bathed in a strange radiance. There were quite a few steps, and twists and turns to the attic. She spotted the painting on the wall up the stairs. At least she presumed it was a painting. There wasn't much to see there. The canvas looked old and shriveled, and the image on it more like mist on a dark and dreary night than an actual painting. But it still fascinated her. Its surface seemed to be fluid, to flow outside of its frame and induce slow flashes of impressions in her mind.

When she blinked and glanced around her she imagined that the long shadow to the right had grown visibly longer. It almost looked like a person, an entity with lips, crooked nose and glaring eyes. She hurried on. There were two more stretches of stairs until she reached the attic. The entire floor, with everything on it appeared at least as derelict as the rest of the building. She saw small holes everywhere, on the floor, in the walls and in the ceiling. The single room stared back at her with a size of a football field, flooded in lights and shadows, interchanging, moving around like living things.

She noticed the larger hole in the wall almost immediately. Birds flew in and out of it, and she felt the powerful draft from their flapping wings. She walked carefully towards it without really making or feeling like she made a conscious decision. The wood creaked and whined under her weight, and she feared she would fall through at any minute, but nothing happened, nothing bad happened.

A bird, a raven landed on the floor in front of her. She stopped. It tilted its head slightly, studying her, before squeaking loudly and flying off.

The chills hit her full force and she stood there, shaking for several heartbeats, before continuing on her way.

She stopped just before the large hole, taking a small step further, and stopping in the hole, neither out nor in. A momentary spell of dizziness almost overwhelmed her when she stared down, at the ground far below.

There was a narrow ledge leading across the roof, to the nearby roof, a path to what seemed to be enclosed space. She imagined that it glowed briefly, in the constantly shifting light. The enclosed space was a mess of derelict, overgrown sheds, poles and what seemed to be the remains of a greenhouse. For just a second there she felt like she was in the wilderness, at the edge of a forest. The smells, the sounds, it was all there. She swayed and she almost lost her footing, before she managed to grab and hold on to the somewhat solid remains of the wall to her right.

She stepped out, into the winds, onto the ledge. The walk, even though she was inevitably cautious was strangely easy. Her firm footing brought her across the building, to the other side of the roof in less than a minute.

She sat foot on the solid ground, on what felt soft and relenting. A kind of door, portal appeared to her, between one blink and another, before fading away, one smelling of forest and trees and burning wood.

Chloe Webster walked through the busy afternoon streets. She carried the camera around her neck. It rested on her chest, dancing up and down a bit every time she took a step. Her observant eyes caught or attempted to catch everything happening around her. Sometimes she stopped, and grabbed the camera, and photographed whatever her eyes had caught. Sometimes she frowned and grabbed the camera again, and did another snapshot, from another angle, paced a bit and chose yet another singular view.

Her eye caught a woman on the corner right ahead. The camera zoomed in on her, but when it had almost completed zooming in on her she was gone, faded like a puff of smoke. Chloe ran to the corner, and stopped there, out of breath, looking to all possible sides and at all angles, but the woman was nowhere to be seen.

Chloe Webster walks through busy afternoon streets, taking pictures, snapshots of reality, fragments of what is or might be. She senses the unrest, the nervous excitement and terror around her, and nowhere is that sensation more pronounced than in her own, sizzling insides.

People returned from their jobs with despair in their haunted eyes. Very few worked in the Pit, at least during the day, but commuted, either to other parts of town or far away. They were happy work was done, but everybody, except those creatures of the night wanted to leave the Pit, leave it behind forever. Chloe caught the haunted look in their eyes through her lens, and her own sense of being haunted increased tenfold. The unseen banshees screeched their whispers in her ears.

Dust whirled into the air from the ground and hit her in the face. She stopped incredulous and then she began coughing, and couldn't stop, and it went on for quite some time, before it finally subsided. Her eyes were filled with tears and she had to blink several times to clear her vision.

A man performed in front of a tavern ahead. He was singing and playing. She was drawn there, like a slew of other people gathering in a half moon around him.

What is that itch in your belly
At the edge of your vision
At the tip of fingers
Reaching out and scratching the air
Somewhere ahead
What is darkness
What is the Void
But a revelation of power and spirit
And everything thereof

He played only guitar and harmonica, but sounded like an entire orchestra to Chloe. Others probably didn't notice, but he communicated far more than the obvious to Chloe.

She couldn't put her finger on what, no matter how hard she tried.

Someone grabbed her right shoulder. She turned and sighed when she recognized the man in front of her.

– There you are, Stephen Farber cried. – Have you any idea how long I've been searching for you? I suspected I would find you in a place like this.

The Pit was definitely beneath his precious standards.

– We are divorced, Stephen, she reproached him, hating herself for being even the slightest bit defensive.

The fact that he had found her gave «credit» to his persistence. She couldn't believe he had. It wasn't like he could afford a bunch of private investigators or anything.

– We belong together, Chloe baby, he stated with his most annoying boyish face.

– Look, Stevie *baby*, she spat, forcing herself to remain somewhat calm. – I made it pretty clear what I felt about you during the divorce hearing. I made it even clearer during your trial, when you were convicted of *stalking* me and ordered to stay away from me, remember that one?

His patronizing laughter revealed, exposed the insane personality beneath the slick exterior. She got the chills and hardly heard the music anymore.

– You don't think something as mundane as a court of law can keep us apart, do you?

– Actually I did, I do, she said, fighting to stay somewhat calm. – That's why I'll go to the nearest police station right now, and deliver proof of your breach of the court order.

She took a snapshot of him. He tried to grab the camera, but she was too quick for him.

– You didn't honestly believe I would welcome you with open arms? She wondered quietly. – You're not that far gone?

He snarled soundlessly and stared sullenly at her. She backed off, holding him in her sight. Even though she didn't view him as dangerous, she had heard enough stalker stories about former, deranged husbands to be cautious. And true to her word, her warning she walked right to the nearest police station.

It was exactly as downtrodden as she had expected, but they took her statement, accepted the photograph and gave her a copy. They even allowed her to fax it to her lawyer (her downtrodden lawyer), and she was in quite the uplifted mood when she left.

She made a sweep the moment she stepped outside, looking for his highness, the stalker, but he was nowhere to be seen or found. She even halfway *looked* for him, before shrugging and continuing on her way.

The street performer was gone. She searched for him in a frenzied mood for a while, before giving up, and entering the nearest tavern, The Green Rose. It was a special place. She noticed it immediately, how it greeted her and gave her the chills. Its heat and warmth struck at her and embraced her, and she felt it all like an actual physical sensation.

She sat on a chair, rocking to the music, its hypnotic rhythm and chords dancing within her. The place resembled a cave, with no electric lights and only candles to light the rooms and cast shadows. Fans created whirls in the moist and smoke-filled air. It was a noisy, distracting room. She sat there and focused her thoughts, isolating herself from everything around her, while still noticing everything. This was power. This was the mind and the body and the Shadow joining and working its Magick.

Two girls by the adjacent table glanced at her. One of them glanced again. On the small, low stage across the room another girl was dancing and singing. Her band stood still as statues. She was moving, half naked, wild and sweaty. Her movements were not fast, though, but slow and deliberate and still wild. The music was all that, and somber and provocative, the fiddle evoking all kinds of strange emotions in Chloe. She listened to the somber, wild rock, and Chloe Webster remembered things past she hadn't thought about in years.

When she closed her eyes she didn't see darkness, but a well of moving images and sensations, both pleasant and terrifying. She saw a large house by a church, a looming and foreboding building, which shadow reached wide and far. In midday, in brightest sunlight, when there was supposed to be no shadow there still was. It was simultaneously both exciting and terrifying.

The music, and the emotions and sensations it evoked stayed with her long after she had left the tavern, everything replaying itself in her mind. She rose. The two girls rose, too.

– We were just wondering… they said, practically choiring, or rather completing each other's sentence, – are you *special*, too?

– In what way, Marion? Chloe asked the girl standing the closest casually.

– My name isn't…

Chloe walked away, leaving the two with a perplexed expression in their faces.

– I could have sworn I know her from somewhere, the other girl, the Asian frowned, a strange longing so very present in her voice.

Noise rose and faded in Chloe's ears as she passed fairly close to the vast, open area leading to the bus terminal and railroad station. This was where the Pit had been deliberately cut off from the rest of the city… or where it had cut itself off. Opinion was split on what was what. But this was the demarcation line, or rather the band making the Pit something singular, apart. She sensed it somehow, sensed the energies or whatever it was making her skin… tingle, making her frontal lobe buzz and her blood flow faster in her veins.

It was possible to walk across, easily at night, or even possible during the day, but not in the middle of the rush hour. Chloe Webster descended into the subway, into the dark and badly lit tunnels.

They were fairly modern, with new or at least recently constructed concrete walls. Electricity didn't work well down here, that's all.

Most people hurried through the tunnels, glancing to both sides with *skeptical* eyes. Chloe walked at a languid pace, cautiously but curiously studying her surroundings. There was something here, there always had been, every time she had passed through. It was faint, like it always had been, difficult to pinpoint, to identify and even be certain existed, but she felt confident… that there was something here.

A whisper howled in her head. She was positive there was no sound. A skull grinned at her. There was nothing there her eyes could see. Its prolonged fangs punctured the skin on her neck, and she cried out in pain. The mirage made her shake and shiver, and it wasn't because of the cold. She was sweating hard down here.

A vent was leaking ahead somewhere. Vapor and steam flooded the tunnels. People hurried on, in both directions, not even looking into the third tunnel, the one leading deeper into the subway.

Chloe stopped, and looked. She stepped forward, into the third tunnel, and her world was filled with smoke and lights and vast shadows.

A hand grabbed her, and she turned towards the man in the workers' attire.

– What are you doing, lady, there's nothing in there, except unfinished tunnels. You risk hurting yourself.

She looked at him, and he let go of her, startled and shaken.

– What do you see? She asked him.

He shook his head, unable to comprehend.

She grabbed him, holding on, digging in hard. He yelped in pain.

– Tell me, *what did you see?*

– Nuthin', lady, he whined. – I saw *nuthin'!*

– I'll tell you what you saw, she stated calmly. – You saw your own fear reflected back at you.

He pulled away. She let him. Her arms fell down. He backed away from her, as if she was a revenant, a banshee haunting his nights.

She forgot about him and turned back, towards what during a brief moment had been a tunnel, but now was only a small hole three to four steps deep filled with rocks and holes.

The steam and vapor dissolved and she saw the wall clearly.

She passed a man on her way back, one she vaguely recognized.

– Do you know what you have done? Do you have any idea how much I want to kill you, now, to roast you over open fire and devour your innards?

He started shaking hard, and in her mind he never stopped.

She walked the streets once more, the streets of the Pit. For how long she couldn't say. It was as if she had never left. She sat on the bench on the square, looking at nothing, having no recollection of having sat down. Chloe takes snapshots of life passing by.

A woman and a boy stopped there, concern painted in their faces.

– Hey, lady, he said, – are you well?

She turned her attention to him with a sad expression in her sweet features.

– You know what they say about the Pit, right? Once you visit it you can never leave. You will remain here for the rest of your life. You have heard that one, haven't you, *boy?*

– Y-yes, the boy stuttered.

– But, you see, it's actually worse than that. The moment you enter its confines, no matter the reason, you forget about the world outside, about your life there, how it was. It is as if you have never been outside at all.

The mother hauled the protesting boy off.

The strange-looking woman sat on the bench, taking snapshots of life.

She drifted around, looking for motives, for things to catch on film (or rather the digital drive). For every new picture she snapped, she studied it, studied the object in question, from all angles. Then she pulled back a little, before starting over yet one more time.

The bench glowed at her, in pale colors, in its normality, its utter mundane appearance. She photographed it from all angles. At home, in the downtrodden apartment she put all the angles together.

She studied the woman sitting there on the bench, studied her from different angles, different perspectives. Her perception of her didn't change. She stood on the bench, and felt like she was rising into the air. Perception changed dramatically, in a single moment. She almost fell. She fell, but managed to land on her feet on the ground, the dusty ground.

The grocery store across the square remained busy, even though dusk was about to settle. Many things settled at dusk elsewhere in the world, but not in the Pit. The store was one of the best supplied Chloe had ever seen, at least when it came to what she was buying. The clerk didn't stare at her when she paid for it all, but she saw right through him. She knew that he knew, and smiled a little.

The stairway was never truly completely dark, and certainly not when it was dark outside. Light shifted in shadow and darkness, and the higher she climbed the better she was able to see what surrounded her.

She searched through her computer, slowly, little by little finding what she was looking for. Symbols and phrases flickered before her eyes. She picked one by one, undressing little by little as she did so. Humming turning into chanting rose from her throat, as she prepared for the ritual. It was always a strenuous task, striving to achieve the right set of mind.

It hurt. It always hurt. She gasped, and the sound of her pain rose upwards with her, to the roof, where wings and birds flapped and flew.

The young cub reporter entered the «newsroom» of «The Color of the Night», walking with uncertain steps to the editor's room. He received her in quite the chivalry way, the very image of support. She accepted his outstretched hand, fighting off a nervous giggle. He sat down behind a desk, balancing his hands against each other and looked humorously at her.

– So, why do you want to work here, Miss Webster? There must be plenty of other places a talented newshound such as yourself would seek work.

– You're being kind, sir, she replied, blushing. – Finding work today isn't exactly easy.

– Ah, an honest bird. I *like* that!

He was old and gray, but had kept his youthful exuberance, somewhat. She… liked that, liked even the fact that he was interviewing her personally, and not through «consultants», an impersonal act that was so common these days.

The conversation went back and forth for a while, covering nothing in particular, and yet she realized afterwards: covering everything.

– I want to turn every stone, she had said boldly. – I want to learn the secrets.

And he had looked at her with sympathy in his eyes, and she hadn't understood why for a long time. She had realized startled, before he had said, or even implied anything, with an excitement threatening to burst… that the job was hers.

She painted herself with the ancient symbols. It had become routine after a few years, even though she knew it was important, crucial to do it right, even though she knew it would be meaningless without the right mindset, without the right person doing it. She knew she was the right person. She had known that for quite a while, for endless years.

Frustration riled her like a mare. She focused on the breathing, on calming down, on channeling the frustration, the raging energies inside her. The symbols resembled Egyptian, Babylonian, Etruscan, but were none of the above. They weren't found in any book of the dead she had ever seen, but were older, more fundamental, closer to the source, or at least to one source.

She knew there were many.

The computer sputtered and died, as she applied the final symbols. There was no need for her to look at herself in the mirror. She was well able to study the woman on the bed without such crude aid, such crutches. The door opened and she walked through it. She ascended the stairs naked, dressed in symbols and paint, carrying her pouch of tricks and tools. A clock chimed, striking twelve times, symbolizing, revealing, initializing the darkest hour. She knew she was being watched, that she was being followed, paying it no heed, ignoring the very thought of it.

– Hi, the nice man by her neighboring desk greeted her, – my name is Stephen Farber. I'm a journalist in this rag, just like you.

She accepted his hand.

– Hi, she replied shyly, – I'm Chloe Webster.

But then he already knew that, you silly girl, she thought.

– Nice to meet you, Chloe Webster, he grinned.

And she melted like butter in his radiant presence.

She mused a lot later, though, about how smooth everything had proceeded. He took her to dinner two days later, and he bedded her that same night.

It was like a storm. It ravaged her like one.

And one day he said, casually out of the blue.

– You want to know, don't you, to know the secrets?

She had looked at him, suddenly understanding his strange glances and veiled observations.

– Yes, she heard herself say.

– I know you do. I saw a kindred spirit in you the moment you first caught my eye, and I think you are ready.

I am, I am, she wanted to shout at him, but she stayed silent, and allowed him to take her hand and lead her to a small closet in his apartment she hadn't been aware of before. They undressed and they sat down there, she suddenly very aware of her nudity.

– This is it, you know, he admonished her. – This is real. This is nothing like the parlor tricks and the hollow games we have seen in countless parties we have visited. I will take you with me to the Other World, and then we will seek further together.

He taught her words, taught her chants and rituals. It didn't come easy and took days of sweating and striving, but then suddenly she felt it, the pleasant and painful buzz of the burning inside, experienced how the world seemed to be fading, and opening up to her in completely new ways and to new thoughts and concepts and understanding. She embraced him, threw herself at him afterwards, kissing him hard enough to make his lips bleed.

They got married the next day. They stood there, before the priest, ignoring his boring words, marrying themselves by the ancient rites and methods, binding themselves to each other forever.

She stepped out on the roof, walking to the special place she had chosen earlier today. Birds rose around her, squeaking and chirping. She drew the wide circle of the pentacle with eased practice, the red chalk resembling crystallized blood in her hand. Her hand brought the rag dolls from the pouch without conscious thought. They seemed to have grown. She placed them at each of four points. At the fifth she placed a candle, but didn't light it. She walked to the center of the star and sat down on her ass there, crossing her legs in front of her.

– I sit here, she said aloud, – in a circle neither golden nor silver, but blood. In blood I wash myself. In the depths of its sea I seek my answers.

A knife, neither golden nor silver formed in her left hand. She grabbed its handle and began cutting herself, splashing the blood around, but not a single drop outside the circle. It hissed as it hit the ground, and the ground seemed to change, to transform from concrete to something soft, malleable, into the sea of blood she pictured in her mind. The air darkened until she could only glimpse what was outside the circle and her surroundings changed, transformed into the remote, desolate place it was.

– I seek the thousand fires, she cried. – I have found many, but there are still thousands left.

She waited a bit, before repeating it, repeating it again and again.

– I name you, she mumbled, turning in turn towards the dollies. – I name you Victor. I name you Marion. I name you Desire. I name you Andy. I gave you flesh. I give you life.

Her wounds didn't heal, and blood kept leaking through the punctured skin. She swayed and moaned in her increasingly delirious state, hesitating, slowly reaching the point of no return.

– I NAME MYSELF! She shouted. – I name myself Beelzebub, Lady of the high and low places. I walk in her footsteps and I become all things. Where do I go? Where do I walk?

A loud thunder drowned her voice. She fell, descended into the sea, the bloody sea. She was rising, seeing the world from above, and becoming the world. Ice and the warm, wet blood filled her, cutting her open, cutting the world open, but she still couldn't see, couldn't...

Stephen and Chloe investigated a haunted house. They had quit the paper and started on their new lives as paranormal investigators, choosing their jobs carefully, usually exposing the obvious hoaxes in advance, earning quite a lot of money, but searching, always searching for what rested Beyond.

– Somewhere, somewhen, he told her, – a resting god slumbers, and we will find it and face it and wrest from it all its answers and all its power.

His intensity excited her. It always did.

The house welcomed them, with its silence, with its snarl. From the moment the door slammed shut behind her she sensed it, almost physically felt it, a malevolent presence of the first order, unlike anything she had ever experienced before, during their many investigations in the long years of searching.

– It's real, she mumbled with numb lips. – They didn't lie.

– Well, that remains to be seen, he contradicted her good-humored.

She realized he didn't sense anything, and she blinked, and stared open-mouthed at his back, as they made their way up the stairs.

He didn't see the cold light emanating from the door ahead. She couldn't think. Her thoughts were a jumble. He opened the door, the right door, the wrong door, and walked inside. She hurried inside after him, stepping into a strange world of pale colors and shadows, one she had previously only experienced in half-remembered dreams.

She swallowed hard, realizing with bittersweet certainty how drastically their world had suddenly changed. They had searched so long and hard for this moment, searched together, and now it had come, and she knew beyond knowing that she could never properly share it with him.

He opened his suitcase and brought out the equipment. It wasn't that much, only the basics of the eager ghost hunter. Usually it would be sufficient to detect any extraordinary, paranormal activity.

Except this time it wasn't necessary, except to determine that she hadn't gone insane.

The place was screaming at her at the top of its lungs. She didn't hear a thing, but the display assaulting her senses made her deaf and blind to anything but its mighty voice.

– You might want to give me a hand here.

She could hardly hear him. He sounded as if he was a million miles away.

– The window, she said sleepily.

– What window? He frowned. – There is no…

He looked at the mirror.

– It's an opening, she said, – a gateway. I feel it. It's invading me, filing me with its secrets, and its power, its beyond majestic and wonderful and terrible power.

The world beyond the gateway looked infinite. It was both there and here, both in front and behind her. She took one step towards it and then more. Ghostly hands reached for her, grinning in anticipation.

He grabbed her, and held on, held her at bay, as she was struggling to reach the threshold somewhere ahead.

The gateway closed. The mirror was once more only a mirror. She looked at him, the mist slowly dissipating from her mind.

– I felt, she said. – I felt…

And couldn't tell whether or not she was angry or grateful.

– This house is clean, she said somberly. – There is nothing here.

In the depth of his eyes, with a frightening clarity she spotted the deepest envy.

Her thunder shook the surrounding air and the concrete and the roof and the clouds above. She fell and hit the concrete, laid there gasping, gasping for life. The human body, the flesh screamed for air, for nourishment, the flames feeding her ashes. She was breathing, breathing in loud heaves. Her wounds healed. From one moment to the next, during the span of a few seconds the gashing wounds closed, and a few seconds after that there was no sign at all of the wounds on the unblemished skin.

She rose, and turned, and stared hard at the boy standing there with a gaping mouth.

He freaked, totally freaked. She saw it, sensed it, and it felt good, so very good.

– Don't fucking LOOK at me like that!

She looked at him with the most intense contempt, with her cold, vicious eyes.

– But in what way do you want me to look at you?

He bolted and ran. Her wicked laughter followed him all the days of his life.

Clarity filled her like ice. Mystery turned to information, information to knowledge, knowledge to understanding, understanding to wisdom and wisdom to mystery. The circle began anew, but awareness had been gained. She knew, knew he had crippled her, given her his weakness and ignorance, pushed her off her path. He had punished her for being superior to him, and she, the poor, disgusting thing had allowed herself to be reduced in stature, to be dragged into the gutter of his resentment. As his resentment had turned to hatred, to possessiveness she had wallowed in her own insecurity and become hardly more than a slave, begging her master's favor. He had abused her, pushed her further and further, until she had snapped, had reached bottom and finally began fighting back.

– You are nothing, she spat, – nothing but rot crumbling under my heel.

She was falling, not through space, but through time. The woman with the cold, cold eyes descended the dark stairs. It was Night. The full moon was up, dancing on a high-wired sky. A dark night, filled with shadows.

There was water all around her. There were no bubbles, only dark, cold, still water. It didn't move her at all, but she moved, slow like icy breath from a corpse, frozen, dead, undying. Every single person in the neighborhood felt her, felt her might and they cowed on the floor in fear.

Chloe Webster was rising from her watery grave, rising bundled in a grin and rotting flesh, and

CHAPTER THIRTEEN

On the third day

She looked through the dusty window the next morning, covering herself in the thick blankets, shaking like a leaf, biting her lip, curling her hands into fists, as her body and mind reeled from her actions last night, the memory of it dim. Sharp as a whip in her mind her gain brought her no relief.

Something was missing, still missing, and it hurt, hurt her terribly.

She went through the motions, making breakfast, eating like a bird, sitting there nude, with the thick blankets swept around her shivering body, wool filling her overloaded mind. Eyes blinked, and in that blink the reoccurring sensations assaulted her mercilessly. It had never lasted so long before. She was close, so close…

But something was missing.

She took a shower. The water was cold again. She didn't mind, but desired, craved the distraction. It didn't help. Her mind was filled with fever and thoughts and sensations of a different existence. She dried herself, rubbed herself, until her skin was dry and inflamed. Her feet moved around in a daze, but she was burning up with movement and an undeniable pull she couldn't resist. She dressed and hit the streets.

Gray surrounded her everywhere. Only in glimpses she spotted pale colors and pale shadows. She crossed the square to the hotel with a determined look in her eyes. The clerk was clearly apprehensive, even though it wasn't the same she had encountered earlier. Her reputation preceded her.

– Hi, she said to him at the desk. – You know the area? I wonder if you can answer a few questions for me?

– Certainly, ma'am, he said nervously, – I'll do my best.

– I'm sure you will, she grinned.

An uncomfortable silence arose between them. She didn't mind.

– I'm looking for The Lady of the Lake, she said.

He looked blank at her.

– Anything you might have on her will be fine, she said gently.

He reddened, both angry and flustered.

– There are quite a few souvenir shops nearby…

– No, she stated solemnly, – not the tourist go-around, the real thing.

– I'm afraid I don't understand, ma'am, he yelped.

– Sure you do, she stated lightly, very lightly, – you hear things, hear whispers in the night and conversation behind corners. «Ask the clerk, and you will find the secrets of the world». The butler didn't do it, you know, the clerk did, if you get my drift.

He believed her, saw it in every little pointed stare she sent in his direction.

– There is a shop at the harbor. He pulled himself together with an effort. – It doesn't cater to tourists, or so I've heard. It's called Mystery Calling. You shouldn't experience any problems finding it. It's…

– I've got it, she said graciously. – Thank you, Oscar, thank you very much. I'll think about you in lonely moments.

And he looked vindicated, somehow, and she felt a little better. She walked through the drafty streets, listening to the voices the wind brought her. The scenery changed slightly. Narrow streets and alleys turned even more so. The light from above hardly reached down here, in this even more forgotten part of the city. The harbor wasn't really a harbor, not anymore. She couldn't even spot the ocean from here. It had been moved half a mile out by development a century ago and a mile longer since then. A population screaming for space had moved in, and abandoned it for yet another new area of greener pastures during the previous decade. The Harbor had joined the Pit and extended its reach significantly.

The sun didn't shine in the Pit, and it didn't shine here, at its newest conquest.

A half digested apple gathered dust somewhere to her right. The garbage cans were not far away, but no one had picked it up. It was old there on the cobblestones. Its red skin had lost its color and its flesh had turned brown. Chloe ignored it, too, and walked on.

A face stared at her from behind a dirty window. It was difficult to see whether or not it was a man or a woman. Chloe saw only indistinct, dissolved features, before it faded away. She walked on.

Mystery Calling pointed a bit to itself in a quiet street. In a row of closed, abandoned shops it stood out. A car with a running engine stood one door away, its red lights reflected in the window, its evil eyes staring at her from the misty world there, making her shudder in fright.

She opened the door and walked inside. A bell called her arrival. She saw no people anywhere. Dust lingered evenly in the air throughout the room. It was hard to tell where the light was coming from. She saw no lamps, but the light was there, present like the dust. Something stirred in the doorway to the backroom, stirred and materialized there. A man appeared seemingly out of thin air. She looked closer at him, at his pale complexion and skinny frame. He looked more like skin and bones than any man she had previously encountered. His eyes stared at her, moved in the sockets as if they had independent life.

He walked to the desk and stopped in front of the visitor.

– Welcome, he greeted her. – Is there anything I can help you with?

There was a strange quality in his voice, two dots she couldn't quite connect.

– I'm seeking the Lady of the Lake, she stated frankly.

– She has always been here, he said.

– So I've heard, she acknowledged, – but I've been looking for her for a long time and haven't found her.

– You have always been here, he said.

She frowned and rubbed her left temple. He made as much sense as a sphinx, and she felt a strong need to tell him so.

– Is there anything I can help you with? He wondered.

He wore completely ordinary clothes and suddenly he seemed very ordinary as well, not the enigmatic figure she had first imagined him to be.

– I'm seeking the Lady of the Lake, she repeated.

Two could play this game. She stared at him. He returned her stare totally unfazed.

– We get quite a few of those, he shrugged. – The Lady can be quite elusive. I know of people who have spent an entire lifetime unsuccessfully seeking her.

– I'm not like most people, she insisted, attempting to sound as casual as she possibly could, before giving it up, before turning pleading and desperate. – I… dream about her and have visions about her, and I recently realized that I have been having those all my life.

The Lady rose beneath the water, rose towards the surface, until she lingered right beneath it, staring at those seeking her with giant dead eyes, and Chloe staggered under the onslaught of her attention.

Chloe blinked and she stared bewildered at a completely empty storage room, in the building where the car had parked outside. It stood there still, with its engine running.

She rushed outside and attempted to open the doors, but they were locked. Hands hammered on the metal until they turned sore and swollen, but nothing happened.

– Let me in, she mumbled. – Let me in, let me in, let me in…

The car drove off. She managed to keep pace with until it speeded up and she was left behind. Exhaust surrounded her for a moment and she stood there coughing until the cloud dispersed and she finally was able to move.

Chloe turned and looked at the door behind her.

– Locked, she mumbled, brightening, – locked.

She entered the shop, the true Mystery Calling, opened the door with intricate carvings, instantly struck by the insides' mundane appearance, its normality. The girl behind the desk looked quite mundane as well. It was the Asian girl she had encountered yesterday.

– I'm seeking The Lady of the Lake, Chloe stated bluntly, before the girl opened her mouth. – I walked into the other shop, the one with the locked door and met the enigmatic man with the beard. I assume I passed the test, and I'm seeking The Lady of the Lake. She's close, now, you know, closer than she has ever been. I feel her in my gut, on my brow.

Desire curtseyed timidly.

– What you say is true, she whispered. – I have been instructed to offer you every possible aid and courtesy.

A warm, warm sensation coursed through Chloe, as she reflected upon the other woman's astonishing and over-the-top reaction.

– I'll be closing the store, the girl said, – and we'll be on our way soon.

She went to the cashier and began counting money. Chloe watched her hands while she did. She was an expert. Her fingers moved fast as the wind, until they became a blur. A horrible stench tore at her nostrils. Chloe was almost overwhelmed with fear and pulled her eyes off the disturbing sight with an effort.

Dust lingered in the air, wherever she looked. The longer time she spent here, the less normal the room seemed. She breathed deliberately, focusing on drawing on her inner strength. Slowly, painfully slowly the panic attack subsided. Whether or not that was a good thing remained to be seen. She wanted to stay, wanted to flee with her tail between her legs.

The wriggling tail felt so real just then.

She waited on the sidewalk, while Desire locked the door. A large sign - CLOSED - covered much of the wood's intricate carvings.

– I can't take you to the Lady, Desire said, – but I can take you to someone that knows a lot more about her.

They walked off, left the downtrodden block of the store, left the «harbor». Desire led Chloe through what felt like an intricate maze of alleys and narrow streets.

At a corner Chloe... stopped. At the corner across the street she spotted a little girl. The girl had pale skin and sunken eyes. She wore a collar around her neck and a chain led from the collar and into the air, where it faded into nothing.

– What is it? Desire wondered.

Chloe hushed her up with a hiss and a move with her hand, her left hand.

The worry, the anxiety she had felt the entire day exploded in her gut and made cold sweat break all over her body, and she knew she looked very similar to that pale girl across the river of the street.

– Hello there, little girl, she said.

– Hello, the girl replied with a hardly audible voice.

– What are you doing here? Chloe asked, feeling both foolish and fearful.

– I don't know, the girl whimpered. – I don't know why I'm here. They don't tell me why they take me wherever they're taking me. I'm just led around in my chain serving my master's desire.

Chloe imagined she could glimpse a hand there, in the shimmering air at the end of the chain.

Suddenly the girl was no longer distant, at the other corner, but on this one, right there, in front of Chloe. The skin on her skull faded away, until it was partly transparent. Chloe gasped in terror.

– Yes, the girl hissed, her face transforming into a hellish appearance, a twisted grin, her voice changing to a spiteful demeanor. – You are correct in your pathetic fear: I am you, you captured and reduced to a bitch to be taken for a walk and displayed among friends on Sundays. This is you like you truly are. Get USED to it!

Chloe screamed. She couldn't help it. It came from her heart and core and filled her ears and surroundings and frightened her beyond her wits.

She gasped, stood there shaking, staring at the empty street before her, behind her, staring at Desire with wild, terrified eyes.

– What is it? Desire wondered. – You had a *vision,* didn't you?

Excitement and worry warred for ascendance in her voice and features.

Chloe nodded, nodded with lips so numb and a throat so raw that she was unable to speak.

– I knew it, Desire said excitedly. – I didn't notice anything, except by looking at you. You are indeed powerful.

– Or I was targeted, Chloe quacked.

– There is that, Desire nodded soberly.

– B-but I've had ample training to withstand a psychic attack, and this was nothing like that. This was something different, something worse.

Desire hesitated a bit before putting a hand on the other woman's shoulder.

– C'mon, I'll buy you a cop of coffee.

Chloe stared pointedly at her, but couldn't stop shaking. Nausea rode her and the mere thought of coffee made her want to puke. She nodded slowly and meekly.

They headed uphill to Grafton Park, another area on the edge of the Pit. The Heights loomed far above them, seemingly totally unreachable from here. Chloe saw the two of them from above and behind like a bird of prey. The change in perspective didn't really startle her. She had experienced quite a few similar events since that first time with Stephen in that haunted house.

«I owned you once», he hissed in her ear. «I'll collar you yet again, like a fish on the hook».

Frosty and sick to the bone she wondered if he was the hand holding the chain.

There was a coffee shop (or something resembling one) at the corner leading to Grafton Park Square. Chloe sat down on a stool by the window and let Desire handle the procuring of the two steaming pots. She grabbed the pot and wanted to drink from it this instant, no matter how much her reason screamed at her to hold back, until the fluid had cooled a bit.

She glimpsed her indistinct image in the window, but what she saw was the deadly pale little girl with the collar and chain around her neck.

Someone had left a half digested apple two seats away. This was fairly fresh, only moderately brownish. She frowned, realizing that someone had left it there only a few minutes ago.

– I have heard that having the Sight can be pretty scary, Desire said. – I can believe that. To say that you look spooked is being kind to the spooks.

– It can be used against you, Chloe said, still frosty, – by those knowing how. And by default you'll see a lot of unpleasant things, because they leave the most powerful imprint.

She sipped a lot of the coffee. The hot brew slid down her throat and slowly, ever so slowly warmed her. A stubborn, defiant expression found its way to her eyes.

– But I wouldn't want to be without it. It has given me a better life, granted me proof beyond proof that there is a vast existence beyond what most people consider real.

– You have a destiny, the other stated solemnly. – It stands to reason that there are people… and forces out there wanting to keep you from reaching your potential.

The kid was… refreshing. Chloe felt a large chunk of ice melt inside.

Where they sat, between shadow and light they looked very similar, with the same hairdo, with dark hair in their eyes, their haunted eyes. Desire was also haunted, Chloe realized.

– You've had dreams, she said softly, – of another existence, where you live a different life, similar, but with distinct variations?

– Yes, how did you…

The girl trailed off, looking wide eyed at the other.

– We're close, aren't we?

The guide named Desire nodded.

They stepped outside. Desire led the way. Chloe didn't really look at her when she followed. She didn't really follow the girl, but the guiding star of the hunger burning within her.

The long alley at the end of the road and the house in the cluster of trees appeared as from a dream. Chloe and Desire walked the distance between here and there. In the course of their walk it turned dark and not a single lamp illuminated the path. The house seemed to be resting in darkness, as if the sun outside was bright enough to cast the deepest shadow. It brought them far away, so distant from where she walked.

Desire rang the bell. The bell whispered in Chloe's ears. It took a while, but they finally heard sounds from the inside. They heard steps and the opening and closing of doors, and the sounds of whispers increased in terms of loudness and intensity.

An old lady opened the door. Chloe looked startled at her, at the familiar face she had never before set her eyes on.

– You come inside, she said curtly, speaking to Chloe, to Chloe only.

Chloe looked at Desire. Desire shrugged. Chloe stepped inside and the old woman closed the door behind them.

The quiet house had a smell. It smelled… old. Chloe frowned. It reminded her of something, something she couldn't quite recollect. She followed the old woman into the living room. It gave off the same, eerie sense as the hall, of age and strange tidings. The furniture didn't resemble any style Chloe had ever seen. The books on the shelves were written in a totally unfamiliar language. Its letters (she saw the letters) looked equally *alien.*

– Tea? The old woman offered.

– No thanks, Chloe replied, a bit distracted.

– It isn't any trouble. The woman looked at her with huge, luminous eyes. – I can make it while we have our talk.

– I don't care much for tea.

Chloe rejected the offer kindly but decisively.

There were a couch, a table and two chairs in front of the fireplace. The flames danced before Chloe's eyes and caused spells of dizziness to wash over her in waves.

– My name is Chloe Webster, Mrs. Haverhsen. I'm…

– I know who you are.

The old woman moved across the room, light on her feet. She sat down on the couch. Chloe sat down in the left chair across the table. The heat from the fireplace made sweat break on her brow in an instant.

– Such a pleasant heat, is it not?

Bony hands reached for the fire, and the fire seemed to reach for the hands as well.

– And it isn't just ordinary fire either. No fire ever is. But the very remnants of the primeval fire present at the very beginning of the Universe.

There was a glow, just outside the range of normal vision. Chloe sensed it. It was pleasant in a way, even though it tore and pulled at her insides like a hook.

– Is it okay if I… if I tape this? Chloe asked eagerly, suddenly feeling excited and ready, in a way she hadn't for a while.

– Be my guest! Mrs. Haverhsen shrugged. – I know how useful such a device can be in hindsight.

Chloe frowned again. What a strange connotation to use.

She pulled the small, digital recorder from her jacket and turned it on, as she put it on the table between them.

The recorder buzzed as they had their conversation, their dance of questions and answers.

– Mrs. Haverhsen… I've heard you have actually seen the Lady. Is that true?

– It certainly is, the old crone nodded. – We have even engaged in a regular conversation. She comes to my house, and asks me questions I can't possibly answer. She's a very curious one that one.

Her head is turned slightly to the side, as if she isn't quite looking at Chloe, or isn't only looking at her, but also at someone to the right, at someone sitting in the other chair. Chloe casts her eyes at it several times, but there is nothing or no one there.

– What questions?

– Are you sure you won't have any tea, my dear? It's quite delicious.

– I'm quite positive, thank you, Chloe responds automatically, glancing at the chair to the right.

The crone seems distracted, as if she isn't really here, isn't quite present in the room. Even so, Chloe senses her, actually feels her like a blade in her gut. She replays the woman's words in her mind, sensing something more about them, another layer of meaning… a device of *hindsight*.

Trepidation breaks on the young woman's brow.

– What questions, Mrs. Haverhsen?

The crone shrugged again.

– Oh, the same questions we all ask, I guess, about the purpose of life, of why we are here and what separates us from the crowd.
– That's bullshit, Mrs. Haverhsen, Chloe said perfectly calm. – Complete and utter bullshit.
– Ah, what a forward young lady you are, Chloe. I rather thought you would be.
Heat from the fireplace reached for Chloe, surrounding her, bathing her in its intense flames. There was a knock, a knock, knock on the door, a loud knock rocking the house.
– Aren't you going to open that? Chloe frowned.
Seconds passed. There was no more knocking.
– What I don't understand is why she is coming to you, asking questions. Chloe consulted her notebook, the blank notebook. – It doesn't make sense, does it?
– A perfectly valid matter to bring up, the old lady nodded. – There is something to wonder about here, isn't there?
Minutes passed. There was no more knocking.
Chloe shook her head, kept shaking her head without moving it upon going through the list of questions she had prepared. It seemed more like a duty than anything making any sense. She realized they no longer made any sense to her at all.
Mrs. Haverhsen often looked distracted, as if she wasn't here at all, but then, suddenly she looked sharp as a whip, as a blade cutting right through Chloe, making her convulse and sweat some more.
– Of course the villagers are weary of me, the crone said at some point, to a question Chloe could no longer recall asking. – They are doomed to be of any of my kind. I bring unwanted guests and chaos, and all things shaking and rattling the feebleminded.
The villagers? Chloe frowned again.
She looked out of the window, the suddenly large, large window, but there was nothing there, except mist and shadow. The young woman shook visibly, unable to hide it.
– I want to meet her, Mrs. Haverhsen.
Chloe suddenly stated.
Then cautiously adding:
– Is that possible?
– Everything is possible, the old woman replied. – In your case I would say it is indeed very possible.
– I had to come here, Chloe said. – I don't know why, but I just had to.
– You're such a curious girl, Chloe. The crone shook her head, the flames from the fireplace dancing in her eyes. – You always were.

And then she turned, and looked, beyond doubt at the person sitting in the other chair.

Chloe still sees nothing, while looking directly at the chair, but while staring into the woman's dancing fires she sees the reflection of a young man sitting there sweating.

– What did you tell her? Chloe intoned, and it didn't seem like her voice at all. – *What?*

– You're such a curious boy, Victor. You always were.

Chloe jumped to her feet, staring at her with insane eyes.

– What *questions?*

– She asked me about The Lady of the Lake. She wanted to meet her, talk to her and gauge her secrets.

There was another knock on the door. This time it was persistent, rocking the entire building. Chloe looked around her, in desperate fear and exasperation.

Mrs. Haverhsen stared at her, stared her down, and Chloe froze, and stood there, still as night.

– Why did you really come here, Chloe?

The girl's voice was thin and wailing when she answered, when she spoke her fevered words.

Everything shifted, turned around, and she saw herself from the outside, her pale face, framed by the dark hair, dominated by the large, pained eyes.

– I'm dreaming of another me, another Chloe Webster, a powerful witch, a creature making Magick and weaving her dark spells. Is it… is she really me? Tell me, tell me what it means.

– Means? Mrs. Haverhsen teased her. – Poor Chloe, so lost and damned.

The knocking grew louder. Everything in the room turned indistinct in Chloe's eyes. She stared at the mirage facing her, her long fangs and claws, and that so familiar elephant trickle hammered down her spine.

– No, not yet, she shouted. – It isn't *fair!*

She rushed towards the hall and the entrance, and grabbed the handle and pulled the door open.

Desire stood there, pale as milk.

– What are you *doing?* She asked incredulous.

– What are you talking about? You told me to wait here, and knock on the door when the time came, but it's *scary* out here. It's just a minute left, anyway.

– A minute…?

Chloe turned and looked back, at an old and wrecked interior, at a house with missing boards and parts of the roof missing, and the two of them stood at the gate, looking at the ramshackle building.

Between the trees, across the road Chloe glimpsed movement and heard the banshee cry, and grew to fully appreciate why Desire was… *spooked.*

She glanced back at the gate. Everything surrounding it had turned dark. Only the path leading to the house seemed somewhat brighter than its surroundings.

Then the misty light slowly faded, and everything around them returned to the dark and remote street it had become.

– What happened? Desire panted eagerly. – What did you see?

– Shut up! Chloe snarled. – Shut the fuck up! Do you have any idea what that extra minute could have given me? Do you?

Tears jumped from the girl's eyes, and she choked and gasped, and suddenly had trouble breathing. Chloe caught a glimpse of the face of *wrath* scaring Desire shitless, and felt both anxiety and fascination.

– I am tempted to leave you here, but that won't do, won't do at all. Come, walk with me, clumsy little child.

She stormed off, her temper, her rage still boiling beneath her skin, within her unruly insides, knowing beyond knowing that meek and despairing Desire trailed her.

The wind whistled between naked branches as they moved down the alley. Everything seemed dead here. They imagined that the short distance expanded towards infinity. Desire sought close to Chloe, seeking shelter within her greater shadow, and Chloe's features softened, and a light touch on the cheek comforted the frightened girl somewhat.

At some point they almost lost their footing. Chloe looked astonished at the even ground, at what, when she squinted her eyes slightly moved like a frothing wave beneath them.

They stopped, holding on to each other for dear life, as mighty forces conspired to tear them apart. Chloe feared she couldn't hear the heart beat in her chest. She realized they had been standing there in silence for minutes. Everything seemed slow, dull. Then she heard the joyous sound of her heart beating, as the world briefly turned itself inside out, as everything inverted and inverted again, to something totally unrecognizable and alien. Branches on the nearby trees looked and sounded like claws gnawing at each other, the trees themselves flashing like the sharpest of blades chopping the air to pieces. The briefest of moments expanded towards Eternity.

A car passed them. The loud howl of the engine hurt their ears and rattled their bones. Raw, pulsing rock music blew at their eardrums from the open windows. They followed the siren call of the rhythm and the melody through busy city streets. Chloe recognized this area. They had returned to the Pit, close to the Square. The Square opened up to them like a peeled fruit, the entire distance they had walked to come here, reach and return to this somewhat familiar place seemed vanished and forgotten in the pervasive darkness surrounding them. She spotted the car. It stopped outside the hotel entrance. Three people stepped out and walked inside the building.

Chloe and Desire followed them, followed them through the vestibule, and followed them down the stairs, through a kind of tunnel, to the bar and dancing area. They played the same melody down there. To them it was as if there was no break in the music from the car and to this smoke-filled room.

Desire waved to three people sitting at a corner table in the deep shadows of the room. They returned her wave. She brought Chloe there and introduced her to the group.

– You know Marion, she said excitedly. – This is Victor and Andy. Guys, this is Chloe.

She threw herself into Victor's arms and gave him a sultry kiss on the lips.

Chloe said hi, and the others returned her greeting, and they sat down by the table, the round table (she realized startled).

She frowned, something touching her mind, before shaking her head in frustration. It had escaped her.

– Chloe and I made Magick today, Desire stated proudly.

– You did, huh? Andy grinned, looking at Chloe as if he was fishing for support.

– We did, she shrugged, staring back at him. – We pulled aside the curtains, opened the pathways to another existence, and faced the Truth Demon at the gate.

He looked hurt at her, as he had clearly expected some innocent, safe reply. She had encountered his kind more than once before. They never appreciated it when their carefully constructed view on reality was challenged, when it threatened to come crashing down around them.

The events earlier stayed with her. She couldn't get rid of the haunting impressions no matter how hard she tried. Sometimes she wanted to, sometimes she wanted to hold on to it all. She feared it would never go away. She feared it would. All her senses screamed at her, so acute and in such a heightened state. When two glasses met and parted across the room she heard it, through the loud buzz and music.

And below, beyond the physical impressions was something far deeper, far more profound… and dangerous.

People talked around them. She heard a lot of shards, incomplete phrases, bits and pieces of conversation, of dark, menacing words making no sense.

– The fire makes me feel the fire, the man by the fireplace insisted, a huge furrow appearing on his brow.

Chloe imagined she sat there by the fireplace, feeling how the flames played with her skin.

Shades of the inferno danced in Marion Dexter's face.

Desire sat in Victor's lap, making out with him.

– I'm subtle, a woman stated slowly, frowning. – I can make people listen to me for hours without anyone having any idea what I'm talking about.

– Gurd! A man jumped to his feet, nodding.

Flames danced before Chloe Webster's eyes, speaking, whispering to her, and for a moment she could almost make out what they were saying.

– Interviewing people can be very tedious, a man with greasy hair sighed. – Nobody is really saying much, you know, not beyond mundane descriptions of everyday life. It's a real drag.

– THE DRAG QUEEN IS PULLING HER HEAVY WEIGHT, the waiter shouted.

Chloe blinked. Their entire time down here had been… weird, but this surely clinched it. People might ignore everything else happening, but surely the waiter's behavior was… excessive?

– I want to kill them, a woman swore, with a loud and menacing mumble, one seemingly originating all over the room. – I want to kill them all.

Chloe stared around her, everything, every impression hammering her, making cold sweat pour from her brow. Desire danced with Victor. The music was low-key, hardly heard, hardly more than felt in the background noise of the room.

– Do you want to dance? Andy asked her.

She nodded numbly, forcing herself into giving him a cute smile.

Chloe danced with Andy, but sometimes he wasn't Andy, but a completely different man. Marion danced with a stranger. Chloe couldn't quite make out his face. Marion grinned at her, and her features turned wicked and vile.

The five dolls danced their stiff dance at their designated base of the pentacle, as the cold moonlight slowly turned red and hot.

Chloe touched Andy's face, attempting to get a feel for it, to see what was behind the mask, the stiff, lifeless mask.

– What's wrong, Victor? Desire cried. – What's wrong with you?

He looked strangely at her. Was anything wrong with him? He looked perfectly all right, except for the deep and lingering anxiety in his eyes.

– Excuse me, he mumbled.

He backed off and set course for the restroom. Clearly that was where he was headed. Chloe followed him, hardly aware of doing so. She stumbled in something, but when she looked down with stunned surprise there was nothing there, nothing that could possibly make her stumble.

Weary eyes searched people standing in her path, behind and ahead to see if anyone had stuck their foot out and deliberately tripped her, but she spotted nothing suspicious.

Victor rushed into the restroom, to the large mirror there, to the sight of his full-figured reflection. Chloe walked in there, after him. She knew it was a wild, crazy thing to do, but made herself ignore the powerful sense of awkwardness. Chloe Webster looked at Victor Matushe's mirror image. Several men walked back and forth in front of her. They ignored her, as if she wasn't here, or as if they weren't. In the mirror she could spot her own reflection, the pale face where her skull was superimposed on the skin, instead of the other way around. In Victor's giant eyes she spotted a different place, a room not a room, but a vast landscape where any human being would be a dwarf, an ant compared to an elephant. Giants walked there. She glimpsed their legs, but nothing more, nothing of the vast body reaching above the clouds.

He walked to a cubicle. He rushed inside and sat down with his clothes on. Shivering hands pushed the door until it closed and locked it. But there was no door. Chloe saw him, saw him clearly, beneath the skin, under the veneer of reason. She studied him with cold, dispassionate eyes.

His pants turned wet, as he peed in his pants, as he sat down on the wet, wet seat. He choked when he finally looked at his watch and realized that an entire hour had passed. His mind felt like wool. His fingers weren't there. His hands slowly faded to nothing. He couldn't think, couldn't hear his own thoughts over the loud, loud beating of his own heart, the gasps of his wide-open mouth.

His hand reached for the handle, before his courage failed him, failed him miserably, and the bone-like hand fell. He could no longer move, no longer do anything but listening to the horrible noises outside, the sounds of mouths chewing, chewing, forever hungry in the darkness.

He looked at his hands, holding them up, his delicate and small hands, with the long, polished nails, frowning at first, then sweating and then shivering uncontrollably, and then gasping, gasping in shock and violent, heart-wrenching terror.

Chloe Webster sat for hours on the toilet seat, shaking violently, not daring to move, totally unable to rise and open the door, and see with her eyes what moved and breathed and grinned outside.

CHAPTER FOURTEEN

On the fourth day

Tripping up, she almost fell when she left the bed.

The old woman sat in her attic and painted. She painted the bridge over troubled waters. Her hand was steady and her brush quick.

Chloe sat up on the bed, reaching for her laptop on the nightstand. It wasn't there. She stared incredulous at the paper and pen that had taken its place.

– I can't see myself, she stated, her voice low and dead.

The light hurt her eyes. During the span of a tiny moment they were filled with tears.

She grabbed the pen, and the paper, and began writing.

A car was driving by outside. She heard the loud music from what had to be over-dimensioned speakers quite well, a lot better than she cared to do. It stayed with her, in the room, lingering in her bones. Ghosts and specters of ancient times rode her brow.

She dried her eyes, and sat still, looking at the floor, until she was finally able to read the note.

– I hear voices, she read, timid and scared, with burning eyes. – I hear them all the time, even in my sleep when everything else is silent.

Other voices whispered, snarled in her ears.

She sat there, writing, doing her best, in vain, to overcome the vicious shaking of her hands.

The pen and paper fell from her hands and to the floor. She rose and walked to the mirror. Chloe looked at her from the world at the other side of the milky surface.

Her phone rang. She turned and stared stupefied at it. It rang a long time before she walked to the table and answered the insistent call.

– Yes?

– Ah, there you are, she heard. – I've tried to get hold of you for days.

– I told you. She rubbed her right temple. – I told you there is no connection here.

– But you still brought your phone, he teased her. – Looks like I was right when I insisted that technology would find a way.

– What do you want? She asked resigned.

– We must meet, he implored her.

She pushed the red button.

– Bad connection, she mumbled and put the phone back on the table.

It rang again later, when she took a shower, and later still, when she dried herself and dressed for the day. Eventually it stopped. She looked at the display with a thin smile on her lips.

NO CONNECTION

The Lake was quiet today. She stopped for a while, taking in the sights, pausing and considering, glancing nervously to all sides, before setting off to her left.

This was a different part of The Pit. It resembled, at least to a point the city, the world outside, with its shops and broader streets. The feeling, though, of decay and entropy remained the same.

She walked down yet another narrow street. It looked cozy on the surface, the very epitome of an old and pleasant tourist trap, but from beneath it hissed at her. There is a cafeteria to the right, with a lamp in one of the windows. Chloe meets Chloe in the reflection of the window, and sees the different street at the other side, one filled with people glaring at her. She walks inside.

The room looks empty at first, before her eyes adjust to the relative darkness inside and discover all the people, all the people glaring at her. There is a couple with a baby sitting by the center table. The baby is crawling on the floor while giving off happy sounds. A woman wearing a hat and trenchcoat sits in one of the corners, her face concealed in shadow. There is the big bartender cleaning glasses, and many more.

– Coffee, please, Chloe tells him.

She counts the ten steps to the bar, but can't recall having walked there.

He gives her her cup. She pays him and walks to the window with the lamp and sits down by the small table there. The coffee is hot, way too hot to drink. The cup warms her cold bones. She lets it rest on the table while looking out through the window, studying everybody passing by.

The cigarette smoke wasn't so bad here, but it still bothered her. She coughed and constantly felt the need to rub her eyes. It was thick as a cloud by the bar. She suspected that this was the only place in the room it was somewhat tolerable.

The baby glared at her. Beneath the smile and the happy sounds there was a monster seeking to devour her. It struck its hand at the floor, THUD THUD THUD THUD, hypnotizing her with its rhythm and menacing quality.

She blinked, realizing that someone had opened the door, and that all the noise from the street outside rushed inside and filled the room.

– Hi, he greeted her, the tall dark man standing by her table.

– H-hi, she returned his greeting.

He sat down opposite her.

– You are drinking coffee, I see, he commented.
– It's good coffee, she said absentmindedly.
– No one comes here to drink coffee, he said.
– Well, I am, she corrected him stubbornly, taking her first sip.
From further inside the place, in the bar there is the sound of loud voices and of glasses meeting and parting.
– Are you okay? He asked, and she wondered if she imagined the taint of concern in his eyes.
– I'm okay, she shrugged. – Never been better.
The putrid stench of ammoniac filled her nostrils. She frowned. It was usually the first thing she noticed when she woke up in the morning. She had searched the entire apartment in an effort to locate it, in vain.
– I look at the wall, she said. – And sometimes I get the crazy feeling that it isn't there. And I see a gallery of faces floating in mist.
She blinked and in that blink she saw an expanding dark cloud, bright as a billion streetlights, and she became the cloud and the cloud became her, and the thousand few voices condensed into just two, no more than two, two joining that of her own, and in that choir, that multitude of voices the world was born.
They sat at the bar drinking. She had fun. She usually had in his company. The bartender had stopped polishing glasses. Chloe coughed every second breath, just as much because of the strong liquor, as the pervasive smoke lingering in the room.
– So, what are you guys doing here? An old fellow that had more than a bit too much to drink wondered. – Except for the odd Japanese bunch and other weird foreigners we don't get that many tourists during these out of season times.
– We're journalists. Chloe, who had had way too much to drink, grinned. – We're investigating the death of David Fallon Somby.
She saw herself wake up in the morning to the sensation of ammoniac.
The room turned dead silent, dark and ominous.
– Somby is dead, the no longer so drunk old man stated.
– Precisely, Chloe droned on happily. – And no one seems to know how. He was dead. Then he was alive, and now he seems to be dead again.
– He was here, the bartender finally nodded, after a break that had lasted seemingly forever. – He sat on the stool before me, like you are doing now.
Suddenly they experienced it as if all the people in the room gathered around them, as the two of them sat there, surrounded by endless chatter. Chloe sat on her stool, rocking to the music, the moody music.

– He came in one day, and stayed for hours, the bartender mused. – Why was never clear, and he never volunteered information of any kind.

– We recognized him, a man mused, mused *a lot*. – Or thought we did. But he had been dead for twenty years, so we figured the guy in question was dressing up or simply was a look-alike of some kind. Somby is quite the hero in these parts. Twenty years ago this was a thriving part of town with packed theaters and clubs.

– He came back here, a woman cried from the darkness, – to relive his triumphs and happiness. He and his wife visited this area often, crisscrossing it through the night, having *lots* of fun. It was a tragedy, a damn tragedy what happened to them both.

Ayes echoed through the room.

Chloe, piss-drunk frowned, striving to keep her head from falling and hitting the hard wood of the bar, and squinting her eyes, staring into the darkness she attempted to glimpse the face of the woman speaking.

Her voice, her voice didn't sound *sincere* at all.

Everybody else sat there nodding, nodding, nodding, but Chloe, poor Chloe sat there with a stupid frown on her face, squinting her eyes, attempting to spot the woman in the smoke and the mirror.

The bartender turned on the TV and that act also turned on the light in the adjacent room at the other side of the building. They saw it cast in a bright light through the open doors. The entire wall slid aside, revealing a lot of open space, lots and lots of poker, Black Jack and roulette tables, and an assortment of other game boards.

The bartender called attention to himself, and he began speaking with outstretched arms and an ironic grin painted on his face.

– The good city council in Jaynagar has, in its infinite wisdom decided gambling isn't legal until after six each day, and now, my good people the time has come. The games will begin shortly, and you will be able to enjoy them until six in the morning.

People filed into the empty space, filling it up. It was large and wouldn't be filled to capacity in hours, when Jaynagar's tired working force and gamblers and wealthy elite alike flocked to the Pit.

Chloe had seen it happen every night. It had surprised her, and the journalist in her wrote a story in her head virtually on autopilot. Her fingers touched the keys and raced across the keyboard.

Her hands moved, and not across the keyboard, but in the air. She sat at the center of the pentacle, and cast spells and mumbled curses and wishes and alien syllables.

She crossed the threshold to the sportsbook room with the male escort by her side. They took their time, arriving as one of the last of those enjoying the pub's hospitality during the last rays of daylight. Jaynagar was far south. Twilight was brief and brutal here. The darkness fell quickly. She sensed it, sensed all the wings flapping in the night. The wheel of fortune was spinning and spinning. Dices were cast.

Chloe stumbled. Her male escort caught her, and she granted him a grateful look.

If she squinted her eyes just right, she could spot David Fallon Somby and his lovely and sexy bride by the tables, he somber, with a constant frown on his brow, and she jubilant and radiant. Somby had come here often after his wife's death. He didn't even look the same. The frown had become deep furrows on his forehead, the expensive clothes wrinkled and dusty, as if he had been sleeping in them for weeks. Chloe saw him, saw him with uncanny clarity, his shaking hands, and flickering eyes, and a sense of profound sadness overwhelmed her.

She stared transfixed at the spinning wheels, the jumping dices, and eventually the cards being flipped at the poker table.

– One turn of a card, he said, – and a life may change irrevocably.

She smiled in acknowledgement to him, while all kinds of strange thoughts roamed her mind. It dawned on her that she couldn't recall his name.

Terror struck her like icy water.

A woman jumped and shouted in joy. The dealer pushed one seriously large heap of chips her way. She began piling them up in an excited frenzy.

Another woman sat there with a deadly pale face. She played with her last few chips. A minute or two later she pushed them into the center of the table. Less than a minute later she had lost. She stood up, smiled and left, left the table, the room and everything. Chloe heard a crack like thunder, and she shook hard.

The two of them had dinner in the restaurant. He raised his glass to a toast and so did she.

– To the tales of mystery and imagination - David Fallon Somby, she said. – May they long reign.

– Hear, hear, he seconded her statement.

Glasses met and parted. She drank, drank deep. Her pale cheeks turned a healthy red.

– It's quite a mystery, she stated firmly, even with a partly paralyzed tongue, where the food didn't really taste any longer. – There is no lack of information here. One might even say there's an abundance of information, but the pieces don't fit together at all. On the contrary: even if you ignore the obvious contradictions and unbelievable details there's still a long list of facts working against each other.

– David Fallon Somby is killed twice, he said, – with twenty years between the two murders, with the same knife, under similar but still different circumstances.

He was encouraged when it dawned on him that she wasn't put off by the morbid subject, but on the contrary was excited by it.

– Logic dictates that one of them wasn't Somby…

– That's true, as far as it goes… She teased him, making him blush deeply. – Using conventional logic.

She waited, pausing, before continuing.

– DNA-samples match… check. Dental work fit… check. Facial details, broken bones, scars… check. There is no sign of plastic surgery… check. Everything… fit. We're not talking about identical twins here, but the same man.

– Except for the obvious, he nodded glumly.

– I expect him to walk through the door any time, now, she grinned.

A shudder of delight trickled down her spine.

Somewhere a white cloth blew in the draft. Drops of blood hit the carpet below. Candles flickered in a dark space without walls.

Pain touched her, touched Chloe Webster. She crouched in her seat. The room began spinning, spinning slowly and nausea hit her like a boxing glove in the belly.

– Take this ring, she said in a bright room, filled with shadows. – Take this ring as a token of my love.

He didn't notice anything. She straightened, the pain leaving her. Only the memory of it remained, a never-closing scar in her mind.

The winner paid for drinks to everybody, which was a considerable number, but the cash she had to put up to do so was hardly more than a pinprick of a hole in her new and bigger pocket. The gambling slowly grinded to a halt, as people turned more and more intoxicated, and the celebration took off. The bartender and casino-owner fought against it for a while, by encouraging people to keep playing, but then he sighed and joined in on the celebrations. He was lucky every night, of course, getting both the money and the joy.

A large man landed on a table, and it broke like china. No one noticed.

In a corner a woman stood and studied Chloe, as poor Chloe downed yet another drink.

The party eventually moved on, as parties sometimes do to another location. A group of drunken people managed, somehow to not loose each other on the street. They waved bottles and glasses in equal measure.

– I'll bet you, a man mumbled.
He took a few more steps.
– I'LL BET YA
People waited excited for him to continue, but the thought seemed to have slipped his mind. A few members of the group wavered and fell off the ship. Where they ended up Chloe couldn't say.
– MAN OVERBOARD. MAN OVERBOARD.
Someone cried.
Hysterical laughter ensued.
– I'm willing to bet you anything that the magistrates would never have tolerated all this waving with bottles and disorder outside The Pit.
A man told Chloe in confidence in a quiet moment between the shouting and hollering.
– Anything? She teased him.
He didn't notice.
The quiet moment stretched out forever to her, as moments sometimes did… to her.
– TO THE PIT! A man shouted and raised his glass (and his bottle). – MAY IT LONG LIVE
– THE PIT! The crowd replied.
She found herself inside, in a rather spacious living room, a place filled with statues. They stared at her. They were all staring at her, the beyond weird statues. She could even swear one of them turned its head.
– The Pit is a p-phenomenon, a woman nodded to her glass.
The woman wasn't truly stuttering. She was merely so drunk that she had trouble speaking clearly.
Chloe passed the many open doors to the balconies. She had never seen so many balconies in one place before. They went around the entire building, like the living room itself. The other rooms were at the center of the apartment, creating an eerie effect, an illusion, making the room seem even bigger than it was. Chloe nodded to herself, downing another drink.
– My head turns to stone, a woman said. – It's true, true. I swear it is. I can't move my toes anymore. I can't feel my toes anymore. I can't see my toes anymore. I look down, and I can pretty much glimpse my erect nipples, but that's about it.
– Have you ever, EVER said anything even REMOTELY sensible? Another woman snarled at her.
There was a lot of sniffing and sobbing after that. Chloe walked on.
The fucking on the balconies had already started. Moans and grunts easily overcame the pitiful sounds of the conversation and drunken games

inside. Chloe walked through the hallway in the secret, inner chambers of the old house, passing by the endless row of paintings.

– They *glowed,* a man insisted. – Every single one glowed the moment I passed them.

– The Pit is a cultural institution, a man declared.

And to that they were all solemnly nodding.

– CHEERS! One man burst out in a hysterical bout of laughter, showering everybody with spit and alcohol.

Chloe painted herself, using her little pocket mirror as a guideline, but wasn't pleased with the result and began searching, searching for the elusive restroom. It took time and infinite patience, but finally she glimpsed the door in the distance. It opened up to her, inviting her in, and she heeded its call. She painted her face in broad and powerful strokes and looked, briefly like a native warrior, before it all faded. The brush fell from her shaking hand, slipped through her weak fingers. She stood before the mirror in the restroom, brushing her hair in a slow, languished mode. It was such a pleasant sensation and made her smile a little.

The image in the mirror returned the smile, with its fangs and cruel smile. Clouds drifted in there, around the creature, the mirror image. A vast alien landscape revealed itself.

Chloe walks in the park, back and forth, laughing with the man with hair by her side. His face is indistinct, shifting, never truly the same. The color of his hair seems to shift as the light shifts.

– I'm all things and none, he says, – and you are, too.

They stumbled through city streets, holding on to each other for bare life. To their left stood crocked an old row of fountains. They had seen better days, just like the rest of the Pit.

– There is water in them, she insisted. – I can hear it. I can't see it, but I can hear it as clearly as I hear you speak.

He said something, but she didn't get what.

The park was bigger than ever, overgrown, reaching out to the city streets around it. She imagined she was able to actually see the branches grow, reach across the gray bed of the street. They walked inside, into the labyrinth of tall grass, trees and uncontrolled growth.

They sat down on a rusty bench. He held her hands, giving her tiny, eager kisses. She reddened.

– Have you never wondered, I mean really, really wondered… what's out there?

He was all over her with touch and kisses, like an eager kid.

The sound of the water pulled her. She walked there, reaching the river bank and feeling the moisture soak her naked legs. She stopped by the bridge. It beckoned her. Just a few steps more, and she would be on her way.

He pulled her back, into his arms. She returned his affectionate kisses, reluctantly at first, then wildly and passionately. They sat down on the newly painted bench in the well-groomed park. In a blur of fevered emotions she noticed he was fumbling with her sweater, attempting to pull it over her head. She chuckled and raised her arms above her head, eagerly surrendering to his persistent advances. He fondled her breasts, fondled them vigorously, as he was breathing into her ear. She sighed and moved a bit on the bench, and as she did she suddenly felt the warm, warm glow grow brutally between her thighs.

– Never? She gasped.

The girl looked at the boy with love and desire in her eyes. She pulled the top over her head, and revealed her swollen breasts. He pulled down his pants. She strived with removing hers, writhing on the uncomfortable bench.

He crawled on top of her, and she forgot uncomfortable, forgot everything but his body against her. She glimpsed his patronizing smile, but it didn't register in her fevered consciousness. He chased away the chilly draft from the black night surrounding them with his tender kisses and lovely smile. She cried out his name, relating it endlessly, not hearing herself say it.

– I have to cross that bridge, she insisted.

He just smiled at her, and kissed her lips.

And pushed into her, lighting a glow in her. She began moving under him, moving, moving, and forgetting everything else. The stench of ammoniac made her nose twitch, twitch, twitch. A woman hummed to herself while she was cleaning the floor in a large house, one with so many floors that, when one was looking up the giant marble spiral stairs there was no end in sight. Chloe fell into a deep abyss, and couldn't, no matter how much she wanted to find her way back up.

As she came, as she fell hard she bit into his shoulder, drawing rust and dawn and dusk and everything under the sun and the moon. In that pint of blood was the Universe. It opened up to her like a flower in spring.

The next morning came and went. The sun crossed the sea in an instant, and the moon smiled down on her.

– I know you from somewhere… don't I? Chloe asked the woman blocking the gateway.

– No, you don't, the woman shook her head. – You don't know me at all. We have, in fact never met.

Chloe walked through the park. Yellow leaves blew around her feet. She walked through the castle hallways, looking at the paintings. One of the paintings depicted an old woman painting the bridge over troubled waters. Suddenly she was no longer in the castle. At least it no longer looked like the castle, but a place filled with stale air. The floor was covered in mud, and the walls looked like they hadn't been cleaned for years. She whimpered. There was a sound behind her. She turned her head and heard the cruel, triumphant laughter, and she ran. She ran so hard that her chest hurt, and her legs turned to jelly, and she feared they would give in beneath her, and that she would fall into the mud, the mud moving and grinning to her as if alive, a grin revealing huge, sharp fangs, and a wide gap.

She moaned in the arms of the man without a face. And there was pain and joy. And that felt right, that felt real. She looked at the woman blocking the gate covered in cold sweat, looked at her with insane eyes. The woman returned a blinding smile. Chloe moaned in fear and joy, and she could no longer tell which was which.

Chloe walked slowly at the water surface, stumbling now and then towards the center of the lake. Her feet turned wet, but she kept walking, kept stumbling. The hotel was on her right, the house to her left. The unknown, so familiar woman blocked the gateway at the center of the lake.

– I'm going to show you what things are like, now, she said. – I'm going to reveal the Universe to you.

Chloe shivered in the cold moonlight.

– You are Chloe, she grinned, and Chloe gasped by the onslaught hitting her. – You are now. And by the snap of my fingers… you may not be.

The Lady of the Lake fell, fell into the Abyss. The waters swallowed her and pulled her down, and all the air in her lungs faded away, and she faded away, as she hit the bottom and lay on her back there forever, fading away like the distant shadows above.

Chloe awoke on the bench, the wide bench. She was nude, but she didn't feel cold. The man by her side was still sleeping, his face peaceful in his deep sleep. She reached for her clothes, but they weren't there. The smile lingered on her face, too. She knew that, seeing her face from a given point beyond herself. Chloe saw herself walk on a trail between the trees, glimpsing the fearful truth, the fangs and claws Beyond. The Woman with her face hidden, cast in shadows hovered before her, clearly just as much at home in the air as on the ground. Chloe felt fear, but she couldn't act on it, couldn't properly express herself. Her attention and wonder was locked on the eternal specter hovering above her… like a Goddess.

– I'm going to show you wonders, and you, like the pathetic creature you are, will crumble under their weight like paper.

A hard, solid hand touched Chloe's head. The Goddess didn't move, but a hand, a third hand appeared from nowhere, and the world changed, transformed around Chloe Webster, into ghosts and shadows.

The scream, the howl shook her, shook her hard, beyond hard. She found herself crouched by a tree, staring at nothing, at herself with eyes big as footballs.

Chloe walked, and walked, not stopping for anything, even though she turned her head once or twice, as she imagined someone calling her name, faintly at the edge of her consciousness. Her eyes, her head began moving, slowly. Unable to stop herself she scanned her surroundings wherever she went, scanned them fervently for signs of life, but she didn't really see anything or notice anything outside the painting she had become a part of. She saw herself become herself, a brush there, a stroke here.

Five people stood on a corner, having a conversation. They seemed agitated, but she heard no sound to add to her imagery. Everything had turned silent and cold. She slid through city streets like a phantom, unable to affect anything around her.

The wind was blowing, a tiny draft or a powerful gust, sometimes warm and sometimes cold, but never lukewarm.

The hand moving the brush painting Chloe Webster stopped, and faded away. Chloe glimpsed a cruel smile in the shadow world beneath the hood. The hand reappeared with a wet cloth, and began erasing the image of Chloe from the painting. The stench of ammoniac ripped her nostrils asunder and made her gag in fright and bile rise in her throat. She faded, even as her surroundings faded, and a completely different picture emerged beneath.

The park with its vast lake was gone, gone forever, and only the city streets with its rough edges remained. She searched for the bridge, but it was nowhere to be found.

She stumbled across Altman Square, across Pit Lake in the gray morning light, towards the fountain at its center. Usually when she looked at it, it was dry and derelict, but sometimes, on rare occasions it was bursting with water, with fire, burning with enough heat to sweep everything clean. It strengthened her, and she reached for it with all the power she could muster. She stumbled and fell, but kept crawling towards the fountain at the center.

They found her there, in the morning, as the first commuters began filling the lake. The first few or hundred ignored her, like they usually ignored all the unfortunate inhabitants of the Pit, but there were those that stopped, just a few of the still river brushing past her.

– What happened? Desire asked. – Please *answer* me.

A hand moved back and forth before her face. Her eyes didn't move, didn't move at all, didn't give the slightest indication of perceiving the moving hand.

Chloe's face was locked in a smile, a horrible, dull smile. Desire squeezed her arm, as hard as she was able, but there was no discernible reaction in either the face or the body. Everything seemed to be… switched off.

Other worried and indifferent faces faded in and out, like the water and the fire and shadow and the mist of the fountain at the center of the lake.

Chloe Webster sat there with an empty expression in her pale face and stared at nothing.

CHAPTER FIFTEEN

On the sixth day

I go, Chloe wrote on her laptop. I go where no one will find me.

She sat on the bed. Eyes are wary when she looks around her, on the bed, on the bed full of dirt. On the floor are large, dirty footprints. Chloe is scrubbed clean. Hair is wet. Skin is red.

Chloe dressed in quick, measured movements. Her suitcase is already packed. The dolls stared at her. She closed and locked the suitcase.

Tianuc Merde is walking down the road, she wrote. Finally! After a long time it's finally happening.

She saw him, the wanderer in her inner eye, too, like she did many things.

The walls hissed at her, and she couldn't get out of here, couldn't flee fast enough, down the murky stairs, across the lake.

A car passed her. She released a panicked shout, and people stared curiously at her. They watched as she rushed through the entrance of the hotel. The hotel guests glanced at her as she walked, somewhat controlled to the desk.

– I need a taxi to the city center this minute, she muttered to the bell clerk, forcing herself, by an act of will to calm down.

– Very well, ma'am, the clerk acknowledged, – but there should be quite a few available cars at Willard Square right now. I can inquire…

– NO! She shouted.

He looked at her with worry in his dull eyes.

– I need a car from the outside, she stated, yet again pulling herself together.

– Very well, ma'am, the man nodded.

He had worked elsewhere in the Pit before he started at his current position, and was used to quite a bit.

She walked to the couch across the hall, and sat down. People stared at her. The carpet moved a couple of steps away. She shook and stared at it for a long time until she was confident that it hadn't, in truth moved, or at least that it wouldn't do so again. A wrinkle remained in the carpet. Her big eyes never wavered from the spot. She found her laptop and opened it. There was an outlet in the wall not far away. She ignored it and turned the machine on by battery power alone.

The computer hummed and worked quite well (and didn't stare at her with ominous eyes). She began watching the photographs she had taken the last few days, across the width and length of the Pit.

She was lost in it, in the images and sounds and smells and the taste in her mouth, lost to the point of forgetting to glance cautiously at the wrinkle in the carpet. The frown on her brow persisted as she looked through the pictures, for the second, third and tenth time.

There was a haunting quality to it all, to every single picture from the Pit. Wherever they had been taken, the Lake, the Harbor, from the rooftops or on street level, inside or outside the many interesting buildings they spoke to her inner self in mysterious whispers and sinister hisses.

But what still startled her were those taken in the demarcation zone between The Pit and the rest of the city, the remote area by the bus station. She had taken the pictures in the afternoon, during rush hour. The place had been filled with crowds, with commuters on their way home from a strenuous day. She had seen them, heard them, smelled them, and tasted their foul flavor in her mouth. A few of them had even dumped into her in their haste, and had spat cruel words at her.

They weren't in the pictures. Not a single person was. She had used the monitor on the camera and looked at the pictures there and then, and had wanted to scream, had taken more pictures, and the result had remained the same. When she had turned the camera and photographed herself she had been a hair's breath from suffering an anxiety attack, but she had been in the picture.

But no one else. Not the insane old woman staring at her from behind. Not the young boy with the sick smile. And not the baby looking menacingly at her over her mother's shoulder.

She looked at herself, at her eerie face and eyes (the deep pools called eyes). They looked like they were bleeding, but she saw no blood. She sat there in the lobby of the old, downtrodden hotel, fearing it was all a mirage.

Steps grew louder. Feet moving on soft carpet material sounded like they were moving on naked floor. She had prepared herself and looked up well before the clerk approached her, and wasn't startled. Chloe stared menacingly at him with her bleeding eyes. He braved the troubled waters and approached her.

– The car is ready for you, now, ma'am, he enlightened her. – It's waiting for you outside.

She didn't voice any reply, only repacked her laptop and rushed outside, leaving him shaken and stirred.

The taxi waited there, with its engine on. She brightened a bit, speeding up her slow walk. Then she frowned again, froze and stopped. The car heaved and breathed, and grinned at her with vicious eyes and a snarling mouth. The car's entire front was a BIG, BIG MOUTH, and it licked its lips in expectation of the coming meal.

Chloe Webster took off. She just ran, ran without care or concern over where she might end up. Her throat was parched in an instant, but she kept running, neither looking at her surrounding space nor listening to its sounds. The foul taste in her mouth persisted.

She found herself with her back to a wall of a building by the subway to the bus station. The wasteland of grinning and loud cars seemed endless to her. The buildings across the road seemed a thousand miles away.

Sweat poured from her brow. It was cold. Each drop froze her skin stiff, making her face immovable, like a mask. She touched it. It felt hard and leathery to the touch.

Her eyes widened so much that it hurt. The silent buzz rose to a roar in her ears, before it slowly, slowly faded. Her breathing returned to normal. Her heartbeat-rate slowed down.

She sat there, on her ass, with her back to the wall. The fear remained, even though the sheer panic subsided. She once again began to notice her surroundings. A little girl had stood still and stared at her for quite some time.

– Are you all right, lady? The girl asked with a thin voice.

Chloe nodded, striving to make the smile work beyond the thin, pale version. She rose. Her back hurt, as if she had been sitting rigid on her ass for hours. She looked at her watch. It had taken a hit and was smeared in blood. It was broken and could no longer measure anything even resembling time.

The girl's mother returned for her, grabbed her hand and pulled her with her, with a few angry words Chloe didn't catch.

People flowed into the subway, heading towards the bus station, heading home. It was afternoon already. Chloe strived to think, to look back at missing hours, but everything had turned into one deep and black hole of nothingness. Her head hurt. Every time she closed her eyes confusing images flooded her mind, but that was all. She couldn't make sense of them.

There was no emotion attached, no… connection. She shook her head in confusion. Her eyes wandered randomly at the swirling mass passing her. She began studying the people closest to her, focusing on individual characteristics. A woman had a mole on her left cheek. It wasn't fake, not a result of carefully applied make up, but real and pulsing and glowing.

Two boys had the same similar silly grins painted on their faces. The grins looked fake beyond words, as true and white as city snow in the north.

Chloe took their picture. She could see them on the digital image afterwards, when she checked.

The commuters and the rest disappeared into the dark subway, fading away into the darkness. She took more pictures, and the commuters were there, not only through her eyes. She breathed easier in stark relief.

The hole beckoned Chloe, and she began moving forward, into the vastness pulling at her.

Then she froze. The hole changed into a big bad grinning mouth threatening to swallow her whole, and she pulled back in horror. After breathing in and out once, twice, she broke into tears, and ran away again.

A million years later she found herself on the lone bench at the center of Pit Lake. Everything seemed changed, alien, and she felt totally disoriented and confused and paralyzed.

She stared at her bag, astounded over the fact that it was still in her hand. The laptop was on, and flashing images in a constant, uneven stream filled the screen. She opened it and sat there with it in her lap, staring at the flashing images with a pained expression on her face.

The computer screen fed her the visuals of her walk around The Pit, returning the memories of the last few days and nights to her, at least partly. Everything felt wrong, felt disjointed. She crouched there on the bench, unable to move from her frozen position. Every time she as much as attempted to look up she saw twisted faces grinning at her, people hissing at her, staring at her with wicked eyes.

She felt smaller and smaller and feared there would be nothing left of her soon.

A hand touched her shoulder. She choked when she looked at it, at its long claws and reptile skin. A long, long time passed, until she looked up and discovered Desire, and imagined that the hand was just a hand, soft and comforting.

– What did you say? She said dumbfounded.

– I called your name, Desire replied. – You looked kinda out of it right there.

– Yeah. Chloe dried saliva off her lips and jaw vigorously. – Out of it.

Desire sat down by her side and touched her cheek briefly.

– Are you all right?

– Yeah. Chloe nodded. – Right as rain.

She chuckled by the joke, the silly joke.

– What *happened* to you last night?

– Nothing happened… did it?
Chloe asked with a tiny, whiny voice.
Then she brightened.
– I walked in the park with… with…
– No. Desire shook her head decisively. – That was the day before. You told us about it before you…
– I can't remember, Chloe whimpered. – I can't remember a *thing,* not even meeting up with you guys. Why can't I *remember?*
– You poor girl, Desire said softly. – I've heard this may happen to someone seeking too hard and too far.
Chloe began shaking and once she began she couldn't stop. It grew progressively worse, and in a matter of seconds she practically fell into the other girl's embrace, totally unable to free herself from terror's brutal grip.
– Come with me. She heard Desire's voice after an eternity of silence.
She followed the girl meekly. They went to yet another coffee shop on yet another corner. The shaking ground wouldn't leave Chloe alone. She had to focus all her strength on standing her ground, staying on her feet while stumbling after the tall skewed-eyed girl.
They sat down by a corner table, where they could see both sides of the street. Desire, too, Chloe noticed had nervous, flickering eyes.
– I'll get us some tea.
– No tea, Chloe said, raising her voice an octave.
– But they have the best tea ever here…
– No, tea, Chloe cried low and dark, with ugly eyes. – Whatever else they may have, even stinking coffee, but *no tea.*
– I understand, Desire whispered, and hurried away.
Chloe sat there by the large window and stared at the monogamous mass racing back and forth on the street outside. She wasn't shaking anymore, but sat deadly still.
The two women sat there and drank their black coffee. It burned in their throat and stomach. That fact felt good, very good.
– I started noticing it yesterday, Desire said, speaking fast and quietly. – Or rather: I wasn't certain I was being followed until two days ago. I've felt itchy for weeks. My boyfriend is a journalist and this has been going on since he started digging deeper into the murder of David Fallon Somby.
A thrill shot through Chloe.
– I've been digging in that hole, too, Chloe said. – And other, related things besides.
– You have? Desire's eyes widened.

– I have indeed, and I can tell you right away there's a lot of uncovered ground on that case. Nobody seems to be digging very deep. Nobody seems to *want to*.

They drank a lot of hot, black coffee. It burned in their stomach, but it couldn't truly warm them. They sat there shaking, to the point of having difficulties holding their cups.

The streets seemed empty, as if all the people walking in all directions around them didn't exist, as if they could be said to be nothing but specters in a deserted and desolate urban landscape.

They looked at themselves in the mirror of a store window. Both of them stared, partly at themselves, partly to the side, a beyond haunted look in their eyes, and they didn't see anything, anything that was there. A man in black stood at the opposite corner, black pants, jacket and a flat-brimmed hat. He had no face. They turned around, spun around and looked at the spot at the opposite corner, and he wasn't there.

Desire crouched there, on the street, unable to breathe. It wasn't like she was under water, where she had to hold her breath, but like there was no air, no air at all.

A hand rested on her shoulder. She looked up through a thick film of pain and tears.

– There is air, Chloe said in a strange, hollow voice, – you just have to learn to breathe, like everybody else.

Desire's vision cleared, staring at the outstretched hand of the other woman.

– Come, Chloe told her.

They headed off, keeping to themselves, slipping between the crowds like quicksilver, walking where no one walked.

The police station was down the road, by the old harbor (no longer the harbor), adjacent to Pit Lake. They crossed the giant parking lot, filled with snarling cars, ascended the stairs to the large building, and for some reason Chloe imagined she heard the sound of running water.

The chill inside the building was a horrible contrast to the horrible heat outside. They headed, very determined for the desk, to the sergeant behind it.

– My name is…

– We know who you are, the woman behind the desk snapped.

– My name is Chloe Webster, Chloe stated patiently. – I'm an investigative reporter with the magazine Colors in the Night. This is my assistant, Desire Watson. We would like to speak to the detective in charge of the Somby murder investigation, please.

– No, we don't have an appointment, Desire grinned.

– Just one moment, the woman behind the desk said sourly.

She took one phone, waited a little while it rang, and then said:

– There are two reporters here to see you.

She put the phone down.

– You may see her, now. It's room 217, up the stairs, and down the hall.

They looked astonished at each other.

The station had at one point been a hotel, and it still resembled one. But that little fact only added to the two women's sense of unreality. Everything, from the sergeant offbeat reaction, to the phone call made them lose ever more bits and pieces of their grip on reality. They walked on a slippery road, and each new step brought them closer to falling.

Room 217 was situated in the other wing, far away from the hectic activity in the main section. Chloe could swear she spotted a spider in the corner of the long corridor. It grinned at her, and she gasped in fear. Desire held around her, and kissed her softly on the cheek, comforting her the best she was able.

There were no cops in the corridor, no people at all, nothing but dust and shadows.

Desire knocked hard, perhaps too hard on the door leading to room

217

A woman with a drawn, very drawn face opened the door.

– Come in, she bid them in a hushed voice.

They slipped inside, and she quickly closed the door behind them.

– I am Isabel Connor, the investigating detective in the Fallon case.

She reached out a hand, and they took it, unable to tell which hand was shaking the most, theirs or hers. They looked at a woman in her late twenties, looking like forty. Her hands shook when she lit a cigarette.

– It helps me… you know… relax. I need to, you know… relax.

On the wall was a painting of a large campfire and of a face, with eyes, mouth and nose submerged in it, of a creature being the fire, staring at the world from that point of seething flames. Isabel noticed their glances and looked even more uncomfortable at them.

She took one look at them and nodded to herself. They nodded, too, hardly aware of doing so. She sat down behind her desk, and they sat down, as well. Chloe noticed the scratches on the edge of the table, and then the woman's ruined nails.

Isabel turned on her computer. Chloe found it… odd that it hadn't been on like office computers usually were. It gave off an eerie, loud sound giving her the chills, deeper chills.

It's only a computer, she thought. Only a machine. A *machine*.

Like the cars, with their large, greedy mouths, with teeth gnawing, gnawing, gnawing…

It took thirty, forty seconds, and a few more keystrokes on Isabel's part, and then images and text filled the windows.

– Journalists come here, have come here several times before. I give them the official version, and they write that. I give them… the spicy details, and they still write the official version. I haven't bothered explaining myself for quite a while…

She looked at them, with an icy stare burning them.

– But when I saw you two… I kinda… spotted kindred spirits, if you know what I mean.

They nodded, not really moving their head, but nodding nonetheless.

The entire time they were in there they heard this eerie sound, like scratching on the walls. It was unnerving, and even more so because of their current unnerved state.

– David Fallon Somby, the infamous movie director, Isabel began, with an ironic twist of her mouth, – was found dead a month ago, after the night of Samhain, November 1. He was found on a bed in a derelict building not far from here, in the worst of the worst slum of East Side Downtown, of the Pit, in a manner the movie director Edgar Allan described as a scene from Somby's movie Dark Shadows in Bright Lights.

She spoke in an even, business-like manner. The discord was hardly noticeable, but to them it stood out, impossible to ignore. In her they recognized themselves.

– He was brought there, and killed there. There were very few signs of struggle. He hadn't been drugged, at least not with anything modern science could discern. Genetic testing and further comparison of physical characteristics found that this was the same man that had been killed twenty years earlier, *the same man,* not a twin. The report doesn't say it explicitly, but if you push the very nervous guys that wrote it that is pretty much what they are saying.

Chloe studied the images, studied the images again. The flow gave her the chills, touching something deep within her, cutting and burrowing.

The scratching continued. She studied the other two in an effort to discern whether or not they noticed it, but if they did they gave no sign of doing so. Either they deliberately ignored it or just didn't hear anything. But how could that be? Either choice was… was

Chloe dried her brow. She did it twice in quick succession, to no avail. The sweat kept coming.

– The investigation took a toll on the investigative team right from the start. The nightmares began almost immediately. Both I and Hesky felt very shitty, but we felt almost okay when we saw the way it worked on Lasko and Monroe. Lasko was a veteran from a dozen rough cases, but we watched him disintegrate before our eyes…

A photo showed Lasko in a padded cell. He just sat there, staring at nothing. They watched a film of him, when the doctors attempted to get a reaction from him. His eyes didn't move. There wasn't the slightest reaction, not even from the pupils when they shone a light at them.

– There is nothing physiologically wrong with the patient, the doctor said on the film. – Nothing we have been able to find, at least. His mind and body have quite simply… shut down. It's all quite… fascinating, really.

The doctor smiled, a quick, nervous smile, devoid of warmth. He turned his head and looked behind him, as if there was something there, something he or the camera couldn't fathom.

– Have you ever walked through empty streets a dark night? Isabel asked her two guests, not really expecting an answer and kept going, kept speaking. – There is an echo, hardly noticeable, as if there is another, putting down his or her foot a moment after you, so synchronized that you can never be certain there is anyone there, no matter how much you fear there is. Then… the nature of the echo *changes*. It becomes more pronounced. There is a bigger delay between your feet hitting the ground and that of the other, behind you. You become almost positive there is someone there, but not quite. But the heart starts beating in your chest, hard enough for you to actually hear it, and you turn your head every second, and you see nothing, but the sound grows louder and louder and louder, until it is close by, and you panic and start walking faster, increasing your speed until you start running, and the panic overtakes you completely, and you run, until the running becomes the only thing that matters in your life, and the cold, cold fear fills you up like a sponge, and you are nothing but your instinct, a scared animal fleeing the predator.

Silence filled the room, as Isabel stared at them with large, eerie, downright creepy eyes. Chloe realized that she held her breath and had trouble breaking the spell. All kinds of thoughts and feverish images danced in her mind until she was finally able to breathe again.

She noticed that the door to the other room stood slightly ajar. There was a bed in there. Isabel slept in her office.

Albert Monroe had hanged himself. They studied dispassionately, paralyzed his bloated face. Carl Hesky had quit the force and disappeared, vanished from the face of the Earth. Misfortune and accidents kept plaguing the investigation, until it was quietly dropped and Connor was finally left alone with her plight.

– And the Cult of Beelzebub? Chloe asked, a strange ambivalence notable in her voice.

– Unknown. Connor shook her head. – They haven't truly resurfaced, not with the presence they once had. There are lots of rumors and innuendo, but nothing aside from that, nothing solid, nothing but ghosts and shadows.

The last part of the sentence made Chloe frown, made her sense even more empathically the presence of the creatures scratching the walls.

– You should join us, Desire said. – Strength in numbers and all that.

– And make myself an even bigger target, you mean?

Connor was very pale when she smiled, clearly out of it, clearly reduced in stature and self-worth.

– You should go with us, Chloe stated calmly. – We can help and support each other, you know.

– Of course, Isabel said suddenly, unexpectedly, – I'll just get my things. It will only take a moment.

It didn't actually take much more than that. She picked a few items from her bedroom, from a drawer there, and put in her purse. Not long after that they were all walking down the hallway. She didn't lock or even close the door to her office.

Chloe realized she was difficult to read. The detective averted her eyes when the other studied her. Even her fear was mixed with something else Chloe didn't understand.

They left the building through the busy entrance hall of the police station. Everybody stared at them, even those turned away. They imagined they saw eyes in the back of people's neck, eyes blinking, blinking, blinking.

The streets felt better after that, somewhat, not so imposing. The buzz, low and insistent was there, but the people were just people, not frightening golems with horns staring them down.

They walked the streets aimlessly for hours, for what felt like days and nights without number. An old woman stood on a corner, playing the violin. It was an old violin, not so well tended, releasing brittle, out of tune music. It haunted them long after they had left the scene behind. They heard it echoing between the old walls.

– She could play, couldn't she, I mean really play?

Isabel sniffed the air, as if the music could be smelled, could be heard through the nose.

– At least she could, once, I guess, Chloe acknowledged.

And the words themselves created such emptiness within her. She wanted to cry. She did, but there were no tears.
– We can go to my place, Desire said, frowning. – There is more than enough room. My roommate hasn't been there for days, and I haven't been able to get hold of her. Nobody seems to know where she is. I know. I've called around.
Tired legs made their way the last stretch up a minor rise. There was a single block of flats there, not too rundown. Someone had even mowed the lawn outside the entrance not so long ago. There was no elevator. They climbed the stairs to the fourth floor. All three were breathing hard by the time they reached the top. The door slammed shut behind them with the characteristic loud and shocking sound.
– I'll make dinner, Desire said tired and weary.
It was a studio, except for the bathroom basically just one room that was kitchen, bedroom and living room. There were two beds. One had been made. The others hadn't.
– She made her bed in the morning, Desire said, – and then she took off, took off without a word.
Desire lived by the harbor, the true, modern harbor. Chloe looked out the window, at the pier across the street. It stretched far out into Peltry Sound. The white benches looked gray under the clouded and dark sky. The light the sun cast through the clouds was pale and virtually insignificant.
At the point of the pier she spotted a tiny shed. Flickering flames seemed to dance behind the window. Chloe rubbed the cold skin on her shoulders. Her fingers felt like claws, but they were only fingers. For a moment there she had imagined otherwise.
A wheeze, a wheezing sound rose from below, from the central heating system that wasn't on, hadn't been on for years. It had been a long time sincc there had been any kind of winter here.
The wheeze sounded almost human, or sounded as if it was coming from a human being.
The three of them grabbed hands, and stood there shaking for minutes before finally calming down.
– Dinner will be ready soon, Desire stated, rubbing them both on the cheek, in a comforting gesture.
They smelled it, smelled the food waiting for them, hungry to be devoured, to be fed the starving humans.
Not long after that they sat by the table, feeding, with shadows in all shapes surrounding them.
– I used to have a life, Isabel cried. – Goddess, how I long for a return to that time.

The other two didn't comment on her outburst. They had enough with their own, troubled thoughts.

It was raining outside. They heard the rain clearly, heard it hit the street through the open window. But when they actually looked the windows were as dry as ever.

– Life isn't straightforward, Chloe heard herself say eventually. – Most people just prefer to think so, think of it as a brick wall, instead of the mist and shadows it is. I have always sought what's… beyond.

– And now you've found it, Isabel spat.

The words and the harshness behind them hurt Chloe. Unable to tell why or understand she just shook her head.

Something hissed at her from the shadows, and she shrunk in her chair. She wondered if she looked as intimidated, scared and downtrodden as her two companions. Slowly her left hand rolled into a fist.

– No, she said.

– No? Isabel frowned. – What do you mean, no?

– We are terrified wrecks, shrinking in both the light and the shadow and darkness, she said, the volume of her voice increasing slightly. – We should be proud, keeping our heads high in the wind. We are Human Beings, not dying *wraiths* waiting for the silence of the grave.

It didn't sound very convincing in her ears, and she feared the sound of her voice hardly carried across the table to her companions, and she wanted to go to the couch and crouch on it, waiting there for Death to claim her.

The two women looked at her, at each other, and she saw something there, the first shadow of a smile, of defiance and…

… and anger, and determination, and a will beyond the body.

They took a shower, feeling a little better. The water felt good, cleansing, as they took their turn in the small cubicle. They dried themselves afterwards, discovering that they had long since passed the point of shyness. Chloe and Isabel didn't have a change in clothes, but could at least borrow underwear from Desire to feel a little better. Isabel cleaned her gun and tested it on an empty chamber, pointing at an imaginary enemy, there, beyond the walls.

– Do you have more of those? Desire giggled hysterically.

– Can you use it? Isabel asked patronizingly, not waiting for Desire's weak shaking of the head and timid expression before turning away.

– It will probably not do much good, anyway, Chloe said with a nasty shrug, very deliberately, feeling strangely empowered by the others' sting of fright.

In the hallway mirror she imaged she saw through to the Other World, where wraiths and ghouls ruled.

They got all sweaty again fast, outside, in the searing heat. Standing still or walking, it made no difference. This was a typical, more than a typical hot late, late Indian Summer night in Jaynagar. The sweltering heat and dry wind imposed itself ruthlessly on suffering bodies and minds. They had all brought their bottles of water, and they needed them to not be left dry husks in a matter of minutes. Standing still did them no good, so they walked.

In the ineffective mirrors of windows, she glimpsed the Other World, where wraiths and ghouls ruled.

She looked around her, studying the rhythm, the confusing pattern of movement in the big city, the dizziness almost overwhelming her.

– Are you all right? Desire asked, clearly worried.

– I feel like I haven't washed for days, Chloe replied angrily, sullenly. – I can hardly keep food down, and I'm sweating like a pig.

And she wondered yet again if pigs did sweat.

She touched Desire's cheek, her hand light as a feather.

They entered the Old City, easily noticing the distinct difference between where they had come from and where they were headed.

– This is the original Pit, isn't it? Desire cried, strangely excited. – The area where it all began, where it started… spreading?

– Yes. Isabel nodded curtly. – This is where it all began going sour.

Several cars had been parked illegally on the sidewalk by the overgrown park. One had the lights on inside. Chloe saw a shape in there, in the driver's seat. In the others darkness dominated totally, and she couldn't see a thing. She shuddered and picked up the pace. Her two companions, with equally flickering eyes joined her.

The building in front of them pointed to itself, really. At least they imagined it did, as they crossed into its shadow. They walked inside and its presence turned even more imposing. It was an old building. They ascended the quirky steps. The old building whispered to them words of warning and ecstasy. It tingled in both Chloe's bones and flesh, and as the walls shuddered, she shuddered with them.

The door to the apartment was off the hinges. A roll of yellow ribbon had been thrown into a corner. The opening reminded her of an open gap. She felt like she was being sucked in.

They entered the dark and dreary apartment. The roof in the hallway was leaking. Droplets of water hit the pool on the floor.

– It hasn't rained for weeks, Isabel stated out of the blue. – Has it?

Chloe wanted to say something, anything, wanted to reply to her, but didn't.

The bedroom looked distinctively different from the rest of the building. The bed and all the furniture they remembered from the photos had been removed, but they could still see it, imagine the scene, as it had been in their feverish minds. Someone had attempted to erase the pentacle on the floor where the bed had been standing, had scratched the floor methodically, had scratched every possible piece of wood, to the point of making a dump in the floor, in complete vain. The five-star figure and the circle surrounding it remained, an indistinct form glowing in black, in shadow.

Chloe took new pictures, and it showed on them, too. They all stared at them, stared for a long time.

– So, it isn't our imagination, Desire mumbled. – That's… that's…

They walked through the rest of the apartment. It was pretty much like the entrance hallway. The roof wasn't leaking, but the floor was pretty much covered in moisture.

– The bedroom is dry, Isabel cried. – Dry as a desert.

They imagined they saw sand blow in the air, there, as they passed it on their way out.

A nude man blocked the exit. They froze. He grinned at them, as he pretended to pick his teeth with the point of the big knife he held in his left hand.

Insane eyes stared at Chloe. He had a large hard-on, pointing at her. Alien emotions shot through her like fire.

– Stop right there! Isabel shouted.

She held her gun steady, pointing right at his chest. Seemingly totally oblivious to this fact he stepped forward, crossing the threshold. She fired. The first slug didn't quite hit him, or didn't seem to. He kept advancing with his eyes fixed on Chloe. Isabel fired again. This time she clearly hit him straight in the chest. They all saw it, saw the red line stand out, in a straight line from his back. He tumbled backwards, back into the hall, and fell on his back there. Blood flooded his mouth. He attempted to catch his breath, but failed and lay still.

They stared incredulous at him, at each other. Isabel stepped forward. Ready for anything she kicked him lightly in the shoulder. There was no discernible reaction. The man remained dead and still. They moved cautiously past him, keeping an eye on him, as if measuring their every step.

– What do w-we d-do n-now?

Desire's teeth hit each other like a machinegun.

– I call it in, Isabel said, – We wait here.
– Absolutely not! Chloe shook her head vehemently. – We must leave, and leave, *now*.
The detective looked like she was going to object, but after a moment or two she nodded.
On their way down all three glanced at the walls. Their eyes never rested on their endless walk. Chloe looked outside through every window they passed. There was no one out there, down there, not a single soul, neither up nor down the street. It was remarkably… empty.
They reached the street without incident, and realized that they had been holding their breath again. Isabel put away the gun, but kept her hand in the pocket. They felt faint when they retraced their tracks, as if they had truly been holding their breath. Ahead awaited them the long row of cars and the overgrown park. They walked through the passage with wild eyes and nervous twitching. Chloe stared at the cars, at all the lit compartments, and the one, dimly lit, and at the shadowy growth at the other side of the street. It seemed like nothing moved and nothing stirred.
But something stirred. Unable to tell whether or not it was outside or inside herself she just moved on.
They walked through empty streets a dark night. There was an echo, hardly noticeable, treacherous, and they wondered if someone was following them, if someone somewhere behind them put their feet down right after them, too close in time for them to know for certain that someone was there.
She blinked, and in that blink she glimpsed a lake under a beige sky and a pale sun. In the middle of the lake was a tree, cast in shadow.
For some reason her attention returned to the one car with the lit compartment. It hadn't moved during the time they had been inside the building. The shape inside was still…
She blinked, and her memory showed her clearly what she hadn't instantly noticed. The car had been empty just now, or at the very least whoever had been sitting inside hadn't been visible.
The nature of the echo changed, turning more pronounced. It was clearly a bigger delay between the time they put down their feet, and that of the other, behind them. She turned her head, and looked, and there was no one there, nothing but the wind and the dust. The sound grew louder and louder in her ears, until it was close by. She started walking faster, and her companions did as well. They speeded up, but had major trouble breathing before they ended up running.

Chloe Webster stopped, right there at the corner. Her companions did, too. And then they heard it, the sound of the thousand feet, everywhere around them. Cold fear filled them as if they were a sponge.
At the other corner, across the street they spotted the man in black. He stopped, and the sound of the thousand feet stopped. Silence reigned in the empty street.
Something sinister beyond words, beyond description engulfed them, made them whimper in fright.
– Who is he? Isabel asked with numb lips and tongue.
– I'm not certain, Chloe replied, – but I can make an educated guess. Can't you? You have studied Magick the last few weeks, haven't you?
Isabel shook her head in disbelief.
– He has many names, Desire mumbled, – The Bogeyman, The Trickster, *Tianuc Merde*. A thousand more.
Isabel paled. In broad daylight, in the warm sun, among the safety of friends and comfortable surroundings she would have shrugged this powerful sense of horror off, but now she believed.
– I have sought him for so long, Chloe mumbled, shouted.
She set out across the street.
– Are you insane? Isabel whispered.
Chloe approached the imposing figure. She felt like she was shrinking, dwindling the closer she came.
His face beneath the mask appeared to her, drawings, wisps in the air.
What are you? Those wisps whispered. Why do you linger here, in this dreary place?
She shook her head, distressed, disturbed, and unable to grasp his meaning.
– Why are *you* here, you bastard? She shouted, close to tears.
I have never been here.
He grabbed his hat, and threw it away. She froze, stared at his head while shaking hers. There was nothing there. She looked for the hat, but she didn't see it anywhere. He began undressing. His upper body faded away, disappeared, as he removed his clothes. She glimpsed the glowing skull, briefly, where his head was supposed to be. In one, swift move she attempted to strike at him, strike his head, his upper body, but there was nothing there, in spite of how he removed the rest of his clothes. She kicked his legs, and the leg was still there, and it was like kicking a brick wall. She screamed in pain and frustration and terror.
Then he was gone. She stared at nothing, except the dust in the air. One gust of wind, and it was gone.
She stood there, shaking, shaking to pieces.

The two other women approached her from behind. She knew they were, even though she didn't see them. They touched her and comforted her, comforted themselves.

The world re-entered the city, its sounds and impressions invading them once again. Cars moved through an adjacent street. Somebody played music in an apartment not far away. They could even identify the exact spot, a loft condo one block away. Three heads moved and looked around in confusion and clarity.

One choir, one multitude of deep, dark voices rose from the ground. They heard people marching, but they saw no one. The choir turned increasingly louder and powerful, as it clearly closed in on them, as they ran, as they couldn't recall having started running, and the terrifying voices threatened to catch up with them.

They ran, without looking back, to the edge of the Pit. It felt like it was such a stretch there, such an infernal distance. They ran and ran and never reached their destination, the salvation far ahead. The Lake was only a brief glimpse, as they crossed it, as they heard water splashing around their shoes and felt their feet getting wet. They reached the vast, open area between the Pit and the bus station. There were a few cars, but they didn't care. They crossed it at street-level, un-choosing the dark hole of a subway beckoning them.

Three terrified women crossed the road, snarling metal mouths snapping at them, hungry for a meal. They ran, leaving The Pit behind, its multitude of voices reaching for them like claws in the blackest night.

CHAPTER SIXTEEN

On the seventh day and night, lasting forever

Chloe woke up with the sound of roaring engines in her ears. She opened her eyes and cried out in pain. Her arm hurt. The lower part by the elbow had been bandaged.

Her back was cold, her front warm, touching the body of the man by her side from head to toe. She beheld his smiling and concerned face. The morning dew covered their exposed skin. A chill fired through Chloe, not in any way influenced by the warm, rising sun.

He yawned and stretched his body. The concerned smile remained even as he kissed the woman on her lips.

– Good morning, he grinned.

– Good morning, she mumbled, a little off, her headache acting up.

The warm, bright and blinding sun hurt her eyes, boiled her blood, stirred a memory she was unable to recall.

– Are you okay? He asked.

– I'm okay, Michael, she replied, a little irritated, hiding it behind a sweet smile.

His smile widened, creating a visceral reaction in her gut.

– It's a good thing it is summer, isn't it? Or we would have surely frozen to death.

He frowned.

– Is it summer?

Chloe frowned, too.

They dressed, with a little help from the other, their clothes being wet and uncomfortable to wear. Their shoes had been spread across the lawn. Chloe found her second one under a bush. They walked arm in arm on the trail between the trees. Michael kicked a pile of yellow leaves.

– It looks so different, now, in daylight, he noted.

She heard the sound of the lake, of its water hitting the shore. It felt so peaceful, so right.

Chloe saw the end of the park between the trees, and then, in no time at all she was back in the streets. She glimpsed Pit Lake and the abandoned, derelict building two blocks away. A strange tingle shot through her. She walked past it, to the parking garage, and her old, dusty car. Somewhere on her way there she had somehow lost Michael. She frowned, striving to think, to reason, frowning in frustration. A sweet memory of lips touching lips flashed through her. She opened the door to her car. It screeched and the screech jarred her mind. She drove away, exited the parking garage and drove south on the wide Motorway 217 between the Pit and the bus station to be. They still hadn't completed it yet. It was one of the major new construction projects in town, and had caused a lot of commotion and dissent before the decision to build had been made official.

She drove on the same M217, along the coastline, towards the suburbs. Her car coughed several times, coughed a lot, but its engine kept running. Cars passed her like blurs on her left, one or two even in the crawlspace to the right. There was, to put it mildly a lot of reckless driving. People were evidently in a hurry. Where they wanted to go they could probably not say, even if asked. This wasn't the direction people drove to work. That was in the opposite lane, and cars hardly moved there, hardly moved at all. One could walk faster than those cars. Using the word «congestion» was in no way sufficient when driving on the road south of Jaynagar.

Marion had a hangover again. Chloe noticed the moment she opened the door. Marion didn't say anything, didn't extend a vocal invitation, but just pulled backwards and left the door open. Chloe hurried inside. The door slammed shut behind her.

The house was fairly neat and tidy, with just a few hints of mess here and there. Marion lived in a beach house close to the famous Wonderland area, with piers and castles down the coastline. An eccentric billionaire had built it decades ago, and then gone broke, resulting in a rainbow backdrop of public and private owners and interests. Tourists and curious travelers from all over the world came here to satisfy their hunger for the different and weird.

The two women had breakfast. Marion hardly ate anything, while Chloe wolfed down food like a ravenous beast. Chloe, being used to the constant noise in the city tilted her head, as if listening to the sound of the mighty waves striking the shore, striking the cliffs hard, pushing far up on the sandy beach. The door to the garden had been left ajar, and she heard the cries of the ocean and the seagulls easily.

– Are you all right? Marion asked her lightly.

– I'm fine, thank you.

Chloe squeezed her outstretched hand.

She stood by the window, looking at the distant pier. People danced there, with glasses in their hands. The red, red wine twinkled in the light from the pale sun. She stopped on her way to the toilet, looking at the pictures on the wall, pictures big and imposing, sucking her in, making her a part of them. A man sat by a table. He seemed to be in such a good mood, practically dancing on the chair. A woman sat by the bar in the same establishment in a very revealing dress, looking very sexy and enticing. She drank orange juice, looking like she had been running, and running hard, her short hair clinging to her sweaty skin.

Chloe's gut reaction at the time made everything turn inside her. The photograph felt wrong, totally wrong and fake. The trickle down her spine intensified and scared her.

Her stomach and arse hurt, and she sat a long time on the toilet bowl before she felt she had managed to push everything out. She returned to the living room feeling all weird and hollow.

She walked out on the beach, and suddenly it was no longer a beach, but a garden. Desire and Marion and Victor and Andy had breakfast (no, not breakfast), had lunch on the lawn of the house, the old house by the lake. Chloe stood there, staring at them, staring at Desire.

– Guys, Desire whimpered. – Guys…

Desire grabbed Victor. She pointed a bony finger at Chloe. The other three turned where she pointed, turned towards Chloe, but they didn't see her. Only Desire did.

– It's her, Desire whimpered. – She's staring at me.

And then she evidently realized that the others didn't hear her, didn't see her, as if she wasn't really there at all. Victor didn't even notice her hand.

– You are lost to this world, Chloe told her, holding the ring with the ruby stone in the palm of her hand.

Chloe stood in the kitchen, watching Desire carry a tray of glass out in the garden.

Chloe sat on the couch. Marion returned from the bathroom, her looks somewhat improved.

– So, what are you doing these days? Her friend wondered.

And Chloe found it amazing that she hadn't asked her that question a long time ago.

– I am camping at the Pit, she replied casually, – seeking beneath its flimsy surface.

– You're not still bothering with that, are you?

– I am, Chloe said stubbornly.

Marion circled the floor a couple of times, before speaking up.

– It's so beneath you.

– Why? Chloe persisted. – Why is it beneath me, or anyone, for that matter?

– It is bullshit, that's why! Her friend spat. – Tales to scare little children and make them behave.

Chloe closed and opened her eyes, smiling slightly.

– If you truly believe that, the joke is on you…

– What, Marion began, forced to stop a moment because she had trouble breathing, – what has ten years of futile search brought you beyond more questions, more useless clues?

– The secrets of mist and shadow don't give themselves up easily. I knew that when I started out.

– Don't give me that, honey. Marion said softly. – This is me you're talking to. Your quest started out as a hobby, a trifle, a night's entertainment, and ended up in a rag like Color of the Night… as an obsession.

The words hurt, like dull blades cutting flesh, and Chloe Webster knew a little about how dull blades cutting flesh felt. She looked haunted at the other woman.

She rose, abruptly. Her legs felt wobbly, like legs felt when someone had been sitting still for too long, and started moving around. Her knee hurt. She walked to the wall. The photographs looked like photographs again. The wall had been dark and eerie. Now, it was only a wall. She walked outside, on the beach, and saw nothing but sand and waves.

– We went to a house, Denise and I. She remained outside. I walked inside, and almost learned its secret.

– Almost? Her friends teased her ruthlessly.

– You don't understand. It was the final proof I needed to know beyond knowing that the paranormal, the Other World is real and true.

– But you didn't find anything, now, did you…

– I'm so close, she insisted. – One final piece and…

– How many times have you *said* that? How many more pieces have you found since then?

Thousands, hundreds, millions… words failed her.

I dream that I am dreaming, about fire burning underwater, about shadows moving through the brightest light. I…

Chloe and Marion walked down Wonderland Main Street. It was indeed a special place, living up to his reputation as being created in an insane man's fertile mind.

At one side was the beach, with the piers and the cafes and small, unique cabins. At the upper side were the castles, in all shapes and forms. It wasn't an amusement park, as the name implied, but a small city, a village with all modern conveniences, and an inherent mystery, a suggestion of far older origin.

What should have been the brightest of days seemed cast in shadow. The sun up there seemed so far away. The terrible sense of dread and apprehension mixed with excitement inside Chloe intensified. It was the same feeling she had had her entire life, only a thousand times more powerful.

A man stood on a stool by a palm tree shouting his skewed vision of the world.

– THE BLOOD OF THE ANCIENTS IS STRIKING THE SHORE

He looked completely… completely wrong in Chloe's eyes.

The entire scenario did.

– Do you see? She said to Marion. – Do you *see?*

– What? Her friend replied annoyed. – I don't see anything for fuck's sake.

Chloe studied the people present and realized that no one but her was able to see the wrong man. A thrill shot through her. Her old, persistent insecurities felt distant and unimportant. Startled, she found herself smiling *patronizingly* to Marion.

– I am right and you are wrong, Chloe stated, very confident.

She repeated it, practically sang it, as they proceeded along the promenade. Her despair from the beach house was like blown away.

– I'm very confident in my position, she added brightly. – It's one I've reached after many years of contemplation and alternative thinking and action.

They sat down on a bench for a while, a green bench warm and pleasant for the body, sat there studying people passing by.

– They stare at us, Chloe said.

– Of course they stare at us, Marion said dryly. – The way you're staring at everyone it isn't strange that they should return the favor.

Chloe opened her computer, waited while it turned itself on, immersed in the rolling text and flashing shadows.

They stare at me, she wrote. I'm not saying this because I'm imagining things or because I'm being paranoid, but because it's *true.*

I know what is real, or at least I glimpse it behind the flimsy curtain. Finally I do. She doesn't. She never will!

The words did something to Marion. They dug deep in her, and didn't let go, and she couldn't understand why.

– Stop, she whispered. – Please, stop.

– I'll never stop, Chloe stated calmly. – Your tactics won't work any longer. You've always held me back with your ridiculous words of caution, but no longer. From this moment on I will never waver from my path.

– You're crazy as a *loon!* Marion gasped, looking at her with hatred in her eyes.

– Goodbye, Marion, Chloe said calmly. – I'm glad I finally realized how small you truly are.

She rose and left, walked away, feeling free and bold, both relieved and sad.

When she turned her head and looked back Marion still sat there, on the green bench, lost and small.

Chloe searched a bit before finding it, finding what burned in her throat and veins and fevered mind, in her thoughts already leaving the other woman on the bench far behind.

A house, resembling a castle, a castle resembling a house waited for her at the end of the road. This was one of the areas of Wonderland where there was a paid entrance. Chloe fumbled in her pocket for a coin. She found it and put it into the machine, the automated system regulating the flow of visitors. She imagined that the guards stared at her, but ignored the tiny voice of fear inside.

One group of twenty had been filled, and those behind had to wait for a while, before being let inside. Chloe and her fellow visitors ventured into the reception hall.

The twenty was a curious mix of tourists and locals, easily distinguished. The locals had the same deep tan as Chloe herself. Such a tan was practically inevitable in these parts, even for people spending most of their days at night, like Chloe. All the others were pale in comparison.

But individuals among both parties shared certain characteristics, such as constantly moving eyes and a more than obvious and familiar restlessness.

The twenty was a curious bunch, period.

– Good afternoon, the young man in uniform said. – My name is Colin. I will be your guide on this gilded tour.

He wanted laughter from his awed audience, and he got it. Chloe found herself giggling, a giggle sounding like a sore and brittle laughter in her ears.

– I'm sure some of you have read *a lot* about this place before coming here, before deciding to visit in person, but I will take you through the essentials, anyway, for the benefit of those fairly ignorant… and then move on to the *juicy* stuff.

In the hallway a lamp blinked, blinked once, and never more. Chloe shuddered.

– Richards' Manor was designed and constructed by Breton Richards to be the crown jewel in his Wonderland Park. Richards had always been seen as eccentric, but this project clinched it in the public eye, especially since this house, this manor was quickly revealed to be an exact replica, down to the last brick of Marlon Caine's renowned place in The Hills…

He was good at this, his punctuations, his humor and underlying excitement. It didn't feel fake. Chloe found herself growing excited.

– Breton Richards wasn't merely rich, but superrich. As an entrepreneur and idea-maker he had earned billions on top of billions in his energetic youth. This was supposed to be his crown, his top achievement, rivaling any other on the planet. But the project was marred with accidents and misfortune right from the start. All projecting costs went through the roof early, and kept on growing to insane levels. And then, on top of everything came the lawsuit from Marlon Caine. Caine sued for compensation and everything under the sun, really, claiming that his Manor had lost value by being copied. Richards countersued, claiming that Caine had stolen his work, that he had made the original drawings of Caine Manor, and that both the drawings and the Manor were rightfully his. To make a long story short: Richards lost, after litigation spanning decades and was ordered to pay an unprecedented amount in punitive damages. Richards bitterly blamed Caine for his misfortune, in a very public display eventually turning into ravings, before he died poor and alone in an asylum for the hopelessly insane.

He retreated into the living room, and the twenty followed him, their eyes and mouths wide open in awe. Chloe did, too, fearing she had lost all sense of proportions.

The flames in the fireplace were fake, but she imagined she saw them burn, saw them dance, and gripped by cold fear she wondered if Marion had been right about her obsession all along.

– I bring your attention to this painting, Colin declared, as if it was the most dramatic thing in the world (and perhaps it was). – It is the infamous painting of Marlon Caine, of course, rumored to be painted by David Fallon Somby. As you know or can observe it isn't signed. Another rumor says Somby painted it the evening of his *gruesome* death, and left it incomplete.

More nervous laughter. Chloe found herself being sucked into the painting, into Caine's huge, ominous eyes.

– Somby *did* paint other works, well known and infamous. Experts have quarreled for twenty years whether or not this is an authentic Somby without reaching anything even resembling consensus. It is Somby and yet it isn't, the skeptics say confused. Somby is yet another mysterious piece of the puzzle in this *fascinating* story.

There was something about Colin's voice, something echoing within her, like a song, a howl in the most ragged of landscapes, evoking memories of something unknown, something she couldn't quite reach. Every time she reached for it the familiar sense of it slipping away overwhelmed her, and she rolled her hands into fists in frustration.

– The fireplace is yet another renowned chapter in this saga. Caine had the stone flown in from the jungle of Asbasos. So did Richards. Strong rumors are circulating that Caine baptized the rock in blood… and that Richards also in this echoed his actions.

The rock looked strange… eerie to Chloe. She had some experience with Magick, and with animism. Bizarre patterns had been carved into the stone, incomprehensible letters forming indecipherable words, meanings. She heard whispers, powerful and invasive. She experimented with holding her hands over her ears, but she still heard them.

According to credible witness reports that she had had access to Caine was into human sacrifices… and so had Richards been. She wondered if this was something the clean cut guide and his bosses wanted to share with the visitors. A thrill of exhilaration shot through her.

– Almost every single object here, in the living room and throughout the house, or rather in Caine's home has significance, in one way or another. We know they are still there, because Caine is quite generous in allowing visitors into his home. There have come a few new things the last thirty years, though, each and every one in turn registered and catalogued by zealous observers. An entire industry has grown in the wake of Caine and Richards' actions.

Chloe took pictures. It was allowed and even encouraged. The owners' revenue didn't come from the objects themselves, but from the visitors' vigorous curiosity, to be kind, the thrill of actually being here.

She noted the small bronze statue in the window, the carpet in front of the fireplace and a dozen other notable items.

Colin the Guide brought them into the kitchen, a vast space of moisture and heavy scents.

– Caine has made some memorable meals in his time, and so did Richards.

Everything was big here, the kettle, pans and knives, spoons and forks and everything.

– Obviously made for a large household, isn't it? Yet, as far as we know neither of them ever entertained large numbers of guests.

Chloe glimpsed the flashing of knives and movement of people, heard the harsh words spoken in foreign languages, and imagined she could actually understand some of it.

They were led into another hall, looking remarkably similar to the first, with another broad marble staircase leading upstairs. In the opposite direction, down the hallway leading outside they glimpsed a setup of two doors.

– Weird, isn't it? Only one of the doors leads outside, at any given time, and which one changes randomly. Yet another rumor states that Caine… and Richards enjoyed placing poison gas in canisters beyond the wrong door, but there has never been any substantial evidence to that effect.

– It looks like Caine and Richards deserved each other, a visitor remarked harshly.

No one commented on his outburst, even though many wanted to. They glanced around anxiously.

Nothing happened. A sigh of heavy relief escaped everybody, as they moved on up the stairs.

– Not all rooms are open for the audience, Colin said with regret. – But those outside the tour areas are mostly used as storage and staff quarters.

Mostly? Chloe attempted to catch his eyes, but failed.

The house had three floors, no basement, no attic. At the top of the stairs rested a natural sized statue of a woman, or rather a female. She clearly had animal characteristics mixed with her human traits. It looked like she would jump at them at any time.

– People claim to have been to an attic in the Caine Manor. Some, never leaving the asylum for the hopelessly insane mumble about stairs going upstairs forever. They remain in the Manor. It never let go of them.

There were paintings on the walls, all over the middle floor, giant wall to wall paintings. Calling them lifelike wouldn't do them justice.

– My Goddess, a woman called out, – I smell seawater.

And it was easy to do that, upon looking at the ship by the harbor. Like it was to imagine that the man with half his face hidden in shadow and the woman standing in the rain behind the window were real, not just applied colors. The paintings looked wet, as if they had just been painted.

– All the paintings are said to be exact copies. Now, anyone with a certain knowledge of art would tell you that that is fundamentally impossible. What I *can* tell you, though, is that Richards hired only the most expensive copyists to do the job. No one we know of knows who the original painters are.

Chloe felt faint, fearing that her legs wouldn't carry her. The statue smiled. The statue in the other room at the end of the hallway… smiled… to her. The long, dark path seemed to go on forever.

– This is so exciting, a man cried. – I knew it would be something, but this is…

He never completed the sentence, but just stood there, lost in the painting of the man with half his face concealed in shadow.

They reached the library, and people found their notebooks, both paper and computer, and began taking notes.

– This isn't an exact copy of the Caine library. Richards was able to get copies of some of the books, but a few of the manuscripts in Caine Manor are so rare that there are no known copies in existence. We have a record of all the books and manuscripts, though, and you may purchase it along with extensive background material in the reception.

He smiled politely.

The upper floor was just the upper floor. Even though that, too felt special, was special they had been jaded and weren't so easily impressed anymore.

But Chloe, and also some of the others heard sounds up here, of wind, and sails being filled and rain against the window, on the cloudless, bright day, even as sunlight flooded the floor and walls and ceiling. They could see the entire Wonderland from here.

Vertigo sized Chloe. She felt like she was miles up, and every time she looked down she felt like she was falling, falling, falling down.

As she descended the stairs, as she headed for the exit, towards the brightness there. She bought a souvenir, a trinket, knowing fully well that it wasn't genuine. Then she left.

She sat down on the green bench down the shingle road, a silent pocket of air in the noise, one she suddenly felt very much in a hurry to reach. Just a few seconds afterwards calm reached her, like she had the bench. People passed her by, but she didn't truly notice them, not feeling them as part of her surroundings at all.

Waves struck at the pier between the two houses across the road. She imagined the sea turning red, and the stench of blood reached her twitching nostrils.

She began writing on her laptop, intensively focused, not looking up from the monitor. The words came easy to her, like they sometimes did. Everything turned to a blur in her eyes.

I remember the girl behind the counter, she wrote. I remember her evasive eyes, and I realized that she had also been studying me when I first entered the hall, and… I realized that she didn't want me there.

She looked at me with hatred in her eyes.

– So, what is «Color of the Night» doing here? I thought you guys had visited this place a dozen times.

He towered above her, blocking the sunlight.

– I haven't, she shrugged.

He sat down on the bench, not too close to her, not too far away.

– Hi, he said teasingly, – my name is Colin Dexter.

– Hello, she replied dispassionately.

She didn't say anything more. He knew her name.

– I noticed you in there, he said smugly.

– I noticed you, too, she nodded.

An awkward silence persisted among them for a noticeable slice of time.

– I was going to have dinner. Would you like to join me?

She considered it, and discovered that she once more felt part of her surroundings.

– I would like that, she replied, a glimpse of a smile in her face.

She had nothing else on her plate right now. Still feeling slightly disconnected she rose, and followed him down the road, to a pier around the corner. She turned and glanced back, at the animated Richards' Manor.

– It leaves an impression, doesn't it?

– Yes, it does, she acknowledged.

– But I'm told it is nothing compared to the original, that skin deep the differences are far more pronounced than they appear.

He pondered. It suddenly dawned on her that she was breathlessly awaiting what he was going to say next.

– I've never been there, never set my foot inside or even approached it. That's pretty strange, isn't it?

– I never have either, she mused, momentarily lost in her thoughts.

Lost, she felt lost, and followed the nice boy.

– Most of the people in Jaynagar, and lots in the world at large have visited the place, but we haven't.

She wanted to respond to him, but didn't find the words.

The pier was uncharacteristically long. It reached out of the cove and made a turn into the next, where there was no road and no houses, a quiet and calm place in the busy area. Somewhere, on the long walk he grabbed her hand, and she let him.

She felt the touch of his skin. It burned her and warmed her.

Large bonfires burned on both sides of the restaurant, the flames dancing without wind, without the slightest draft in the air, mirrored in the open windows. The flames welcomed her. She imagined they greeted her and spoke to her, and their language almost made sense.

They chose a table for two outdoors. For some to them unfathomable reason most of the guests had chosen to be seated indoors, but that felt completely wrong to them. They sat down, the wood making up the table legs made a screeching sound, resembling how a banshee might sound, if such a creature had existed. The glowing disk in the sky had passed behind dark clouds. Only far at sea, at the western horizon the sun sent pale light through the clouds. She frowned, faintly recalling another pier, another day of pale sunlight, before brightening, and smiling at the boy. It was such a dark and lovely day. She looked boldly into Colin's eyes.

The waitress made a quick trip to their table, leaving the menu. They picked it up. She looked at it, while glancing at the windows, at the pale mirror image of herself and her companion, and the few other people sitting outdoors on this fine, chilly day. Half expecting to see gooseflesh break on her skin she took a look at her arm, but there was nothing there.

The warm air practically made the skin sizzle in her sensitive ears. Her sharp as hawk's eyes spotted easily droplets of sweat grow between tiny hairs.

– … so I took this job to pay for my tuition, he said, eagerly confiding in her, while they were eating. – It felt right from the start. I got the job from several thousands applicants. The boss said I was the perfect choice…

– You obviously enjoyed it, she remarked. – I think the most insensitive person in the world would see that. The various stories seemed to come alive while you were telling them. How you can remember it all without aid is beyond me.

– I am winging it a little, he admitted and grinned, – not telling everything about everything, and there are hidden teleprompters, but aside from that… what can I say? I have always benefited from a close to photographic memory.

– There are hidden teleprompters? She said agitated.

But he easily saw through her mask of indignation to the jokester beneath and smiled his boyish smile.

– Sorry…

She returned to somber, to sad.

– I wish I had an ability like that, she said. – I always forget everything.

From day to day, night to night, forever.

She swallowed hard, closing her fist again, resisting the need to strike the table.

– I've read all your articles in Color of the Night, he stated somberly, grinning some more to take the sting out of the moment.

– You have, but that's…

– Granted the magazine is a rag, but your articles are different, clearly standing out from the rest. You are indeed their star reporter. In the short time you've worked there, you've certainly made your mark. They would be *nothing* without you.

He just kept piling it up. She turned hot and queasy.

And then he took her hands. She managed to hold on to the knife, somehow, but the fork fell from her hand and hit the plate with a loud, high octave sound.

– Does that sound like inside, in a room to you? She asked him.

He looked astonished at her.

– It does, he whispered.

He looked almost stricken.

The waiter distracted her. He asked them if they were pleased with the food. They both mumbled pleasantries.

The moment had been lost. She felt it slip through her fingers yet again.

They continued eating. It was fish, salmon from the sound, or so the advertising said. Constantly preoccupied she couldn't tell whether or not that was right, whether or not she liked the food or not or if she cared or not. She could tell that she enjoyed the occasion. He noticed her hungry look and blushed, and it was so sweet and she gave him the hottest of stares.

The other people around them didn't really seem to be there, to be present at all. She, for one practically ignored them.

They drank wine, red as blood. Glasses met and parted.

Wine is red as blood, she thought unprompted.

She drank some more. It burned in her stomach, like all red wine did.

– I own a boat, he declared.

She kept eating, determined not to make it easy for him.

– It used to belong to my esteemed father, but he handed it over to me, officially binding and all… two years before he disinherited me.

– I read about that, she nodded. – Quite the funny story.

– I forget that you *are* working in a newspaper, with access to the wire services, he acknowledged. – Very few outside the professional collegiums of journalists had a change to read it… before it was killed.

She wanted to say something, but waited in breathless anticipation for him to continue.

– I would love it if you join me on my boat today, and sail up the coast with me.

– I'm told the coast is quite beautiful this time of year, she replied lightly.

There was something underneath the light banter, the small challenging stings, but she couldn't identify it.

They paid, put a few bills on the table and left before the waiter approached to pick them up. The fire burned Chloe's back as they walked away. She wanted to ask him if it burned him as well, but she held her tongue.

– I live on the boat, he said.

That didn't come as a surprise or wasn't news to her, but she appreciated him telling her. He was refreshing and mysterious and deep. He was attractive to her, in more ways than one. His riddle attracted her, drew her to him, and she let it happen.

It was quite a walk to the pier where he hid his boat, but she didn't mind. Less ghosts disguised as people surrounded them. They left Wonderland behind, and it dissolved in their mind like a mirage.

– Tell me about my articles, she begged him. – Tell me about my first.

They reached another cove, one with one single pier, one that had holes in it and had seen better days. There was only one boat there, hidden beneath a large plastic wrapper, difficult to spot, perhaps, between the two big rocks, for people not looking for it, but Chloe was, and spotted it easily. She noticed Colin sign to someone hidden on land, and she glimpsed someone signing back.

– That was my roommate at the university campus, Colin said, so pleased that she had noticed the setup. – We do each other services, what friends do for each other.

He pulled off the wrapper and uncovered the rather luxurious boat.

– It's twenty feet long, and quite valuable, he said.

– It sure looks that way, she grinned. – If I was a wide-eyed teenage chick I would be quite impressed. It isn't exactly the worst place in the world to sleep.

She had seen worse, a lot worse.

He folded the wrapper. It covered surprisingly little space when he was done. He packed it in a compartment at the front and signed for her to come aboard.

It was about a step of a gap between the pier and the boat. She was a little nervous, even though she shouldn't be, but made the jump easily. He pushed a button and that was all it took for the process of disembarking to start. The poles with the sails began straightening and the anchors were pulled from their spot at the seabed, and stopped when they rested at their rightful place at the side of the boat. He pushed, pushed hard away from the pier, and suddenly, in mere seconds they were far away from their starting point.

They walked down the stairs in the cabin, into what felt to her like an eerie, twilight world. The sunshine hardly reached them at all here.

He started the engine with what were obviously trained movements.

– We need to get far enough away from land to reach the wind. It will take us north.

She knew she left her car in Marion's garage, but didn't care.

– Your first case was about a neighborhood besieged by an elusive stalker exposing himself to little girls. The police couldn't catch him. Years passed by. It had practically become a legend, one with what in certain circles had paranormal properties, but too long time had passed even for magazines such as yours, and that's why your esteemed editor sent a newbie to cover the story. It had been covered countless times, but with fairly few new cases to print your editor felt it was time to yet again recycle the story.

He was good at this, good at this, too, with conveying the right kind of irony and mild sarcasm, and still hold her interest. She felt the story be born into the world. This time he used no manuscript, no hidden telemetry, but spoke solely from his memory. Excitement riled her when she pondered it and realized what it actually meant, to her, and in terms of how he viewed her.

– The first night of the stakeout you spotted the stalker and called for help, and a lot of others got a good look at him, too, before he ran away. Even a couple of police officers did, as they chased him across several blocks of bright city streets. A phantom drawing was made from people's description…

The wind began taking hold of the boat. They returned to the deck. He had to untie the ropes and set up the sails manually, but he did it with ease.

– But even though the man was put on newspapers' first pages and television broadcasts he remained elusive. No one recognized the man.

She looked at her companion with wonder and fear in her eyes.

– Not until you began researching decades' old news-clippings, and found him there. He had died fifty years earlier.

They had returned to the cabin. She didn't realize that at first.

– No officials would admit to such an unmistakable fact, of course, but it was more than enough for your editor. He saw in you a change of legitimacy, for at least a step or two up the ladder of the established media hierarchy.

– I saw him, she whispered, with her hands covering her face. – The stalker appeared to me. He grinned *viciously,* before fading away before my very eyes.

The wind grabbed the sails, filled them to the max, and she felt the pull.

– It felt like a dream the next morning, she said, speaking in a low voice, – and in time I convinced myself that it had been, but I never stopped the hunt for absolute, beyond anything convincing proof and certainty.

They moved further away from land. She saw him plot a course, one that would put them far away from any reeves or possible landmarks.

He turned towards her and walked to her, and grabbed her, staring into her wet and burning eyes.

– The other visitors, even the keenest among them were at best dabblers, children playing at a frog's pond, not knowing what they were doing or where they happened to be, but not you. I *saw* you! In the Richards' house I saw how you reacted on all the hot spots, even those not in official and unofficial overviews. I knew about those because I felt them, know them myself, far, far better than the back of my hand. What do you think I've been doing while spending all that time in that house?

The gooseflesh finally broke on her skin, and it was a doozy, creating a surge of heat and expectation throughout her body.

He kissed her and she responded, or the other way around. None of them could tell which was which.

The twilight of the room turned even more distinct, surrounding them, and she felt one with it.

One with him.

– Goddess, he exhaled, – You're so beautiful. I love your smooth, dark hair on your tanned skin. It's so damn enticing and sexy.

It could have been a totally, beyond stupid statement, like something out of a romance novel, but the intensity and implied brutality behind it made that impression going away quite fast.

He began unbuttoning her black blouse. Skin felt black, too, now, like all of her, burned to ashes in the swathing fire. She exposed her teeth, her fangs to him and began tearing at his sweater, his thin, thin sweater, where the skin underneath was easily seen. He raised his arms above his head and she pulled off the tiny fabric in a swift, brutish move, scratching his shoulder, breaking the skin there, drawing blood. He removed her blouse and her top, and she stood exposed before him, her breasts and nipples swelling and hardening untouched.

They clinched. He kissed her so hard that she feared he would cut her open like he would a fruit. She sucked at his shoulder, sucked the blood into her mouth, swallowing it with a thirst beyond any possible anxiety, anything reasonable. They slipped further down the stairs, descended deeper into the boat, surrounded by the sea, by endless waves striking at them, as it constantly struck the boat, the thin wall protecting them from the deep, deep water. They were completely nude, in bed, with more than enough space to spare.

– I read a police report once, or something that could have become a police report, about Caine and Richards. Would you like to hear about it?

– I would *love* to.

Her dazzling smile wasn't even a smile, but a snarl, a hunger so vast that she couldn't deal with it.
– They sacrificed children in the basement of their castles, or so the saying and the witness reports went. But there *is* no basement in either of the houses. So the charges were dropped before they could gain anything even resembling validity. But the rumors persisted.
– Rumors again…
– And get this: at least two people I have spoken with claim that David Fallon Zombie's children weren't killed by the fire, but in a satanic ritual led by Zombie's good friend and producer Marlon Caine. Seeking payback Zombie tracked down the parents of the other victims and planned his vengeance with them, but they were all killed like him before they could complete their task. One man was found with his eyes missing, a woman without her breasts. Others without arms and feet.
– So, she whispered into his ears, – is there smoke with the fire?
She kissed him and stopped him from speaking before he could respond. Crawling onto his lap she pushed her breasts at his face. One nipple found his mouth, and he began biting it, sucking it. She growled pleased in his ear. They began touching each other for real, hard and invasive and potent and with an intensity beyond anything they could remember felling. One hand found his cock, squeezing it. It hardened and grew. He pushed his hips upward, pushing himself between her moist thighs. They tumbled down on the bed, face to face. He pushed himself into her, and her shout of pleasure shook the ship, the ship sailing the seven seas.
– No one connected the dots, she mewed, – except you.
– And you, he whispered. – You connected your dots and…
– … you yours, she stated, breathed without breath, as they began moving, becoming one beast, in two interconnecting bodies.
His hands squeezed her thighs. Her nails broke his skin. Prolonged moans and growls filled their ears, and beneath it all, beyond the moving of the ship and the dance of the waves, they glimpsed the shore. They smothered each other in touches, in kisses and sounds and hisses and warm breath and taste and scents. Hips rolled and moved and created waves in the heated air. Thoughts rolled through their fingers like grains of sand, falling like tears and rain.
– Chloe, he cried, he mumbled, – Chloe, Chloe, Chloe
She heard his weak shout from far away, closing and opening her eyes as she dipped up and down on her lover.
At the shore, at a high point Marion looked through binoculars and followed the boat, as it sailed up the coast to its inevitable destination. It seemed to be standing still from her point of view. She laughed or

chuckled or cried. Chloe couldn't tell, there on the boat, riding Colin Dexter. Pain invaded her, sweet, sweet pain, as everything took off, rose to unfathomable heights, fell to unimaginable depths, into the palest of shadows, the most colorful darkness. She knew that he was real, that the hard thing moving inside her was a fact and not her imagination, but the rest of the world kept blurring around the edges, kept fading in and out like day and night, and the boat was nothing but a thin veil surrounding them as they rode through a vast, infinite space.

CHAPTER SEVENTEEN

She saw herself enter the subway between the Pit and the bus station, the underworld below the billions of coughing cars driving up and down M217.

Through a series of fever visions she became all the people behind the wheel, looking at the world through a thick fog of misery, despair and desperation.

The boat sailed the sea, avoiding, sometimes narrowly the occasional ragged reeves. It was a cloudy day, fairly bright clouds, thick enough to hide, conceal the sun, but not significantly diminish its light.

Chloe Webster opened her eyes. He did, too. They stretched, enjoying the moment and closeness, the sounds of the sea below echoing pleasantly in their ears and minds. The light burning through the small windows provided more than enough illumination, even though she still noticed a strange quality in the air. It was bright as day summer twilight.

She kissed him on the lips and headed for the shower, wriggling her butt as she walked and glanced back at him. The bathroom was large and luxurious, still was, in spite of the obvious signs of age and neglect. She turned on the water. It hit her hard and potent. She panted a bit in surprise and enjoyment. Touching herself didn't really return her heat. He had fucked her good, sated her.

The slow, enjoyable cleansing lasted a while. She dragged it out a bit, by default, studying with open eyes the millions of droplets falling around her and on her. It was the strangest thing… in each of the raindrops she saw a world, with its people and history. She practically experienced how each hit the ground, and flooded it, and the river rose, flooding all shores, all times.

He was still in bed when she returned to the bedroom, when she began drying herself in his honor, toying with a giant towel, hiding and exposing her body as she did. Her nipples remained erect, touchy. She enjoyed that, like she enjoyed everything during these fleeting moments.

– Come here, he called to her.

She rushed to him, joined him in bed. Lips met and burned, skin to skin. She half waited for him to become aroused as they played with and teased each other, but it didn't happen.

He kissed her and left the bed and headed for the shower, his large cock dangling between his thighs, and then, as she heard him in the shower, and pictured him behind briefly closed eyes, she did become slightly aroused, her need burning on a low, pleasant flame. She attempted to count how many times they had mated earlier, but she could never quite get the number right.

Her mind kept drifting, soaring, descending into the deepest shadow, where she might glimpse everything, her thoughts a chaotic rubble. She sensed how the boat moved around her, how its heart hammered in its chest. Wind picked up for a brief moment, seawater hitting the windows, obscuring her vision.

As it sailed the vast sea.

He returned and began drying himself in front of the onlooker, like she had done, and she watched his nude body, like he had watched hers.

– I better check the charts, he said. – The automatic system isn't necessarily reliable.

– So, you're saying it's mere luck that we haven't crashed, she teased him.

– It's never a good idea to stay distracted for too long, he teased her back.

He began dressing, and she, leaving the bed did, too.

They ascended the stairs, rose into the boat's upper level. He began checking the instruments, disconnecting the automatic functions.

– We're way off course, as is usually the case, he snorted. – My father had a lot of shares in that technology development company and bragged about it endlessly, of course.

Chloe rose up between his arms, his arms with hands around the wheel. She pushed herself at his body and rested her head on his shoulder.

– We're on our way to Jaynagar, aren't we? She said in a tiny voice.

– Yes, we are, he acknowledged.

– Can't we… can't we just sail on, go north, and just keep on sailing?

– You decide, he said.

He stepped back, leaving the decision to her.

She hesitated, choked and made a fist, and then turned the wheel in her hand. The sails changed position and she felt the mighty ship under her feet change its course.

– I choose this, she declared, – choose this path, this fire and shadow and mist and life.

She sensed his affection.

It began as a tiny rumble, but rose quickly to a low roar in her ears. The coastal landscape changed, as the first signs of the urban backdrop that was Jaynagar appeared. A few houses turned many.

– I'll pick up your car tomorrow, he said. – And have Johnny drive it back here.

– Don't bother. It's a wreck and will certainly not keep moving forward for much longer.

She sounded strangely confident when she said that. He didn't comment on it.

The Jaynagar harbor appeared abruptly behind a cliff. Almost the entire inner city revealed itself to them, and they felt nausea strike them from their belly. The Hills, with the mountains towering behind. The financial district, with its tall buildings. The Pit, with downtown and Deeper Pit. And the Harbor, most of it not really a harbor anymore, but ugly, square blocks of flats, what the mayor had called «modern architecture». They sailed past a vast array of large ships and tankers parked in the deeper waters, the rust visible at the ships' sides and its stench tearing at their nostrils.

There were also a few smaller boats, all of them sailing, and sailing in different directions. The sight made her dizzy, like she was pulled in many different directions simultaneously.

The trip lasted forever, in her experience, filled with details and dilated time.

They reached the shallow waters of the inner harbor, the marina, where the small boats had been parked along rows of piers.

Colin's father had given him a lifetime space to his boat, another gift impossible to rescind. Chloe knew that without him saying anything. She realized she knew many things, as she took the wheel and began handling the boat quite easily, as one who had clearly done so before. The designated space was just across the street from Desire's apartment. She knew that, too. He looked wide-eyed at her.

– I didn't know you could handle a boat. It isn't like driving a car, but much trickier.

– I've always done it, she mused, a dreamy smile touching her face.

It was practically quiet here, like usually was the case. Collin had no problem folding the sails and anchoring the boat. Chloe parked it on its spot with an elegant swing of her one hand on the wheel. The anchors hit the sea bed and they had arrived at their destination.

The dark-clad woman shuddered involuntarily.

They disembarked. He reached out a hand, and she did, too, allowing him to take her hand with a murky giggle. She noticed that the pier shook slightly under her feet, like a ground, as if mighty waves shook the solid workmanship. Dark eyes slid across the still waters.

Nothing moved for a moment. The seagulls hung suspended in the air. People stood frozen in all directions.

Chloe blinked and the world rushed back in.

And she knew there had been people that hadn't been frozen, hadn't been moving back and forth right before, but had been standing still and looked in her direction, had been staring at her with cold, merciless eyes.

She looked for them, as unobtrusive as she could. They were nowhere to be seen, and she wondered if they had ever been there at all.

– They know we are coming, she said.

He glanced at her with nascent worry in his eyes.

She kissed him, making the dread go away.

People stared, she was certain of that much. When she studied them she discovered the oh so familiar dark gleam at the edge of their form.

It was a hot and busy afternoon in the Harbor. People on their way home bought fish for dinner, made a bargain at the many stalls. The stench of blood and death was almost overpowering. The music rose with the striking of the drum and faded away again with its passing. She shivered a bit, inevitably, as emotions cursed through her like thunder. A woman bought a lot of fish. She carried two full bags with her across the street, to the waiting car. The car's windows were dark and impossible to look through.

Its dark red lights were reflected in the nearest store window. One light blinked, winked at Chloe.

She and Colin crossed the street, to the apartment houses along the harbor. The sense of urgency persisted, even on this slow, languid day. They stopped outside Ocean Avenue 108. The entrance door was slightly ajar and skewed, evidently impossible to close properly. She noticed Colin's look and grinned ironically.

– Yes, I know, she said. – The entire place was ravaged and didn't look like much for a long time afterwards. The entrepreneurs buying it has never truly made any effort to repair it fully, in spite of countless complains. They have even changed the numbers of the entire block in an attempt to fool people into moving in here. Go figure. This was originally 112.

– Real estate people are nutters, he acknowledged.

They walked inside. Walking up the stairs in the fairly mundane building intensified Chloe's eerie mood. To her it didn't look very mundane at all, but like a dark and dank cave, something surrounding her and invading her on all sides. Someone played a fiddle somewhere, playing music set in the gypsy scale. On the walls she saw shifting shadows and in the shifting shadows she glimpsed images and mouths whispering in her ear with haunting and intense voices.

She rang the bell in front of her. They stood there, waiting. The door opened and Desire's happy and enigmatic face appeared.

– Visiting me on this fine day, are you? Well, know that you are welcome. Please step into my humble abode.

Colin glanced at Chloe.

– She has played a lot of Shakespeare lately, Chloe grinned.

They entered the hallway. Chloe passed the mirror, glimpsing an indistinct version of herself. The other wall, so close on her right seemed so far away in the mirror.

She stopped momentarily, swallowing hard upon looking at the dark smile of her mirror image.

Marion stood by the window. She smiled to the two of them as they stepped into the living room.

– I reckoned I would catch the two of you at this spot…

She held a set of car keys in her right hand.

– I thought I should do you a service by bringing your car here. It fit my plans, and everything went well. There isn't a single scratch on the sweet baby.

She threw the keys through the air. The metal twinkled as it spun, passing through indistinct rays of sunshine reaching it from the outside. Chloe caught them, and held onto them.

– That's awfully nice of you. I'm very grateful. Thank you.

Marion shrugged and waved her off.

– Don't mention it. As stated I was on my way here, anyway, and I hate riding the bus.

– I was about to make dinner, Desire said brightly. – It's no trouble if you want to join in. I can just as easily make for four.

The entrance door closed in the hallway, much later than expected. The wheel above the handle turned and turned and gave off a very distinct sound.

Chloe noticed Marion's flickering eyes behind the nice smirk.

They heard Desire plunder in the kitchen. This was a fairly large, though worn apartment, with a separate kitchen.

– She got the place cheap, Marion smiled to Colin. – The entire block has quite a story, you know. They had to sell it well below perceived market-price.

– I know. Colin coughed. – I heard.

– Of course you did, Colin.

Marion said.

A lot of seagulls squeaked outside. Chloe heard them. The walls squeaked. She heard them, too. The fiddle played its song outside. It haunted her.

A hole appeared in the very air somewhere. She saw it, experienced it as if she was there.

Something passed through, a shadow, something indistinguishable and alien.

She shook as Colin touched her on the shoulder. The smile she granted him felt unfamiliar on her lips.

They sat down by the table. Desire served them all, insisting on doing it without help. She did a marvelous job, flowing between moments, until all the food and all the plates and forks and spoons and knives rested in front of everybody. The four of them sat there eating, with black candles burning on the table, to the sound of twinkling metal and the distant fiddler's tune.

The lemonade burned in Chloe throat, as if she had the beginning of a cold, but she knew it wasn't so.

The food and spices marched on light feet through her mouth and hit the stomach like rain, so detailed an image, such a powerful sensation.

– So, when I walked through the harbor earlier I felt like I was standing still, like the streets and buildings, the very city was moving around me.

A mist floated outside the window, or so it seemed, dancing on the airwaves, obstructing her vision.

– I've read up on Jaynagar recently, Desire said excitedly, her eyes lit like the dark candles. It's *old,* rumored to be here even before the first settlers arrived.

The flickering lights of the candles overpowered that of the daylight outside. They all sensed that. Chloe discovered it when she studied their wandering gaze.

– This entire area was a desert, before people began irrigating it, but the city and its immediate vicinity was green, like an oasis, and at its center was a lake, one large and deep.

Her voice, or her words or both did something to Chloe. She felt something… give inside.

– If it was green it hardly was a city at all, was it?

She heard herself speak, from the other side of a long tunnel.

– It was probably a village of some kind, Marion shrugged.

– But there were no people, Desire said dumbfounded.

They had lemonade, a lot of lemonade, and finally some cider. The ice-cold cider burned in Chloe's throat. They had spicy meat and vegetables, and a selection of fruits. It was a relaxed meal. Chloe remembered that much, in the dark tunnel and hallway later that night.

– My compliments to the chef. Colin took a sitting bow. – The food and drink were delicious.

Desire blushed like an apron.

– Any witch with a minimum of self-esteem can cook, she snorted.

– That's right, Chloe winked to him, – we must be into herbs, and thereby, by extension food.

Marion stared at Colin, as if she was angry or something.

– Is it just me, or do any of you find this eerily familiar? Chloe wondered.

– It's you.

Desire chuckled aloud, and almost doubled over on the chair.

– What do you mean? Colin asked her, suddenly somber.

They looked at each other. Chloe looked at all of them, one by one, and in flashes she saw them in a different light, in a setting not at all familiar with a nice dinner-setting a warm summer afternoon.

– This isn't today. It is long ago… before… before…

She strived, but couldn't get the last part right.

– But not exactly. That isn't right either. Not… not completely.

– Not today? Marion grinned. – What day is it supposed to be then?

Chloe shook her head, relenting in dismay and frustration, giving them her best smile, the one she had practiced since early childhood.

The mist outside the window drifted off, dispersing in the sizzling afternoon air.

They slid through the hallway again. Marion and Desire joined them on the streets. The hallway, the streets, it didn't seem to differ much. There was the same silence, the same quiet noise. The cars slipped past them like ghosts. They walked through the subway to the bus station. The modest lights on the walls didn't really brighten the tunnels very much. It felt like sort of a pleasant change compared to the shiny daylight.

The afternoon rush had just started and people were all around them, on their way home after a long and hard workday. The subway wasn't that long, even though they imagined it to be. It was just designed to bring people below M217, below the roar of cars in Chloe's ears and to the bus station, and did that excellently.

She watched the lights, watched them flicker. For moments between moments it was dark and a special sort of restlessness spread among the commuters. The relief was sculpted in their features when the lights came back on.

The four emerged with the crowd into the bright hall. The flower boutique and the magazine sales outlet were on the right, the burger chain restaurant to the left, three of many stores and restaurants and coffee shops. This had indeed turned more into a shopping mall than a bus station.

Chloe saw herself walk this stretch long ago, before it had turned into a shopping mall. She saw herself walk it again today, now, saw the people around her shimmer and burn in the shadow of her vision.

– I'm looking for something she said aloud, – but I can't remember what it is.

She glanced at the others. They didn't react in any way, and she realized that they hadn't heard her.

They reached the other tunnel, one leading to the bus departure and arrival area. It was a long straight stretch with stairs, side tunnels numbered from 1 to 50 where buses departed to and arrived from the entire greater Jaynagar area and West Coast.

– Why is number 6 closed? She wondered. – It makes no sense.

– You're looking for the world to make sense? Colin teased her.

He was correct, of course. With that realization a shudder, a deep, deep shudder passed through her, and it was as if she saw, yet again the world with new eyes.

There was no passage numbered 6. It wasn't merely closed, but blocked by a wall of concrete. If one looked carefully one could easily see the difference, the demarcation between where there once had been an opening and the older wall around it.

They walked up the stairs to platform 7. There were a few people there, but no buses. Desire looked impatiently at her watch.

The bus station was also an enormous parking garage. Above them were three levels filled with cars. Chloe could sense how their weight strained the concrete. Everything was under roof here. But there were no walls. The hot and cold draft made hair move on people's heads.

A bus arrived. Desire brightened, until she realized it was headed for platform 12.

A flute played somewhere. Sometimes Chloe wondered if it was just in her head, other times she could swear she heard it from somewhere on her left. Even when she turned around it was still on her left.

A new bus arrived, and it was headed in the right direction. At one time it would seem that it was still turning and choosing one of the other platforms, but then it shook its head defiantly and drove towards them.

– About time, a woman five steps away swore, – it's half an hour late.

Chloe shook puzzled her head. It hadn't been that long, had it?

Victor stepped off the bus. Desire rushed into his arms and smothered him with kisses.

Chloe looked at the electronic clock on the wall. It said

2.17

She looked at the watch on her wrist. It said

5.17

They walked up one floor, to a street bridge leading to the Railway Station, another building in the vast complex that was Jaynagar City Station. The bridge was completely closed off, with glass walls. Chloe looked down, at the people and buses and cars passing in both directions below.

The cafeteria, at the center of a large atrium was packed with people. Everything was fairly low-keyed, except for the intense music played through speakers somewhere. It wasn't loud. People could have a conversation without being bothered by it.

It sent chills through Chloe.

– Coffee or tea? Colin asked.

– Coffee! Chloe replied, very decisively.

The others agreed. For some reason the mere thought of drinking tea had an adverse effect on them.

They sat down by the window. Here, too the entire wall was glass, and it disoriented them. It was as if there was nothing between them and the edge, the free fall to the street below.

The place was filled with art, all kinds of weird, eerie sculpting and paintings, provoking and evoking all sorts of reactions in people. Most of those present pretended to ignore it. They were exposed by their anxious glances and constantly turning heads.

At the opposite window was painted a transparent eye. It looked like it was moving as people walked across the room, as if it was following everybody moving back and forth between the restrooms, the cashier and the two exits and entrances.

A statue in front of the restrooms had stuck its tongue out. It seemed to be moving, taunting everybody passing by. A large bird flapped its wings. A recorded sound of flapping wings played constantly in the background. A gust of wind hit people standing in front of it, and they imagined that the stone was moving. A piece of red blood meat hung from its beak.

Or so people feared.

– Look at them, Chloe said.

Her companions looked at her.

– Look at the people gathered here. Listen to them. Their conversation, even between friends is as dry as paper. There is no spark there, no excitement, nothing beyond the mundane of daily life.

She saw them without trying, noticing their empty eyes and words, the lack of variation, deviation from the pattern, and the wind from the stone wings blew straight through her.

– The entire bunch looks like carbon-copies, Desire giggled solemnly.

The eye seemed to be cast in shadow. Chloe imagined it looked at her and winked to her.

She saw its mouth's wide grin and sharp fangs.

The sound hit her from nowhere. It touched her earlobe and burned her skin. Pain cut through her stomach. She doubled over.

– Are you okay? Marion asked her.

– Yes, Chloe replied, – it's just my stomach acting up again. I'll be right back.

She hurried to the restroom, fearful of running, afraid that the shit would push itself out if she exerted herself in any way. It was packed with people in there, *packed*. She looked bewildered around her. Every single stall was taken and there was a queue in front of every single one. She stood there indecisive for a few moments before leaving. Desire only had eyes for Victor and didn't see her when she waved, but Colin did. She pointed to the passage, pointed at the bus station. He gave a thumb up and smiled encouragingly to her. She left the restaurant and headed for the other restroom across the street bridge.

There weren't many people on the bridge, a fact that encouraged her. Pain shot through her again, as another contraction rose from her stomach and the shit once more threatened to erupt from her second lower hole. The restroom, her second and final hope was almost empty. She rushed into the nearest stall, closed and locked the door, pulled down her pants and panties and then, just as she sat down the liquid content flowed freely into the bowl, and a sick sense of relief almost overwhelmed her. The door changed color from deep red to pale green.

It burned when she dried herself. The toilet paper practically drowned in shit and fluids. She had to use twice as much paper as she usually did. After she had flushed the toilet some of the paper still showed.

There was no one there when she opened the door. She imagined she heard suspicious sounds from the farthest stall, but couldn't be positive. In the wall to wall mirror the room seemed unnaturally large.

She splashed water in her face. Her pale face reflected in the plushy mirror stared back at her. She realized that she had forgotten to pull up her pants and had dragged her feet across the partially wet floor. Her attention was drawn to the dark bags under her eyes. In this distinct light they were particularly visible.

Stephen waited for her outside. She stopped startled.

– There you are, he snarled. – I knew you were hiding somewhere around here.

– I'm not hiding, she said fairly calm.

– Of course you aren't, he snorted, – you'll only sic the cops on me again, won't you?

He grinned, a twisted, sick grin.

– But that won't work, he said matter of fact, – not anymore. That's what I came here to tell you, seeee. They can't guard you every minute of the day, and they don't even bother with that.

He looked completely insane. She couldn't hide the glum face. He was right, damn him.

– They have better things to do with their day, seeee, than guarding an unfaithful ssslut.

Then he was gone, and she couldn't with confidence say he had ever been there.

She stood there for what felt like a very long time. It was like she was outdoors. The wind blew around her. She stood still by the window and looked at the vehicles passing back and forth below. There were no windows. She crossed the bridge slowly. A bus turned the corner to her left. For some reason she stopped and studied it, as it approached her, approached the bridge. The buzz in her ears, the sound touching her rose to a painful wail. The bus disappeared under the bridge. She turned and looked in the opposite direction to see the bus appear on the other side.

It… didn't. She rushed to the other side and stared down, but saw no bus. Somehow, it had… *vanished* between the north side and south side of the bridge. She ran down with her heart beating hard in her chest, ran down the stairs. The walls were transparent glass all the way. She had a comprehensive view of the entire street almost immediately.

The wind shook her when she stopped on street level, eyes wide and filled with incredulity, with wonder and confusion and fear and cold sweat covering her skin.

Cars, other buses, people passed back and forth under the bridge. People looked at her with worry in their eyes, reacting to her burning stare.

She walked back up in a daze. Time passed, she couldn't tell how much, as she stood there, leaning towards the window, looking at the cars and buses and people below, both north and south. No one or nothing vanished (and she stared hard) as far as she could see, not anymore.

It was like everything moved around her, moved like the wind. Everything stood so very still, and she was the only one moving.

She easily noticed the others' glances when she returned.

– I had a really bad stomach, she confessed.

And made them notice her even more.

– It can't have been that bad, Colin said pleasantly. – You weren't gone that long.

She closed and opened her eyes. It had felt like hours.

Marion laughed at her behind the sweet exterior.

Chloe stuck out her tongue to her. Marion's nice mask cracked in incredulity.

– What are you doing?

Chloe sensed it, suddenly felt it like something tangible, not something touching her, but something inside of her reaching out, touching the world, and slowly, slowly she began smiling.

– It was very bad, she admitted willingly, – or at least I thought so at the time, and also for a considerable time afterwards.

The world changed around her, details in the room transformed into something different. The statue moved, and its tongue turned pink. The eye grew a twin on the opposite window.

But most of all her impression of it changed. She feared she was dreaming, and was scared to death that she would wake up somewhere, not remembering anything and shaking in fright.

– I see myself walking down a dark hallway, and I'm not afraid, but *excited,* like in my best moments. When do we lose this in our lives, the ability to laugh in the face of adversity?

She once again closed her eyes briefly, but she didn't feel like that, didn't feel like she closed them in denial, but that she was opening them to all kinds of possibilities. When she opened them again she wasn't looking at one of them, or even two, but all of them.

– Something is happening, she stated solemnly. – A force is sweeping the world and I have touched it. We all have, to some degree, and in turn it has touched us. That is inevitable. The Other World is reaching out to us. We are reaching out to it. Two forces are meeting each other in the middle. There are bound to be consequences.

They looked at her with the familiar skepticism shadowing their concern, but for the first time in a very long time it didn't bother her. At least right now it didn't.

– I have looked for what is *hidden* my entire life, long before I knew I was doing it, and I have paid the price, ridden with self-destructive doubt in a society denying all the dark and pale shadows of the world. Yes, Mystics going deep *are* troubled, but it isn't necessarily a bad thing. It can just as well be a sign, a clarion call for the coming *transformation.*

She stared back at them, shaking inside, ready for their laughter, their kind and rational disrespect.

In the short time since she had stuck out her tongue to Marion everything or at least something major had changed, something she had always known was there, but in doubt-ridden guilt had ignored.

Images assaulted her, terrifying sensations making no sense. She rejected Colin's offered hand.

– It's an old truth: Power changes with the tide, and now the tide is coming. Come with me!

They looked startled at her.

She spotted Andrew Fallon and Isabel Connor the moment they appeared by the western entrance.

Remaining drained and nauseous she rose from the chair she couldn't recall sitting down in, and they rose with her, a study in contradicting emotions.

Isabel looked horrible. Andy had to stop her from falling several times. Chloe walked to Isabel and grabbed her hands.

Her friend crumbled before her eyes, but held on.

The small group moved on. They followed the reverse migration back to the Pit, approached the subway to the other side from the railway station, as the first rays of light began to fade and twilight began asserting itself. Chloe's shoes felt tight, uncomfortable, as if she had walked for miles, and the others didn't exactly look much better.

– They just won't leave me alone, Isabel choked.

– I know, Chloe said, – we'll deal with it.

They descended into the tunnel. The darkness received them with a gentle touch. Chloe's eyes flickered in the pleasant shadow.

– It's just a subway, Marion insisted.

Chloe's smile widened.

– It is Friday, isn't it? Isabel wondered. – I think, even if I'm not sure that it is Friday.

That would have been evident to the most confused person. People had already started drinking, stumbling forward with bottles in their hand. It was the end of a long, draining week of work and people set out to forget. Especially down here, in the dark, even somewhat sober they dared things they would never do most other places. Chloe sensed the energy… of the enslaved shaking their chains. It made her shiver in delight and disgust.

– Look at them, Isabel spat. – They just want their Friday fix, and never yearn for more.

The group exchanged glances.

– We do, Chloe assured her, and assured them all, as if attempting to convince herself.

She couldn't help noticing the catching in her throat.

– Where did you park the car? Colin asked Marion.

– Not very far away. She smiled sweetly to him. – Not very far away at all.

Pit Lake revealed itself to them. They looked to their left, at the hotel, and to their right, at the old, derelict building.
– This is where the original settlements were, Desire said, – circling the lake. This was an oasis in the desert then.
– That's hard to believe, Andy said, clearly skeptical. – Shouldn't there at least be *some* evidence, some results of the countless excavations? Granted there are miles and miles of sewers down there, but…
– Who says there isn't? Desire countered.
There was something between them, between them all, a wound never closing, never going away.
They entered the hotel lobby. A sense of frightening familiarity almost overwhelmed them, but they pressed on.
The clerk greeted them with his professional smile.
– Hello again, Andy greeted the smiling man.
– Hello, Mr. Fallon. How nice to see you all again. May I presume you want your old rooms back?
Now, he didn't sound like a clerk at all, but like something completely different.
– So, it's quite okay then? We didn't exactly plan on spending more nights here.
– It's a slow season. We haven't even cleaned your rooms I'm afraid. If you will wait here we may do so. It won't lake long.
– No, that's okay, Chloe said hastily. – We'll manage.
– No luggage? The clerk smirked.
– No luggage, Andy confirmed.
He stared at the man, looking for anything resembling smugness or triumph, but there wasn't any, not any that he could discern.
The clerk rang the bell.
– We know the way, Marion emphasized. – There's really no need…
– The bellboy shows the guests to their rooms, the smirking clerk insisted. – That's the rule.
The freckled and eager bellboy led them through dark and long hallways. The lights dimmed further. Everything turned completely black for a moment, before the dim lights blissfully reappeared and blinded them. Marion sought close to Colin. He put his arm around her, and squeezed her gently.
Their rooms hadn't changed. In fact they looked exactly the same. The beds hadn't been made. They checked out all the rooms with a nervous flicker in their eyes.
– Color me wrong, but isn't everything exactly as we left it?
Victor shook his head in dismay, and more.

There were three interconnecting rooms, really, making up what the establishment called a suite, a redefinition of the word for sure.

– This is okay, Colin shrugged. – It will serve us well.

– We need equipment, Victor said, – but I have no idea where we can get any… on our budget.

– We need some equipment, Marion giggled.

– It blinked, Desire said, clearly shivering. – It turned completely black.

– Yes, I know, Andy said. – But it isn't exactly a surprise that the electricity is failing here.

– You don't understand, Chloe said. – You *know,* but fail to understand. Perhaps you still don't want to, in spite of everything that has been happening.

– Enlighten me, then, he said with a stubborn stance.

He convinced no one.

– It didn't just turn dark, there in the hallway, Desire said, with shivering lips. – Everything *went away*. The ceiling and the walls, and the very floor we walked on were gone.

– As if someone turned a switch, Isabel choked.

She sat on one of the beds, staring straight ahead, at the nothing in front of her.

– We don't need any fucking equipment, Desire said. – We don't need a crystal ball to confirm the obvious.

She dried saliva from her lips and jaw and vanished into the other room. Victor hesitated a moment or two, before following her.

– Hold me, they heard Desire's sexy, but now so thin voice.

They heard her sigh, heard the sound of wet kisses. Colin and Chloe looked out the window. Chloe studied the small ants crawling away down on the street, down there at the dry harbor, far from the sea, the wet, vast sea. Colin frowned as he traced the lines of the western horizon, the distant harbor, the sea and the low cliffs where the sun fell and boiled the deep, deep water.

– Squeeze me, Desire whispered. – Wring me like a sponge.

Everybody imagined how she fell on the bed, how she writhed on it and performed enticingly and sensually, making Victor hard as rock below. They heard gasps turn to moans and small happy screams, and the distinct sound when sweaty hips collided.

– I've never seen clouds so black.

– Huh?

Chloe frowned, looking at Colin frowning, as he stared at the western sky. Distracted to the point of being oblivious to her surroundings she began zoning in on his voice, following the line of his vision.

– They seem to be *moving,* he said incredulous.

She looked, looked at the swelling black mass, moving in from the north and the west. Desire released a loud, horny snort, and Chloe imagined she smiled in exalted happiness and expectation, and that her face wasn't turned towards Victor at all, but at some point beyond the wall, beyond the confines of the building.

– Did it… did it just turn cold in here?

Colin's voice came from far away. The black mass grew arms, a head, feet and slowly, slowly a face formed, and it was close by, suddenly, irreversible.

– That isn't clouds. Come!

– What..?

– Trust me, we must go, *now*. We must…

– *Time,* a voice said, chilling her blood. – *There is no more time.*

The cloud, no longer a cloud had entered the room. It had taken a form and size of a human being, and stopped right in front of Chloe, a creature of smoke, of mist and air and the nothingness it had come from.

Desire released a loud, prolonged moan, as she and Victor fell on the bed and a beyond happy smile lit her face.

Isabel fell on her knees, a terrified and ecstatic expression shadowing her face.

The creature… entered Chloe, slipped into her like the non-material thing it was. Her entire form turned dark. She looked at her companions with surprise and awe in her eyes. Her eyes turned inside out, turned white. She heard the sound of Andy's camera as he snapped pictures, many pictures. The shock in the others' expression hurt her. It hurt her terribly. She fainted. Everything turned black, turned shadow. Consciousness left her, even as sensation embraced her. She fell, slowly, fast, and hit the ground on her back, landing in the pool of dust and twilight. The others rushed to her, but they felt remote and far away. She imagined them through a haze of distance and loss.

CHAPTER EIGHTEEN

Tianuc Merde is walking down the road. Once, long ago he created himself from the smoke and dirt of the Earth. Chloe mumbled his story, as she crouched there in the vast darkness.

The vast darkness wasn't complete. She was able to see, to glimpse movement and creatures and human beings in its pale shadows.

The man missing an eye stumbled through darkened streets.

– Have you seen my eye? He asked everybody he met. – I need to find my eye, and it is nowhere to be found.

He stopped absolutely everybody, moving in a fast, furious and frantic way.

But he met only specters, people more or less ignoring him, with no more substance than a passing thought, and he stumbled on.

The dark-clad woman and her companions entered the dim and dank room passing for a dining hall in the old, forlorn hotel. There was quite a number of people present, whispering among themselves in hushed hisses, with excited expressions painted on their worn faces.

– It's quiet, Andy whispered.

– Not really, Chloe said quietly.

She heard it, heard it all, a choir filling her ears, her mind and slowly rising in volume and intensity.

Her companions glanced at her, doing their best not to stare.

They glanced at each other, at the pale faces, the sunken eyes, and terror took hold in their hardly beating hearts. The bleak fear that had grabbed them earlier in the day held them in its fist.

A man sat by a table drinking. He drank fast and intense, like he was drowning in a desert of water. Andy studied him, or tried to. There wasn't much to see, really, except yet another drunk getting drunk.

They sat down by a table, the only table available in the room.

– What truly happened to David Fallon Somby? Desire wondered, looking down in her newly acquired glass. – Will we ever know, ever even come close to what is hiding behind the world?

– Heat is real. Victor shrugged. – Cold is real. But you can't touch it.

A man sat by a table drinking. He drank fast and intense, like he was drowning in a desert of water. Andy studied him, or tried to. There wasn't much to see, really, except yet another drunk getting drunk.

– The Other World is real, Chloe said with a deep, hollow voice. – It's just a little less accessible, that's all.

Colin grabbed her hand, and held on to it, as if he feared it would slip away, would vanish before his eyes.
– Are you okay? He said, clearly concerned.
– I'm okay, honey, Chloe replied.
– We shouldn't have come here, he swore.
– I'm glad we did, she said, her eyes deep pools of ebony radiance, her smile light as a feather.
The man at the other table kept pouring liquor into his mouth, He quickly changed from being drunk to being totally wasted. Only during the fairly short time they had watched him he had consumed enough to kill most ordinary people.
– WAITER! He shouted, belched like an elephant in a pawn shop.
No waiter arrived or was forthcoming. The man stared into his glass with a dull expression in his eyes.
– It doesn't work, he sniffed. – Nothing does!
– We are nowhere, Marion whispered.
– We are here, Isabel said with deep color in her cheeks.
Chloe looked curious at her with her huge, opaque eyes.
The drunk rose abruptly, and pushed his chair across the floor, until it hit the neighboring table. The people sitting there jumped in their seats. He walked on unsteady feet towards the bar. Halfway there he crashed right into another table, and several people fell off their chairs. A ruckus of another world erupted. The victims of his bad navigation wanted to strike him, but realized quickly there was no point. He was far beyond their potential retribution.
Someone played a piano somewhere, haunting, eerie music. It rumbled through the hall and hallways, and they heard it as a kind of enhanced, not fading echo, enchanted like a forest… or a dance. The chords, the very sound of it sent shivers through them all.
– Where is the PIANO? The man on the floor wailed. – I never saw a fucking PIANO here!
The seven chuckled a bit. Chloe looked at Colin with her vast-deep eyes.
– I'm okay, you know, she told him. – I feel so much better now.
She rose, still sweating cold droplets, still troubled, still calm like ice.
– I have to go to the bathroom.
– Certainly, Victor said, sipping his drink. – We will just sit here and relax while you are exerting yourself.
– Do you want me to follow you? Colin asked concerned.
– There is no need for that, my dear, she grinned. – I can manage.
Everybody laughed, a little uneasy. Colin felt a little wounded by her rejection, but he concealed it, and was about to nod encouragingly to her,

when he realized she had already turned her back on him. He spotted her by the bar, on her way to the restroom.

The piano music changed. Somehow it metamorphosed into lengthy organ tones. There was no transition or sense of transition. One moment a piano was playing, the next the organ.

– Did you guys hear that? Denise said.

– Hear what? Marion asked.

– The transition. It was practically flawless.

She looked at the piano player turned organ master. He looked perfectly normal, even average. A frown deep and wide cut her brow.

Desire sat there, anxious and alone, desperately attempting to put her worry into words, but no words came.

Chloe stepped into the bathroom. There were other people there, but she discarded them like yesterday's laundry. Her attention took her elsewhere.

She touched the woman, the mirror image facing her.

Andthenshewasalone

And then she was alone, as she changed and the world changed around her. Small shady dots flowed slowly from her body, surrounding her. The mirror image changed, into the vast, alien landscape she recalled so well. Then the restroom part changed, too, joining the wasteland in the mirror. But the two identical women facing each other remained the same.

– Hello, they choired. – It's so nice to meet you.

And the landscape no longer looked alien, but strikingly familiar.

– Things are two, like everything is two, at least that. They are many.

Chloe returned, her walk confident, her eyes calm, a large pool of calm.

– Have you seen our friend, my dear? Victor wondered.

She looked inquiringly at him.

– The drunk? Victor explained. – We can't seem to locate him anywhere, not even if we had actually been trying.

– So, he has vanished, then? She nodded. – Good! I didn't care much for his loud act.

She smiled, and bent down and kissed Colin on the lips. He felt her hard nipples stab his skin further below. There was an odor coming from her he couldn't quite identify, so familiar that he was amazed that he didn't recognize its imprint.

A man, another man screamed. He wasn't far away. They saw him, when they turned, saw him sit in his chair, saw him fall off it, and hit the floor.

– NO! He howled. – NOOOOOOOOOO

He kept repeating it, not letting up, not getting up, but remaining on the floor as if his ability to walk or even stand had been taken from him, been plucked brutally from his brain, and he no longer even had the actual ability to use his legs, or even remembered that he had any.

A man hit the man beside him. There was no evident history there. He just hit him, from out of the blue.

A woman sat by the bar, drinking. A row of glasses had been lined up in front of her, and she took on them all, and there seemed to be no end to her endurance. Her long and greasy hair hung from her bowed head, and occasionally it swept the floor, and picked up even more dirt.

The floor had clearly not been cleaned for days.

– Let's leave. Chloe shook her head in disgust. – The clientele here isn't exactly desirable company, and certainly not up to our standards.

She smiled, a smile freezing tongues and larynxes, keeping voices from being heard.

The others, sick to their stomach, were only happy that someone finally took the initiative, and they could hardly wait to get up and walk off, out of there. The woman in the bar, with a downright eerie smile started throwing the glasses at the mirror. It broke, and broke again, until it was in a thousand pieces, but yet had to fall off the wall. Desire looked into the mirror as they passed it, and she frowned at first, but then she shook, hard and viciously in Victor's arms. One glass, with a great throw by the woman hit the bartender in the head. He went down like a felled tree.

Victor walked behind the bar, grabbed a couple of bottles and six glasses, and they were off. They didn't see the bartender or anyone resembling a bartender anywhere. He wasn't on the floor, where they had believed him to have fallen. There was nothing but dust there.

The hallways were as quiet as always. They half expected the bellboy to join them and insist on following them to their rooms again, but they didn't see him, didn't see him anywhere.

They glimpsed the clerk, on his post, grinning at them with his faceless smile.

Colin grabbed Chloe and shook her.

– What was that? What *happened* in there?

– I don't know, she replied weakly. – I'm not certain.

– We should leave this place, Desire said, turned towards Chloe. – There is nothing for us here.

– I believe you are correct, Chloe nodded. – Let's leave.

– Ok, Marion agreed, – let's just go collect our things…

– No, Chloe said, – we don't go back up there. No way! We leave.

She walked away, left the lobby, the hotel altogether, and the six followed her.

They stepped outside, into the fleshling night. There was no noticeable change in the air. Inside and outside were the same.

The Lake looked different, somehow, stirring beneath the surface. They imagined they could see it, as if the bricks had become transparent liquid.

– What do you think happened? Victor asked.

He had been paying attention. Chloe acknowledged him with slight smirk.

– People fear Chaos, she frowned, a frown slowly turning ecstatic, – but they shouldn't. They should embrace it, with all their hearts.

– What does that mean? Marion asked. – What?

– That should be self-evident, even to you, her old friend replied softly.

She began walking.

– Come, she told them.

They followed her, across Pit Lake, returning to the subway under the passing highway, returning to the bus station, walking in the opposite direction of virtually everybody else.

– I'm glad we left the hotel, Desire said. – It had nothing good in store for us.

– It is a bloodthirsty hotel, Chloe acknowledged. – It would have left us in pieces, but it won't, not this time.

She could sense the incredulity in Colin, Adam and Marion. She chose to ignore it. So close, so close, now to what she had chased for so long.

A long and broad metal stairway had recently been added to the wall outside the bus station building. It ran from the ground and all the way to the roof.

They ascended slowly, rising above the ground, above the closest parts of the city, with its lower buildings.

The car stood there lonely, and left alone, far from the other cars.

– How? Marion said, almost enraged. – How did you know where to find it?

– Like I told you, I know things. I remember pieces of the puzzle, events that never took place, and where many a dog buried his bones.

She paused a bit, hesitated a bit.

– I feel it, you know, she told them all. – I have always felt it, but now it's finally close enough to touch and taste, and not only to imagine. It's time, for that crucial final step

She produced the car keys from her pocket. Marion looked astonished at the display, searching her pocket for the keys. They weren't there.

– How did you…

– I lifted them when I bumped into you.

A light bump, a swift move with the hand had been all it took.

Laughter, so good, so nervous.

Marion had been about to throw the keys to Chloe, but had changed her mind and said smugly:

– I think I'll hold on to these…

Chloe unlocked and opened the driver's seat door. The air striking them had an indistinct stench making them pause and cringe. Chloe sat down in the driver's seat. She opened the other doors and everybody joined her. There wasn't really room for more than four passengers. Desire and Marion sat in Victor and Colin's lap. Marion leaned against Colin, smiling sweetly to him.

The car started with a roar. Chloe needed only one attempt. The engine coughed a bit, but its sound was loud and strong. She drove off the roof (but not off the roof), down the tailspin road to street level whistling a tune evoking a range of emotions and impressions in the six people traveling with her, visible in their faces and in the depth of their eyes.

Chloe and Marion gazed at each other in the rearview mirror. Marion shrunk in Colin's lap.

– Where are we going? She wondered, with a weak voice. – Where are we going?

Chloe ignored her and drove on, leaving the Pit and its immediate area behind, seeking the higher elevation at the base of the mountains. Buildings and houses changed into Mansions as they reached the Heights, the place to live for anybody that was something in society in Jaynagar. Chloe's wreck of a car passed dozens and dozens of stylish vehicles, the next usually even more elegant than the one before it.

And then they reached the area where the cars weren't parked along the road, but on vast estates where they could only glimpse mansions behind high fences and thick clutches of trees resembling forests.

The open space they arrived at was a square of sorts, with two buildings opposite each other. On one side was the church, on the other was Caine Mansion, both shiny and well kept buildings, old architecture renovated to stand tall in modern society. The seven people in the car shivered a bit. They could hardly take their eyes off the stately mansion ahead.

– I've had dreams about this place since I was a little girl, Chloe mused, her voice shaking. – I've never been able to tell why.

Here there was parking, an entire parking lot in fact. It was almost full. There was a queue lined up to gain entrance to Caine Mansion.

A part of it was open for visitors from nine to nine every day, even on Sundays.

– The revenues from visitors keep the house shiny, Marion said. – Even Caine, with his vast resources would be hard pressed to keep it afloat without that. He keeps stating that there is no basement in the building and no treasure, which in turn makes people even more convinced that there is one, the sly old bugger.

Chloe parked in one of the few available slots, with an elegant swing of her left hand.

They stepped out of the car.

– And people can pretend to be rich here, of course, Colin remarked. – For a few hours they can, for a fairly non-expensive treat pretend to be one of the successful, the rich and famous. Every rich and famous individual has dined here and spent the day here.

– They, too come here, looking for something lacking in their lives, Chloe said.

There was something in her voice, something not quite evident, in the subtext of the words.

Seven people turned their backs to the church and made their way between all the cars, towards the looming building.

– It's pulling at me, Isabel whimpered, – pulling me bad.

– Look at the lights, Marion said, almost lost in thought.

There was one line of lampposts reaching from the start of the driveway and to the entrance. They all stared apprehensive at it, like they did at the building itself. It was a strange landscape revealing itself to them all. They all shared a sense of unreality.

– They look like fireflies preserved in amber.

Marion sounded completely insane, but the others hardly reacted, except by finding themselves nodding.

The image forming before them seemed to be reflected on the ground, as if the lawn and the driveway and everything below reflected what was above and all solid matter had turned fluid and flexible.

Seven people crossed the road, and reached the gate. It was open, as the queue reached almost off the estate.

They slipped inside and joined the line of people journeying towards the Promised Land.

There was a little boy with his parents there. He hardly reached up to his mother's hand. A young girl had taken advantage of the warm weather and wore almost nothing. What she did wear could hardly qualify as clothes at all. She reminded Chloe of a model on a catwalk, clearly showing off, expecting to be assessed and appreciated.

Dozens more, all blurring, but yet so clear in Chloe's mind.

Caine Mansion seemed to rise, to flow from the ground, from the Earth itself, and far into the sky, as it towered above them. The selling of tickets far ahead seemed surreal to Chloe, only more so, as they appeared closer to the finish line.

A man, bleeding from a gauging hole in his left eye-socket stumbled forward.

Chloe blinked, and he was gone. Waves of chills assaulted her.

The revolving doors kept turning. There were no revolving doors here, but she still saw them, whirling air brushing people's hair.

They stepped inside. Caine Mansion welcomed them, whispering random delights in their ears.

– It's a living, breathing thing, Chloe whispered, – like a heart beating.

No one heard her, or if they did made no sign of having done so.

Sunlight, fading to red shone through the large window in front. Moonlight, gaining ascendance flooded the floor, and the people crossing the large entrance hall.

Chloe's shoulder hurt. She rubbed it with a little distant look in her eyes.

A dog barked somewhere. The bark didn't sound like that of a watchdog or anything, but more like a yelp of utter fear and desolation.

A cat stood on the second step of the staircase leading to the upper floors. It looked at all the visitors with a calm, collected stare, so proud and independent and free.

The clean-cut kid in uniform greeting them by the stairs didn't seem to be aware of the animal at all. That didn't seem very likely, since the cat made very much a nuisance of itself, but the kid didn't look or even glance at him.

– Hi, the clean-cut kid said. – My name is Kevin. I will be your guide tonight. Let me start with welcoming you to Caine Mansion. It's an honor.

– Do I sound like that? Colin asked Chloe anxiously. – Please tell me I don't.

– You don't, Chloe told him, very accommodating.

She was a bit preoccupied. The cat walked up the stairs, but she wasn't looking at it, but studying the others, her fellow visitors.

Logic suggested that at least some of them would automatically look at Kitty while she moved, but no one did. They didn't raise their eyes at all.

– We have a great evening ahead of us, Kevin said, – one you'll never forget.

Was there truly a wicked grin somewhere in his boyish smile, or was she only imagining things?

Her awareness seemed to have increased dramatically since she had stepped inside. The details of the hall practically *assaulted* her, burned themselves into her memory.

She looked up the straight, broad staircase to the upper floors, to the mist and indistinct details at the top.

– The stairs seem to continue… beyond the mist, don't they? A boy shivered. – To go on *forever?*

– It's a very successful optical illusion, a girl snorted. – There's nothing more to it, nothing more to it at all.

The statue of the goddess Beelzebub stood up there, at the center of Chloe's vision.

Pulling her perspective back down, she saw clearly the souvenir shops and paraphernalia associated with any respectable haunted house. But up there seemed unreal and distant, as if it wasn't really a part of the building at all.

– I feel like there is someone standing behind me, she said aloud.

Nobody seemed to be hearing her.

She turned and took a peek, but there was no one there, no one she could see. The sensation of being watched was almost overwhelmingly powerful.

– If you good people will follow me, Kevin said pleasantly.

Twenty followed him into the living room. The place had a pervasive, smoldering heat felt on the skin. The flames reaching out from the fireplace burned Chloe to cinder.

– There are no records of Caine Mansion ever being *built,* Kevin related. – There are other records, though, referring to it, the first being just a few decades after the first settlers arrived. Whether it was built by the first settlers or was already here upon their arrival or just appeared out of nowhere one day is open to interpretation.

Nervous, very nervous laughter.

A lamp blinked, slowly, time stretching out to eternity. Chloe blinked, too, and saw colors and blackness and whiteness, and an endless gray, a ragged landscape defying description. The fireplace transformed into a vast well of fire covering most of what was an entire valley.

– I bring your attention to this painting, Kevin declared, as if it was the most dramatic thing in the world (and perhaps it was). – It is the infamous painting of Marlon Caine, of course, rumored to be painted by David Fallon Somby. As you know or can observe it isn't signed. Another rumor says Somby painted it the evening of his *gruesome* death, and left it incomplete.

More nervous laughter. Chloe found herself being sucked into the painting, into Caine's huge, ominous eyes.

There was something about Kevin's voice, something rusty, something dead, like a saw blade being dragged across metal. He didn't seem engaged at all, not to her, no matter how most of the visitors ate up everything he said.

– The fireplace is yet another renowned chapter in this saga. Caine had the stone flown in from the renowned jungle of Asbasos, where a lot of stone used for great monuments has been taken from.

His voice sounded fake. This was the retouched version, nothing about the great scandals and perceived or possible horrors surrounding Marlon Caine's life, or at least just enough of it to keep the audience's attention.

An echo of his voice seemed to come from the stone, from the fireplace, from its roaring fires, so loud that it occasionally didn't sound like an echo at all, but the original voice. Chloe imagined she saw a face, even faces in the rock, heard a choir of suffering voices.

She dried her muzzle, and her hand turned red with blood. Marion stared astounded at her for a moment before her face once more turned stoic, impassive and Chloe couldn't be positive the change in expression had ever been there.

Her attention, like that of everybody else's was drawn to the painting.

– I bring your attention to the remarkable work of this unknown artist, Kevin declared. – The art world is ripe with speculation over who the artist is.

– Isn't it more or less proven, like you pointed out that David Fallon Somby painted it? Chloe asked sharply.

It took a heartbeat or two before Kevin pulled himself together.

– Implied perhaps, he laughed nervously, – but not proven.

– It is rumored that Caine can't even stand Somby's name being mentioned in his presence, Colin said to Chloe, and thereby to the entire assemble. – And certainly not here, in his Mansion.

– That's more than a rumor, a man snorted.

And that was probably more than right. During their years of feuding in the courtroom Breton Richards had used every opportunity to mention David Fallon Somby, and Caine had been visibly shrinking every time.

– Marlon Caine is a collector of objects… Kevin began hesitatingly.

– And people, the same man cried with poison in his voice.

– … and in this room you'll find a collection unlike any other place, Kevin continued, clearly strained.

Chloe saw pearls of sweat form on his forehead.

Everybody glanced nervously around, as if an angry stare studied them from above, but nothing happened, and they visibly relaxed.

– Marlon Caine is having a drink here in front of the fireplace every night at nine. People observe him sit in his chair as they pass by outside.

Hopefully you will understand that that makes this room and surroundings off-limits then.

He smiled politely.

She took pictures. So did most of the others present. She noted the small bronze statue in the window, the carpet in front of the fireplace, the poker above the kitchen door, the umbrella holder by the window, the stained glass in the window and dozens of other objects. The statue emanated a dark glow, its eyes pulsing in an even stranger flicker. Everything here spoke to her in a louder voice. They were distinct, too, hissing and whispering seductively to her.

Kevin the Guide brought them into the kitchen, a vast space of moisture and heavy scents. The slabs of meat the employees worked on and cut to pieces looked animated, alive to Chloe.

– Here is where the best chefs on the West Coast prepare your evening meal, one worthy of kings and gods.

– I can believe that, Desire nodded awestruck. – Everything looks shiny here, as if it has just been cleaned.

– One has a hard time knowing food has been prepared here at all, Andy noted wryly.

The talkative man from before let out a howl of loud cackling.

They were led into the other hall, one looking remarkably similar to the first, with another broad marble staircase leading upstairs. In the opposite direction, down the hallway leading outside they glimpsed the setup of the two doors. A lot of saliva gathered in the cavity of Chloe's mouth. She attempted to swallow, but couldn't do it.

– Not all rooms are open for the audience, Kevin said with regret. – But those outside the tour areas are mostly used as storage and staff quarters.

Mostly? Chloe wanted to ask him, experiencing a horrible sense of Deja vu, studying Colin with an anxious stare.

At the top of the stairs rested another natural sized statue of a woman, or rather a female. She clearly had animal characteristics mixed with her human traits. It looked like she would jump at them at any time.

There were paintings on the walls, all over the middle floor, giant wall to wall paintings. Calling them lifelike wouldn't do them justice.

– My Goddess, a woman called out, – I smell seawater.

Chloe had difficulties breathing. The stench of seawater was so powerful, evoking such vibrant sensations. The Cyclops with one visible eye stared at her. She ventured that he wasn't really meant as a Cyclops and imagined she could glimpse his other eye there in the shadows to the left, a red glare in the darkness razing her skin, her overworked mind. The woman in the rain hammered her fists at the window. A piece of the floor by the stairs had turned wet, a puddle of moisture threatening to become a pond. People glanced uneasily at each other.

– It's a deception, of course, the loud man snorted. – They make sure the floor is wet before each tour.

They reached the library, and people found their notebooks, both paper and computer, and began taking notes.

– Yes, Kevin said, very snotty, – this is the famous Caine Library of Rare Books and Manuscripts, many being the only known copy in existence.

Most of the books were placed on the shelves, but a few were protected by glass, and even fewer were enclosed in dark glass, protected from light itself.

– There is the Secrets of Time, a collection of scrolls said to be written thousands of years ago, a rare survivor from the library in Alexandria. We have The Spells of Ruins, a diary of a Viking sorcerer. Then the true gem: the Assyrian Book of the Dead, supposedly a first edition rumored to have been bound long before Gutenberg made his invention. These three and hundreds of others.

Chloe looked at the book hidden in the dark glass.

– What is it? Colin asked.

– I just wonder if Marlon Caine has read these books, and if he found anything truly useful in any of them.

She attempted to hide the yearning in her voice, but failed miserably.

– I don't think he did, Colin said. – He's more of a collector, not the fanatical seeker.

He bit his tongue, but he couldn't undo his words. Chloe sent him a smile to assure him that his indiscretion didn't matter. She tried very hard to make it work.

For some reason, just then she saw Marlon Caine sit in front of the fireplace in the living room. She stood on the outside, looking in. There was a flicker of glass between them. He looked big and imposing. The short grass on the lawn whispered to her, as if it was long and dry.

– There are negotiations, Kevin kept droning on, – between Mr. Caine and the city about making at least some of the collection accessible to the public. Mr. Caine is very conscious of his elevated role in society and is, as always eager to contribute to it in all ways available to him.

There were quirks and groans, low keyed, but unmistakable, as if a mighty wind rocked the building, as if a storm raged outside. But everything was silent on the lawn and in the garden. No branches on the trees or leaves of grass moved (but it still whispered). She stood on the inside, looking out.

Kevin brought them deeper into the Caine Mansion, up another floor, to where they finally reached the ceiling of the two halls. Like on every floor there was a hallway connecting them, one lit by lamps, but darkened by an inexplicable, pervasive ebony glow.

He brought them to an atrium, one that made them gasp in awe. This was the dining hall. A long table reached from one end to the other. Waiters were doing the final settings, placing plates, forks, spoons and knives in the correct order. The guests for the evening sat down in their designated seats. Every seat had a name. Chloe looked at hers, studied it even, before shaking her head and sitting down with the rest.

A variety of appetizers were offered to them. They could choose one or a selection of them, what they experienced as a smorgasbord of cooking, of food and drink. Chloe said no tea, even though the waiter offered it twice, its stench sticking in her nostrils.

– Don't drink the tea, she told her companions.

They looked bewildered at her, but acquiesced more or less willingly to her special request.

The meal… began. Chloe enjoyed it, perhaps even more so than the others, even as her eyes kept wandering back and forth, up and down. She kissed Colin unashamed on the lips, and laughed aloud afterwards. It was a great five course dinner, a meal to remember. The visitors had come to this place to experience something special and they did. At long last they got a taste of delights lingering in their dreams.

She watched the other guests devour the tea with great enjoyment. They chewed the appetizers with a happy gleam in their eyes. This was a highlight in their lives, something to strive for.

A husband and wife practically jumped up and down in their chairs, clearly having a great time.

Chloe glanced around with her keen power of observation, her eye for details, and her cruel ability to look inward, outward.

In the twisted mirror surface of the spoon she glimpsed Chloe Webster's drawn face, the blood-red lipstick, the bags under the eyes, enclosed by the short, shining dark hair.

Colin raised his glass to her, and they had a toast. The sound as the two glasses met and parted echoed in her… in her mind?

– What's wrong? The very perceptive man asked.

She hesitated a bit, before looking steadily at him.

– How many times have we had dinner today?

She asked him quietly.

He looked thunderstruck at her, attempting to give her an answer, unable to do so, doing the math, attempting to solve the unsolvable riddle. She saw him shiver in his bones, from his fingertips to his toes and back again, and she nodded to herself.

The main course was served, yet another multi-choice within the greater meal.

– The chef and crew must be hard at work tonight, a red-faced man bristled.

An image from the kitchen came to her, hidden in mist, faces of the chef and his hard-working crew. It felt increasingly real, as if she was standing right there, two steps away from the big man with the thick arms and giant chop-knife.

He didn't notice her. At least he made no overt sign that he had.

Marion looked radiant on Colin's right side. She flirted with him, and showed off to the very best of her ability, and that ability took her far. Her doll-like face agreed quite well with the light in the dining room. She had had her hair done recently, and she had kept it tidy. It revealed and framed her sweet face in excellent ways.

Chloe shrunk in her chair, fearing she was turning invisible. Her hand actually looked transparent for a moment, and she choked in her anxiety.

Sore eyes were, for some reason drawn towards the chair, the empty chair at the end of the long table. It was different than the rest, bigger, more elaborate.

– That's Caine's chair, Desire said in a hushed whisper. – It's there, in case he should join the guests, but he never does. They say it's only for show.

– I know, Desire, Chloe said absentmindedly.

Something in Desire's voice, in her demeanor… hooked her. She smiled at the empty chair. Her eyes twinkled.

She rose from the table as one of the first.

– I've had so many dinners today, she declared.

The man in the chair frowned. That pleased her, for some reason. It sent a shudder of exhilaration through her body and her glowing mind.

She walked to the window and looked out, at the peaceful, elegant suburban landscape.

– It looks like a painting, doesn't it?

– It does, Colin said behind her.

He grabbed her from behind and began kissing her on the neck, slowly making his way forward to her face and lips. She smiled, clearly showing that she appreciated his effort and writhed sensually in his arms.

She looked at the neighborhood. It seemed to go on forever beneath their feet. Not Jaynagar, only the immediate neighborhood surrounding Caine Mansion.

– I feel like I am falling, she whispered, – not through space, but through time.

A cat ran across the lawn, a huge, dangerous animal, a familiar born of Magick and darkness. Its shadow covered the entire lawn.

– But that isn't quite right either. There is more.

People finished their dinner. Some had trouble moving afterwards, because they had eaten well beyond their capability. Several of them burped, unable to keep it contained or hide it for their fellow man. Chloe would have chuckled if she hadn't smelled the stench of tea in her nostrils.

It was almost visible as mist in the air, and she had trouble breathing properly.

– There will now be an opportunity to go exploring on your own, Kevin said with his nasal voice. – Please keep to the designated areas and return to the west wing hall in an hour.

People hurried off, in a rush of motion. Chloe and companions took their time, deliberately, like a slow-moving train.

– We are here, Desire said, turned to Chloe. – We are finally here.

Chloe found herself nodding. For some reason she didn't question the strange look Desire sent her.

– What do you mean? Marion wondered. – This is nothing special. We could have gone here any time.

They ignored her. Chloe walked down the stairs, to the first statue. It grew in her vision before she reached it.

The walls shimmered in that eerie light again.

She walked to the statue, circling it, kissing it on the black lips.

– Are you standing here alone? That is so rude. They shouldn't keep you from each other. How many shores have you visited, in search of the Other?

The deep, soft voice carried far, into distant corners and shadows.

They walked through the dark, seemingly narrowing hallway, to the other side, to the three paintings.

One of a man with half of his face hidden in shadow.

One of a woman standing in the rain outside a window, hammering on it to get in.

The third of a ship sailing the sea, approaching a distant harbor.

Hectic activity ruled the harbor. People boarded the ship and left it back and forth in something that certainly wasn't an orderly pattern. Some reappeared, while others were never seen again.

Chloe looked at the painting of the ship anchored in the busy harbor, blinking once, twice, thrice. The large waves struck its sides, like on the most troubled sea.

She looked at her watch, and saw only an indistinct mass.

The harbor shook under their feet, when yet another powerful wave struck land.

She began checking the closed doors. They were all locked, except for the one leading to the restroom. She pondered if she should be peeing, but felt no pressure below, no pressure at all.

On one door at the top floor a most peculiar inscription revealed itself.

NO ADMITTANCE EXCEPT FOR CREW

They walked, they knew they did, all over the house, back and forth, endlessly. Chloe had that special look in her face. She knew she did, could see herself, as if there was a moving mirror following her everywhere. Sometimes she would swear she even glimpsed herself in the shimmering air, not just in the flickering shadows on the wall.

She glanced at her watch again, and again not long afterwards. The hands moved so fast, like the wind. No one could read them, could catch their breath, and certainly not she.

They returned to the library. There wasn't anyone else there. An empty, eerie quality dominated the room. Chloe rushed to the spot where the Assyrian Book of the Dead was locked down. She tested the solid lock on the side, shaking it as hard as she could. It didn't budge the slightest.

She stepped back, breathing hard, her face sweaty, and her hair in disarray. In her mirror image she saw it, the bulging eyes, and the dull expression in her face. She frowned slowly, painfully.

– Has the library… grown?

It looked like that to her, when she cast her attention across the room, at what appeared to be more shelves and a wall farther off.

Marion let out a mocking laughter.

It echoed in Chloe's ears, so cruel and disturbing, and no matter how she strived to focus her thoughts and attention, she couldn't do it. A roar deafened the sounds in her mind. To her inner eye appeared Marlon Caine. He sat in his blood red chair in front of the fireplace and had his nine o'clock drink, in the living room, not the library.

The loud bell shook the walls and tender ears. Chloe gasped in pain. The hour was up. She heard the sound of steps in the hallways, as people hurried down the stairs to not miss the deadline set by the illustrious Kevin.

Chloe pulled herself away with the others. She stopped briefly in front of a mirror by the door, a mirror covered by strange letters, forming words she strived to understand.

– Come, Marion said gently, taking her arm, – there is nothing for us here.

– But this is important, Chloe sniffed. – I *know* it is.

– They are just meaningless symbols scribbled on a mirror, her friend shrugged.

Chloe made her way down the stairs after the others. Every step felt painful and very much like an uphill battle. She imagined that her companions walked far ahead, an unbridgeable distance to cover. Everybody else was present. She was the last to arrive.

Kevin the Oracle bid them farewell with a professional smile and encouraging parting words.

– Thank you for coming. I hope we will see you all again soon.

She leaned against Colin, as they made their way towards the double exit. The yard outside looked so bright, meeting them with an almost blinding light.

– What did he say? She wondered. – I didn't quite hear him.

Colin looked at her with worry in his eyes.

– I saw him, she insisted. – I saw Marlon Caine sit in his chair in front of the fireplace with his none o'clock drink. I saw him as clearly as I see you now.

No one deemed her or her words worthy of a reply. She choked in misery and despair.

They made their way towards the exit, but it seemed to be miles away.

CHAPTER NINETEEN

They found themselves outside, heading for the parking lot at the other side of the road with the other visitors.

– I thought there would be something in there, Chloe said, her voice faltering. – I thought…

She made her way to the car with the others, with her companions.

As she closed and opened her eyes briefly, the image of Elliott Lasko in his straitjacket appeared to her, making her release a mute moan.

They returned to downtown. Chloe's hands shook, as they clutched the wheel. The parking garage rose in the urban landscape before them. Traffic was light towards the city. The few other cars on the road buzzed like angry wasps as they passed by.

Chloe drove the car the tailspin road up to the roof. She parked the car at its center, where the ground was calm and didn't shake so much. The longtime companions walked back down, to the bus station, through the subway to the Pit.

– So swift, Chloe mumbled, – like a striking dagger.

She recalled the buzzing wasps on the road.

The derelict building rested dead and still. Nothing seemed to be moving in there. Chloe imagined she sensed movement somewhere on its upper floor, but wasn't certain. She sought it, helplessly, walking up the stairs.

Her old apartment hadn't changed much. She even imagined she could glimpse the imprint of her body in the dust on the kitchen table.

But she couldn't say for sure.

The entire place seemed to be filled with dust, including the very air, from floor to ceiling. Distress caught her, as she caught sight of the five dolls on the couch. One, two, five seconds passed while she studied her six companions. There was no notable reaction in any of them. She relaxed again, returning to her somewhat constant form of unrest.

– Please, feel at home, all of you, she giggled darkly. – There is no lack of room here.

The furrow on her forehead was so deep that it hurt, but she was unable to find out the reason for it, what she had forgotten.

– Some place, Victor commented dryly.

Shapes formed in the air, in the dust. Chloe reached out to touch them, to grab them.

– What is it? Colin wondered.

– Can't you see them? She whispered. – Can't you…

He couldn't. None of the others could. Despair grabbed her again.

She entered the bedroom. A window was broken. A wet spot akin to a small pool had formed on the carpet beneath it.

A note, a message had been left on the bed, glued to the sheet with long term humidity. The occasional burst of wind didn't really touch it.

3.15 am

M

That was all.

Suddenly she had difficulties breathing. Violent pain in her chest made her want to double over. She clutched herself with both hands while wild, violent fear coursed through her.

Pushing her hands at her chest brought no relief, but was simply a reflex, a choice where there was no choice.

She walked past them, her companions. They walked through the streets, on busy sidewalks haunted by the noise of the angry four-wheeled machines in the stone river between. They glanced at each other with anxious eyes, understanding eluding them. Chloe kept walking, charging forward with the painful catching in her throat.

Across the street a sign declared with large letters:

TEA FROM THE WHOLE DAMN WORLD - MUST TASTE

Through the large windows they saw the people inside devour the various tea brands with great enjoyment.

– I have such a craving, Andy said hoarsely.

– No tea! Chloe stressed, repeating it with a taint of desperation in her voice. – *No tea!*

They walked on.

On the next corner, across the street another sign called attention to itself:

TEA FROM THE MOST EXOTIC PLACES YOU CAN IMAGINE

No one said anything this time, but pushed on.

They found a combined Coffee and Whiskey bar in a dark, hidden away alley in the deepest parts of the Pit, after walking the streets of the Downtown East Side, where beggars and homeless fought for their attention. The mood was different, muted. At the entrance was yet more meaningless words scribbled on a mirror. They found, after some soul-searching a quiet place in a corner in the deepest parts of the bar. Seven sat down. Seven enjoyed steaming hot and tasty coffee.

Victor looked around him with a look of happiness resting on his face.

– This is great, he exclaimed. – I can't for the life of me understand why so many people have a preference for tea.

– It's one of life's great mysteries, Andy agreed.

As the hours passed away the place was slowly filled with people. Moisture began condensing on the windows. Chloe nursed her third cup of coffee. She studied the room and its people, as was her want.

– What do you *see?* Isabel asked her, filled with excitement.

Chloe looked at her, as if seeing her for the very first time.

What do I see? She closed her eyes, an image of the room and its people forming in her head.

The girl with a hat on her head sat by the window, a silhouette superimposed on the streetlights.

The drawings, or rather prints of darkened human forms on the walls.

The man sitting by himself, all alone in the other deep corner, drinking whiskey.

And so on, everybody and everything else encircling her in a vortex, a whirlwind of time and change.

The buzz, the voices around her formed words, like those scribbled on a mirror.

A man moved a bit in the corner by the window, half in shadow, half obscured by gray light.

She grabbed the glass, sipped the drink a bit.

– Sometimes I get the feeling, the suspicion that I'm cursed, that I took a completely wrong turn somewhere.

The strong whiskey burned in her mind, making tears form in her eyes.

She blinked, and shook her head in confusion. The man was no longer there.

Isabel and Desire looked at her with reverence in their eyes. She realized startled that they had always done so. They looked at her completely different from everybody else.

She stood by the broken window, her left foot right by the widening pool on the floor. A sudden draft surrounded her with a breath of fresh air. She stared down into the pool, into the lake.

They waited for her in the living room.

– What just… happened? Andy wondered.

– Yes, what just happened, Andy? She asked him calmly.

He laughed a bit, clearly embarrassed.

– Nothing, I guess. For a moment there I imagined I was somewhere else, that's all.

– That's quite a common phenomenon, Marion sniffed. – You hear sounds, smell familiar spices and you connect them with somewhere you've been before, and presto your senses have fooled you.

– C'mon, Marion, Desire said wickedly, – you don't really believe your own shit, do you?

Marion looked utterly lost then.
– I just had to go here and take a look, Chloe said. – I'm ready to leave, now.
They descended the stairs. There were strange echoes and sounds they couldn't place. A man sat on the bench at the center of Pit Lake. He played the flute. They saw him through the dirty windows on their way down, and heard the music loud and clear in their ears. It seemed to them like he sat only a couple of steps away from them.
It was a chilly late afternoon. People pulled their open coats hard around themselves. A draft seemed to originate from the fountain at the center of the Square. The water twinkled in gray, in rainbow. People rushed back and forth, like they always did. A woman rolled a stroller across the Lake. The baby in it kept crying.
Chloe glanced around at the peaceful scene. Everything looked okay, looked normal, but when she blinked…
People stared at her, with hard, condemning eyes. She returned the stare, stubbornly, and it was as if they… they faded away, as if they weren't there at all.
The man playing the flute was gone.
The sun disappeared, vanished for a while, for a moment, and Chloe saw a completely different scenario, not the city at all, but the desolate landscape of her dreams and visions. She gasped, even as she strived with all her will to avoid gasping.
– Did you guys…
They looked at her, not really looking at her, not really bothering.
– Didn't you guys see that?
She studied them. They seemed totally unconcerned, as if they hadn't seen anything of what she had seen.
– I saw *something,* Desire said, suddenly, – but not anything I can put into words. What did you see? What did you see?
Both she and Isabel stared attentive at her, as if they expected her to reveal some horrible secret.
– I saw the sun vanish in the sky, Chloe replied with shivering lips, both comforted and increasingly fearful. – I saw the desolate landscape from my dreams and visions.
– Your power, Desire whispered. – Your power…
– It is growing, Isabel nodded. – You're changing, becoming yourself, like release, like pain.
And her words obviously comforted her and scared her witless.
Her comfort, her terror mirrored Chloe's insides.

They walked through the park, passing the green bench on their right. Behind it someone had put up a sign

JUST PAINTED

– Someone has a lot of paint on his or her back, Marion giggled.

Someone clearly had to have. The imprint of a human body on the newly painted bench was a dead giveaway.

For some reason they looked at each other's backs to see if there was anything there, but there wasn't.

They laughed in their uncertainty, their nagging doubt. When they reached the next fork in the road Chloe turned and looked back at the bench. She stopped briefly, imagining she saw a figure sit there, sit there and rise, with a lot of green paint on its back.

A heap of newspaper sheets took flight in the wind. The entire street they walked through was suddenly filled with flapping paper. There seemed to be no lack of papers to feed the flow. When they passed the heap there was still a lot of it to go around.

Chloe passed it. A chill down her back made her turn. She imagined she had seen a face beneath it all, one pale and cold, but when she turned to look, there was nothing there.

A door slammed somewhere. It was such a strange sound, as if it slammed right in their faces. They even stopped momentarily, before driven forward by their own momentum.

The small group walked a long and dusty road, one that didn't seem to be a part of the city at all. Chloe recognized part of the harbor, but that didn't seem right, either. The half digested apple to her right gathering dust seemed bigger, younger and vibrant. The car outside the shop Mystery Calling had a distinct grin on its front. The face staring at them from the window looked more like a painting than an actual face.

– I'm seeking the Lady of the Lake, she said.

– So you are, Desire acknowledged. – But why?

– Exc-cuse m-me?

– Have you ever stopped and asked yourself why you seek the Lady?

– I have been dreaming about her my whole life. I…

– No, no… Desire shook her head. – That is, at best a secondary motivation, not the true reason.

The long alley at the end of the road and the house in the cluster of trees appeared as from a dream. Chloe and Desire, and the rest walked the distance between here and there. In the course of their walk it turned dark and not a single lamp illuminated the path. The gate seemed to be resting in darkness, as if the sun outside was bright enough to cast the deepest shadow. It brought them far away, so distant from where she walked.

– There used to be a house here, once, Chloe said. – There isn't any house here, now.

She kept walking, having a sense of the others following her, not looking back to confirm it.

The briefest of moments expanded towards Eternity.

A car passed them. The loud howl of the engine hurt their ears and rattled their bones. They followed the siren call of the rhythm and the melody through busy city streets.

They hurried through narrow and dark city streets. Each block seemed to stretch on forever, the distance from one corner to another something akin to infinite.

The eyes stabbed her back again. She turned, but there was no one there. It was such a familiar sensation.

They entered a new part of the city, and it was a completely unknown part. There wasn't a single building or landmark that looked familiar to them.

The fire in the sky froze them, chilled their skin. Down here darkness surrounded them, ice burning their bones.

When they stopped, at what felt like hours later they were breathing hard, and sweat was pouring from every inch of their skin.

– I think we're lost, Colin gasped. – This isn't any part of town I've ever seen.

It was something in the way he said «lost» that made everybody stare at him.

– In Central Jaynagar? Andy said. – Don't be silly. I know this place better than the back of my hand.

They stared at him, too, and he returned a confused look.

– You're correct, Colin acknowledged. – I can't for the life of me believe this is Central Jaynagar.

– But where *are* we, then? Marion said nonplussed. – I don't recognize anything. It seems more like another town to me. Where are the fucking mountains?

She tried to look above the buildings, but couldn't. The houses weren't really that tall, but above them was only sky. She looked east, or where she surmised east was, but there were no mountains, no mountains no matter what directions she looked.

The whimper rose in her throat, and she sought closer to Colin. She looked at him, but he looked away.

– The city is growing, Isabel said frostily, – growing like cancer, reaching out to ever new untouched areas.

They kept walking, often running, looking around with pained, bewildered stares. Thunder rolled, but not in the horizon, under their feet.

– Oh, no, Victor groaned, – oh, NO!

It started raining, a tiny drizzle at first, then it was pouring. They ran for the nearest shelter they could find.

There was a ruin, or a construction site, it was difficult to say which right around the corner. They almost cried in relief, as they huddled under the incomplete roof. Water flowed around them on all sides, and made the floor more of a pool than a floor, but they remained fairly dry.

They looked at each other with misery in their eyes.

– At least we found cover, Andy said upbeat.

– This isn't a cover, Victor groaned some more, – but more of a shed, really, leaking like a… a *tea* strainer.

They looked at each other with terror in their eyes.

The evening cold invaded them. They began to shudder, and then shake, seeking closer together in a useless attempt at keeping warm.

– This is insane! Marion said exasperated. – What's happening to us?

Chloe saw everything, everyone from all sides. It wasn't confusing, but clarifying.

– We should gather wood, she said slowly.

– Wood, here? Colin said dumbfounded.

– There, she said and pointed.

And when they looked they spotted a little corner, across the site, where there were lots of dry material and not so much water flowing down.

Victor began laughing in relief.

– How come we didn't see this before?

Colin shook his head, paused a bit and did it some more.

– Who CARES?

Victor ran through the rain, across the site, into the quiet corner of the world. The others followed him, reaching their destination even more wet and cold. Victor began assembling paper and wood in a heap, and found matches in his pocket. A match lit up. The bonfire lit up. The flames seemed to hesitate a bit, one moment, two, three, before finally burning with a tall and steady flame.

There were three dark windows on one of the walls. Chloe's attention was drawn to them, and she let it, let herself be immersed in the eerie, beyond strange surroundings. There was a pain in her chest, and she gasped.

– Are you all right? Colin asked.

– He is ever the attentive boy, isn't he? Desire said wickedly.

– I am, she assured him, touching his hand lightly.

A broken mirror flashed and burned opposite the three dark windows. Pieces of it on the ground twinkled in angles and shadows, and glimpses of the Other World.

– The fire is so warm, Isabel mumbled, – so pure.

Chloe held her hands closer to the flames, and the dancing protuberances and her fingers seemed, briefly to touch and mingle and become one. Claws of heat and icy cold reached for her from all sides, not only from her front. The darkness behind their backs and the fire in front touched and mingled and turned into one, singular entity.

It stopped raining, slowly. They noticed it, as they looked up, how the heavy showers faded and dark blue sky above reasserted itself.

The water kept pouring from the many cracks and openings in the derelict building.

– Come, Chloe bid them.

They walked through the city streets again, crossing the endless wasteland.

It felt like they had been walking forever, for two eternities, not just one. They walked and walked and walked, and saw no end in sight.

– Are we there yet? Andy gasped.

– Not quite yet, Chloe said brightly, with a sick shine in her eyes.

– I'm not hungry yet, Marion said. – Shouldn't I be hungry? We have walked the entire day… haven't we?

And as if on cue a restaurant appeared around the next corner.

– Come to think of it we should get some food, Victor nodded. – Yes, I think some food is definitely in order.

The buzz in Chloe's head, the pale light at the edge of her vision grew brighter.

– It's right, right ahead whatever it is, she hummed, impossibly enough.

There was a sort of opening ahead, a brightening of the dense air. Chloe recognized the place, rejoiced and choked by the sound of bubbling water in her ears and mind.

The restaurant faded away, from both their vision and consciousness. Hunger prevailed.

The lake appeared before them. On their left was the house, on their right the hotel, across the wide, vast lake the small, cozy village. A boat sailed the water. The sun shone from a cloudless, deep blue sky.

It was a sight cutting into them all. They looked confused and bewildered at each other.

Dog-tired feet kept moving forward. Strangely light-headed they walked down the road to the hotel by the lake. People walked in and out of the entrance. The building was basically made of bricks, like a castle, transformed and refurbished to fit modern taste.

It was hot in the sun. They began sweating almost immediately. When they stepped inside, into the air-conditioned colder surroundings they quickly felt better. The clerk met them with his sleazy smile. Andy frowned.

– Would you like rooms, ladies and gentlemen? The clerk asked them. – You may have one each, two for the price of one, a special offer. We've got plenty of rooms here these days, you see.

– Rooms would be fine, Andy squeaked. – Rooms would be…

– Excellent, she clerk cried enthusiastically. – The bell boy will show you the way.

– This is… off-season, isn't it? Victor asked.

– On the contrary, sir, the clerk beamed. – Times are great and even more people than usual seek out our excellent hotel, but we've got…

– … plenty of rooms here, Chloe completed his sentence.

And it pleased her to see a glimpse of fear in his lizard eyes.

The young, inexperienced bellboy stepped forward, offering his services to them.

– My name is Oscar Lerner, he recited, as if from a book. – I am at your service. If there is anything you need, please tell me.

– Oh, we will, Chloe said lightly, playing the tease. – Rest assured we will.

He turned red as the ripest of tomatoes.

– Everything changes all the time, from one moment to the next, Marion moaned. – Who can live like that, in a constantly changing environment?

They followed Oscar, the bell boy down the hall, and into the murky hallways.

The painting of Marlon Caine was right there, at the beginning of the long display wall. Chloe shivered as she glanced at it, as it overpowered her senses.

An old woman opened one of the doors they passed. She looked totally insane.

– She's a witch, she cried in pain. – She casts spells on us, and curses us to our last soul. I hear her, hear her mumble her incantations, hear her swear, and I see her dance on the hill, around her fire.

She slammed the door shut again. Chloe heard her mumble and swear behind the door.

Oscar unlocked and opened the doors to the seven rooms and they stepped inside. Victor held around Desire, his tongue playing with the exposed skin on her neck. She blinked, and in that blink she saw him hang from the ceiling, his face bloated and black.

Chloe touched Oscar under the jaw, making him look at her with worship in his eyes.

– I don't have any need for you at this time, she said, – but I might have later.

He faded away before her eyes, so very, very attentive.

Isabel walked back and forth in her room with a happy smile on her lips.

Andy pushed Marion at the wall, kissing her on the lips in a very possessive move, but she was unresponsive and evasive, clearly not interested, and he let her go.

– Everything feels so familiar, she cried in frustration. – I know I have never been here before, but I still can't free myself from a powerful sense of familiarity.

The seven of them had breakfast in the restaurant across the bridge, crossing the bridge moving (not shaking) under their feet. The waiter showed them to the corner table, by the large window, where they had a nice view of the lake and its surroundings.

– There is a car outside the house, Marion said. – Someone has moved in.

They followed her line of vision over there, witnessed the activity behind flickering curtains, apprehension cutting them like a drill.

– This tastes like SHIT! The woman by the neighborhood table shouted.

She stared miserable at the delicious ham and cheese sandwich.

– No, that's not true, she sniffed. – It doesn't taste like shit. It doesn't taste at all.

She started crying. Huge tears fell from her eyes and wet the table cloth.

– Would you like some tea, ma'am? The waiter offered generously.

– Yes, *please!* She sniffed.

He poured her cup to the brim, and the moment he stopped pouring she grabbed the cup and started drinking. It had to be hot, scolding hot, but she drank it all in one swallow, and leaned back in her chair with a happy, happy smile on her face.

A deep chill trickled down Chloe's spine.

She and her companions chewed the delicious sandwiches, drank the fresh orange juice, and enjoyed their time there, at the corner of the lake.

They took a lazy stroll through the village afterwards, quite enjoying the scenic tour.

– This place is so different, Marion said, – so different from the city. It looks unreal, like a painting.

– Did we walk here? Victor mumbled. – I can't remember walking here.

Desire rubbed his cheek with a tender glance, as she spoke in wonder.
– It is like a flash, isn't it, like from one moment to the next?
Two people rowed a boat across the lake.
– «I watch them from below», Desire said in a voice not hers, – «as I rise in the boiling waters, terrified of what I'm becoming».
They all frowned, shuddering in the warm sun, in the glow of the cold moon walking in their midst.
– This is peaceful, Marion insisted. – We should have gone here long ago.
The echo from all sides made her shrink in her tracks.
The man and woman in the boat went to shore and approached the village. They joined their friends enjoying the warm afternoon sun in the village market.
Chloe and her companions headed for the market, for the square ahead.
– We should return to the hotel, *now,* Marion stated.
The others looked incredulous at her.
– But it's such a fine day, Andy said.
– I forgot something there, she said, close to hysteria. – Yes, I forgot something. We need to go and *fetch* it.
They reached the market. People whirled around them, indistinct and unreal. The vortex spun and erased their surroundings. The circle of benches and the four people sitting on them were the only real images in the whirling mist.
The painting was one mundane, with crystal clear colors and faces. Andy, Marion, Desire and Victor looked at themselves as they froze solid at the busy, free-moving marketplace.
A dark laughter pushed itself from Chloe's itching throat. The others tore themselves free from the haunting image ahead and stared at her.
– Don't «worry», they can't see us, she admonished them. – They aren't of this world.
– What are you talking about?
Andy didn't scream, even though he very much wanted to.
– Don't you see? She said. – We're back at «Caine's Manor». In truth we never left. Tear the blindfold from your eyes and wool from your mind, people, and see the world as it is.
And with that inevitable realization the world changed or rather stood revealed before them. Streets and alleys metamorphosed into the dark hallways they thought they had left behind.
– No, Marion whimpered. – NO!
They stared at the painting, at their mirror images.

– Do you like it? Chloe asked with her ghostly voice. – I painted it myself, meticulously, using the smallest brushes, sometimes only one single hair, creating the most vibrant details…

– What IS this? Victor cried. – What has *happened* to us?

– It's the house. Chloe turned towards him, towards them. – It catches everything and everyone coming its way, the unaware and aware both. The world is Mist and Shadow, and so is the house.

– But w-we l-left?

– Did we or did we just believe we did? The house can be very accommodating, you know, showing its tenants what they believe they see.

– You knew about this?

Colin shook her with his anger.

– I did, she replied, – even before I knew I knew… just like all of you…

Her skin, her very being, pulsed in a sick glow.

He wanted to say more, but couldn't form the words. She wanted to go to him, but steeled herself.

– It seemed so real, Andy whispered.

– It was, she acknowledged. – It is. It's just a different part of reality than most people encounter. If anything everything is more real, more potent here at this place, this nexus.

– What are you *saying?*

– Haven't you been listening to what I've been telling you? She asked him softly. – The house that isn't a house catches, traps everything and everyone it encounters. It's old and vast, existing outside time and space. Can you *imagine* everything it has seen?

Her sickly smile stunned them, made fear gnaw at their bones.

– My God! Victor exclaimed. – This cannot be true. It can't!

She struck out with her arms. The hallway and its very air brightened visibly around them. They could suddenly see far and wide again, at both ends of the corridor. Chloe walked to the statue, touching it, kissing its lips, releasing a tiny moan of pain, before stepping back, staring at her companions with rigid eyes.

– Come with me, she bid them, commanded them.

They followed her in a daze down the stairs, to the entrance, the doorway they had walked through so long ago.

– There is a third saying about the Pit, she said, said to the air in front of her. – They say people come there, people of mystery and imagination come there, not to forget or be forgotten, but to remember, to stare horror in the eye, and look back at the Abyss.

She stopped in front of the door. It was bright daylight outside.

Victor rushed past her.
– I wouldn't do that if I was you, she said, with her ordinary voice.
He stopped abruptly, unable to tell why.
– There is a cloud out there, he said dumbfounded.
– That's no cloud.
They saw it as it grew, as it expanded to fill their view.
Everything turned pitch black outside.
– It won't let go of us that easily, she said. – I didn't think it would.
Colin stared at her. She sensed his eyes in her back, hearing his unasked questions.
She turned to face them.
– Something is… happening to me, she said. – I'm close, now, so close that I can actually reach out and touch what has always been out of reach, *hidden*. I saw myself, another me walk through the subway towards the bus station, crossing the bridge over the raging river, and all the world's secrets opened up and revealed themselves to me, *to me*.
She stared at them with pale burning eyes, her face changing, not changing.
He looked so lost just then. Her resistance faded and she took one step forward.
Everything turned black.
She stood there alone, all alone. The blackness burrowed into her. A moan escaped her lips.
– Hello, she cried out. – Hello? Can anyone hear me? Please respond!
There was no response, nothing even resembling any.
She stepped forward, or she tried to, but there was nothing there, nothing for her foot to stand on. She whimpered and pulled it back.
The darkness lasted forever.
There was nothing in it, nothing that her senses could fathom at all. She stood still, frozen, for an eternity.
Suddenly there was once more light, if ever so little. It reached her from behind her left shoulder, and when she turned a path revealed itself. She glanced around. All other directions were closed to her. She took a step forward, sick with relief when she touched solid ground. Whether it was floor or not she didn't know.
She walked through pitch black darkness, a traveler on a dark and lonely road, but she didn't really have a sense of moving forward, at least not very fast. There was nothing there, on the black wall ahead of her. Then she was able to glimpse something, a shimmer of change, a pattern, a texture in the Void. First there was something, a swelling that might be a nose. A heartbeat, two later she knew it was. Then the mouth appeared,

full lips like hers. The lips and nose together, and the eyes, far deeper than everything that was the pitch black darkness, that was the Void.
Through the eyes she glimpsed something, someone.
She recognized Andy, as if through a veil.
– Reality is hidden by a thin veil, she said aloud.
He didn't hear her. She kind of recognized the place. It was her bedroom in the old house by the lake.
The others were there as well, gathering information, researching what looked strikingly familiar.
A card rested upside down on the bed, white, against the white linen.
He turned the card and he read what was written on the other side.
I KNOW WHO KILLED DAVID FALLON SOMBY
Andy handed the card to Desire.
She crouched, as if in pain the moment she touched it.
– No, she said aloud, – that wasn't what the note said at all.
She turned the card again and read what was written on the other side.
I KNOW WHO KILLED CHLOE WEBSTER
– The third side reveals the truth, Isabel said.
She and Desire smiled at each other.
Chloe fell against the wall, as if gravity pulled her there, and slid slowly horizontally towards the distant door. When she looked back there was no window there anymore. Panic grabbed her, and she attempted to claw herself through the wall, hold onto it for dear life, but everything was smooth and hard, like ice.
She hit the door, and stumbled into the next room.
It was the dining room. Marlon Caine sat there in his chair, at the end of the table. Chloe recognized several of the dinner guests. They sat there with a distant look in their eyes.
– Poor Chloe, he said, foregoing the greeting, his usual thoroughly polite self, – born to such potential and squandering it on trifles. Do you enjoy being helpless, being weak, to be nothing but cattle anybody can run over and stamp on?
– No, she said, – no, no, no!
– Poor girl, he said sympathetically. – You look tired. Have a seat. Rest a bit.
There was one available seat. She pulled out the heavy chair and dumped down in it.
Everybody looked at the host with dull eyes, and it dawned on her that she was, too.

The husband and wife sat there with empty eyes and drawn faces. They, like most of the people around the table, reminded her of people that hadn't slept for weeks.

Even though she couldn't truly say what they looked like.

– Behold, Caine said to her, – this is you after an eternity or two. It will take longer, but the end result will be the same.

He raised his glass, filled with a smoking brew. He drank. Everybody around the table, except Chloe drank.

His drink… invigorated him, even as the others changed into dry husks.

He turned towards Chloe. She stared at him with dry and hollow eyes.

– Don't you want some tea, my dear, *wonderful* green tea?

– No, she replied angrily, – no tea!

– Suit yourself, he shrugged. – In time you will crave it, won't say no to the oblivion it offers.

She rose with an effort and rushed off. There was no door to the atrium, not really. She just faded away into the growing darkness.

– You will crawl for me, he bellowed. – CRAWL FOR ME!

An image entered her mind. She was dancing for him, sweet and enticing, a whirling mist in his cruel eyes.

She ran faster, her throat turning parched like desert sand, and she longed for tea, green, sweet tea.

– Everything here is symbolic, you know. Your problem is that you're not very good with symbolism at all.

His voice haunted her, angered her, scared her witless. The frown deepened and ever more thoughts she couldn't fathom churned through her mind.

The clerk waited for her behind his desk. She stumbled and almost fell, but managed to grab the desk and stay on her feet.

– Greetings, madam, is there anything I may help you with?

– I would like a room, she gasped.

– Very well, madam, he snorted. – May I see madam's reservation?

– I regret to say I have no reservation, she said to his face, – but I would still like a room.

– I'm afraid that's impossible, madam, he said, shaking his head.

– Listen, you pompous little ass, she said, – I have traveled far, and I'm dog-tired, and I would appreciate a room. I'm even prepared to pay for it.

– This is a decent hotel, madam, he snorted. – We require pre-reservation or no, *no* cigar. Is that clear?

Her fist struck the desk. The wood cracked and split in two. He looked absolutely stunned at her, and for a moment there was naked fear in his eyes, until it faded and only anger and smug arrogance remained.

– We *follow* the fucking rules here, he shouted, tomato-red in the face.

His words echoed in her head long after he had faded away and she continued her walk through the endless hallways.

She wondered, briefly what he had seen, what had evoked such naked fear. There was an image of herself, one enhanced and empowered, seen through his eyes, his perception, there one moment, gone the next. She sniffed, drying eyes and lips, continuing on her never-ending path.

Loud, horrible noises reached her in the dark, as she hid and covered there, of teeth chewing, chewing, chewing. She crouched on a naked floor, and there wasn't a wall in sight, not in any of the four directions, the vast space. Her feet moved again, hit hard the ground she ran on. Silent steps covered miles in a heartbeat. She chased something on a dark path, something elusive, fading every time she reached for it.

It didn't register at first. She didn't realize she was in the Library until she spotted the book. It was exposed, open, no longer inaccessible, locked in a box, its secrets no longer hidden to her. She began reading, her attention glued to the strange letters forming on their own before her very eyes.

The book was empty. The moment she opened it, there were lots and lots of empty pages. It wrote itself and turned its pages as she watched.

One text among many caught her attention, and the moment it did the fast writing slowed down, the turning of the page stopped, until there was only one page, one text:

> «In the Book of Fate there is everything, all events, all ages, everything that has been, that is, that will be, everything that can be…»

Heart jumped in her chest. There was nothing more. The pen or whatever it was that wrote the letters had stopped. Nothing more was added.

– Something is missing, she cried. – Something is *missing!*

The book had stopped, stopped completely. She slammed it shut in frustration. The dust blew across the room. She breathed it, in and out, observed how it flowed from her mouth. The dust was Shadow, dancing in the air.

She stumbled in a coil, one turning into a hissing snake. Her arm and body moved on its own and bent down and picked it up, and it turned to dust in her hands, and she breathed its sweet nectar.

Her feet moved. Rows of books filed past her, each copy's content known to her. She stopped briefly by the door. There was no mirror there, neither to the right, nor to the left. She passed through the doorway and appeared into the hallway. A push in her back kept moving her forward.

She embraced it, as she walked up the stairs, frowning, heading up the staircase far beyond its natural length. Fear stuck in her throat, but she moved on.

She appeared in a very familiar bedroom. When she turned there was a door there, one that hadn't been there when she first had glimpsed the bed, the bed with white linen. The statue to the left of the door stared at her with its black eyes. The clock on the wall said

3.15

There was the other door leading into the apartment. A tree whispered outside the window, its branches stretching far and wide, blowing in the wind. The bed had been used. She noticed, a bit distracted the imprints of two shapes on it. Across the vast lake the hotel lit up the other shore. On the large pillow rested six big life-like dolls.

She glanced at the note in her hand.

3.15 am
Marion

A creak in the floor made her turn. Marion stood there, her face pale, the skin bordering on white, on translucent, her lips quivering and the big eyes gray like stone, her hands buried in the deep pockets of her jacket.

– Ah, there you are, Chloe said relieved. – I wondered if you would come.

– I went for a long walk, Marion said in a hushed voice. – I walked on the balconies, round and round and round…

The lights blinked, slowly. Chloe managed to blink during the momentary darkness. It was as if an eternity had passed, but nothing had changed, nothing at all. When she looked around her she could easily confirm that to herself.

– I know this room, she said amazed. – I know it like the back of my hand.

Marion began walking forward, her face frozen in a beyond rigid expression. She pulled her right hand from her pocket. Chloe was astonished to spot the knife in her hand.

The floor creaked, creaked loud and strange. Marion walked close to her. In one swift move she plunged the knife deep into Chloe Webster's chest.

CHAPTER TWENTY

Marion plunged the knife time and time again into Chloe's chest with deadly accuracy, cutting her heart to pieces. At the final plunge she twisted the blade brutally as much as she possibly was able, before pulling it back out with a swooping sound.

Chloe stepped back, and fell backwards, on the bed. She lay there bleeding to death, soiling the white linen, gasping for breath, until she stopped and stared at the ceiling with dead eyes.

Marion dropped the knife. It hit the floor with a dump sound.

She stood there sniffing, drying her face with a bloody hand.

– Everything is okay, now, she said to the body on the bed. – I can marry Colin, now, and we can go away together.

The smile transformed her rigid features.

– I love Colin, love him to death.

She began swaying, then dancing, turning round and round until she stopped by the window, looking at her own, double mirror image.

– It was such torture, seeing you with him, but I bid my time, forced myself to be patient, waiting for the right moment to strike, and tonight the perfect opportunity presented itself, didn't it?

The double mirror image smiled some more. She played with a piece of her hair, slightly distracted.

– I can see us, imagine us together. We'll both be studying at the university, of course, work for each other, pay for each other's tuition as we do, as we love each other.

There was movement. She glimpsed it in the dark window the very moment she heard the creaking of the floor. She whirled around, her attention at the body on the bed. It lay still, and she breathed in stark relief.

There was nothing here, no one in the room beside herself and the bloody remains of Chloe Webster on the bed.

Chloe didn't move.

The branches of the three outside touched the wall. Marion almost jumped out of her skin and cried out loud.

Marion shook like a leaf.

The statue blinked. Marion gasped in fright, as it stared at her with its unmoving eyes.

The eyes blinked again, slower this time. Its left arm moved. It took one step forward. Marion watched in fearful fascination as the statue resembling Chloe Webster transformed into a living, warm-blooded woman.

– I remember now.

The voice was rusty, hoarse, as if hadn't been used for ages.

– You did it. You did it again. Thank you. The chains are off, now. I'm free! In death there is life.

By the beginning of the last sentence her voice had almost returned to normal.

Marion wanted to move, to run, to flee, but was frozen solid on her spot, beyond fear.

Chloe smiled to her.

– I remember everything, actually, every single second and moment of my existence. Can you imagine how that feels? Do you have even the slightest clue?

Marion stood there shivering, unable to stop. She looked at Chloe on the bed, from unmovable Chloe, to the warm, vibrant creature in front of her, glancing back and forth between the two, unable to stop her flickering eyes from flickering, from hurting in a tearing, horrible pain.

– Cat got your tongue, huh? Perhaps that isn't so strange. You've always been quite unimaginative, unable to grasp what is outside a given mundane reality.

Chloe turned towards the bed, reaching out, touching the body. Both bodies shook slightly, before standing Chloe let go, and dead Chloe lay still again.

Standing Chloe looked even more vibrant, even more alive.

– It wouldn't have worked, you know…

– What are you *talking* about? Marion whimpered like a spoiled child, finally able to articulate at least some of the horror resting within her. – I havc planned everything.

– Oh, the murder will work perfectly. No one will place you on the scene or even suspect you. There is no motive. You did a great job of concealing your obsession with Colin, and you will wait quite a bit, more than long enough before you start *comforting* him. I'm talking about you and Colin together. You've got nothing in common, really. After the first, initial sweetness he will grow tired of you and go to others, and it will end badly.

Marion screamed, or at least she imagined she did, a wrenching sound rising from her depths and never truly letting go. Tears filled her eyes.

– And you will know beyond knowing, beyond the tip of your tongue that I am there, with you, waiting even more patiently than you did, to punish you, to let my wrath loose on you.

Chloe grabbed the sixth doll on the pillow, petting it, giving it a sweet kiss on its lips.

– Run, now, little Marion, go to your balconies round and round and round.

Marion fled. She ran and kept running, and would never stop.

The doll burned to ashes in Chloe's hands. Her hands didn't burn. They didn't seem to be affected by the flames at all.

She packed the five remaining dolls in the large shoulder bag and went on her way, leaving behind the bloody body on the bed.

There was no room, no path. She walked through the hallway, down the stairs at Caine's Mansion.

– You look the same, she said softly, – unchanging, forever, ever new and eternally changing.

It replied to her, sort of, its walls forming words, emotions, expressions.

There was a long row of statues in the entrance hall, leading to the living room, all of them staring at the world with blind eyes.

On the mirror by the door was written a few sentences in fire and shadow:

> «In the Book of Fate there is everything, all events, all ages, everything that has been, that is, that will be, everything that might be, everything that might have been».

A thrill of excitement and expectation rose from her center and warmed her, ever so pleasantly.

She saw through the wall to the living room inside, didn't even have to strain herself.

Marlon Caine sat in his red chair in front of the fireplace.

He was shaking his drink, but didn't stir it.

She stepped through the door without opening it. It dissolved before the glowing hand moving through the air.

He rose startled and almost spilled the drink.

– Do you want me to dance for you? She said softly.

He opened his mouth to speak, unable to do so.

– Aye! She nodded. – I think I will do that, one, final time.

She started swaying, started dancing, turning around and around, jumping graciously from one foot to the other, in perfect balance, perfect movement.

Dust rising from the floor, pulled in from the walls flowed around the whirling form, the creature of Mist and Shadow performing in the limited, infinite space, drawing him in, freezing his attention, mesmerizing him, until all of him existing focused on her.

He bowed before her, offering the smoking brew in his hands, his shaking hands clutching the cup.

She struck it out of his hand. It fell and hit the floor and broke in a thousand pieces.

He stared stunned and horrified at her.

– What have you *done?*

– What is my right, my province.

Her dance continued. Her body whirled into the smoke rising from the floor. She pulled all of it into herself, breathed it, and absorbed it through the skin, skin glowing briefly before returning to normal.

He crouched, coughing, coughing hard, unable to keep it at bay.

She saw herself through his eyes, as the smoke cleared and she stood there radiant and beyond powerful. He could hardly bring himself to look at her.

It was just a tiny moment she stood there and acknowledged his presence, but to him it felt like forever.

– How is that for symbolic? She spat.

She turned and headed for the door.

– Please, he begged her.

She turned halfway back.

– Why are you kneeling before me? We are equals, now, just like you desired.

She laughed short and sharp, the laughter echoing in potent waves between the walls.

– Perhaps perception truly is reality.

And walked away.

A hand reached for her, and the frail and old human form froze in exactly that position, leaving him shrinking in her tracks.

She returned to the hall. The walls trembled around her.

– Don't be afraid, she said softly. – There is nothing to be afraid of. In Death there is Life.

It hissed at her. She shook it off with a shrug. Her senses reached out, to all the lost souls within its vast domain. She moved through a dark alley in the Pit, recognizing it easily as an afterthought, a mirage. There was no sound as her feet touched the ground, but her steps created an echo, so much louder than the sound others made.

They weren't hard to locate, even though they remained hard to actually find.

She found the five at the end of the long row of statues, where she had left them so long ago. Their movements, what was left of it were slow and dull. At the moment of her appearance something changed in them. They turned back into living, breathing people.

Desire and Isabel fell on their knees, looking up at her with an ecstatic smile on their flushed faces.

– The Lady has returned triumphant, Desire declared, – at long last. Behold her Power!

The two of them had known all the time, even when it hadn't been clear in their mind, had seen what was happening to Chloe Webster, what was still happening.

The boys looked just as bewildered as she remembered them, Victor and Andy angry and scared, Colin hurt and fuming and a host of less identifiable emotions.

She grabbed his head and kissed him on the lips.

– It's time, beloved, she said, – for everything under and beyond the moon.

The cold fire of the moon stared at him, seething under the calm surface.

She kissed them all, embracing them all, as she raised them up, as she made them stand.

The nearest statue blinked, and then the next did, as well.

– There isn't much time, she stated. – We must make haste.

Her speech and demeanor was different, was the same.

They rushed up the stairs. The use of their limbs felt so good, so indescribably good.

For each of the many floors they passed they saw more of the flashing images and sensations, sensed it filling them, their endless void.

A ship sailed the sea.

Groups of strangers gathered around the campfire in the wilderness.

A tribe reached a derelict hut at a remote coastland.

The atrium glowed in an eerie light.

– Here we will dine, what was Chloe Webster told them, told the five. – Here we will feast.

There was no table here, not anymore. She stepped out on the naked floor. Dark wings flapped and ravens screeched. She drew the wide circle of the pentacle with eased practice, the red chalk resembling crystallized blood in her hand. The others stepped inside the circle. She welcomed them with open arms and a snarl of bloody fangs.

– The world beyond the veil will overload your mind at first, she told them. – Endure, and the reward will be great.

Her hand brought the large dolls from the pouch without conscious thought. She placed them at each of the five points.

The five knelt at each of the five points, the whispers speaking to them, revealing their task.
She placed herself at the center of the star, facing its north point, where Colin knelt.
– I stand here, she said aloud, – in a circle neither golden nor silver, but blood. In blood I wash myself. In the depths of its sea I find my answers.
She pulled the bloody knife from her bag, holding its handle in a firm grip. In one, two, three swift and brutal moves she began cutting herself, splashing the blood around, hitting her dolls of flesh and mind, not a single drop hitting outside the circle. It hissed as it hit the ground, and the ground seemed to change, to transform from concrete to something soft, malleable, into the sea of blood she pictured in her mind. The air darkened until she could barely glimpse what was outside the circle and her surroundings changed, transformed into the remote, desolate place it was.
– We are the thousand fires, she cried. – One among thousands.
She waited a bit, before repeating it, repeating it again and again.
– I name you, she mumbled, turning in turn towards the dollies. – I name you Victor.
A clawed hand reached his brow.
– I name you Isabel.
She touched the girl's brow. Isabel nodded in acceptance.
– I name you Desire.
It touched her brow. Desire shook in delight.
– I name you Andy.
She touched his brow.
– I name you Colin.
She kissed his brow.
– I gave you flesh. I give you life. I claim it in my service.
Her wounds healed, the blood froze to rubies on her skin and on her clothes, her ragged and elegant clothes.
The shadow in her eyes danced in cold light.
– I NAME MYSELF! She shouted. – I name myself Beelzebub, Lady of the Lake. I walk in her footsteps and I become all things.
A low thunder accompanied her voice. Gasps filled the room, the Void. She fell, descended into the sea, the bloody sea. She was rising, seeing the world from above, and becoming the world. Ice and the warm, wet blood filled her, cutting her open, cutting the world open, filling her, filling it to the brim, and she knew everything, all there was to know, to sense and ask.

She was crouching, there, at the center of the pentacle, slowly overcoming her pain, straightening her body, reaching out with her hands, her claws.

The air was like a wall. She focused and raised her hands and pushed at it, pushed through the veil, to the world beyond. The air above and before her turned liquid, like the surface of a pond, a mirror image turning into a mirror, one in which she saw herself and them, expanding beyond three dimensions and even four, even five, six, fifteen…

The Chloe Webster of the Other World stared back at her, one with physical scars and a dark luminance in lupine eyes. A thousand coincidences roamed and rolled into one, singular possibility.

– I accept you, the two choired. – You are a part of me.

WE ARE ONE!

Chloe looked incredulous at her hands, as they moved and drew patterns in the air, symbols long since lost to the world.

A small, translucent pool appeared on the floor, the uneven ground. She bent down and pushed both hands into it. When she pulled them back up, she held five golden rings with a ruby stone in her wet hands.

She turned towards her five companions, her fellow travelers on the Shadow Path. When she looked at one she looked at all.

– Take these rings, she said in a dark room filled with shadows. – Wear them as a token of my love.

When she walked to one, she walked to all.

– I don't understand, Victor whimpered. – How long have we been here? I don't understand what's going on, don't understand any of this.

– You've always been here, the woman says.

She grabbed his left hand and put the ring on his finger. A shadow was lit in his eyes, and they were filled with knowledge and dark cunning, and a smile lit up his lower face, reducing his insecurity and anxiety to a tiny ember, his ashes fading in her dark brilliance.

Desire, kneeling with bowed head and an exalted smile raised her left hand.

– You took us, and made us yours, she said solemnly, – and we're so very, very grateful.

She gasped in clarity and joy when the Lady put the ring on her finger

Isabel shook and accepted the dark gift in silence, in mute abandon.

– Why? Fallon gasped. – Why… choose me?

– Because you are among the last of a dying breed, my dear Andy, Chloe chuckled. – You're not content to sit still, and let life pass you by. You have to go out there and *experience* it. I need that. I want that.

And she put the ring on his finger.

Colin held up his hand half up, not quite there, holding back, before choking and surrendering it to her. She placed the ring on his finger. Its ruby glowed. He looked astounded at it. She rose him up and kissed him, rose up and kissed them all. Her kiss was like fire, like poison, sating their thirst, wetting their parched throat, like cold water one burning hot day.

The walls shook, shook hard.

– It's time, she told them.

They began their descent, down a distance cut in half every second. It felt like flowing, but their feet hurt.

– What are you? Colin asked. – Who are you?

– I'm Chloe, silly, she replied softly to him. – I'm the Lady of the Lake. Why ask for answers to questions you already know?

She looked up and away a bit, clearly pondering something.

– I'm becoming more and more her the longer I stay, the more steps I take, her destiny becoming mine.

– I understand, Victor said, shaking his head, – but there are still unanswered questions… aren't there.

– Aren't there always? She teased him.

She looked almost ordinary, now, except every time they tried to focus on her, and glimpsed the Lady behind the curtain, behind the veil of ordinary existence.

– Don't you see, don't you understand? The last piece will never fit the puzzle. There will always be loose ends. Eternity beckons us, even more than it does everybody else that doesn't heed its call.

Her words, but even more her smoldering shadow shook them.

The house, and this time it was clearly the entire house that was shaking, was shaking itself apart.

– RUN!

She shouted, and they were astounded to hear fear in her voice.

They reached the base of the stairs. A giant piece loosened from the ceiling and blocked the entrance. They rushed on, past where the long row of statues had been, where there was now none. Chloe led them through the living room, the dark living room without a fire, through the totally dark kitchen where the only thing even resembling light was Chloe's Shadow and into the other entrance hall. They ran towards the open doorway, where several of the others had already passed through.

– Stop! Chloe said casually.

Because they were so attuned to her they stopped in an instant, stopped in time, just before the grinning jaw in front of them devoured them raw.

Several of the others also stopped, casting their attention on Chloe, a glimmer of recognition in their eyes.

– If we choose this open door we will be lost in the maze of the Manor forever.
– You, too? Desire wondered, clearly terrified.
– Especially me. It wants me more than anyone else, *hungers* for me with everything It is.
Another loud rumble shook the house and more of the ceiling was coming down. Two ran in panic through the opening ahead.
Chloe ran first at the wall, stumbling in a plank that stuck out from the wall, but fell through what had seemed like solid matter. Desire and the four others followed right behind her.
They stood outside, looking at her, while several others stumbled out from what from this side clearly was a door.
– Walk! Chloe snapped. – And keep walking.
She had injured her foot, and had to limp off. Colin and Desire grabbed her and supported her.
– I'll heal, she mumbled. – I'll be okay quite soon.
Large chunks of the wall fell. One man was hit in the head. He fell to the ground, and he dissolved as they looked at him. They saw him be pulled back through the wall.
Everybody ran, towards the gate, seemingly so far ahead. There was something about the gate, a glow they all recognized. A tiny piece of dusty rock hit Colin's arm and burned it. He screamed in pain, but kept running.
A rather large piece of glass from one of the big windows hit Chloe's shoulder and cut deep into her body. She gasped as she felt the paralysis and death spread throughout her body, her very self. Colin met her eyes and realized they were fading, fading. He screamed again, but in frustration, in passionate rage.
They pushed through the gate and fell on the ground outside. The six and the rest of the people escaping lay there, gasping for breath, for the fire, the nectar of life filling them once again.
Colin stared at Chloe's shoulder. The piece of glass that had been stuck there was fading, as if it had never been there at all. Boundless relief flooded his being.
The Lady returned the look with profound fondness in her shadowy eyes. She rose, her health and vigor returning, the wound closing as he watched.
They looked back at the house, and were stunned to behold a derelict building, an age-old ruin covered by moss and growth with a large hole in the roof, as if it had fallen decades, not seconds ago.

The entire neighborhood had fallen on hard times. The church was hardly more than rubble. All the houses and even the road and sidewalk, where such beasts existed at all were in a serious state of disrepair.

The dust settled slowly, on the ground, and on them, and they were breathing it, feeling the vitality rise further within them.

– No cars? A man said perplexed.

There was one, missing all four tires and doors.

– But I put it on the parking lot last night.

The parking lot was a field covered with tall, withered grass.

No one cared to explain it to him.

– Will he get it? Victor, not looking so hot himself asked Chloe.

– He should, she replied. – The secrets of reality are at his fingertips…

She turned towards the five, the ring-bearers.

– Like they are at ours.

– Some people are just dense, I guess, Victor shrugged.

Their laughter shook the ground, the very ground they walked on.

– So, what happens now? Colin asked Chloe.

She seemed to be considering his query, his request a bit, before deciding to reply.

– I don't know.

– Surely the Lady jests? Desire said humbly.

– I have a certain idea, of course, but I can be wrong, at least not perfectly correct.

They walked in silence for a while, as they made their way back to the city.

– It's a game, she said aloud. – Perhaps it's somewhat ordered like chess or a lot more random, chaotic, but a game none the less. We need to play it, but more: to appreciate and enjoy it. And most importantly of all: to make our own rules.

– Don't leave us, Lady, Isabel begged. – Pretty please!

The Lady turned towards them all, even as she kept walking, even as she embraced them all, and spoke in their dreams.

– I'll never leave you.

2

– It isn't her, a voice in the darkness, belonging to Stephen Farber said.

– But how is that possible, Wynyard cried. – She looks like her, talks like her and is her, beneath the shell.

Chloe Webster left the Pit the morning of November twenty-fifth. She heard the two men speak, knew their precise location, too. It was easy, just a matter of focus and will.

She descended into the subway under the highway. It was dark and dank down there. The very thought brought a smile to her face.

The repair-work wasn't quite finished yet. The tunnels were filled with steam and smoke. People were coughing a lot. She slipped through it all, among the commuters heading the other way.

She met the repairman again. He didn't recognize her.

– What are you doing here, lady? He asked irritated. – This is a restricted area. You shouldn't be here.

– I'm looking for a mirror, she said, more or less ignoring him and his bullying.

– There is no *mirror* here, lady, he said exasperated and shook his head in contempt. – Are you daft or what?

– Sure there is, she shrugged. – Look, there it is.

He followed the line of her vision, and froze in shock.

There, right ahead was it, the mirror, levitating in the smoke and steam, not really hanging on the wall or anything, but much more an integrated part of the air they breathed, their very surroundings.

– I see my own worst fear reflected back on me, she mused, – and it's no longer a big issue to me, but more like a pleasant memory of times past.

She turned to the stricken man, curiosity lit in her eyes.

– What do you see?

He didn't want to look, but she forced him, forced his hand, pushed him into confronting himself and his life.

The scream rising from his throat quickly turned high-pitched and banshee-like. He turned and ran, completely beside himself.

She walked on, choosing the detour to the railway station. It, too, was busy, but it didn't faze her. She slipped through the crowd like a ghost.

The station was old, far older than the building itself. People had been killed here since time immemorial. The ghosts didn't frighten her. Their hateful whispers were slightly irritating, but no more than that. She saw the blood being spilled and soaked it up. It strengthened her. She drank more of its sweet nectar.

The ghosts and spirits backed off when they realized their folly, when they realized what vast power was hidden in that finite flesh and blood form of hers. They bowed down to her.

To her.

She walked up one floor, to the atrium, to the cafeteria. It was packed with people, as usual, with busy people meeting other busy people, or others, taking a brief break in their busy schedule.

The eye glared at her. She glared back, and it closed in pure fright, shedding tons of tears.

And it pleased her.

She sat out across the bridge. It shook under her feet. The water in the raging river underneath hit the banks on both sides. She felt it as a quiver at her fingertips. There was daylight, but a strange form of daylight. She saw no sun, but lots of shadows. Chloe felt haunted, no matter how much she resisted and spat at the very notion of it. She turned her head and looked back, and there they were, the two men, Stephen Fraser and Jason Wynyard chasing her. Old fears and horrors rose in her. She rejected them, but they still threatened to overwhelm her. The glass dissolved and she stood exposed on the naked bridge, at the mercy of its brutal winds.

Perception is reality, a wicked voice whispered in her ear.

It was as if she froze, there, on the bridge, and shrunk to nothing.

– You won't get away, baby, Stephen shouted in a bright room without shadows. – I'll never let you go.

His features were dissolved into anger, spite and wicked triumph.

She heard him, no matter how hard she tried not to, and she choked in despair.

Her legs felt like wool, like she couldn't even stand still without falling, and she was falling, not through space, but through time.

She finally reached the other side, weak and powerless, sweating and gasping and stumbling.

– Don't you cry, sweetie, Dr. Wynyard whistled cheerfully in a room with bright lights and pain. – We'll have you fixed in no time.

She ran, or tried to, but it was like she was moving through quicksand. Even the very attempt at moving was hard and slow. She descended the metal stairs towards street level.

– Where is it? She mumbled. – I can't see it. Why can't I *see* it?

Below is the raging river, the boiling waters.

– Below is the raging river, she mumbled. – Below are the boiling waters.

She stopped, instantly sensing it, the Rise within, and it was that easy, and there was no more doubt.

Perception is reality!

Her fists began glowing in shadow. It felt so good.

The bus turned the corner. She noticed its dark glimmer instantly, like a long lost, dear friend.

The dark glimmer appeared in front of the bus, under the bridge, in its hissing foam. The bus drove into it, and faded away. She rose in the air, and pushed herself forward, even as she was pulled into the seething vortex.

The giant frame of Beelzebub broke the surface of the lake.

She reappeared in the hallway beneath the bus-station, before passage number six, previously blocked by concrete, a passage now opening up with the new reality she created, the old world already fading away behind her. Chloe Webster placed her left foot on the first step, and power coursed through her anew.

– The final piece, she cried. – THE FINAL PIECE!

Her form grew, even as it was standing still, even as it was ascending the stairs, even as it remained the same. It grew in a way no one could fathom, if they didn't see and sense and experience what she did.

The old her far behind her in an expanding universe Chloe Webster reached the top of the stairs, the dark glimmer surrounding her, a never-fading part of her.

The bus waited for her, its quiet engine running, wind filling its sails.

– Not yet, she giggled, giggled wildly. – Not quite yet.

To move, to fade away and reappear at another location was like flipping a page.

Stephen Fraser and Jason Wynyard stood frozen at the start of the bridge, not even wet on their feet. She waved a hand in front of them, and everything was in motion again, the world once again *was*.

The two of them watched her appear from open air, a mirage at first, then solid, potent. Wynyard gasped and took a step back. Fraser wasn't exactly frozen, but she still kept him in place somewhat.

– Hello, Stephen, she greeted him.

He wanted to speak, to charge her, but she kept him from doing so, and it was the easiest thing in the world.

– It has come to my knowledge that you are looking for me.

She kissed him on the lips. The kiss burned, and he yelped in pain.

He stared at her, knowing, not knowing, crouching at her feet.

– You'll be pleased to note that you made me feel so small, like less than nothing, made me freeze and shrink, right there, on the bridge of destiny, and just because of envy, of spite because you couldn't follow me beyond the veil. You both did.

Hands flickering in dark glimmer touched them under the jaw.

– I'm not telling you anything you don't know, though. You enjoyed every moment of my degradation. You'll be quite displeased to realize that I've put it all behind me, that I've crossed the bridge, and grown beyond your wildest imagination.

Farber turned to Wynyard, enraged, impatient, cocky, arrogant, so eager.

– What are you waiting for, man? Get *on* with it!

Wynyard looked at him, totally confused and incredulous.

– Do I know you, man?

Farber grabbed him in the collar with both hands and pushed him at the wall.

– Are you out of your mind? God damn you if you choose this moment to play games.

– Look, man, Wynyard gasped. – I don't know you, don't know any of you. Just take my money, but please don't *hurt* me.

– WHAT ARE YOU TALKING ABOUT, MAN? Farber shouted, beyond loud. – HAVE YOU CRACKED?

– He has, you know, Chloe told Farber.

She spoke to him and him alone, and he knew it, and turned to her with a more than haunted expression in his eyes and features.

– He is out of his mind, at least the mind you remember. He doesn't remember anything, anything of your big plans or his former life.

– Former life? Farber quacked.

– Yes, I erased it, she grinned. – I erased all of it. He is nothing more than an ordinary country medical practitioner, now, quite boring and unimaginative, really.

Farber began sweating, truly began sweating, as the implications of her words and the empirical evidence of the situation dawned on him.

– I made certain you remembered everything, though, or almost everything. The Lady of the Lake can do that.

She flashed her fangs, and he shrank in her presence.

– You coveted my gift, not me, never me, both of you, but it will be denied you. You try, in your vain hope to twist reality, turn it around, to make it do your bidding, and fail miserably, because you don't understand, don't even see what's right beyond the thin veil, and that's so *easy*. The desert walk will be your home, you running forever in circles.

– You're both INSANE! Wynyard blurted out.

– No, we're not, Jason, she countered softly. – We quite simply have information you lack, that's all.

He wanted to leave, to strangle her, but was unable to do either.

– I have never, *never* laid my eyes on you before, he said in what was a state of pain beyond pain, the deepest despair in a place deep down, where he indeed knew.

– But you have, she said wickedly. – You just don't remember having done so.

– I don't *know* you, lady. Why won't you *listen* to me?

– But you do. You know me so well. At least you used to. You used to know a lot of things, being a wicked and notable wise man, but now you don't anymore. You used to be feared. Now, you aren't anymore. Now, you're lower than the worms in the ground you used to express such contempt for.

He fled. He finally managed to get his feet to respond to his brain. Neither of the two remaining watched him leave.

– You should be happy for me, Stephen, she said. – You would have been, if you were worth the effort.

– What are you? He whispered.

The smile felt so familiar on her lips.

– I have finally become a true creature of the night, a true Human Being, ready for whatever existence throws at me. There is the ice breaking on the river in spring, the celestial mist formed by gathering galaxies, the scream of a newborn, the final gasps of the dying, and that's merely a fraction of everything I am. I am the center of the Universe. Wind and time are blowing through me.

Stephen Farber grabbed her. She let him. It wasn't exactly pain he felt, but something far worse, something inconceivable, at least for him. He let go of her. His hands just weren't there anymore, and were only slowly, slowly returning to the right spot at the end of his arms. He wanted to scream, but even that was denied him.

There was brief silence, at least to him, as she pondered something, something catching her attention, momentarily tying her to this spot.

– Tell me, Stephen… do you know how it feels to have the building blocks of the Universe at your fingertips?

He looked blank at her.

– No. She shook her head. – Of course you don't know how it's like…

She pulled the lips back in a snarl, exposing her fangs.

– You'll never know.

She looked at him with regret.

– You were nothing but playthings in my dream, and now you are even less than that.

She looked at him with pity.

– I CAST YOU OUT OF MY WORLD.

She embraced him in her raging storm as she took her leave. He knew, for the briefest of moments how it was like, and then he forgot, always to remember, but every time, when he reached out to grasp it, there was nothing there.

The broken figure rose, and stumbled off, unable to stop choking.

– You're one of the few vestiges remaining of Chloe Webster's Earthly life. I think I'll hold on to that, and to you for a while, as a reminder. And a Goddess needs to be entertained.

He heard her, heard nothing but the whispers in the wind.

People crossing Altman Square, popularly called Pit Lake frowned at the sound of waves hitting the shore echoing in their ears. There were those that would swear they had seen the Lady, in the water or in the air or at the center of a dancing flame. Those sightings were reported far beyond the Pit.

The Lake was no longer dead and still, but boiling in fire, mist and shadow spreading from below to its vast and distant shores.

CHAPTER TWENTY-ONE

Colin and Ethel dined at her apartment in the Pit, with candles burning on the table. Her blonde hair with a touch of red turned all red cast in the light of the flickering fire.

Glasses filled with wine, with blood met and parted. They drank.

– So, she believes you are on a *business* trip? Ethel chuckled.

– As far as I know, she doesn't suspect a thing, Colin shrugged.

– But how can that work? How can she be so… stupid?

He considered that, hesitating a bit.

– I suspect sometimes that she does know, but she has always been very selective considering what part of reality she accepts, you know.

– Perhaps she's planning on killing you? Ethel chuckled wickedly.

– Very Funny…

– Cheers! Ethel cried.

She raised her glass with a solemn, loving expression in her eyes.

Glasses met and parted anew. They drank and dined.

Colin knew that they, at some point, soon would end up in bed. He saw it happen, saw every move before it played itself out.

– Will you leave her? The woman whispered in his ear.

– I will leave her, he replied. – If I ever felt anything for her, it's long gone. Sometimes I can't understand why I married her in the first place.

– She endeared herself to you, in your grief, didn't she, filling your emotional gap?

– My Goddess, he exclaimed, – she did, didn't she?

– I do believe she did, Ethel nodded sadly.

Dinner was salmon, baked in vegetables. It filled his belly, but still made him hunger for more.

They were dancing to low-key music, faces slowly being pulled to each other, kissing with wet lips.

The loud sounds from the Pit didn't seem to matter, sounding distant, immaterial.

Shadows moved in bed, on the couch, on the floor, and eventually lay still and dreamed quiet dreams.

He awoke on the couch the next morning with a splitting headache and in good spirits. Only a slight sweat revealed the existence of his intense dreams. Ethel lay snoring by his side. He rose quickly, looking around, looking into the bedroom. The bed showed signs of having been used, but there were no one there now. The house was silent, the construction work outside the window loud and noisy. He awoke in bed, finding Ethel snoring by his side. It was a quiet morning. No sounds, unfamiliar or not, disturbed the peace. He rose quietly without waking her, without even making her stir. He had long practice. The smile rested on her lips. He looked at the watch and then took a look out of the window, at the setting sun. Hmm, late afternoon already. He grinned. They awoke on the floor, her wet kisses waking him up well after he had opened his eyes.

– Beloved beast, she whispered in his ear, loving him with her expressive eyes.

He sat up, patting her cheek.

– I'll make breakfast, she said and sat up, too.

– No. He shook his head. – I must go.

There were still ten, fifteen minutes until the bus arrived. He took his time dressing, savoring every sensation of cloth touching the skin. Outside, as he closed the door behind him, he breathed in the polluted air and coughed hard.

It was early late Saturday afternoon in the Pit. People had just started to arrive for the night revels. He walked more or less in the opposite direction compared to most people. The lake sighed as he crossed it. He heard the sound of water sighing below and dreamed himself away. The fountain at the square's center point split the light in a thousand directions.

A twinkle on the ground made him stop and wonder. Someone had lost a ring, a most peculiar ring, golden with an eerie ruby stone. He bent down and picked it up.

Take this ring, as a token of my love.

He put it on, feeling ridiculous, glancing around to see if anyone had truly spoken to him. There was no one, among the many people swimming in the lake he would pick as a candidate for the enticing voice.

The ring made a perfect fit, as if a goldsmith or someone had made it or adapted it for him.

He walked through the subway, to the bus station. There was a baker there. He looked at his watch and decided there was still time. There was a queue, but not a very long one. He forced himself to relax, even as he kept looking at his watch.

– You love this, don't you? The man behind the counter, the baker said.

Colin looked at him.

– The bread? The baker said, certainly a bit taken aback by Colin's pointed stare. – You buy it often, especially on Saturdays.

– Oh, Colin said, suddenly unexplainably relieved, – it's my wife. She loves it, and she most certainly loves fresh bread in the morning.

Suddenly he was very grateful for the fact that the baker didn't look at his watch.

Colin paid and hurried to the bus. It was on platform 6 today, for some reason. Usually it was on platform 5, but that one was closed today. He shrugged and paid for the fare.

An old man with a cane entered the bus a few passengers behind him. He didn't reach an available seat before the driver drove off. The old man fell, and there was a loud sound as he clearly broke his leg. He screamed, a loud whine entering Colin like a snake.

Everybody else sat down. They had to. Several other people, including Colin almost fell in the next curve. The old man screamed louder. Every time he attempted to stand up the bus jumped through another curve.

– Will you please stop? A man sitting close to the driver cried anxiously. – Can't you see that people are hurt?

– No can do, the driver shrugged. – We're on a schedule here, and I won't be too late and loose part of my salary, no, sir.

At the next stop five people entered, enough time for people to help the old man up and to a seat. They had just returned to their own seat when the driver speeded up again.

– HEY, MAN, a young girl shouted from the backseat, – THIS AIN'T A TAXI. YOU DON'T NEED TO ARRIVE BEFORE YOU LEAVE, YOU KNOW

The driver turned visibly red on the neck, but took no action, except pushing the pedal even harder. People held even harder on to their handle.

– It has finally happened, the man sitting next to Colin said in a hushed voice. – The capital has totally submerged people's needs and wishes, finally ignoring them with impunity.

Ten minutes later, after a long row of burned rubber incidents and near misses, the miracle happened: the bus slowed down. There was a long whine of burned rubber, as the driver pushed the breaks, not the gas pedal. The bus wavered from side to side. One man said a prayer. The bus stopped right before it crashed into the car ahead.

There was a queue of sorts. They saw smoke and mist far ahead.

– An accident, a woman said, – an honest to Goddess accident.

– Probably a bus or two or three, her companion said and shook his head.

The driver shook his head in distress, close to tears.

– THERE GOES YOUR BONUS, the girl cackled from the backseat.

It was a major accident, involving several vehicles. There was blood and shrapnel everywhere. To Colin it looked like someone had punched a hole in the very air in front of them. All loud voices seemed to be set on mute for Colin after that. The police had organized a drive-by on the sidewalk, where only one row of vehicles could pass simultaneously. It was a slow and dreading process. They drove into the mist and the smoke and people howled in distress and pain.

Round and round the major vortex span. Car tires, wreckage and twisted metal pieces had been spread everywhere, everything visible from the air and in the light cast by the powerful spotlights, like an indistinct shimmering twilight where all sharp edges were hidden. A curtain in a bedroom where light and shadow constantly moved. Indistinct phantoms becoming something alive, something tangible.

To the left he saw the remains of what had briefly been known as Caine Manor. There was a giant hole in the roof, and the entire «estate» was overgrown. A large tree grew out of the hole, its branches reaching far and wide.

The former church to the left didn't fare much better. A

FOR SALE

sign could be glimpsed behind all the dense growth.

The bus passed the final obstacles. Colin looked through the back window and imagined he spotted someone there, in the whirling mist, a face, eyes cloaked in shadows.

Then the woman was gone, as if there had never been a woman there at all.

– This looks promising, the woman sitting next to Colin said, whistling a false tune. – With efficiency standards such as these this transport company looks like an excellent investment object. Most transport companies waste billions by being horribly inefficient every year. Billions!

He studied her in an attempt to gauge whether or not she was being sarcastic. He couldn't convince himself one way or another.

– I blink, he shouted quietly, – and in that blink I see an expanding dark cloud, bright as a billion streetlights, and I become the cloud and the cloud becomes me, and the thousand few voices condense into just two, no more than two, two joining that of my own, and in that choir, that multitude of voices the world is born.

– What?

Colin blinked, rubbing his temple.

– What are you saying? The woman said, very insulted. – You aren't attempting to be funny at my expense are you? Because if you are, know that I WOULD NOT take kindly to such rude behavior.

He ignored her, or better, pretended she wasn't there at all, and when push came to shove, he wasn't certain that she actually was.

– You're making a serious attempt at unhinging me, aren't you? The woman whimpered. – I know you do, but it won't work. I swear to you that it won't work, you cruel *bastard*.

Her childish, muted shriek faded in the wind, the air outside.

Minutes passed, minutes that felt like hours. These bus tours had always taken their toll on him, but today it felt worse than ever.

The bus made one final turn, and the familiar neighborhood appeared and his immediate surroundings also seemed to become more tangible, more real. Voices and sounds and shapes entered his consciousness.

– Are they *ever* gonna complete that crossroads work, a guy two seats behind him said to his companion. – I feel like they have kept at it for years.

– Try centuries, the other guy replied, shaking his head.

A lot of people were evidently shaking their heads these days.

– You see, that's exactly what I am talking about, the first guy continued. – They have kept it going for so long, now, that I don't know what I will do if they finally stop. Perhaps I have grown so used to it that I will never be able to sleep in peace and quiet again. I fear I will go crazy, and that they will lock me up somewhere.

– What *are* you talking about? His buddy said.

– Am I talking? I wasn't aware that I was talking.

And then, a few minutes later:

– It's these bus drives. They drive me nuts. I swear the bus changes routes several times a week. I *swear*.

For some reason Colin looked at his watch.

06.02

It said.

The construction work was particularly bad by the bus stop. The noise hammered his ears and mind the moment he stepped outside. The sun hadn't quite set yet, its rays still bright, even though they already cast long shadows. He began shuddering, unable to fathom what was happening, unable to shake off the feeling haunting him.

Marion met him in the door, embracing him, kissing him hungrily on his lips. He gave her the bread and she brightened like the sun outside, casting long shadows like it did.

She ran to the kitchen and began making sandwiches, humming a melody. It jarred in his ears.

They sat by the dining table in the living room, and had sandwiches and orange juice.

Her hand shook.

– Someone called me today on the phone, someone I didn't know.

She looked at him in distress.

– Oh, what did they say?

– «Your time is up». It was a woman, a very vile woman. She said «your time is up».

– You didn't recognize the voice at all? It wasn't in any way familiar.

She shook her head fearfully.

– I have never heard it before.

They sat there for a while without speaking.

– Who can do such a thing? Who can imagine doing something like that?

– It's a cruel world, he said, frowning, not quite pleased with his reply, and striving to add something, in vain. – It's a cruel world.

She looked at him, stared at him, clearly hesitating before speaking.

– I have felt… haunted lately, she admitted. – There have been small things, many small things. I don't sleep well, and a voice is speaking in my dreams all the time.

– What does it say? He wondered, taking a bite of the sandwich.

– «Soon», she whispered. – In all my dreams, every time I close my eyes that's' the only word I hear.

It was like she was imploding there, in front of him, like she was tearing holes in herself with the nails of her own fists.

– Listen, he said, taking her hand across the table, – people get crank calls all the time. We should definitely go to the police with it, at least if it continues.

There was a subtext to his words that made her look even harder at him.

– How can you be so… relaxed about this? She whispered.

– I'm not, but you said it yourself, your nightmares… perhaps you should consider…

… getting help, she completed the sentence for him.

He didn't have to confirm it. His expression said it all.

She rose, abruptly.

– Are you aware of how that sounds?

She didn't wait for his reply, but started pacing the floor, in ever more erratic movements, her hands constantly moving, seemingly independently of the body.

He rose, too, keeping his distance.

– I'm not the only one acting *strange* lately, am I?

She choked, both her hands rolling into fists.

– How many business trips can a lowly accountant and «web consultant» be sent on, before it gets ridiculous?

The guilt was written on his face, all over him, in his body language. She smiled.

– My God, she spat. – You stink of body juices. I'll bet you didn't shower. You're not even trying to *hide* it!

She walked to him, fingering with his collar, pouting her lips.

– Any respectable man practicing infidelity would, you know, at least until the children was out of the house, but you, you look so guilty, so guilty all the time that it's pathetic.

The dawning malice slowly asserted itself. She looked at him in contempt.

– I certainly protected my secret well enough…

– What secret was that?

He didn't think before asking that question. It just slipped from his mind and his tongue.

Suddenly she was the one looking guilty, or at least defensive, very defensive.

He opened his mouth to speak, but no word or sound manifested.

Something dawned on him, something a long time coming, unrealized to this day, this moment.

He stared at her. She averted her eyes, and then, beyond knowing, he knew. He knew!

– You killed her, he said softly. – You really killed her.

He knew the answer before she voiced her reply, her contemptuous laughter.

– Yes, I did, sweetie, she whined. – I had to, of course. You didn't have eyes for anyone but her, your beloved Chloe.

She spat the name as if it was something vile and hideous.

– I had no other choice if I wanted you to notice me, and you did, you fell right into my lap, you silly bugger.

Her ugly side came out in full force, a dark glimmer ascending in her eye.

– You didn't *suspect,* did you? A horrible smile lit up her sweet features. – You didn't even suspect me, even though it was kind of obvious. I would say that was sweet… if it wasn't so fucking stupid. How stupid can you get?

The contemptuous laughter shook the room.

– I wasn't very selective when choosing a husband at all, was I? My friends from school chose prospective bankers, lawyers and policemen, but I chose you, *damn* me…

There was a whistling sound, the kind one hears when something is plunged really fast through the air. It ended in a loud SWOOP, as the large kitchen knife in Colin's hand cut into Marion's flesh. She looked at him in absolute astonishment and incredulity. There were more swooping sounds. He cut her several times, until the final, deep cut, where he was unable to pull the knife back out, and he let go of the wet, slippery handle, and Marion fell backwards, and hit the floor with a dump sound and lots of blood splashing all over the living room.

She lay still. Dead eyes stared at the ceiling. He looked at her for a while, at the woman with a knife sticking out of her chest, as if committing the sight to memory. Then he turned away, and left the house with fast, furious steps. He used the backdoor, looking neither left nor right, stumbling into the small garden, fading away in the ever-gathering darkness of his invisible path.

TWENTY YEARS AGO TODAY

The group, the crowd, six people walked through darkened streets late in the evening, an unfathomable purpose, a riddle out of context that didn't belong.

They charged through countless darkened streets, driven beyond driven by a force slowly, abruptly making itself clear to them. Hazy eyes changed, turning huge and opaque and filled with sinister purpose.

Carter John stopped at a crossroads, taking the measure of his followers.

– We were deceived, he cried.

– DECEIVED, they choired.

– But no more. Now, we declare our undying love

OUR UNDYING LOVE

– Beelzebub, our eternal Goddess awaits impatiently our acts of devotion and sacrifice. Let it be.

– LET IT BE

– Make it so!

– MAKE IT SO

The decision made, they made haste, walked in a fast, furious pace through the urban landscape, passing numerous luxurious estates on their way.

A man walked down a long driveway, to the distant gate and was let out by the sentries. He was about to reach the waiting taxi when he was approached by Carter John and entourage. The man looked a little anxiously at them, and looked back at the sentries by the gate, but they seemed to ignore the scene completely.

– You're a photographer? John asked with his very intense demeanor.

– I take pictures, the man said, and jokingly referred to the camera hanging in a strap around his neck and the tripod in his hand. – Name's Marsten, Evanard Marsten, I take pictures, all kind of pictures.

He still wanted to catch the attention of the indifferent guard behind the gate, to scream for help, but that need was dwindling ever so pleasantly.

– I see…

John seemed to be pondering something, before putting a hand on Marsten's shoulder, a hand and an arm eventually crawling (like a snake) all the way around the other side of the neck.

– You take baby and birthday pictures, that kind of stuff, right? And once in a while you're allowed to take pictures of the rich and famous, and their icky children?

– That is fairly accurate. Marsten nodded, a little put off, insulted. – I wouldn't put it quite that way, but yes.

John looked at the road ahead of them, making Marsten look in the same direction.

– But you long to be a true photographer… an artist, one making art, instead of cheap documentation, am I right?

The road turned indistinct in front of Marsten. He felt an almost forgotten excitement rise within. The loud, penetrating thud of the taxi's horn sounded distant and far away.

– Are you French or something? He wondered, feeling dizzy. – You sound funny, for a white guy, even though you have an English name.

The taxi drove off. Marsten found himself walking with John and his strange entourage, three women and two men in outlandish clothes. They surrounded him, as they walked further on their way, and he joined them.

– You have sufficient amounts of memory for your pictures, yes? John hissed pleasantly in his ears, both his ears simultaneously, as if another, invisible John stood at his other side. – There is no need for you to procure more?

– I always carry more than sufficient amounts of «film» with me, Marsten snorted, more than a little insulted. – More than sufficient amounts for days of work, actually.

– That's a good boy, John said cheerfully, patting his back, suddenly speaking like a true English gentleman.

– You're very handsome, one of the women said sweetly. – Have you ever considered having your own picture taken?

– No, not really, he replied. – I…

She appeared before him, walking backwards towards him, just as easy as most people would do normal walk, embraced him and kissed him softly on his lips, his eyes drawn to her exposed breasts and erect nipples.

And just like that she had lifted the camera off his neck. The sudden lack of pressure felt like an enormous relief.

– Hey…

She took his picture.

– Smile, she said enticingly.

He smiled.

She took another.

– Don't smile, she whispered. – Look at me with those sweet eyes of yours.

He did, his tongue hanging out like that of a dog.

– That's enough, John told her, good humored. – Give the man back his camera. Return the tool to the professional, to the artiiist.

French, Marsten thought feverishly. Has to be!

– Here you are, she said, and handed him the camera. – Thank you, sweetie.

They walked on, with steps light as feathers. Marsten began, as they climbed further up the Heights to feel a remarkable happiness. He began taking pictures, photographs of the group, using his double-angled flash, reducing the flat light an ordinary flash created. They moved in a strange way, strange pattern he, as an observer couldn't help but noticing, moved in relation to each other, to him and the surroundings.

Marsten knew when they were there, when they had reached their destination. He looked at the shining church to the right and Caine Mansion to the left. It hardly came as any surprise to him when John led them right through the gate, and just walked right up to the door and opened it. Marsten imagined he heard a screeching sound, even though it was clearly mute, clearly was no sound at all, except the marching feet of John and his five followers.

The seven rushed right to the living room. Marlon Caine sat there and watched television. There was a movie on, Dark Shadows in Bright Lights, David Fallon Somby's undead classic. Marsten glanced at the clock on the wall. It said:

11.45

Marsten felt the seconds tick away towards midnight.

Caine rose from his chair and looked irritated at them. Marsten realized with a shock that he wasn't afraid.

– You're not supposed to be here.

Carter John stopped in front of him with a very determined and hateful stare in his huge eyes.

– That's where you're wrong. This is exactly where we're supposed to be.

The five rushed forwards and grabbed Caine. Caine, being a big and strong man fought against them, decked two of them before the others struck him to the ground and began beating him up in wild and brutal ways. They kicked him from all sides, until he was subdued, and they pulled the half unconscious man back on his feet, and brought him before John. Marsten photographed it all, a strange detachment growing in his mind.

– You have been found guilty of crimes against Beelzebub, the Supreme Goddess, John declared. – You will suffer and die for an eternity, and serve the Goddess for the rest of your existence.

The five began a low chant, something rising from their throats, making Marsten dizzy and delirious.

– You guys didn't give me anything, did you? I just can't recall if you actually gave me anything.

They began drawing… symbols in the air, invisible at first, but then, incredibly enough symbols becoming smoke, becoming visible.

– You'll pay for this, Caine swore. – Damn idiots! You don't know who you're *dealing* with, the horrendous consequences of your actions, both to yourself and everybody else.

He was about to say more, but something seemed to be happening to him, something freezing him in place, making him unable to move or speak. He tried, with sweat flowing down his face to move his hand, to form symbols of his own.

They broke his fingers, all of them, in several swift and brutal moves. He released a low cry. The sight of pain in his eyes spoke far louder than the sound.

And then Marsten froze, shaking his head, not certain what he actually saw.

Fleshhooks in a line of putrid skin grew from Carter John's body and buried themselves in Caine's flesh, turning into jaws, devouring skin, burying themselves deep within Caine's powerful frame. This time the scream, even though muted reached deafening proportions.

The heavy body was lifted effortlessly into the air and pushed at the wall, skewed, its upper body pointing slightly down. The five instantly found their hammers and nails and stuck him there, in a frenzy of hammering and nailing. John pulled his fleshhooks back and returned them to himself. Blood flowed from open wounds a bit before almost stopping.

– The poison I injected into you will ensure that you will die slowly, John explained to Caine. – It's important that you don't die before we, and the Lady are through with you.

Marsten unfolded his tripod and considered the angles.
– So many choices, he mused, – so many great possibilities.
– Then explore them all, John told him generously.
– You… mean that? Marsten said, frowning. – You're not kidding, not fucking with me?
– Most certainly not, John snorted. – Get to it, artist. We've got time, all the time in the world.
– Thank you, Marsten cried, tears in his eyes. – THANK YOU!
He kept snapping pictures, kept moving the tripod, his happy dance turning happier by the second.
– With the tripod everything gets better, he explained to no one in particular. – By using the tripod to prolong the exposure the light, the skin tone and everything become more natural. Then I can use the flash and prolonged exposure in combination. I don't need to use the flash at all, for that matter. Oh, this is SO great!
They tore off Caine's clothes, every single piece of them, including his underwear. His large cock hung like butchered meat. The women made loud noises with their lips. They tore off their own clothes, and the males didn't wait long after that, Marsten hesitating only a moment. John removed his clothes, too, a bit more controlled, walking to Caine.
– You may speak again, now, if you wish, John shrugged. – Be aware that the spell will strike you the moment you attempt anything worthwhile.
– You can't do this to me, not here, Caine sobbed. – I'm protected. There are safeguards…
– That protection has been rescinded, John said curtly, proudly. – And the Lady is here, with us, of course, to protect her servants and make sure her will is carried out to her satisfaction and pleasure. The Lady is everywhere. Praise the Lady!
– THE LADY IS EVERYWHERE, the other six choired. – PRAISE THE LADY!
One of the women began rubbing the hanging cock.
– I take your strength, she chanted. – I suck it out of you with my hose and my Magick.
The cock began growing, began hardening.
– No, Caine whispered. – Please, no!
She slapped him, and kept slapping him.
– Do not protest, she chanted. – Do not resist. Give your strength, your very life with a happy smile on your face and joy on your mind. Yes, that's it, sweet boy, sing the Lady's praise. Soon you'll be in her presence

and pay tribute to her exalted being ever after. You will be collared and led in a chain, nothing but a slave singing her praise.

He moaned, moaned again, and then the smile broke on his face. When he ejaculated on the floor in front of the woman he gasped in profound happiness, and the light faded a tad more in his eyes.

– There is no replenishment or healing, she said proudly. – Everything just vanishes, and leaves an empty shell.

They started working on him in earnest, with knives and blunt instruments, cutting large chunks of his flesh off his body, tearing out his eyes with their bare hands, tearing him slowly apart. He peed on himself and shit himself and threw up. There was a slow hissing sound, as if the air was let out of a balloon. They drew symbols on the wall and on the floor, using blood and fat and saliva, and semen and piss and shit and vomit and tears.

Someone played a slow whistle somewhere, one filling the room, the flesh of those present and the entire manor from top to bottom and from bottom to top. They began chanting to match the music, the soundless fury and profound happiness stemming from everywhere and nowhere.

The photographer's face lit up as he worked, a study in ecstasy. They posed for him, to make the photographs as good as possible. The women smiled to him and the men hummed his praise. He was given the opportunity to engage in every single fantasy or wet dream he had ever had as a photographer, and he took it, grabbed it with both hands (and feet).

– It is as if you are all puppets in my strings, he gasped, - doing my bidding in all things.

– We are. One of the women kissed him with burning lips. – The Lady understands and cherishes High Art.

He stood there, before his objects, gaping in awe.

– A death in beauty, he choked, – a death in ugliness and beautiful despair.

Time just slipped away, while he worked with his camera and his hands.

It wasn't easy to say exactly when the sacrificial lamb actually expired, or there wouldn't have been, if they hadn't felt it, felt the powerful sensation as it happened.

Then, at exactly that moment Carter John finally plunged the sacrificial knife into the body's heart, completing the picture.

Their loud, wicked chuckles rose to the ceiling, the higher than high ceiling.

The sensation grew, impossibly yet another notch and filled them to the brim, like sex, like wild, unadulterated pleasure. The males jerked off time and time again and the females splashed the floor continuously for minutes.

It felt endless, and every time they believed it would end, it just kept growing stronger.

– That's a wrap, Marsten cried, Marsten gasped a while later, exhausted but yet bursting with vigor.

All of them rose, as the power kept burning inexhaustible within.

The dance, the final part of the ritual began.

– My hands are bleeding, they sang. – We are breaking you to bits, and our hands are bleeding and poisoning your putrid flesh and hollow mind. In Death there is Life. Praise the Goddess. Praise the Lady of the Lake.

– What I wouldn't give for a video camera right now, Marsten said, with longing in his voice.

Then he shrugged.

– I better not be greedy. Want not, need not, as they say.

Before throwing himself into the dance with his six new friends, all far more vigorous than before they had started on their wild abandon.

They saw the Lady, in tiny glimpses lasting an eternity. She was everywhere in the room, no matter where they looked with their glazed eyes, blazing with awareness. They sang and they danced and forever and ever fucked each other's brain out in the moist darkness.

They partied on all night.

Initiated in 2001, started in earnest 2004, completed 2010-02-17, the 58. night 12065, in the tenth year in the time of the Twilight Storm
Printed version ready 2012-01-10, the 20. night 12067, in the twelfth year in the time of the Twilight Storm

Author's word

This is a first, in many ways. It's the first novel I completed in six years since I finally managed to end Night on Earth in 2004, the first I've written in English right from the start, the second I've completed solely on the computer and the first in my personal genre of something I call Existential Horror. You decide what it is. I don't know when the next book in that «genre» will be written. Perhaps never.

I would suggest you ignore both words and look at both of them simultaneously, as a whole. That would be or might be somewhat helpful.

My other novels have always been read by others prior to publication, people providing valuable input and contributing their insight in whatever subject they desired.

This is the first without any external input whatsoever. Here I can safely say that one hundred percent of the book is mine. There has been no proofreading by anyone, not even a glimpse of the story for anyone… except myself. It was an approach I decided upon early on, in an effort to make the book even more different from my previous books and every other out there.

And equally interesting: it's the first novel I've written where the main characters aren't both demonic and idealistic versions of myself, clearly a major change in approach. Some of them have my knowledge and skills, of course, but they are basically made from scratch.

I've always strived to be original, for my books to not even resemble any other books and I know I've succeeded. This is even more a step further in that regard. If my other books are special, are «far out there» (and they are)… this one is even more so…

While I've strived to have a certain consistency in my previous novels, to have connecting dots and logic and coherence and logically composed connections between scenes, I have kind of made an effort to not have those things here. And while there is a certain internal logic, there is one quite different from what you might expect.

It isn't at all what you expect.

It never is.

All my books become something quite different from what they appear at first, but in this one that effect is far more pronounced. You might think you know what is going on at any given part of the story, but you would probably be very much mistaken.

I wrote three possible blurbs and story descriptions during and after I completed the book twenty-three months ago. They are fairly good descriptions of parts of the book, but none of them can be said to cover its total, complete story. In those twenty-three months I've made repeated attempts at writing a fourth blurb covering it all, in vain and have sort of given up, at least at this point.

I will use all three off and on, at various settings.

Story descriptions usually come fairly easy to me these nights and have for a number of years after I first managed to overcome an initial resistance to it, but not on this one. It's okay, really. The story is and was supposed to be not easily grasped from I first started out on its vast labyrinth.

It is a story, even one making sense to me, slowly, as I was writing it, but I am the author. I know where the shoe drops and the flower grows and the hidden lake flows.

People reading it will really have to dig deep to find something to hold on to. A friend of mine has called this my psychotic novel, a description as good as any. And he hasn't read a single word either, just listened to my descriptions of the story and the methodology behind it.

Will there be some kind of understanding, a glimpse behind the veil of rationality in the end? Perhaps, perhaps not. There will be a journey, somewhat enjoyable, with a kind of reason and rhyme, whether or not the end is the beginning or the end. You may experience illumination, you may not. When you close the book and sit there sweating hard after having completed it, you may breathe a sigh of relief, and be comforted, telling yourself that the jigsaw puzzle that is existence, is reality, is the world makes sense.

But probably not.

Good luck with that.

Other published and upcoming novels by **Amos Keppler** from **Midnight Fire Media:**

The Defenseless

The two rivers meet and join in the city of Denver, becoming one...

The two dark brothers, growing up with their sister Linda in a mundane, average suburb, a place well entrenched in modern United States and the world, have since their moment of birth been at odds with the world... and with each other.
Mike and Ted Cousin are not who they are. There is a mystery here, one of birth and upbringing, one of fate. Violence and death, blood and fire follow them all the days of their lives. The fire is resting somewhere inside... waiting for the Spark.
Their parents know something, but are not telling it. The policeman Mark Stewart and their aunt Trudy do, too. Everybody knows something, pieces of the whole, but nobody knows the whole truth, nobody telling it.
The ancient power is returning to the world, a world massively suffering from physical and spiritual poison, on the brink of collapse and a collective tailspin suicide run without its like in human history.
Magick is returning from its long exile. Thus begins the story of the wild beasts rising from their ashes.
The Spark is struck, horrible and terrifying.

First book of ten in the Janus Clan series: Ten stories of the wild man in the modern world, forty years of wandering, before the Phoenix is rising from its ashes.

ISBN 978-82-91693-08-8

Shadow Walk

The world is changing. They know this, in their core of cores, where everything moves and shifts. Night and fire have followed them all the days of their lives.

What they carry inside has always scared them, always intrigued them...

They have always felt different, apart from the crowd. And here, now, they get the confirmation they have always wanted, always yearned for, that they are truly different, a breed apart. The metamorphosis begins. Their minds, their bodies are changing in shocking and unpredictable ways, as what's on the inside is brought to the outside. And as they themselves are changing they are also changing the world.

Danger awaits them, Life awaits them, in the small, backward New England town. Magick and Mystery may be found beneath unturned stones.

People, young and old, are descending on the small, insignificant town of Northfield, New England.

Boys and girls, students at the school of Life, Seekers, yearning for what's different, what's hidden.

They're seeking within and without, high and low.

And here, in this dusty, remote place they're finding it, turning the stone, finding the strength within themselves to be themselves, to break out of confines, to the world beyond. And in time, after the initial, tentative steps, pushing down paths new and undreamed of.

And the present day order sees them for what they are... Agents of Change, a threat to any establishment, any imposed reality. The heatwave, the worst in living memory, is nothing compared to the boiling within the human heart. The Indian Summer heralds the twilight of mankind.

ISBN 978-82-91693-12-5

Your Own Fate

From The Book of Fate:

In the Book of Fate there is everything. Every incident, all times, everything that has been, that is, that will ever be, everything that might be, everything that could have been.

But who is writing it? Who is penning it? Who is turning page by page, too many to be counted, blowing in the wind? Does it perhaps write itself, with a pen moving across the yellow sheets? Or is it a hand moving the pen, one unseen, one stretching back into the past, back to the time before everything was created, creating itself from nothing?

Timothy Joyce is an enigma, a man without a past, appearing from nowhere, to go on a rampage in an astonished world.

Jeremy Zahn is hunting Timothy Joyce. It seems like he has always been hunting him, from old London, from the island of angels, where it is said they met for the first time, to the city of angels, California, the new world.

Here, on this shaky ground, following confrontations spanning the globe, its time and space the two will fight for the last time.

And the world is watching, its people shivering in their frozen hearts.

ISBN 978-82-91693-05-7

Night on Earth

This is said to be the age of enlightenment and reason...

A culmination of thousands of years' development and illumination.

The hunters are dying off, they say. Their day is done, in favor of the new, enlightened time of neon lights, technology and civilization.

But a hunter is stalking the streets of London. A creature without form, eyes and skin. In a city on the brink of chaos, of social and economic collapse, it is stalking cops, killing them in ever more horrible ways.

Sheila Watts is a hunter. She's a cop.

Sheila is lost, losing herself further by the second. She's losing herself, finding herself, as she's closing in on the creature of the night, as it is closing in on her.

Sheila Watts can taste the sweet blood in her mouth...

ISBN 978-82-91693-07-1

Dreams Belong to the Night

New, emerging urban rebel guerilla groups, freedom fighters, called terrorists by enraged authorities are overwhelming Europe.

What is, in truth terrorism? Who does it to whom?
How much can a human being take of bondage, injustice, degradation and destruction of spirit... before being fed up?

Present day society is a wound not closing.
In a modern world society destroying everything making life worth living there are those, who, through coincidence and fate, have decided not to take it anymore.
And as they are making that decision, together and as individuals, they are also starting on a journey, a journey back to humanity's roots.
Judith, Sivert, Kim, Willhelm, Anya and many more.
A handful of people against an entire world.

This is their story...

ISBN 978-82-91693-11-8

Experience the defeat of civilization, of tyranny, of anti-life in:

Thunder Road - Book One: Ice and Fire

Damon Terrill is the Storm Child. He is born into the life hostile civilization's last years, as humanity starts on its return to nature, return to Life.

It started with the need for Freedom, the passion of life, and went from there, in new and unforeseen directions, in one, final attempt to get it right.

– It's the human being's path through life, Anya told them. – What challenges, destroys and strengthens it.

The Thunder Road is making a turn. It always is. Burning Ice, Biting Flame...that is how life began. And that's how it will renew itself. No matter where humans are going. And now the blade is laid bare, ready to be tempered once more. Humanity's idiocy, their hubris has finally and fully been visited upon them. The End Time, the final hour, Ragnarok is here. The sea is rising, winds are increasing in strength. A thoroughly rotten society is collapsing under its own weight.

Humans are natural nomads. Now they become nomads anew, pulled together in small tribes once more, pulled into a fellowship of fate in a final, desperate attempt to survive, to live the life humans are born to live. Finally. Damon, Anya, Andrè, Myriam and many others have started on their way Home.

To be published June 21, 2015

AFTERGLOW DUST

She has died a million times…

Someone is stalking her. She knows this, knows it at the edge of her vision, where nothing really is seen, only dreamed. Her nightmares give her no peace. She turns and looks behind her. There is nothing there her eyes can see. But in the wind she can hear the wailing cry, the cry of Death. Sniffing that wind, she can smell the blood in her nostrils.

There is truth in flesh, they say… and there is truth in that. But there is also substance in what cannot be seen, cannot be touched. Claws and fangs cut ceaselessly through the night, looking for her. A silent cry is heard in the dark.

Someone… or something is stalking her.

She remembers a kind touch and a slap in the face, and hardly anything else.

Kathryn Caldwell is Afterglow, a woman of undetermined age, a strange creature wandering the dark corners of the world. Something happened to her once, something horrible, something she can never forget or put out of her mind. It is haunting her every second of her dark days, every moment of her pitiful sleep. She has become an empty shell, a pale imitation of the human being she once was. Long ago, as she measures time, she lost everything valuable in a human being, saw it fall through a crack, irreversible, never to be found again.

So she is wandering the darkened streets of the modern world, aimlessly, adrift, hardly ever seen, hardly ever there. People cannot see her, but she is there, present in their daily lives, an open wound that will never close.

No one is safe for Afterglow…

To be published April 30, 2015

FALLING

She can not rid herself of it, the sense of falling. It is lurking in her dreams, every time she looks at the world from the edge of her vision. The old, cruel oracle at the fair did not tell her anything she did not know.

Janet of the Blue Flame is born a sorcerer, one with powers of the mind and the body far exceeding those of most others, one in a line reaching far back in antiquity.

In this modern age she, like many others is virtually unaware of the potential resting in the murky parts of her being. She may know, deep down, but she is not aware… not until the day Malone the Sorcerer comes for her.

Malone is dark and powerful. His skills and might are unquestionable. His power speaks to her, to her murky depths, roaring in her consciousness like a storm. Janet is only Sweet Sixteen and is overwhelmed in Malone's presence. When he offers to train her, for her to become his apprentice she consents with an eagerness of a mule chasing the carrot. He is everything she is not, everything she has ever dreamed of being. She leaves her friends and family, leaves behind everything she knows and joins the mighty and enigmatic sorcerer on his quest. His harsh teaching takes her far away, into the nine realms and beyond.

He gives her her devours, gives her everything he promised and more, wishing her good luck, leaving her to pick up the pieces of her life

Janet of the Blue Flame is ready for the world.

To be published October 31, 2015

www.ingramcontent.com/pod-product-compliance
Lightning Source LLC
Chambersburg PA
CBHW060605310726
48982CB00008B/1243/J

9788291693132